THE
MADEMOISELLE
ALLIANCE

THE
MADEMOISELLE
ALLIANCE

A NOVEL

NATASHA LESTER

BALLANTINE BOOKS

NEW YORK

Ballantine Books
An imprint of Random House
A division of Penguin Random House LLC
1745 Broadway, New York, NY 10019
randomhousebooks.com
randomhousebookclub.com
penguinrandomhouse.com

A Ballantine Books Trade Paperback Original

ISBN 978-0-593-72653-2
Ebook ISBN 978-0-593-72654-9

Printed in the United States of America on acid-free paper

2 4 6 8 9 7 5 3 1

BOOK TEAM: Production editor: Jennifer Rodriguez • Managing editor: Saige
Francis • Production manager: Sarah Feightner • Copy editor: Caroline
Clouse • Proofreaders: Andrea Gordon, Claire Maby, Deborah Bader

Book design by Jo Anne Metsch

The authorized representative in the EU for product safety and compliance is
Penguin Random House Ireland, Morrison Chambers, 32 Nassau Street,
Dublin D02 YH68, Ireland. https://eu-contact.penguin.ie

*To every man, woman, and child who's fought
against oppression for their freedom, and
especially those who've lost their lives in the
struggle. To those who are fighting still. Above
all, to Marie-Madeleine Fourcade. Hero.*

She first made contact with the outside world when she emerged, paralyzed with cold and cramp, from a sealed diplomatic bag. This had been carried in the boot of a car to Madrid by a compliant Vichy courier who had crossed the Pyrenees in mid-winter. Reports to London that her Nefertiti-like beauty and charm (she was then thirty-two, mother of two children) were equalled by her total dedication and executive capacity proved unexaggerated. Fact had outpaced fiction in producing the copybook "beautiful spy." This was Marie-Madeleine.

— MI6 COMMANDER KENNETH COHEN

Uncatchable

Aix-en-Provence, France, July 1944

I hear their boots first. *Ack-ack-ack,* like machine guns firing in the stairwell. Then the roar: "Gestapo! *Aufmachen!*"

That's when I remember—I forgot to lock the door.

I've run so often these past four years that I think I can make it; that if I fling the bolt into place, I'll have time to escape out the back. And I do make it. The bolt is in my hands, but the door is bulging from the force of the bodies trying to break in, and my fingers are hysterical with adrenaline and can't make the lock catch.

The wood cracks. The door shudders.

It flies open.

Two dozen Nazis burst in.

This is the moment everyone in London warned me was coming. Capture. Torture. Death—but only if I'm lucky.

In front of me is a wall of submachine guns and menace. I should back away, far away, but my feet are ready to charge straight through the guns and out the door and toward my three children so I can hold their innocence and their love right up against my body for what could be the very last time.

It's not his intention, but a plainclothes *gestapiste* saves me from that mad act. He demands, "Where's the man?" rousing me back to sense.

The man. He's here for one of my three thousand agents, then. Not me. Not yet.

Which means I have to take hold of myself, become the name on my papers: Germaine Pezet, a provincial housewife. Hérisson, the little hedgehog I take my code name from, must scuttle away. If this performance is anything less than my best, they'll find the agent they're looking for. And I'll never see my children again. Or Léon.

Where are you, Léon? Please God, let me find him.

The *gestapiste*'s gun clicks. I make myself step toward it, cackling.

"Where's the man? Oh, please find me a man. With a face like mine, they're in short supply." I gesture to my jutting chin, thankful that I let MI6's dentist make me a prosthetic disguise to alter my face so completely that I'm unrecognizable as the woman on the *Wanted* posters who leads the Alliance network.

It's the only weapon I have, so I wield it, winking at the Nazi and pointing to a cupboard where, six days ago, stacks of documents couriered across France from my agents were hiding. "Perhaps he's in the armoire."

When the soldiers fling open the armoire, they find nothing. All the papers stashed there have long since been coded and sent to London.

I expel adrenaline with another cackle. "Make sure he's a good one."

The leader glowers. But doubt flickers in his eyes like the match I hold to a nonchalant cigarette and I start to hope: Maybe I'll get away with it. Perhaps I won't even be taken to prison this time but will be overlooked as an ugly peasant woman who has nothing whatsoever in common with so-called beautiful spy Marie-Madeleine.

The Nazis fan through the apartment, probably hunting for Lucien, head of my Provençal sector, who was here earlier, both of us part of a network the Germans call Noah's Ark because of our animal code names. Probably also hunting for the stack of intelligence reports Lucien delivered, which is sitting in plain sight on the table.

I inhale smoke, exhale fear. I have to hide those papers. But there are five machine guns still trained on me. I leer stupidly, call out, "I prefer brown hair. Brown eyes, too."

Léon's eyes are gray-green jasper. *Forever,* I told him the last time I saw him, ten months ago.

Thankfully, my guards join the search, leaving just one SS officer in the room. The second his attention shifts to his companions, who have the fun of hunting out Resistance quarry rather than the bad luck to be stuck with me, I snort revoltingly into a handkerchief. The guard shudders, turns his back, and I leap forward, scoop up the papers, and toss them under the sofa just before the plainclothes *gestapiste* returns.

"Have you seen a tall man with fair hair? He's part of a network of terrorists. We were told he'd been here." The officer speaks politely, but I know this is the moment before his temper breaks.

I have to stop it from breaking on me.

I heave my shoulders into a witless shrug. "The only blonds here are your soldiers."

"Then why did you try to bar the door against us?" he shouts. Spittle and frustration punctuate the air like angry stars.

My hands tremble.

I shove them in my pockets, cast a sly eye at the furious Nazi. "If I'd known you were all so handsome, I'd have flung the door wide open—and my chastity belt, too."

I want to be sick. The *gestapiste* wants to hit me. But his soldiers have found nothing. He hits the table instead.

I swallow, breathe, swallow again as, miraculously, incredibly, the Nazis shoulder their guns and walk away from the leader of the largest Resistance network in France.

Two minutes more and I can drop to my knees on the floor.

But . . .

One of them sweeps the room a final time and, as if the devil has control of them, his eyes fall to the space beneath the sofa where piles of coded messages wait like traitors. Now I do almost drop to my knees and cry out that deaf and futile word, *Non!*

"*Lügnerin!*" the Nazi screams as he pulls out fistfuls of paper. *Liar.*

Now I stumble. I'm so tired, don't think I can do this anymore. Defend myself and my agents, pretend and perform, rescue myself every time. Where's the damn D'Artagnan the storybooks promise you, the rebel trickster who saves both the day and honor, too?

Six soldiers advance, machine guns pointing at my head, my chest, my throat. Others tear the sofa to pieces, the footstools, too, which are crammed with more intelligence reports. Rifle butts smash tables into splinters of bone.

The ringleader seizes me by the shoulders. "Who are you?" he rages, shaking me so viciously I'm terrified my prosthetic will fly out, revealing both my disguise and the answer to his question: *I'm the woman you've been hunting since 1941.*

I'm the D'Artagnan. And no matter how scared I am or how tired of fighting and mourning my murdered friends and the children I never see, I have to fight some more. There's time for despair only when I'm lying alone in my bed at three in the morning and no one can see how I have to grip my hands between my knees to stop them from trembling.

I fling out my last-chance dice.

"I'm a spy," I say, the guise of silly housewife lain aside, the self of Hérisson still hiding. "London sent me."

The *gestapiste* tries to interrupt, but I keep talking the way Marie-Madeleine, the airplane-flying, car-rallying daredevil iconoclast, would have spoken five years ago.

"I'm the stag you catch when you were just out hunting rabbits. And I'll only speak to the master of the house, not his gamekeeper. Find me the most senior Gestapo officer in Provence, rather than his underling," I sneer.

My heart is a maniacal drumbeat. My common sense is screaming at me to find a better solution than to let them arrest me. But I need to get away from the guns. If I'm taken to a prison to await a Gestapo commandant I have no intention of facing—because a commandant will know exactly who I am, and he won't be so kind as to shoot me—then maybe I can escape. Guns kill, but prisons *can* be escaped from; that's a fact I've learned firsthand.

The officer frowns, worried. What if he lets his men kill me, but then discovers I had valuable information that could have been tortured out of me?

He pushes me toward the stairs. "The regional commandant will be in Aix-en-Provence tomorrow morning."

The boneless relief of being allowed to live for a little longer almost makes me stumble again. But what hellish prison will they take me to? And how will I get away before I have to face a Gestapo commandant, or before they serve torture for breakfast?

I'm driven to the Miollis barracks and shoved into a punishment cell. The men occupying it are ordered out, leaving behind the stench of urine and sweat. I brace one hand against the wall, but it isn't enough to ward off the stink and the terror, and three seconds later I'm retching into the bucket so violently that perspiration drenches my body and I want to claw my skin off my bones.

Empty and exhausted, I sag against the wall, close my eyes, draw on the memory of Béatrice's and Christian's faces the last time I saw them, over a year ago. I picture the tiny baby, Léon's child, whom I had held for only a week before I had to give him up.

He will have just turned one.

How many more birthdays will I miss?

It's the kind of question you should never ask yourself when you're alone in a prison cell with a capsule of cyanide hidden in a locket around your neck. Not when the man you love is missing. Not when lives of your three thousand agents, as well as the freedom of your country, are at stake.

By morning, the Gestapo will have read enough of my papers to know who I am, and they'll punish me in ways so cruel I can't even imagine them. If I'm to swallow the cyanide MI6 gave me, it has to be now. Back in London, the priest told me that God would forgive me.

But will I forgive myself?

If nobody warns Lucien that the Gestapo are onto him, he'll be captured. His sector, almost all that's left of the Alliance network after the last brutal months, will be torn to shreds. And France, fighting with everything she has for her freedom now that the Allies have finally landed, will feel the Nazis' guns press right into her skull.

So I pull myself up, remind myself that I'm a little hedgehog wearing a dress of spikes.

It's five hours until dawn.

I start at the window. It's up high, one meter wide and perhaps double that in height. No glass covers the opening, just a heavy wooden board with a gap at the top through which I can see thick metal bars.

A gap.

An opening.

A space where the light gets in.

My breath comes faster. I'm balancing on the thin line that exists between madness and hope when I shove the cot beneath the window and empty the bucket, gagging again from the stench.

I upturn the bucket on the cot.

In Shanghai, where I lived in the French concession as a

child, my father told me about burglars who greased their bodies so they could slip easily into houses at night. It's summer. The cell is an oven. My body is drenched in sweat. Rationing and running from Nazis for four years means I'm as thin as a needle.

But am I slick enough and thin enough to slide into the gap between the board and the bars and then through the bars to freedom?

I slip off my dress, grip it between my teeth. Then I climb onto the bucket, reach up to the window and try to believe that I'm like a ray of moonlight, able to crack open the darkness and pass through anything—uncatchable.

Part One

ADVENTURER

1928–1941

*. . . what chiefly struck me was the apathy
of the younger women. I asked them if they
had a garden, and they shook their heads
wistfully, saying that there were no gardens
in Old Fez. The roof was therefore their
only escape: a roof overlooking acres and
acres of other roofs, and closed in by the
naked fortified mountains which stand
about Fez like prison-walls.*

— EDITH WHARTON, *In Morocco*

1

I Never Want to Leave

Morocco, 1928

'm eighteen years old and I'm standing in a street with my husband of just two days beside me and I wish my eyes were cameras and could capture everything I see. The turquoise domes that crown the buildings, the white cloths that helmet the heads of the men. The veiled women who are permitted only a thin net strip to look out onto the world. Do they revel in the anonymity, or do they want to tear off those claustrophobic skins and expose their faces to the bright, hot sunshine of Tangier?

Above me, perpendicular streets cascade through a tangle of houses with filigree balustrades wreathed like lace around them. To my right are laden donkeys and motorcars, a bazaar selling silk and leather, olives and guns. Guards with stories engraved on their sword belts stand in the niches of temples. Naked men wail incantations to a worshipful crowd. Through it all, a descant melody hums: the muezzin calling in tongues I don't yet understand, but that make my musician-trained body shiver as if I've just heard Bach for the very first time.

"Can we explore?" I'm already lunging toward the scent of cinnamon and saffron, wanting to taste it on my tongue.

"There's more than enough heat, dirt, and poverty waiting for us in Rabat."

The voice of my husband, Edouard Meric, is brusque and I stop.

It's the first time he's spoken to me with anything other than amusement, affection, or pride. He's eight years older, an army officer working for the French Intelligence Service in Morocco. His dark eyes and brooding air made me think of a breathtakingly real Heathcliff the first time I saw him, but right now he looks more glowering than gothic. He's the man some might say I've given up my dreams of being a concert pianist for, but I can barely recollect that, now that I'm in Morocco and the adventurous spirit born within me years ago as I explored Shanghai with my amah is quivering like the plucked string of a cello.

"We need to get there before dark," he says, tone conciliatory now.

I climb into the car. The driver punches the accelerator and we lurch, stall, restart.

I almost whisper that I'm a much better driver and could probably take on the task, but my sister advised me to introduce Edouard to my unconventionalities one by one. So I settle for peeling off my gloves and discarding my shawl and hat, which isn't proper in public, but layers are meant for a less tropical climate.

Through the Spanish zone, the roads are so brutal it feels like our car is being tossed from trough to crest of a twelve-foot wave. Edouard's expression is grim, so I take his hand and his frown recedes. Such is the power of love—one hand woven into another's banishes all unhappiness. I smile and his lips turn up in response.

When we reach French Morocco and the roads level out, it's easier to speak. Edouard flaps a handkerchief back and forth. "God, it's hot."

It *is* warm, but not in the humidly oppressive way of Shanghai or even Marseille, where I was born. This heat sparkles like diamonds.

"Take off your jacket," I say, glad of my sleeveless dress, which allows my bare arm to bask on the sill of the open window.

Jacket gone, I undo Edouard's cuff links and roll up his sleeves. "Better?"

"Better," he agrees.

I rest my head contentedly on his shoulder until Rabat rises up before us, like a crown atop a cliff the color of fire, having burned down everything in its path to reach this place of triumph.

"Look!" I cry, thrusting my head through the car window.

Then I turn around and seize my husband's hands. "I love you," I tell him, a vow more urgent than anything I said on our wedding day. "And I love it here. I never want to leave."

When I lean over to kiss him, he shakes his head. "Not here." Then he winks. "But definitely later."

I don't think I've ever smiled the way I do now at the foot of Rabat, ready to throw myself into my next two adventures—one that will take place in this country, and one that will take place in our home, between the two of us, wife and one very handsome husband whom I'd give my heart to, were it possible to pluck it from my chest and hold it out in the palm of my hand.

2

How Lucky I Am to Be French

Paris, 1936

"Third place!" I cry, bursting into my apartment in a way I never would have dared had I still been in Morocco. It's taken four years for my body to learn not to check itself. But anger never greets me here. Instead, my children do, and they're eager to know if I won the Monte Carlo Rally.

"Maybe you'll do better next time," my six-year-old son says, and I laugh, as does my mother, who's been looking after Béatrice and Christian.

"Do you know how many people wish they'd come in third?" I crouch down to my children's level, hugging them close.

"People with small dreams," Christian says as Béatrice winds her fingers into my hair.

I look up at my mother, trying to hide the furrowing of my brow. Have I given them great expectations when I should be encouraging a less constellated outlook?

No. That's why I left Morocco. So my children could grow up believing they could reach not just for the moon, but for universes longed for and unknown.

I grin at Christian. "Next time I won't come home unless I win."

I tickle his sister, who looks momentarily worried that I mean it. But these two are the North Star of my existence. I would *never* abandon them.

"I left before breakfast so I could see you before bedtime," I tell her.

"Before breakfast?" repeats my four-year-old daughter, eyes like dinner plates. Breakfasts at the Monte Carlo Beach Hotel are her idea of paradise, and only the most unswerving devotion would make someone skip such a feast.

"That's how much I love you," I tell her, and she giggles.

When I stand, my eye falls on the headline of the newspaper on the table: *Le Chancelier Hitler Dénonce Versailles: Les troupes allemandes sont entrées en Rhénanie.*

Yes, Hitler has all but torn up the Treaty of Versailles and occupied the Rhineland, right on the border of France, an act akin to war. "That's also why I left Monte Carlo early," I murmur to my mother, exuberance gone.

She squeezes my hand.

Perhaps it was silly not to stay for the awards ceremony because of something happening hundreds of kilometers away. But while my marriage vows might be all but shattered, the one vow I'll never break is the one I made when I fled Rabat—that my children matter more than anything. I need to be in Paris with them.

"Let's get ice cream," I say. "Race you!"

We dash out the door as fast as if the police are chasing us. Christian wins, whooping, and Béatrice and I come in equally last; we both suffer from a congenital hip condition. Mine worries at me like a mistrustful husband if I don't venerate it enough, and hers has always been worse, making running difficult.

"Really, we came in second," I tell her, and she beams.

Soon our hands are sticky; Béatrice's face is pink and Christian's chocolate-stained. Mine is smeared with love.

My sister, Yvonne, hosts an evening salon that attracts artists, journalists like me, military intelligence officers, and men of influence. They'll all be talking about Hitler and the Rhineland, and if I want to find out what it might mean for my family, then I need to attend. So I pull out a red silk dress, something to lift my spirits, dimmed by France's and Britain's responses to Hitler—gutless shrugs. Since when do you allow a bully to keep what he's stolen?

I'm too familiar with tyrants not to know they never reveal their true ambitions until it's too late to stop them.

My hip spasms, dampening my mood further, and I know I'm going to have to work hard to hide my limp tonight. But the cure for that is to step into the dress and make up my face with lipstick and a smile.

"*Maman!*" Christian says when I stop to kiss him good night. "You look so pretty."

His words see me out the door with barely a hitch in my step.

Yvonne greets me with kisses before taking my arm, which means I'm not disguising my limp as well as I'd hoped. But it's a relief to lean on her for a moment. Until she deposits me with a group of women discussing why it's essential to own a country home so their busy husbands have a place for repose.

"Let's see how long you last." She grins before slipping away.

If only it were possible to commit siblicide with a champagne coupe.

Thankfully, after my only having to pretend to listen for a few minutes, my brother-in-law beckons me over to the fireplace. As I slip away from the wives, I hear them whisper, "Separated."

I wear the scarlet letters of that word like a scar. Edouard does not. He's a man in the military, whereas I'm just a blonde. Of course our separation must be my fault, meaning some of the women see me as a threat, the men as an invitation. I haven't helped matters by daring to become a journalist here in Paris in defiance of the view that mothers should be at home with their children. But I love my job at Radio Cité spinning tales about the latest Chanel gowns or interviewing fascinating women I find on the margins of parties like these, women who'd otherwise be ignored by the conservative French newspapers. All of which makes me an excellent party guest: I bring scandal, conflict, and never a dull moment. I have no idea which of these entertainments Georges hopes I'll add to his group, but judging by the yawn he's smothering, I'd say all three.

"My sister-in-law, Marie-Madeleine Méric," he announces. "And the family daredevil. Just returned from a third placing at the Monte Carlo Rally."

"What do you drive?" the man introduced as Navarre inquires.

I know Navarre by reputation; he's a military intelligence officer and hero of the Great War. I'm surprised he's bothering to speak to me at all, let alone about cars. But then, not all military officers are like Edouard.

"Just a Citroën Traction Avant," I say.

He almost looks impressed.

There follows a debate about whether I might have won in a Peugeot. All yawns are forgotten as I describe the thrill of the last white-knuckle charge into the town square, where I was, in fact, beaten by a Peugeot, until another man smirks. "You're welcome to drive my Peugeot any time."

Ah, he's hoping for scandal. But I'm good at this; I've had to learn to be. "I always find Peugeots disappointingly lackluster," I say with innocent eyes. "No staying power."

Georges guffaws, as does Navarre. The flirt takes it on the chin and laughs, too.

Soon the conversation shifts to Hitler and our group expands. Navarre gestures furiously as he explains how much information he's all but scribbled inside the prime minister's eyelids over the past few years, outlining Hitler's unabating preparations for what can only be war. Our government has ignored it all, he says.

My stomach twists. Hitler's taken the Rhineland. What will he do next?

Tempers flare over that very question.

"It will never work," Navarre blazes as Lieutenant-Colonel Charles de Gaulle, another military man of a similar age to Navarre—about fifteen years older than me—proposes assembling a French strike force to push the Nazis back into Germany. "Hitler's army is too strong."

"You want to keep hiding behind the Maginot Line," De Gaulle shoots back. "It's time to stop relying on ideas conceived two hundred years ago."

Navarre nods sharply. "That's one thing we can agree on— the French military is decades behind. Unless we act quickly, France will be wiped off the map."

"But is the France we have now worth fighting for?" the flirt from earlier asks with world-weary cynicism, and I say adamantly, *"Bien sur!"*

Everyone turns, faces expressing amusement or condescension. I'm the only woman in the group and I should be over in the delicate chairs discussing my husband's needs. But Navarre, who looks curious rather than patronizing, indicates that I should mount my defense of France.

A good journalist knows how to spin a story. So spin I do, because my children's futures depend on everyone's believing in France like I do.

"I grew up in the French concession in Shanghai," I begin, "and I've lived in Morocco, too." I keep my voice soft to match the fire-lit air and the cherry-red Beaujolais and the lilting notes of Satie's "Gymnopédie No.1" drifting from the gramophone. "I've spent seventeen of my twenty-six years standing on different ground than that beneath our feet right now. Maybe that should have made me love France less. But . . ."

I pause. Everyone is listening, perhaps because they've never been to such places as I've been lucky enough to know. So I continue.

"The expatriates in Shanghai and Rabat all spoke of France as a place of romance and heroes, a country so epic that it meant something. It meant people who'd endured invasion since the beginning of time. People who'd fought off every attack. People whose language is a synonym for poetry, who've created a culture admired all over the world, who've built cities that everyone longs to visit just once before they die. Living away taught me how lucky I am to be French, and how blessed I am to call this resilient and beautiful land my home."

My throat is suddenly too tight for speech. I lift my glass to my mouth, trying to swallow down the tears that have come from a strange sense of loss—but what am I losing?

"We *are* blessed," Navarre says quietly.

But De Gaulle says, "Blessings don't win wars."

The next day, the children are at school and I'm making notes for an interview with Édith Piaf, but I can't sit still. It's not my legs but my soul that's restless—as if it wants to be let out of the prison of Parisian quotidian life I didn't know I'd trapped it in. I thought I was keeping myself alive with flying lessons and car rallies and working at a job rather than on my manicure; adventure, but not enough to taint my children. But this morning I can feel—like the night before I met Edouard, the dawn of the day Christian was born—that change is raising a hand to knock on my door. Where once I would have flung it open, now I hesitate.

When did I become so fearful?

Hitler, who at the very least is a liar, a thief, and a murderer, is invading land just over the border. That's why I'm jumpy. But what can *I* do about Hitler?

Except—isn't that what cowards say?

What if Gustave Eiffel had never believed that one man could build a tower so famous the whole world would know of it? What if Coco Chanel had told herself that women preferred wearing cages to letting their bodies move freely? What if Joan of Arc had sat in her salon with her door tightly shut?

But while I love a fine dress, I'm no visionary or saint.

The phone shrills, startling me.

"*Allo?*"

"Madame Méric," a voice says. "Navarre. We met last night. There's something I'd like to speak to you about. Something I'd prefer to keep between the two of us."

I almost groan aloud. An affair isn't an adventure. It's a mess.

At least I can hang up; it's the propositions at parties that are harder to shake. So many men interpret *non* to mean *oui*. I'm now good at finding the tenderest part of a man's foot with the heel of my shoe.

But something stops me from disconnecting the call. Navarre and my brother-in-law were deep in conversation when I left the party, and I find it hard to believe Georges would have given Navarre encouragement to call me with an indecent proposal. And while Navarre had shown himself to be a passionate man compared to the dour De Gaulle, he was enamored of his country, I'd believed, not me. So even though his words are suspicious, I relent and invite him to visit. But I take the precaution of changing into a plain gray suit, something nobody could mistake for an invitation.

It seems I've finally learned to judge a man correctly, because Navarre's first words are, "This meeting must seem irregular and quite possibly dishonorable. I assure you it's the first, but not the second."

I smile. "Well, I'm intrigued now."

He sits with the air of a king installing himself on a throne.

Indeed, his carriage and tone tell me he's used to having power. But his face is avuncular, rather than handsome or regal.

"If you let me know why you're here, then I can decide whether to throw you out or offer you a cup of tea," I say.

He laughs and I relax. Navarre might be an imposing figure, but his laugh comes from his belly. Edouard spat his from his mouth like rancid meat.

As though summoned by my unwanted recollection, Navarre starts talking about my husband. "Georges told me you helped your husband with his intelligence work in Morocco. That you . . ." He considers his words. "You gathered information from those your husband was less skilled at talking to."

I hold his gaze but don't reply. I might have told Yvonne and Georges that I helped Edouard, but I have no idea why it interests Navarre. Then he says, "You paid close attention to the conversation last night," and I feel change crack open the door.

Now I decide to step through it.

"What's happening in Europe frightens me," I tell him. "But when I'm frightened, I prefer to do something about it, rather than hide. In Morocco, I wanted Edouard to understand the other side to the story of brutal tribes who hated one another and the French most of all. But I don't know what to do about Hitler."

Navarre's reply is, "I want to tell the other side to the story of Hitler and the Nazi Party. I want people to join me on a crusade for truth."

A shiver flickers along my spine. Crusades are both deadly and noble. One takes part only if one believes. But in what?

The other side to the story. It exists somewhere. Everything I've witnessed living in colonized countries where power is held on to by force and fear tells me it does.

"The situation in Europe is worse than I could say last night," Navarre explains. "To force our government into taking action, I nccd everyone to understand what Hitler is capable of and what he plans to do next."

He leans toward me, intent and magisterial; if ever anyone could lead a crusade against Hitler, it's this man.

"I'm starting a newspaper. You're a journalist and you understand something of the intelligence business. I need those skills. And when I tell you what I need above all else, then you can finally decide"—his smile is brief but contagious—"whether to throw me out or make me that cup of tea."

My laugh is cut short by his next words.

"A friend of mine has some secret dossiers that prove the intentions of the German high command. I need you to drive to Brussels and collect them. We'll publish them. And our government will finally have to act against the Nazis."

On the mantelpiece behind Navarre is a framed photograph of my children. For their sake, I should refuse to collect papers someone has smuggled out of Germany—papers the Nazis could be looking for. But it's because of my children that I don't even consider saying no.

When you've spent your formative years somewhere like Shanghai, then you grow up fascinated by the world. While other people might think of the danger, I think of standing on the banks of the Whangpoo River, agape at the sampans and junks weaving their way through the freighters, emerging on the other side fast and free, sails filled by the wind. I think of how that moment was the first time I'd felt the immenseness of the world and its inexorability—dynasties might end and kingdoms fall, but the ocean connecting us all endures.

Hitler wants to keep the junks in the harbor, wants to close the oceans and trap the winds, wants to stretch out his arms and crush it all to him so there is no wonder left, only possession.

I refuse to let him.

The Jewish journalist I meet in Brussels is more ghost than real. His eyes dart like startled birds and I only know he's the right person because he's standing where he said he'd be—outside the antique shop in the Promenade Saint-Hubert with a red umbrella under his arm. We don't even speak; he just pushes a folder into my hands, then hurries away.

"Wait!" I call.

He looks back and shakes his head furiously. There's sweat on his brow—and I suddenly understand exactly what it means to flee Nazi Germany with incriminating documents.

He's spectral because fear has eroded his flesh. He's learned to slip like a shadow into a crowd because to flee a place implies a chase.

This crusade I've embarked on is more than politics, land, and ambition. It's people running, turned into phantoms.

It's Nazis hunting for the documents under my arm.

I sit on the folder and speed as if I'm in another rally all the way back to Paris.

A fortnight later, Navarre's newspaper, *L'Ordre National,* is published with the information I collected, which shows, chillingly: Hitler is preparing for war. He's making tanks and guns and warplanes in quantities that suggest Europe will soon be overrun.

Then the man I met with is kidnapped by the Nazis.

At last, people begin to talk. And worry. And send us more information.

One dossier leads to a discussion leads to a movement. I help it swell, certain the government will no longer ignore Hitler, that a crusade has truly begun.

This is the world of intelligence and I am hooked.

3

Sepia Love

Morocco, 1929

can't honestly say which I prefer. Exploring the great Kasbah of the Oudayas in Rabat, where the sky is painted across the walls in ombré swathes that deepen from peacock to sapphire . . . or riding a camel behind my husband to visit the tribes he needs to befriend so they'll tell him about local unrest before it escalates into another Rif War.

I watch him command our retinue, smiling back at me the way he'd smiled across a dance floor a few months ago. That night, every man had asked me to dance except him. It was almost midnight when I approached and asked him why.

"I was scared you'd say no. And that would break my heart," he'd said.

If swooning hadn't gone out of fashion last century, I might have been tempted to try it. I didn't dance with anyone else for the rest of the night.

By morning, as I told my mother about him, I knew it was the kind of love you'd drink poison for; the kind that would make you step in front of a train if it ever died. The kind of love my mother and father had shared before he died six years ago.

Today, the powdered sand of the desert we're traveling across is a hue I christen sepia love: a passionate red that's gentled into something softer, like the phase our marriage is moving into now—an epoch I hope will be even more beautiful than the quick fall into love.

Halfway to our destination, we find a market erupting with scarlet pomegranates. Alongside are rugs and daggers, silks and *kouskous* arrayed like jewels. I dismount, bargaining for cakes of black soap, using the Arabic I've learned of late, my polyglot ability with languages making the stall holder come out from his tent and summon everyone over to behold the blond French woman who speaks their language.

"Get back on your camel." Edouard's hand is on my arm, showing a protective streak that's a little too vice-like. His eyes are the same color as the soap. "You have no idea how dangerous it can be here."

The stall holder turns away, leaving us to the banality of our domestic dispute. A single cloud wafts overhead, leaving one dark shadow to tarnish the red sand, which looks more like anger now than love.

Not long after, I see a twisted shape by the road. A mule, not watered properly and left to die and then burn. Morocco is both ruthless and beautiful, the blue sky and innocent white buildings hiding the fact that, out here, the sun is a weapon, trained on us.

Edouard was right. It *is* dangerous. I've always been too apt to see the waves sparkling on the water, not the ships and bones that lie beneath.

When we reach the village, Edouard helps me down from my camel and holds my hand and everything is as it was. He even claps when I ask in Arabic for the name of a woman's child.

"This is Aderfi," she tells me. She wears so many amulets and coins around her head that she sounds like a tambourine when she moves, and the pianist in me thinks how lovely it would be if I could wear a skirt made from piano keys so that any child of mine would know lullabies and music right from the start.

I touch my stomach very briefly, then I take the child and pass him to Edouard, which makes the mother—Ghislaine, she tells me—grin. Soon, we're sitting before the fire and I translate for Edouard as the chief speaks of his grievances against the French. We eat a tagine that tastes of sugar and spice, and I know that no meal at any time in my future will ever surpass this one beneath a navy Moroccan night sky with my husband smiling beside me.

It's only near the end that I realize I'm the only woman at the fireside. The rest are positioned farther back, in exile.

I pick up my bowl and take it over to the women who are washing up in a bucket, leaving the dishes to dry on the sand. Ghislaine slips in beside me speaking so fast that I don't understand the Arabic at first. When she repeats herself, I listen with my musician's ears and the words translate to, *The chiefs of the tribes are meeting next week. They don't want the French to know. But I don't want another war. My brother died in the last one. I don't want Aderfi to die in the next one.*

Then she relieves me of my bowl and I'm left standing there with a secret I don't know what to do with.

If the French find out afterward about this meeting, they'll be angry and afraid. Fear makes nations do terrible things.

Fear makes humans do terrible things, too.

I remember back in Shanghai when our amah took me and my sister to another house to play. The mothers sat in the parlor, the children in the nursery. The amahs went to another room, out of sight. It was only when I was about ten that I understood the amahs weren't French and some people thought that made them lesser. I asked my mother about it and she sighed and said, "I tell myself we're giving her a job, and many others, too. But what if they don't want our jobs? What if they don't want us at all?"

The Rif War should tell me plainly that they don't want us. But now I carry a mother's pain whispered in my ear, reminding me that things are more complicated than I've allowed myself to see. Aderfi's mother has betrayed her husband and her tribe by telling me that secret. But, in doing so, she's trying not to betray her son.

"Marie-Madeleine!" Edouard calls.

Time to return to the colonizer's side of the fire.

Later, I persuade Edouard to drag our bedding out so we can sleep beneath a firework sky. As we lay blankets on the ground, I tell him what Aderfi's mother said and he wraps me in his arms, saying, "When you're an outsider trying to get people to trust you, it's a definite advantage to have the most beautiful wife in the world by your side."

"I think it was because I asked about her child."

Her expression, when she looked down at the brown cloth that attached the baby to her like another limb, was the same as my father's whenever he looked at me. I can't wait to smile at someone the same way.

So I tell Edouard, "I'll have to ask her about the sling. Because I'll need one in seven months' time."

My husband beams, then tightens his embrace, whispering in my ear, "I love you so much I can hardly bear to let you out of my sight."

4

A Wild Child

Paris, May–November 1940

"France will lose," Navarre says, grim-faced, on the threshold of my apartment.

Navarre never lies. But if he's right, then I—a woman known to have helped publish an anti-Nazi newspaper—am in real trouble.

And I've put my children in danger, too.

Indeed, Navarre's next words are, "Send your children away. Your mother, too. Go to my house at Oloron-Sainte-Marie. It's close to the Spanish border, safe. My wife is expecting you. I'll join you when I can and we'll find some other way to fight."

Behind him, the Nazis' bombs have recolored the sky. It's dark at midday. Ash falls down like snow, as if Paris is a crematorium.

"In what kind of world does publishing the truth put me in a position where I have to send my children away?" I cry despairingly.

"A Nazi world," Navarre says, his voice hard. He's been in prison for two months, put there by our government for saying that one and a half million Germans would come crashing through the Ardennes. He was released just days ago when that prophecy came true.

If he can rejoin the troops that are trying to defend the country that threw him in jail, the least I can do is find a little courage.

"Be safe," I call after him as he leaves.

"Be safe, *mes enfants*," I whisper as I pack Christian's little brown bear that he sleeps with and Béatrice's favorite blue dress, which I've mended and washed and pulled over her head a hundred times. For seven years, I've come home at night to this apartment and kissed my children, their embraces like arithmetic, multiplying my joys to infinity. But now . . .

My mother, working quietly beside me, interrupts my thoughts, saying, "If Navarre survives, join him. Do whatever you can to stop all of this. But do it carefully. He carries a target now. You might, too."

"What power do I have against tanks? There's nothing—"

I cut myself off as my son and daughter creep into the room.

"The girls at school say Hitler eats children," Béatrice whimpers. Beside her, Christian's eyes are huge.

It's like watching their innocence peel away, leaving them unshelled and vulnerable in a scalding world.

I gather them in my arms. No, Hitler mightn't eat children. But he's given his doctors powers to execute anyone with physical and mental disabilities—starting with newborn babies.

"I would never let that happen," I vow.

Béatrice's relief is immediate and immense. She really thinks I can save children from Nazis. *I'm just a liar who's imperfect and weak and afraid,* I want to tell her.

I catch my mother's eye and I wonder—how many times did she want to say the same thing to me after my father died? How often did she have to hold on to her tears so she could soothe mine?

So into my daughter's hair I whisper, just as I do when her hip hurts and she asks when it will feel better. *Bientôt*—soon—I always say. "I'll see you very soon."

In truth, I have no idea when it will be safe for me to see

them again. Nor whether the lies I tell them then will still be small and white.

"Hug me as hard as you can," I say and they do, pressing in as if we each want to stand inside the other's heart.

I try not to cry when they carry their suitcases out the door, on their way to the island of Noirmoutier. The echoes of our goodbyes ring on as I wait in Paris, hoping the French will push the Nazis out of the north and my children can return home.

Soon, a strange parade marches through the city: young women wearing cropped trousers and riding bicycles laugh gaily, scarves knotted madras-fashion on their heads. Families push barrows filled with grandfather clocks, mirrors, and caged parrots, as if knowing the time, looking one's best, and a sharp beak are all you need to fight the Germans. An old woman carrying two suitcases and leading a little white dog tells a man who offers her a place in his van that she's happy to walk to Orléans.

Orléans is 130 kilometers to the south.

I like her optimism. I like the fact that everyone retreating south is smiling.

Navarre is wrong. France won't lose.

But on the twelfth of June, the radio announces, "The French government has left Paris and declared it an open city. The Germans are thirty kilometers away."

Run, the voice in my head urges and I do. I run out onto the street, and what I find there makes me stop.

Not a single car. A row of apartment buildings that nobody enters or leaves. Only abandoned dogs and concierges remain. No sounds, either—no scrape of chairs on a café terrace. No shrill from a policeman's whistle. No laughter from a child's mouth.

From somewhere above, a piano sounds out an A, melancholic—a one-note symphony for a city bereft of harmony.

It's time for me to leave.

Running south is like funneling a tidal wave through a crevasse. Millions of people clog the roads. Horses, too. Cars, many with broken axles, line the roadside, as do the slumped forms of people who've fainted from heat and exhaustion. The sun is as merciless as any Nazi and people are wearing their entire wardrobes. Suitcases make a strange accounting of fatigue—there are few abandoned near Paris, but as the kilometers march on, more appear, their contents strewn like petals. People must realize at some point, with the Stukas shooting at us from above, that all they need are their lives—not madras scarves, which flutter like exhausted birds in the dirt.

My car sputters, protesting the heat and the strain of low gear. Just as I stayed in Morocco too long, hoping for . . . not even miracles, just regular, ordinary love, so too did I stay in Paris, believing that the Germans would be pushed back by France's courage.

I've always had too much faith in mirages, something only dreamers and optimists ever see. But is it really better to turn away from beauty just so you'll never be guillotined by the agony of disappointment? Isn't it better to believe that if we live in a world that can cast Moroccan sunsets onto the sky, it's possible to find hope and magnificence around every corner?

Not today. Around today's corners are mothers writing names on their children's smocks. Around another corner is a stricken woman screaming the name *Gisèle* over and over, and I realize the scribbled names are a way to make everyone believe that, should they become lost in the swarm, they'll be found a little later on down the road.

If I hadn't sent Béatrice and Christian away, that mother might be me.

Right now it's impossible, even for me, to believe in sunsets.

I reach Navarre's house in July. The pain in my left hip from sitting is so bad that it takes me more than five minutes to climb out of the car. I stand there holding on to the door for a long time before I trust my leg to bear my weight. I don't bother to hide my limp—I can't. It'll be days before I can do anything more than shuffle.

Adrienne, Navarre's wife, comes out of the house and flings herself on me. "Is he all right?" she sobs, and my gut twists. I thought she'd have news.

I tell her what I believe. "Navarre's immortal. He'll come."

My belief is rewarded when, a fortnight later, word comes through that he was wounded and captured but escaped a German hospital and is now missing. Adrienne sobs anew. I spend the next two weeks comforting her, wondering where the hell Navarre is, and walking up and down the fields to ease my hip back into functionality. That's where I see Navarre when he staggers in at last, having journeyed under cover of night for hundreds of kilometers. Both his flight and his injuries have cost him forty pounds.

"Thank God you're here," he says, embracing me for the first time ever.

Things are truly bad if even Navarre is getting sentimental.

And yes, things couldn't be worse. Marshal Pétain is made head of the "French state," whatever that is. He petitions Hitler for an armistice: a fancy word for giving up. Thus five and a half million French soldiers are defeated by just half a million Germans. As if that's not enough, Pétain also agrees to pay a daily tax of four hundred million francs to the Nazis for the pleasure of having them occupy us.

We're broke, defeated, and ignorant about what the armistice means. But on the streets, people cheer, "God save le Maréchal Pétain!"

The Great War has made cowards of us all. People would rather surrender than lose more husbands and fathers and brothers. I want to tear up the Pétain pictures, muffle their celebrations, scream at them that we've made a gift of ourselves to an evil man, but I remember the mother in Morocco who gave me her husband's secrets for two years because she believed it would save her family from war.

We're all selfish when it comes to those we love.

I walk into town to get a salve and bandages for Navarre's wounds, and that's where I hear people saying that Pétain, hero of the Great War, is only pretending to side with the Germans. Eventually, he'll fight back. For now, they applaud the deal he made with Hitler, a man who stood in his parliament and said that war was the means to exterminate all Jews.

All the work Navarre and I have done over the past four years to prove the Nazis were megalomaniac monsters has been futile.

Back at the house, questions for Navarre press into my mouth like bile. *You said we'd find some other way to fight—but what? And who are we fighting against—the French officials who gifted the country to the Nazis, or the Nazis themselves?*

But I can't accost an injured man who looks like he weighs less than me now.

I help Adrienne nurse him like I nursed my father through the ravages of cholera when I was thirteen. While he sleeps, I write furious letters to my mother. *I miss Papa. How he'd hate to see France butchered like this.*

I can't send them. Noirmoutier is in the Occupied Zone— Pétain has let the Nazis carve up France, giving the Germans a large Occupied Zone in the north. The French get a much smaller zone in the south, where Pétain rules from Vichy, having persuaded parliament to give up sitting and gift him all its powers. No mail is allowed from the free zone, or *zone nono,* where I am, to the Occupied. My children are in the lion's den. So is my sister, Yvonne, and my brother-in-law, Georges; they're both still in Paris.

Forehead resting in hand, fingers smudged with inky tears, I surrender to self-pity as I imagine my mother's reply: *Your father would hate it. So, for him, and for Christian and Béatrice, you have to put France back together.* I add a fantasy postscript: *One day you'll love someone like I loved your father. He'll be an adventurer, too. And you will be his life's one true adventure.*

Reunifying France. Falling in love. They're as unlikely as Hitler's surrendering. But if *I* surrender, then France will forever be a Germanic province. My daughter will be told to aspire only to *Kinder, Küche,* and *Kirche*—children, kitchen, and church. And my son . . .

In 1938, we published a report about the Death's Head brigade, composed of boys only a little older than Christian. The boys were taught how to kill, how to maim—and how to enjoy both.

So I wait for Navarre to recover with a patience that's almost impossible for a buccaneer like me to practice.

In the evenings, I help him out to the porch. We stare at the Pyrenees, which stand like warriors against the flames of sunset, as we listen to the radio tell us that coal, fuel, and food are rationed. That Pétain has proclaimed a new motto: *travail, famille, patrie.* Work. Family. Fatherland. But only the men are to work. The women must make babies.

Patience expired, I snap my fingers, a castanet click announcing a tempest. "Gone."

"What is?" Navarre's equanimous expression is the opposite of the urgency that convinced me to work with him back in 1936. He's been away somewhere for the past two days, and I expected him to come back with a plan. But he hasn't.

"War isn't only about a dictator and a demarcation line," I cry. "It's about forcing one set of beliefs down a culture's throat. I'm everything Vichy France abhors. Do you think they'll shoot me or stone me when they find out I'm estranged from my husband? That I left my children with my mother? Meanwhile,

Charles de Gaulle is the only Frenchman who's declared he'll fight Hitler. He's in London, but we're sitting here like old women!"

You wear your emotions like a bright red dress, my husband once told me. *Too obviously, and like something most men will want to remove.*

I still haven't learned to cloak them.

But Navarre doesn't retaliate. He says something ridiculous. "We're going to Vichy."

"That isn't funny." Obviously we're not going to the town where Pétain's set himself up, along with the impotent government of the new Vichy French state.

"I visited Pétain yesterday," Navarre continues. "Told him how sorry I was for my treasons. He received me as one receives a son. He gave me a job."

My God. I haven't seen Christian and Béatrice since May. And the man I thought I was on a crusade with has turned out to be a collaborator, too.

I whirl around, thankful only that my hip is better and I can stride rather than hobble to fetch my keys.

"I'm an official of the new Légion française des combattants," Navarre calls. "I'm to turn a hotel in Vichy into a reception center to rehabilitate returned soldiers to civilian life." A beat. "It's the perfect cover."

I halt. "You have about five seconds to explain what you mean."

"I mean," he says, the crusader's gleam back in his eye, "that the only way to overthrow a government is to find out their secrets. We're going to create an intelligence network to dig up every last one. Then we'll give those secrets to the Allies, who'll use them to help us take back France."

"So which is it? Are you rehabilitating soldiers or starting an intelligence network?" Despite my skepticism, I sit down.

"Every ex-soldier who comes to the reception center is a potential source of secrets. We recruit the like-minded ones, eavesdrop on the rest. Which means"—he points at me—"you need to get into the habit of deceiving people."

Haven't I been doing that for the past seven years? I step into a salon with my blond hair and blue eyes and reputation as an estranged wife, and people think they're getting a racy flirt they can play with like a hand of baccarat.

Then Navarre leans forward and says the most preposterous thing yet. "I have to make Pétain believe I'm trustworthy. So you'll be the one recruiting the agents."

The warrior mountains are hidden now by night, but I need more than nightfall to hide my incredulity. "Recruit military men? I know what they're like—I married one. They'll either laugh or spit on me if I try to recruit them for anything other than a date."

"Then wear a raincoat and laugh right back."

"That's so easy for you to say!" I jump to my feet, cross to the balustrade, brace my hands against it. "You're one of the most well-known military intelligence officers in the country. Nobody's ever spat on you."

"Spoken by a woman who's never seen a battlefield."

It all comes down to this, doesn't it? The knowledge I can never lay claim to because of my gender. But—*I have seen one,* I almost retort. My heart bears the scars of the most personal battlefield of all: marriage.

But wrapped around Navarre's neck is a twisted scar from the German bullet that almost killed him last month. My skin is porcelain smooth.

I close my eyes, confronted by a picture from a long time ago. A *wild child,* the Shanghai mothers called me—the ones who wore white lawn day dresses and who always knew where their hats were. If anyone said it within my father's earshot, he'd take out the dictionary, turn to the *w* section.

"*Wild: a free or natural state of existence,*" he'd read. "*Passionately eager.*"

I'd lean in closer so I could make sure he wasn't inventing these descriptions that were all the things I wanted to be—all the things I was.

"*Deviating from the intended or expected course,*" he'd go on. "*Having no basis in known fact.*"

I took it as a compliment and a motto—I'd live a life that outran expectations, like a ship blown into a new ocean not needing the stars to find its way. There was no *way* to find except the one I chose.

And now it's time to choose. For me. For my children. For my country. We deserve more than to be condemned to *travail, famille, patrie*—and Nazis.

"Being a woman is the best qualification of all," Navarre says. "Who'd ever suspect—"

I open my eyes. "A woman."

Once upon a time I didn't know how to fly a plane or play an étude. But anything can be learned if you want it enough.

I'm thirty years old and the mother of a ten-year-old boy and an eight-year-old girl who I hope will have futures of airplanes and music and freedom and awe.

"Then I'd better get a raincoat," I say. "Or learn to spit."

I see my first Nazi on Rue du Parc in Vichy. He's on a white horse, surveying the town from on high, uniform sleek and gray—an elegant rat. Some passersby stare, others nod deferentially; two young women smile.

Around us, women in pastel dresses shop and lunch at the Hôtel du Parc as if they're subjects in a Belle-Epoque painting. Their husbands either are part of the new ministry of Nazi collaborators or are here trying to gain the favor of those collaborators. Do these women really have no idea that the government ran away while French children were strafed by the Luftwaffe?

Their ignorance and their husbands' groveling makes doubt flare. What if everyone believes Pétain has our best interests at heart—that he even has a heart? What if they think only inconsequential things have changed: menus written in German, the Nazis having first choice of the couturiers' silks?

Finding people who want to help us dig up the Nazis' secrets might be harder than I'd thought.

Sensing my dismay, Navarre indicates the Nazi. "Uniforms dirty easily."

"So do white horses," I reply.

We open a reception center for the Légion française des combattants at the Hôtel des Sports. De-mobbed French soldiers come in ready to eat, to talk, to receive financial and career advice and medical care. My job is to ensure the supply of fresh flowers, hot food, and warm fires—the atmosphere men expect but never wonder how it happens.

"Be invisible," Navarre tells me. "Eavesdrop. Take anyone worth talking to up to the first floor."

I'd like to believe I *could* be invisible. But it takes only a day to know that's impossible.

"*La maîtresse,*" I hear one ex-military officer say.

He could be referring to my role as mistress of this establishment, but his tone tells me otherwise. These men, all at least fifteen years older than me, can't think of a single reason why I'd be here other than as Navarre's mistress. France is ruled by Hitler, but all they want to talk about is who's sleeping with whom. Their eyes travel like advancing armies over my body—a simpler kind of covetousness than Hitler's, but it comes from the same impulse: to be the one with the most power. Being a woman means either accepting weakness or learning that anything can be repurposed as a weapon.

I pick up a lukewarm coffee pot, trip on a flat piece of carpet, and spill the coffee over his lap. Chaos ensues. So much for being invisible.

"We're not going to defeat Hitler with espresso," I say to Navarre at the end of our first month, when the quantity of coffee I've served to self-important officers is significantly greater than the quantity of information I've gathered.

I pour us both a brandy. A double.

"The Germans are building sentry boxes along the demarcation line and manning them with armed soldiers." My voice is flat, the brandy too delicious. "I heard you'll need an *Ausweis* to cross into the Occupied Zone—and that getting an *Ausweis* will be about as easy as climbing the Eiffel Tower without a rope."

"Did they reach Mougins?" Navarre asks, redirecting the conversation.

I nod. He's referring to my mother and children, who've arrived safely at our Riviera summer home in Mougins in the *zone nono*. The Nazis allowed refugees, excepting Jews and foreigners, to cross the demarcation line for a short period to return home. I can breathe again.

Navarre swallows his brandy. "I heard from a friend yesterday that our Renault workshops are now making German tanks."

"And I heard that the ports in Bordeaux are being modified to house U-boats. U-boats in France." My brandy vanishes, too.

"The Allies need to know that."

We're slumped in the comfy leather chairs of the empty reception room, firelight illuminating our despair rather than making the night feel cozy, the hothouse roses sagging in their vases in mimicry of our posture. Our plan in coming to Vichy is to gather enough information to impress either the British or De Gaulle. We need support to build a proper intelligence network, and they have money, supplies, and arms.

I shiver. What would we do with bullets and arms?

With my arms, I want to hold my children.

Which means believing that the woman who gathered information to show her husband the Moroccan people wouldn't just accept the Berber Decree can do this, too.

"All right," I say, trying to convince myself as much as anyone. "We have three pieces of information. U-boats, Renault workshops, and demarcation line fortifications. So we have more than we did yesterday."

Navarre picks up the brandy bottle and tips another finger into our glasses, voice emphatic—the military leader returned. "Here's to making sure that each day we know a little more than the day before."

I go for a walk in the evening blackout, trying to find inspiration for tomorrow. But everything in Vichy is strict, regimented—the trees spaced at precise intervals along the main street, the soldierly lampposts. There's no hot, red sand. No bazaars or souks. No music.

One awning, different from all the rest, catches my eye. It's adorned with yellow stars just bright enough to be visible in the dark.

Raoul Théret, Astrologue.

I've believed in stars since the night my father took me outside and held me up in his arms and told me the stories of the constellations hanging above Mount Moganshan in China. The story of Callisto, or Ursa Major, the she-bear forever hung in the sky beside her son, just as I would like to be forever alongside my children. Perhaps that's why I enter—the sense that I'm failing at everything. I'm not with my children, nor am I doing any good here in Vichy.

Monsieur Théret indicates that I should sit on the banquette, where I blurt out, "I want to know about France's future."

"*L'Autrichien mourra de manière violente,*" he says without hesitation.

THE MADEMOISELLE ALLIANCE   33

The Austrian will die a violent death.

Hitler. It has to be.

I'm about to ask, *When?* but the astrologer says, "You cannot change what's written in the stars. But you can use your cunning to arrive at your destiny."

"My destiny?"

"Vous irez jusqu'au bout de votre route."

You will go to the end of your road.

"What road?" I whisper.

"Madame," the astrologer says solemnly. "You will make it to the end of everything."

The room is black-draped, like night. Celestial charts paper the walls, bringing the moon and stars inside. For a moment, I feel as if I'm hanging in the sky, a brilliant tear in the darkness, able now to see.

I press myself up with such fervor I surprise even the future-seer. "Thank you."

Cunning means being inventive. I don't have to speak to the men Navarre wants me to talk to. I'm good at weaving a story that enthralls people—that's where *my* experience lies.

Tomorrow I'll find a group I have something in common with. I'll put down the coffee pot and be an enchantress instead.

Only as I'm about to fall asleep do I remember the astrologer's other prediction: *You will make it to the end of everything.* What exactly is written in the stars that glitter above me, like the dust left by once sparkling lives?

5

You're a Go-Between

Rabat, 1929

One drawback of Edouard's brooding Heathcliff personality is that he's less sociable than me. He retires to his bureau after dinner and people come to see him, but it's for work, not pleasure. I'm left to float around our villa, gramophone on low, dancing alone, worried I might forget how to waltz. The piano tempts me, but Edouard asked me to use the dampener if he had people over, and a tamped-down sonata is like an unlit candle.

"Why don't you meet them at your office during the day?" I ask him one night when he comes to my room, bemoaning his meetings for having kept him away when he could have been here in my bed, kissing my neck.

And it's there in my bed that he gives me an introduction to intelligence work.

"Because there's a chain," he says. "You need someone at the top, which is me." He draws me beneath him and I laugh.

"What am I, the *larbin* at the bottom?"

He kisses me again. "You might be under me, but you're not an underling. You're a go-between."

"I don't know if that's innuendo or explanation," I say, still laughing.

"We could make it the first"—his hand slips between us—"but I meant the latter. Do you really want to know, or is this your way of trying to seduce me?"

"I don't think I need to try very hard at that. But you know what I'm like when my curiosity is piqued."

Edouard groans. "If quenching your curiosity will get us back to your neck, then I'll tell you that the go-betweens are the ones who come here at night. I'm known in Rabat, so if they come and see me during the day, it's obvious they're passing on information. They find out things and bring them to me. Like you found out something from that mother. She can't come to my office. So I need go-betweens. Cultivating them is the biggest part of my job. But now that I have one in my bed . . ." His lips are no longer on my neck but everywhere else. "I don't intend to talk about my job anymore."

I take advantage of Edouard's good mood to persuade him to go dancing the following night at the French Club, where all the expatriates gather.

I slip into a cream and gold crushed-velvet Vionnet gown that I adore. It's so contoured that this is probably the last chance I'll have to wear it until after the baby is born, and I twirl for Edouard when he comes into my room.

He frowns. "Isn't that dress just for me?"

I press a kiss onto his lips. "This is definitely not a house dress."

His frown disarranges his entire face.

"You don't really want me to change?" I hate the tentativeness in my voice, as if I'm actually considering complying.

He points to his watch. "You've taken too long already. We're meeting your friends at eight. Although, how you can have friends when you've only been here a few months, I'll never know."

"I talk to people, for a start," I tease, trying to cheer him up. "Why don't we walk through the *medina*? It'll be romantic."

"*La curiosité est un vilain défaut.*" The curiosity that only last night Edouard had enjoyed has suddenly become my fatal flaw. As if to drive the point home, he continues, "You only go to the *medina* after nightfall if you want to be robbed. There's a reason they lock the gates of the city each night. We aren't . . ."

In France. I mouth the words he says most days. Before tonight, I'd have grabbed his hands and cried, *But that's exactly why we should explore! We don't know how long this will last.*

Meaning, *how long we'll be in Morocco.* But now an uncomfortable doubt writhes in my stomach.

I rediscover my smile when we enter the club. The group of officers and wives I've made friends with in that way you do when you're all far from home—swiftly and intimately—calls out, "Marie-Madeleine!"

Rather than join us, Edouard says, "There's someone I need to speak to." Then he's gone and my hand is empty.

I sit beside Marguerite, who, along with her husband, Maurice, has become my closest friend. They're both divinely beautiful, overflowing with high spirits, and have taken me under their wing. She's a princess and he's the duke of Magenta, as well as an officer in the air force and a flying ace. I've gone with her to watch his aerobatics displays and been spellbound by the extraordinariness of flight.

"My husband is trying to persuade someone to be his navigator for the Morocco Car Rally," Marguerite tells me. "But I don't think many people besides me enjoy having their bones rattled into dust on the twelve-hour return trip from Casablanca to Marrakech." She gestures to her stomach, which is the rounded ball of a near-full-term pregnancy. "Even I'm not daredevil enough to want to give birth out in the desert, which is a more certain outcome from all that jolting than him coming first."

Maurice laughs. "Now you've set the challenge."

"What does the navigator do?" I ask.

"Tries to keep everyone alive and heading in the right direction." Marguerite smiles.

"I'll do it," I say as something sparks inside me that's been tamped down by long nights at home and silly squabbles with Edouard. "I've been driving since I was fourteen. My mother has a property on the Riviera, and after my father . . ."

I try to say it as unemotionally as I can, but my words still hitch. "After my father died and we came back to France, I'd drive the truck to take hay to the animals. I know most women don't drive, but I'm a good driver and . . ." I grin. "That sounds like an adventure."

The duke lifts his glass. "To adventure. And to us coming in first."

"I don't care how pregnant I am." Marguerite holds up her glass, too. "I'll be at the finish line in Casablanca cheering you on."

We clink glasses exuberantly because—this is life. The fast riff of a saxophone as you find a kindred spirit in a Moroccan nightclub. The gin tickling your tongue like anticipation as you discover the next trail to blaze.

Maybe I can eavesdrop for Edouard in Casablanca, too.

My feet start moving to the music, my shoulders as well. I look around for Edouard but can't see him.

"Dance with Maurice," Marguerite says. "I'm too big to move."

The duke kisses his wife, trails his fingertips over her stomach, offers me his hand, and we have so much fun dancing to a Spanish *pasodoble* that we continue on to the next song—nobody here thinks it's improper if you dance with someone other than your husband. In fact, it's almost encouraged.

Stops us all from getting bored, Marguerite had said to me once with a devilish wink. Then she confessed that she didn't think she could ever be bored of Maurice, even if they were

married for a thousand years. I'd been smitten by the romance
of it, determined to be the one saying those words to the next
new bride in Morocco.

When we return to the group, I ask Maurice to tell me how
it feels to fly upside down, and soon all the officers of the Armée
de l'air are good-naturedly competing with one another for the
right to take me up in a plane, when I feel a grip on my arm, just
like when I'd wanted to buy soap.

"We're leaving."

My eyes search the room for the source of Edouard's anger
even as the voice in my head whispers, *He's mad at you*.

"We haven't danced yet," I say, thinking I can cajole him
back into being the dashing man who'd gone down on one knee
on a dance floor in Paris after only a few weeks. "This is a dancing dress, remember?"

"You didn't wear that dress for me." He tugs me to my feet
and steers me across the room in front of everyone. They all
stare—even the Arab waiters, who never make eye contact with
the French.

"Drunk," I hear someone whisper, and I flush. I've had one
glass of gin.

In the car, he doesn't let go of my arm. I'm speechless, have
no context for what just happened. I know what flirting is, and
it's not what I was doing. I adore dancing. And laughter. And
friends. What an idiot I was. If he can barely tolerate my dancing, he won't agree to my going to Casablanca, much less navi-
gating in a car rally.

When the front door closes behind us, Edouard barks, "What
do you do in the afternoons?"

"I go to Marguerite's!" I cry. "She can't walk around the city
now, and she's bored. Maurice sometimes joins us and I talk
to him about flying, the same way I talk to Marguerite about
dresses—"

He cuts me off. "That's the problem. You're too open. You

wear your emotions like a bright red dress. Too obviously, and like something most men will want to remove."

My mind grapples with the metaphor. How can anyone be too open? Or too happy? Or too in love?

I touch his cheek and tell him the one truth that should matter the most. "I love you. Like Marguerite loves Maurice, and like he loves her. We married fast and sometimes we surprise each other, but if I could spend every afternoon with you, I would. If I could dance with you every night, I would—"

This time, he cuts me off with a kiss and I'm so glad I almost weep. Everything will be all right.

Later, when Edouard's asleep, I climb out of bed and cross to the windows. From the streets below, a snake charmer's flute plays, a siren call for hips that like to move, for souls that like to quest. That's when I decide.

Marriages require compromise. So I'll forget what happened at the club—unless it happens again. But for better or for worse, I'm going to be in that car rally.

6

Like I'm Seventeen Again

Vichy, December 1940–February 1941

bypass the high-ranking men at the Hôtel des Sports and eavesdrop on those closer to my age, stopping when I find a group sharing war stories about falling from the sky. One of them, small and spry like the foxes that roamed the western Sahara, is recounting that, back in June, the air force sent him up in an Arsenal with almost no fuel because they'd run out. It stayed airborne for just ten minutes.

I wince. Arsenals are made of plywood. "That must have been like crash-landing in a cardboard box."

He grins. "You sound like you know airplanes."

Now everyone's eyes are on me. A woman who knows airplanes is as common as a heroic Vichy politician.

"I used to fly a Caudron," I tell them. "Until a friend borrowed it and mistook the Loire for a landing strip."

They groan and ask how I learned to fly. I tell them that the duke of Magenta, a name known by all pilots, is a friend of mine. They're fascinated to hear of our exploits in Morocco, of the time he took me up and, without warning, performed an avalanche, throwing the plane into a snap roll at the top of a loop.

Everyone gasps. Pulling off an avalanche in 1928 was, for

anyone other than the duke, suicide. "I made him promise to teach me when I learned to fly."

"And did he?" someone demands.

"Of course."

The man who crash-landed the Arsenal offers me his seat at the head of the group with a sweeping bow. I settle in, ready to trade more aerobatic tales, when he says, "If you've lived outside France, then you must have a different perspective on what's happening here now."

The mood shifts. Eyes dart from him to me to the officers by the fire. Air is held in lungs, waiting.

Is he testing my loyalties? What are his?

But if I don't take a risk, I'll never know if any of these men could be Navarre's intelligence gatherers. Without intelligence gatherers, we'll have very little to give the British, who, the newspapers tell us, are being bombed to rubble by the Luftwaffe.

"My perspective is a bit like when you're upside down in a plane," I say very quietly. "You have to have faith that, despite gravity and everything else that's working against you, you can turn yourself right again. Like you going up in that Arsenal. You knew it would crash, but you went up anyway because you believed you could turn things around for France."

I stand, hoping I've said enough, but not too much to attract the attention of enemies. "If anyone would like to talk about turning things around, I'll be upstairs."

Once in my office, I freeze. A year ago at the newspaper there were no consequences for running an anti-Nazi enterprise. Now there are. Neither Vichy France nor the Nazis will tolerate treason.

Then my friend from downstairs appears in the doorway, another man beside him.

We stare at one another.

I need to say something because the silence has gone on for so long that it is its own musical score.

Think of each piece of information as a twig, Navarre said to me the day the Hôtel des Sports opened. *One is inconsequential. But gather enough and you can make a bonfire.*

Which makes me the girl in the forest collecting firewood, always on the lookout for wolves. How do you spot a wolf?

They have yellow eyes.

The pilot has eyes the color of chestnuts: Christmas and family and warmth. His hair is neatly combed and his trim little mustache looks to have just been smoothed down with water.

You only present yourself carefully if you're worried you might fail. *Oh.* He thinks I might reject *him.*

He has no idea I need all the help I can get.

The man beside him is so young. Maybe the same age I was when I went to Morocco, back when I didn't understand that my husband's black eyes disguised the fact that his love was a weapon, trained on me.

This man's eyes are as round as medals, lending him the same air of principle.

"Come in," I tell them.

"Maurice Coustenoble," the brown-eyed one says. "And this is Henri Schaerrer. Ex-navy."

From out of his pocket, Coustenoble pulls papers scribbled with names and addresses. "These people all want to turn things around for France. But not *Vichy* France."

I reach for the pieces of paper. Every name listed is a potential go-between who'll find people out there who know how many pens are being built in the new U-boat nest in Bordeaux, which factories are now making munitions instead of cars. I'll teach them all to eavesdrop, to memorize everything, to never carry notes.

I *do* know what I'm doing.

Coustenoble says, "If every Frenchman really wanted to let

the Germans rule us, then the air force would have saved the Arsenal. I'm on the side of anyone who thinks flying an almost empty airplane is an act of hope. I decided to find others who believed that, too."

"We've been talking to people on trains and in bars, writing everything down," Schaerrer finishes.

These two are exactly what I need: people with the optimistic conviction that scribbling names onto a piece of paper will make a difference, and the indefatigableness to do it in the first place.

"No more writing things down," I say. "Or, if you do, use tiny pieces of paper that you can slip into a slit in a seam. I'll show you."

And so it begins.

Under the banner of the Légion française des combattants, we're relatively safe in the free zone. The Vichy government doesn't have any idea that people are working against them, and only Nazis from the Armistice Commission are permitted here. So I interview the men from Coustenoble and Schaerrer's list and enroll some in our crusade.

They all know of Navarre, the Great War hero turned rebel. He's the reason they come. When they discover they're meeting a woman, some flee. Others try to strong-arm me into a kiss, but they don't know I've seen plenty of street fights in Shanghai and Morocco and that a pair of scissors from my desktop makes an excellent substitute for a dagger.

Coustenoble, having heard another scuffle upon his return from recruiting truck drivers, bursts into my office, but the offender is already making a hasty retreat.

"Problem?" Coustenoble asks.

"Solution," I say, holding up the scissors.

I'm making myself more of an outcast than ever, but I'm

happy upstairs among the mavericks and life livers. Soon I have fifteen people sending me information.

I send Schaerrer to Marseille—where ships, supplies, people, and secrets enter and leave France—to find someone who could start an outpost there. I hang maps on the walls and I mark the locations of the munitions factories and aircraft manufacturing plants the informants tell me about—all potential bombing targets for the British.

If we can get in touch with them.

That's Navarre's job. Mine is recruiting, which I do well into the new year, until an air force commander enters the Hôtel des Sports one day in February. His height is what makes me look up, my attention caught by the head above the crowd. And what a head it is, as perfectly sculpted as a Rodin visage.

Mon Dieu. In seven years of separation, while I might have occasionally admired a handsome face, I've never compared one to a masterwork.

Before my thoughts run any wilder, I retreat upstairs. The man has arrived with General Baston, a former air force general who's running a statistics department for Pétain and who's also one of Navarre's informants. I expect Baston will follow me up shortly and he does.

"This is Commandant Léon Faye." Baston gestures to the man beside him. "Deputy chief of the air force in North Africa. Fifteen minutes ago, I had to stop him from punching Pétain. I told him he'd find fools of similar temperament here."

Baston doesn't know what to make of me. Pretty women, he told me at our first meeting, belong at their husbands' sides. He shies away if I get too near, worried my unorthodoxies are contagious. But he's doggedly loyal to Navarre, and we need someone in the Vichy government on our side, so I ignore the comment about fools.

Léon smiles at this assessment of us and I can't help but return the gesture. His position in the air force explains his self-confidence and air of command, qualities that would make him an ideal agent in North Africa. The fact that he also has a strongly cast jawline and thick, dark hair is absolutely redundant.

I push myself up from the desk, flee to the cognac decanter even though it's barely midday, and pour out three glasses.

"What brings you here from Algiers?" I ask, fixing my attention on business.

"I came to ask Pétain for more men and money for my squadrons," Léon says, a hint of fire still sparking in each word.

He doesn't sit and nor do I, although Baston drops heavily into a chair. A dozen sheets of paper flutter with agitation.

"I thought there were patriots in Vichy who'd want the air force to be equipped to fight for France when the time is right." Léon swallows the brandy in two gulps.

"Pétain refused," I guess.

Some military men, who've been trained to fight for their country—to lay down their lives for it—believe Pétain is planning to equip the armed forces to rise up against the Nazis. Léon Faye must believe that, too. But Pétain will never bite the hand that's given him a banquet. No, he wants to gorge himself—while taking away our ability to eat.

Abortion has been declared treasonous, punishable by death. It's now illegal for women to work in the public sector. Laws from forty years ago that prohibit women from having control over the money they earn have just been reintroduced. And divorce laws have become more restrictive, which means that if Pétain and the Nazis stay in power, I'll have to live out my life as Edouard's wife, never knowing the kind of love that makes you feel as though a symphony has been played on your heart.

I almost surrendered myself to my husband seven years ago. I have no intention of surrendering to Hitler.

I take a seat at my desk and Léon sits opposite me. "I don't need Pétain," he fumes. "You're here with Navarre because you think there's still a fight to be had. Well, I have the air force on our side in both Algiers and Tunisia. I've secured the navy's assistance, too. And I'm working on the army."

"To do what?" I ask, unable to stop myself from leaning forward. I'm speechless at the audacity. Navarre's always said intelligence is the only weapon we have right now. That we'll fight with real weapons later. But Léon is saying . . .

"We can fight the Germans now. Starting in North Africa, with the French forces we have there."

It's the most reckless plan I've ever heard. "You're mad."

Baston finally agrees with me on something. "*Il a une araignée au plafond.*"

Yes, Léon Faye definitely has spiders in the ceiling.

"Better to be mad and right than sane and submissive," Léon fires back, tapping a cigarette from a case as furiously as if it's the French prime minister he'd been prevented from punching earlier. "If I settle for the latter, I'll be dead in a few months when the Nazis pour into Algiers and occupy that, too. They will, you know. But if I attack first, then I at least have a chance of living through it."

Baston rumples his hair to the point of almost tearing it out. "I'll get Navarre."

But I'm worried Navarre will fall for Léon Faye's damn fool plot, too.

Baston gone, Léon and I regard each other over the desk, partners in aims but enemies in methods. The hand gripping his cigarette relaxes a little and he says, "You called me mad and I called you submissive. I'm not making a good first impression."

I smile. "Maybe you're impassioned rather than insane."

"Well, I'm happy to accept any description that has the word *passion* in it," he says with a grin, and I laugh. He's flirting, but in a way that's more charming than annoying.

Except that, beneath the banter, we're talking about launching a coup in North Africa.

It's time to ignore the charm. "I agree there's a fight to be had," I say. "But not yet. Right now we need to gather intelligence and wait. Most of all, we need someone in North Africa."

He leans back in his chair, one restless hand turning a Gauloises pack over and over. Instead of discussing my proposal, he asks, "How did you like Morocco? I was stationed there for years. The duke of Magenta is a good friend."

If Léon is a friend of Maurice's, then hopefully it means that whatever he knows of me, it's that my greatest fault was loving my children, and of believing myself to be more than the one thing my husband allowed me to be: Mrs. Edouard Méric.

"I adored it. Occasionally I hated it."

Léon's smile is surprisingly gentle for a man who's just sparred with Pétain. "Brutal and luminous," he says.

Yes, I want to say. *Exactly.* But he shifts the conversation again, asking, "What are you fighting for?"

He's the first person who's asked me this and I almost snap a retort at the condescension that probably lurks beneath the question. But Léon's expression is curious, as if he's looking for someone who wants the same thing he does.

"I have two children," I say very carefully, because thinking about how long it's been since I held them makes me want to cry, and speaking of them is the hardest thing of all. "I never want . . ."

Béatrice's blond hair unfurls in my mind. My hands quiver, wanting to braid those tresses. Are they still long, falling to the middle of her back?

Mothers should know those things. But I only know this: "I never want my children to believe that their mother taught them to sit back and accept something that they know is wrong."

I almost don't add this last thing, but it spills out. "My youngest is a girl, and I can't bear her knowing only a world that shuts women in a trap from the moment they're born. Based on what's happened in Germany, the Nazis are readying that trap for France."

Léon is silent for a moment, staring at the empty glass in his hand. Then he says softly, "That's worth fighting for."

Our eyes meet. In his, I see, hopelessly, the glitter of stars in the black Shanghai sky. "What are you fighting for?" I ask, voice low.

"My father was a policeman," he replies, mouth quirking at the surprise that flashes across my face. Like Edouard, like General Baston, like Navarre, most high-ranking military men come from a narrow band of moneyed society who have the pedigree to get into the École superiéure de guerre. A policeman's son has no pedigree at all.

"I joined the army at seventeen, didn't even finish high school," he says, unabashed. "But I was a great pilot. When the air force invited me to apply to the École supérieure, I buried myself in books for months to get in. And I prefer what I had—a knowledge from the cradle that I could achieve anything I worked at, a knowledge of what was right and what was wrong, and the belief that I should do whatever I could to stand firm with the former. I don't want all the other small boys in small towns in France to grow up mistaking evil for honor."

He pauses, but I sense he isn't finished.

"And?" I pass him another cigarette.

He shrugs, but the ferocity is back in his voice when he replies, "My older brother and my brother-in-law, two people I was closer to than anyone, died in the Great War fighting the Germans. If I do nothing, it's like saying they were worthless cannon fodder."

A man who thinks not just of himself, but of those who might come after him and those who came before him—ghosts who will never force him to pay that debt of honor—is someone I want to talk to more. But I shouldn't. A man driven by the kind of love that drives Léon Faye—love for honor and country—will be a fine soldier, but a fine heartbreaker, too.

Then he adds, "Now I'm also fighting for you—so that *your* wish might come true."

Through the window comes the sound of a string quartet playing in the neighboring hotel, where Nazis dine with Vichy collaborators. I keep the window open because they play delightfully and, I like to think, subversively. Today they've chosen Mozart's *Dissonance* quartet, and they go straight into the Andante Cantabile, four stringed instruments singing as if they're on the edge of weeping.

I close my eyes. There is tenderness. There is passion. There is darkness. There is all of life in the touch of a bow on a string. How can we make something so exquisite—and then turn around and kill our neighbors?

"I love this piece," I say, opening my eyes. "I like to think they're playing it because it's the only way they can cry. It's their protest, perfectly hidden in music."

"Just like you hide your protests behind an officer's club and . . ." Léon hesitates only as long as the beat of a semiquaver before adding, voice low, "a beautiful smile."

I never flush, not anymore. I gave it up the first time my husband ordered me to stay at home. But now I flush like I'm seventeen again and have no idea that love is just the same as war.

Like Navarre, I live at the Hôtel des Sports. I get up around five in the morning, accustomed to my son Christian's sparrow-like hours. I use the bathroom down the hall before anyone is awake, hurrying through my ablutions—one of the elderly guests is either deaf to the sound of someone in there or determined to catch me *au naturel*.

Alone in that tiny bathroom, lit by one bulb and shadowed by black mold, I dwell on the things I miss. Freshly squeezed orange juice. In Morocco, I used to drink it with breakfast, and I planted an orange tree in our courtyard when I returned to Paris. Cosmetics. I have half a lipstick left and my face powder's almost gone.

I glide the barest hint of color onto my lips, decide I can go without powder, and know I'm thinking about these unimportant things to avoid thinking about the things I miss most of all. I'd give up orange juice, lipstick, warm baths, and almost everything else for my children. And my mother and sister, too.

Yet here I am in Vichy, not giving up this work.

I run from my reflection in the mirror, almost knocking over the old gentleman outside. "Perhaps that will teach you to knock," I snap.

Which is my pain talking.

"*Désolée,*" I whisper before hurrying downstairs to where the truck drivers are arriving, bringing in food for the Légion and messages from our agents. I sit with them in the kitchen, drinking ersatz *café nationale,* smoking cigarettes, and enchanting them with Moroccan anecdotes. I catch myself sometimes, the colonizer making the colonized into a fable, treating their culture like a curiosity. Today is one of those days, and the shame makes the chicory sit like wood in my stomach and my desperation for a real coffee drunk at my kitchen table with my children almost unbearable.

But, to gather enough intelligence for the Allies, I have to tell stories. The truck drivers love them, and I need them to keep bringing me tightly folded pieces of paper. So I persuade myself it's indigestion that's bothering me, rather than my conscience.

The drivers prefer gruesome tales of pomp and splendor arrayed around violence, so I describe the ceremony of the Sacrifice of the Sheep, where a rider galloped from the *msalla* into

Rabat with a sheep that had had its throat expertly slit slung across his saddle. If the sheep was still alive when it reached Rabat, it was a good omen for the Sultan.

"Not so good for the sheep," I conclude. They howl and pass me little squares of paper, warmed by camaraderie, and I know they'll return next week with more.

By late morning, I'm in my office reading through the notes, which tell me about decoy airfields the British are bombing because they don't know the locations of the real ones, and rumors the Nazis will invade Russia, their ally.

"That can't be true," I say to Navarre when he passes by, shocked that even Hitler would attack his friends.

"Find out more," he says, and I cross to my map, considering which of the fifty agents we now have in our ranks will be able to tackle such a risky piece of sleuthing.

That's where Léon Faye finds me. He's returning to North Africa and his mad but audacious plot, which Navarre, just as I'd feared, has given his blessing to. But he's also agreed to become the leader of our new North African sector.

Léon holds out a package. "For you."

I try to nonchalantly unpeel the paper but end up tearing off at least half. Inside, I find a cake of Moroccan black soap, like the one Edouard wouldn't let me buy. I inhale the scent as deeply as if I'm planning to eat it.

I look up at Léon. He's watching me with a smile I don't know how to interpret. Does he think that with one bar of soap I'll tumble into his arms? Or is he happy because, for a moment, I was, too?

"You brought soap with you from Algiers," I say as I rewrap it. "You were planning to seduce someone?"

"I was just hoping to talk to someone besides pilots. Most of them don't use soap." His tone is easygoing, his expression intent.

It's almost impossible to look away.

But . . .

"Coustenoble!" I call.

He bounds in.

"Give this to one of the men." I pass him the soap, hiding my reluctance beneath a quip. "I'm sure half of them haven't bathed since the occupation."

Léon surprises me by bursting into laughter. Coustenoble leaves with the soap and a bemused expression. And I tell Léon, "I'm married."

Despite not having seen my husband for seven years. Despite knowing I'll never see him again.

"That's why I only offered you soap," he says, eyes two licks of flame that suggest he has so much more to offer me than soap.

It's a look that makes even my insides flush.

How many men, when wanting more, take nothing—but give a little instead?

"I *will* see you again," he says when he leaves, and it sounds like a future rather than just a dream.

The following week, I stare at papers, foot tapping restless staccato beats on the floor. Our agents have told us so many things. But Navarre says we still don't have enough to approach the British.

This is why men plot coups and get thrown in jail for treason—doing something bold keeps you from thinking how it would feel to lose. Thankfully Schaerrer appears before I do something reckless too, and I realize this is like being a mother. Some days you do the most minute tasks over and over, no matter how futile they seem. Someone has to find agents and collate their information so that there's something left to fight with if the coups fail.

Schaerrer's face is so lit up he needs his own blackout shade. "I found someone in Marseille who wants to talk," he bursts out.

It's my turn for boldness, at last. If I can set up a successful

Marseille sector, then we'll be able to tell the British the movements and cargo of every ship into and out of Marseille.

I ask Schaerrer to set up a meeting, and he's only just left when I hear Navarre marching down the hall. "Look!" he shouts, holding out a newspaper. On the front is a photograph of Pétain shaking hands with Hitler. Beneath are the words, attributed to Pétain: *I enter today on the path of collaboration.*

"Our Marshal will now officially collaborate with the Germans across all zones," Navarre says, fury in his voice. "He's going to let the French police work with the Nazis to ferret out any opposition."

Which means they suspect that, somewhere, there *is* opposition.

The danger of what we're doing has just increased a hundredfold. But I airplane the newspaper into the trash can.

"More people might join us, now they know Pétain's true colors. Someone in Marseille is interested. And we have all of this." I gesture to my folders of intelligence. "Maybe it's time to go to the British."

And Navarre finally agrees!

But the obvious question is: *How?*

The government will notice if Navarre vanishes for what's likely to be weeks. Britain is enemy territory. It's forbidden to travel there. He'll have to take a ship to Morocco, then stow away on another ship to Gibraltar, where they might well throw an unauthorized French traveler into prison as a spy.

"I'll tell Vichy I'm ill," he says, hands still clenched into fists of fury. "That I need to rest and recuperate. But the burden will be on you to charm them if they come to investigate. You'll be directly in their firing line."

Yesterday I'd have waved that off. But after Pétain's announcement, Navarre's words are like a cloud bank swallowing up the plane you're flying. The only thing you can be certain of is that the cloud is a cold knife pressed against your neck.

7

Full Throttle

Casablanca, 1929

Never have I ever done anything like this! The Rally of Morocco is as bone-rattling as Marguerite warned, but the red desert stretching on to Marrakech steals my breath and then my heart. It's the emptiest place on earth. No villages. No nomad tents. No life. Just skeletons and a glittering red-rock road. Only out there is it possible to get a true sense of the great, ungraspable sweep of the world. How perfect every corner is, even with its flaws. If it weren't so empty here, you would never feel so full of awe.

When we reach Marrakech, we hear we're in seventh place.

"Ready to give it our all?" Maurice asks.

"Nothing less."

We race back to Casablanca at an even faster pace, Maurice at the wheel, me watching for potholes and boulders, deer foxes and polecats—anything that might cause a mechanical catastrophe in the middle of nowhere.

Atop the hill into Casablanca, I look across at Maurice and we both shout, "Full throttle!" before we fly into the city half laughing, half terrified, careening around every near-blind curve, me using the map to call out warnings, Maurice braking just enough for us to survive each one.

When we pull into the Place de France, I see Marguerite

waving frantically. Maurice leaps out, picks up his delicate wife, and kisses her passionately, the two of them like a rhapsody played on French horn: colorful, tonal, ecstatic. Like I thought I would be, like I sometimes am with Edouard. And in the midst of such radiant joy, I imagine Edouard will be just as proud when I tell him I came fourth in the great Morocco Car Rally.

"You look like aliens," Marguerite says, gesturing to the red dirt caked over us.

I groan. "I think I left my backbone somewhere near Settat. You can be his navigator next time."

"You won't do it again?" The duke looks at me quizzically.

"Next time, I'm driving." I grin. "And maybe I'll even beat you."

We drag our aching bodies back to the Hôtel Excelsior, where I have a luxurious bath. Then we go down to the brasserie with the other drivers and navigators and the European sophisticates who populate Casablanca to celebrate having beaten thirty other cars.

Our group is mid–extravagant conversation when Marguerite seizes my arm and excuses us.

Her belly parts the crowds. Once we're in a corner, she asks, "Did you tell Edouard?"

I stare at the floor. "I told him I was coming away with you. I invited him, but he said he was busy. And the rally part . . ." I look up at her. "I thought forgiveness would be easier than permission. I will tell him."

"Marie-Madeleine," she says gently, "he's here."

"Maybe he just missed me."

Marguerite can't hide the pity on her face.

"Come back to the table," she urges. "He won't make a scene in front of Maurice."

But Edouard marched me out of a nightclub in Rabat. I can't bear to be dragged from another room. Because I promised myself I'd do something if it happened again. Now that it's a possibility, I can hear the sound of my promise breaking, little shards of my self-worth scattering onto the floor.

"Don't let him empty you out," Marguerite whispers before I flee to the elevator.

Edouard enters my room about twenty seconds behind me.

"I should have told you," I say, reaching for his hand. "I'm sorry."

He doesn't even see my hand, intent only on the anger that's driven him here.

"When you need money, ask for it." He takes my purse from the table. "You're to only go out with my driver. No more dancing. It's bad for the baby. And you're never to go near a car rally again."

"You can't . . ."

I drop onto the bed, gut-punched by realization. He can.

Per French law, my husband owns my money. He can order me to do whatever he wishes.

For the rest of Edouard's life, I will never be free.

I thought he was a dashing young captain bound for Morocco and that marriage to him would bring adventure and love. I never thought about what it would cost.

I swipe my hand over my cheek and wish with all my might that the child inside me will be a boy. Edouard will never let a daughter live the kind of life I want her to have.

The baby comes in a headlong rush that I'm unprepared for. It's all-consuming, and I hardly remember anything of the thankfully few hours it took for him to be born. All I remember is the instinct. Edouard might have been my first love, but this child is my second, and it's an altogether more ruthless kind. I understand now the love that Ghislaine, my informant, has for her son.

Which means keeping the peace at home. For my son to

thrive, he needs to know the love of a father, just as I knew the love of mine.

I'm lying back on the pillows, utterly spent, my beautiful boy asleep at my breast, when Edouard puts his head in. "Here's your son," I whisper.

He glances at the baby and I watch his face, wanting to see him fall too, but his expression doesn't alter. *"Bon,"* he says, as if I've served him dinner rather than a child. Then he looks at me and his face does change. It softens, love evident in his eyes.

I'm about to invite him to sit beside me and meet Christian properly, but he says, "Some officers are due to arrive in Rabat in a fortnight. I want to take them out to that village where you made friends with that woman. There's a dearth of information coming from the tribes. Maybe you can talk to her again. Or charm her husband with your Arabic." He kisses my cheek.

And I understand. I'm allowed to be myself when it benefits him.

There have been so many nights in this bed when we were like some celestial bit of happiness I mistook for love. But now I know—for Edouard, love is possession.

And my heart withers like the body of the parched donkey in the desert, gasping for just one drop of tenderness.

8

Good God, It's a Woman!

Vichy, February–April 1941

As Schaerrer and I walk along Vichy's tree-lined promenade bound for Marseille, I want to look back over my shoulder. Something's making my skin prickle—not the subzero wind, but the sensation of eyes fixed on me.

Schaerrer's head turns a centimeter, too.

"Can you feel that?" I whisper.

Immediately I wish I hadn't spoken. It's too female, relying on premonitions and feelings. Navarre would never pay attention to a goose bump on his neck.

But Schaerrer says, "Yes."

"Vichy officials have been visiting the hotel more than usual," I murmur. "I don't think they're coming for the turnip soup. I'm not sure how much longer I can persuade them that Navarre isn't taking visitors."

We don't say any more as we reach the station and step onto the train. The carriage smells of unsoaped bodies. Everyone looks more frayed than a year ago, when we all consumed coal as freely as bread, when nobody dreamed we'd be eating turnip soup and wearing shoes with wooden soles. My gut feels just as ragged. What if our days at the Hôtel des Sports are numbered? And why didn't I realize that a group of people plotting against the Nazis wouldn't be able to remain in one place for long?

Now that I've started worrying, I can't stop. In Vichy, I have Navarre's presence behind me. It makes men comfortable, knowing he's there to clean up any mistakes the woman might make. But today, it's all down to me. We either get the Marseille sector up and running—or we deliver the British less than Navarre will be promising. Perhaps I shouldn't have worn lipstick and a sapphire-colored Schiaparelli dress. But would bare lips and a homemade dress make me seem any more trustworthy?

I'd still be young and blond.

At the top of the massive Saint-Charles staircase outside Marseille station, I inhale deeply. This is the place where I was born. On the breeze, I can smell mussels as if they're being cracked open beneath my nose, can taste anise from the Provençal *pastis* you need drink only a few mouthfuls of before every part of you—even your fingernails—is warmed. The stall-holders' cries drift up from the Marché de Noailles, as does the fragrance of the spices they're selling.

I tip my head back, take it all in.

Beside me, Schaerrer's stance mimics mine. But his eyes are wide open, staring straight at the sun. When I try, my eyes shutter instantly.

"How do you do that?" I ask.

"It's something you learn as a sailor," he explains.

I try again but the sun is too dazzling. "Can you actually see it, though? Is it . . ."

I almost don't finish. It's something Navarre would never even wonder, let alone ask. "Is the sun as beautiful as everyone thinks it is?"

Schaerrer replies with the peculiar wisdom that's so at odds with his apple-cheeked youth. "The harder it is to see something, the more beautiful it has to be."

"Like freedom."

Every worry vanishes and a smile like a brilliant "Ode to Joy" plays across my face. *Freedom*. For Béatrice and Christian. That's why I'm here. And it's why I won't fail.

Schaerrer points to my smile. "Me, Coustenoble, the other men—we can all see how much this means to you. You don't hide it. Not like everyone else out there who pretends that France still exists. It makes us all want to do our best for you."

I shake my head. "You're all here because of Navarre."

"I've hardly spoken to Navarre."

Maybe that's true. But the *idea* of Navarre is enough. And when you've been told by the man you married that the openness that's as natural to you as breath is actually a sickening character flaw, it's nice to have someone tell you it's your greatest attribute.

"Shall we?" I ask, still smiling.

Schaerrer leads the way to a café in the Vieux Port.

Inside, it's lively with conversation, red wine, and the foot-tapping songs of Maurice Chevalier. The smell of fishermen's bouillabaisse is strong—saffron, fennel, and garlic, like a Proust madeleine that sends me hurtling to Mougins, where my children are with my mother, who makes the best bouillabaisse in the world.

I push the memory aside as Schaerrer approaches a man who takes one look at me and shouts, as if we're pulling in nets amid the hubbub of the port rather than holding a clandestine meeting, "Good God! It's a woman!"

I might as well be a hippopotamus. I think that would shock them less.

My smile dies. He won't be interested, now he knows I'm a woman.

But then I think—*Am I still interested, now I know that my being a woman has shocked him?* The purpose of this meeting was for *him* to prove himself to *me*.

Sometimes being a woman feels like you're hiding behind an apology.

Not today.

I sit, crossing my legs, refusing to hide my femininity, and lift one immaculate eyebrow. "You're observant. That's a good start for an agent."

He bellows with laughter.

Ah. A sense of humor. I can work with that. I summon the waitress over. "We'll have *anchoïade* and bouillabaisse."

"For everyone?" she asks, round-eyed at my temerity to order food for the men, rather than waiting for them to choose what I eat.

"For everyone," I clarify, and Schaerrer grins, enjoying the spectacle of lady David trying to slay the Goliath of convention.

The man watches all this with blue eyes that are incongruously delicate atop a stocky, no-nonsense body. He's wearing neat trousers and jacket with a dirty old fisherman's cap and a bright red cravat, as if he once ruled the city, or else was a pirate. On a pirate's ship, a woman is bad luck—unless she's a naked and silent figure stuck on a prow—and he seems to think the same lore applies here.

"Tell me what you know about intelligence," he asks.

"I know that I have plenty—in both senses of the word," I shoot back.

He laughs even more heartily and holds out his hand. "Gabriel Rivière."

I think I'm halfway to passing his test. Now I need him to pass mine.

The anchovies and stew are placed on the table. Beneath the raucous chatter of this place that's been well chosen to render our conversation inaudible to eavesdroppers, I ask him to tell me about himself, wanting to know what he thinks is the most important thing to say in this moment.

"Nobody in Marseille despises the Germans more than I do." Rivière attacks the bouillabaisse, keeping the broth and the fish in their two separate plates, drowning his bread in the liquid and chasing it down with a good chunk of meat.

My father ate it like that. As do I. My gut makes another of its sudden judgments. This man is someone I like.

Especially when he says, "I know a grain dealer who has access to shipping manifests and cargoes. I know the police and the Marseille underworld. I know someone who can operate a radio, if you get me one. But for this to work, we need a cover story like you have in Vichy. I propose we buy a fruit-and-vegetable business. It gives me a reason to be traveling around the city. The warehouse can be the meeting place for agents and couriers. My wife will serve in the shop."

It's a great idea. We'll have to reappropriate almost all of our Légion funds, but Navarre's always seen Marseille as the linchpin for the British.

Through the windows, palm trees dance and the afternoon sun casts glitter onto the white wicker chairs, which look like evening gowns at rest. My spirits dance too, and I think I've sealed the deal, until Rivière asks, "Whom will I report to?"

A flock of gulls sink their claws into the wicker chairs the same way Rivière's words puncture my optimism. But Rivière isn't the only pirate at this table. I'd wager a bet that I've traveled more oceans than he has. "You'll report to me."

He doesn't reply. And I don't look away.

I can sense Schaerrer willing me not to be the one who blinks first.

The urge to throw more words at Rivière is almost impossible to subdue. But I remain as still as if one of my children has fallen asleep on my chest. Only my mind shifts, wondering—*Is he thinking still?* And if he is, do I want someone so ponderous? No, I want someone like Léon, with whom affinity was instant. But no other man will be like Léon, and that's a good thing. We need thinkers as well as adventurers, I muse, smiling.

It breaks the impasse. Rivière summons over the waitress and orders *pastis*. He raises his glass. "If women are now waging war, a woman it shall be."

I leave Schaerrer in Marseille and take the train back to Vichy, watching the sea, thinking of all the wonders that hide beneath the blue—lost cities and ghost ships, sea stars and white whales, a queen conch waiting for the wind to play a trumpet voluntary. Just like my dreams for France's freedom are concealed beneath my blouse, sweater, blazer, coat, hat, and scarf. Despite the layers, I'm shivering in the January chill until I hear the sound of Béatrice and Christian diving into the waves so vividly that my head whips around.

But no. I'm alone with strangers, and a twenty-foot wave crashes down upon me.

Every night when I lie down in my single bed in my spartan room at the Hôtel des Sports, which bears no decoration beyond the framed photograph of my children, the same wave slams against me and I wonder how it's possible to spend each day with so many men but to feel so very lonely. My hand presses against the center of my chest where the pain feels most acute. In Morocco, I'd worried my heart would wither. Has it? Is that why the ache of missing my children hasn't killed me?

No. Because the biggest secret of all is that while I love my children, I love this life. Nazi airstrikes have killed or wounded more than fifty thousand people in Britain alone. But in Marseille, Rivière and Schaerrer are meeting with the grain dealer, who'll send me shipping manifests so we can tell the British which ships leaving France carry German munitions. Those ships can be destroyed before the weapons kill more people— and we'll be one step closer to freeing France.

Even so, I wrap my arms around myself. Stare at the dusk, that slip of time between my days, which are made up of secrets, and the nights, full of memories of when my arms were like blankets enfolding my children.

Pierre Laval, Pétain's deputy and well-known Nazi lover, visits the club three days in a row. On the third day he says to me, tongue flickering like a snake, "Madame Méric. I hear you're caring for our friend."

The inflection on the word *caring* suggests it's a synonym for harlotry.

But that's the least of my worries. *The burden will be on you if they come to investigate,* Navarre had said.

Laval's here for Navarre. But I have no idea where Navarre is. Still at sea? In prison? Or—*s'il vous plaît, mon Dieu*—in England? It's been weeks since he left, and I've heard nothing.

I say in my most Nightingale-like manner, "I'm about to fetch his chamber pot. He can't even walk to the toilet. You can go up and see him if you can bear the stench."

Laval shudders. My gamble works. But he takes a seat and doesn't bother to hide the fact that he's watching me for the next two hours. I daren't go up to my office, where intelligence from the agents we now have in Marseille, Grenoble, Chamonix, Lyon, Dijon, and Périgueux is stacked in towers that rival the Eiffel.

That night, I start packing boxes. When Schaerrer returns from Marseille, I ask him to locate a pension in Pau—near the Pyrenees and away from watchful eyes—to house us, just in case.

The next morning, a peculiar-looking blond man appears in my office. It takes me a moment to realize it's Coustenoble, that he's dyed his hair.

"You make a terrible blond, Couscous," I say, laughing.

"Believe me, little one, if I had a choice, you'd be the only blonde here."

He's taken to calling me *la petite*. From him, I allow it. And I can't object to him nicknaming me if I call him Couscous, which suits him so much better.

But my mirth evaporates when he says, "We're being watched. The guards at the station have noticed how often I come and go."

Then comes the sound of feet pounding up the stairs.

"Laval," I whisper, hardly knowing whether to hide Couscous or the papers first.

We brace. The door flies open.

But it's General Baston.

"They've just fired Navarre in absentia," he says, panting as if he's just run all the way from the Hôtel du Parc. "You're all done for. A warrant for his arrest is imminent. Then they'll come for you."

My heart feels like a piano lid being slammed closed again and again and again. It's the only sound I can hear, urging me to pay attention to it and nothing else. But the thing about being a mother is that no matter how much you might be panicking at the sight of your child covered in blood, you can never let it show.

I stand.

"Get Schaerrer," I tell Coustenoble. "We'll move everything tonight, before the warrant is issued."

Couscous runs out. I scramble for a box of matches, ready to burn the papers I've memorized, expecting Baston to flee. But he picks up a stack of papers. Secures them in a box. Then another stack.

"I'll do it," I tell him, snappish with fear, not understanding why a man who ordinarily treats me like the grippe is packing treasonous papers into boxes, an act that would cause him to lose more than his job if he's caught.

"I'd like to help," he says gravely, continuing to pack.

My heartbeat slows. I rest my hand on his. "Thank you."

"Today the Nazis arrested a Resistance group in Paris for the first time," Baston says. "Two were women. I cannot let a mother be taken to prison."

His words are like the match in my hand, lighting up the dark corners and making me see that this is the last moment where I have plausible deniability. If I leave right now and return to my children, nobody will come after me. But if I flee and continue working for Navarre . . .

It's dark outside when we hear the sound of a motorcar.

Is it slowing down?

It is.

I'm about to hide us in the larder when the car continues past.

"Hurry," I urge.

The fire burns all night. I carry box after box to my Citroën. I nod to Baston as he leaves. Then I send Schaerrer to Pau and Coustenoble to Dijon, knowing we need to stay away from one another for a fortnight and lay low. Our evacuation will not go unnoticed.

Out on the road, my head turns constantly from side to side. What does a Vichy government intent on arrest look like? How far will they go to track Navarre down?

Every time headlights bear down on me, panic just about bursts out of my chest. I ready myself to turn the car in to a field, but it's always just a milk van, a delivery truck.

In the moments between headlights and panic, the truth is a mallet, striking me—*I failed. Badly*. I should have made everyone leave the hotel the first time Laval came in. He gave me three warnings, for God's sake.

I have no idea what I'm doing and my ignorance is deadly.

The need to escape self-recrimination makes me turn south and do what my heart most wants.

On a narrow road leading up to a house about five kilometers north of Cannes, I draw to a stop. It's early spring and the mimosas beckon; the peach and cherry trees are abuzz with bees.

Sunshine envelops the house, as do memories of happy days spent here together.

This is what I'm fighting for.

"*Maman!*"

Tumbling out of the house come Béatrice and Christian, my two tiny miracles.

But they're not so tiny now. Béatrice's head nestles into my ribs and Christian's is only just below my chin. They've grown so much, but they smell exactly the same. I inhale deep, gulping breaths of their hair, their dirty fingernails, the music of their voices.

"I love you," I say, trying not to weep, trying not to make this moment about the pain and the lost days, but about the beauty of the three of us, together.

Christian draws back. "You didn't write."

Now this moment *is* about the pain. Of course it is; they're eleven and nine and they have no father and they want me to be the wave they dive into, the soft sand that breaks their fall, their steadfast, beautiful sky. Instead I've left them because of a faraway man called Hitler and a nebulous idea called freedom.

I grip Christian's hand, hold fast to Béatrice, too. "Remember after the Monte Carlo rally when I joked that next time I wouldn't come home unless I'd won?"

Christian and Béatrice nod.

"In war there isn't a second or third place," I tell them, trying to make this ugly adult thing into something child sized. "There's only a winner and a loser. To have the best chance of winning, I have to play a game, like the one Béatrice plays every night at bath time." I kiss her forehead. "Thank you for teaching me how to hide. But imagine if you sent a letter when you were hiding— then we'd know where you were. So I can't send letters. And I have to win, because then we can go home together."

"You need to make yourself very small, *Maman*," Béatrice says, eager to help. "Otherwise your foot peeks out and they'll find you."

Christian's frown is too old for his face and his question should never have to be asked by an eleven-year-old boy. "Is it dangerous?"

Last night I ran away from the police.

"Only for my foot if I leave it peeking out."

That night, my mother and I sit outside, backs against the terra-cotta-colored stacked-stone walls. Every few minutes, I tiptoe down the hall and peep into my children's bedroom, drinking in the smell of the crushed rose petals my mother puts in their bath water, the dark honey shade Christian's hair has deepened into, the kitten-like sigh Béatrice makes as her fingers wrap more tightly around the rag doll I made for her.

When I step outside, there are tears on my cheeks. "What if I can't make myself go back?"

My mother wraps her arms around me. In that embrace is everything that's good about the world—flowers and red wine and garlicky citrus, compassion and tenderness and love.

"Do you remember the Graf family from Vienna?" she whispers. "They lived next door to us in Shanghai. I had a letter from them in 1939. The Nazis beat Tobias and every Jewish man in their building one night. They did something to his back that made it impossible for him to stand. I haven't heard from them again."

I hold on to my mother even more tightly.

"The Nazis didn't even try to hide what they were doing, *ma chérie,*" she continues. "They hit and they kicked in full view of everyone. If that's the kind of violence they enact in the open, imagine what they do when they think no one is watching. Be the one who watches, Marie-Madeleine. I'll keep your children safe while you do. *That* is love. Not staying here and doing nothing while innocent people are beaten beyond repair."

My knees buckle, but she holds me up and I know that if a troop of Nazis marched in here and told her to hand me over, she would never let me go.

"Little one!" Coustenoble calls when I arrive in Pau.

Schaerrer gives me a bone-crushing hug. "What do you think?"

The inn he's found is called, providentially, Pension Welcome. It's screened from passersby by a walled garden and a wide porch with a creaking wood floor that will alert us when anyone arrives. It's perfect, so I set about charming Josette, the innkeeper, into believing we're establishing a branch of the Légion française des combattants, which is why so many men will come and go—and that she doesn't need to keep registration papers for us.

She winks, pulls a pistol out from under the desk. "I'll shoot the dirty Boche if they come here."

That night, it's not me but Josette regaling us with tales of what she did as a child to German soldiers during the Great War, adding ground peppercorns to their tobacco tins, for instance. Needless to say, I give her a place on our team. Our first female recruit.

When I notice Coustenoble gazing at her with liquid brown eyes, I whisper, "Do you still have the soap from Commandant Faye? You could give it to Josette."

He blushes but recovers quickly. "Why? Is Commandant Faye bringing you more?"

Now I'm the one blushing.

Within days, the pension is like a schoolyard. What was once the dining room is now the operations room. My maps hang on the walls, with areas colored red where we have people bringing us information and green where we need to find people. Recruits sort the intelligence the couriers bring. They always arrive at dinnertime, devouring the trout Josette's son, Lucien, catches from the stream. My gramophone plays a mix of jazz and classical, and the air is thick with cigarette smoke and the scent of Josette's cooking.

Soon, Baston sends me a note: *They're still looking for Na-*

varre. Luckily no one thinks "Navarre's mistress" is worth questioning. What knowledge would she have, besides how to crease the bedsheets?

I hope you know I don't believe you occupy that position, Bastion's note continues. *Not just because Navarre loves his wife. But because I've come to see that you are honorable.*

It makes me soften even more toward the traditionalist with a revolutionary's heart.

But April arrives with no word from Navarre.

Where are you? I think for the millionth time. Without the money the government gave us for the Légion, I can't pay our agents. I emptied my bank account for last week's wages. We need money from the British, not just for practicalities, but for hope. Today, there's only the stale smell of last week's Gauloises in the air. The couriers come in with messages and leave without the usual gift of a pack of cigarettes. We've run out, and I don't know how long the men will keep coming if we give them nothing.

So I take out my diamond earrings—the only jewelry my father had the chance to give me—and I walk to the pawn shop. I return with enough money to keep us supplied with food and cigarettes for a couple of weeks. The agents race into town whooping. When Schaerrer returns, he drops a pack of Gitanes onto my desk.

"You didn't have to," I protest.

"Of course I did."

April marches on. I still don't know whether Navarre's in an English prison or on his way back to France, and I'm wondering if I can sell my Cartier purse for funds, when the telephone rings.

"The Allies have agreed to work with us," Navarre says.

9

A World That Has No Need of Women

Rabat, 1932

"I'm going out to see Hachem," Edouard says to me over breakfast. "You'll need to come and translate. Find out if they're really planning another protest or if his wife is just imagining things."

Hachem is Ghislaine's husband. Their son Aderfi is dead. He died last year from kala-azar, a disease caused by sand fly bites and poverty. Ghislaine has three more sons now and no time to either mourn or imagine anything.

I want to tell Edouard that I'm done with the go-betweening, done with listening to him derogate Ghislaine and use her for information all at the same time. The last time I saw her, more than six months ago, I told her we should stop, because now her sister, who lives in Rabat, and a couple of her cousins, all equally eager to save their sons from another war, are involved, too. But Ghislaine stared at me with disgust and said, "The only people colonial pity is good for are the French. It makes you believe you're moral. It gets me nothing."

She stalked off and I was left with my despicable pity, a sense that my education meant nothing at all and that Ghislaine understood more about politics than I did.

So I nod at Edouard, dress for a day on camelback, then give my son an extra-long hug goodbye.

Most days, I play with Christian from the time he wakes and throws his chubby arms around me until I tuck him into bed at night with a story to sweeten his dreams. He's insatiably curious and loves to investigate everything, which drives Edouard mad and makes me smile. I go out only when I collect notes from Ghislaine's sister and cousins, always meeting them at the souk around midday because Moroccan women aren't permitted out at night. It means I'm able to see Marguerite and occasionally the duke, too, the two of them having become my partners in stealth, taking me out to lunch—somewhere where there's no danger of running into Edouard—or to explore the abandoned *medersas,* their loveliness still evident in the ruined skeletons of columns or the broken frame of a mother-of-pearl mirror. They've even snuck me into the duke's airplane a couple of times.

Today's journey is more sedate. We reach the nomad camp in time for dinner, where I sit between Edouard and Hachem translating.

"Tell your husband he's getting fat," Hachem says. "His pretty wife will lose interest in him." He grins at Edouard, making it clear his words are only amusing to himself.

I'm used to this. The power play. Edouard wants something only Hachem or someone like him can give. And Hachem wants something too, from Edouard and the other tribal leaders. They each give as little as they can. I don't know if either of them truly has their country's best interests at heart, or if their lives are devoted to the frisson of gaining the upper hand.

This is why wars happen.

I can't believe I ever lay in a bed and laughed about go-betweening.

When we return home, Edouard's in a benevolent mood. He has information that cost him fewer francs than he'd expected, having no idea that his thrift means that this year or next, Ghislaine's other sons might die from kala-azar disease, too.

The thought pounds in my head beside images of the children at the camp with the round bellies and thin legs of the malnourished. My own son's skin is plump, his cheeks rosy. We can afford food and medicines because Edouard is good at a job that exists only because of the conqueror's need to spy on the conquered.

The next morning at breakfast, I take the biggest risk I've contemplated since I had Christian.

"I'd like to assist at the women's clinic," I say, trying to sound careless, as if it doesn't matter if Edouard refuses. "I'd overhear things that could be useful for you."

I have no intention of telling him anything but hope the falsehood will be persuasive and soon forgotten.

He agrees.

Two days later, I'm holding a woman's legs while she gives birth to a baby boy.

Soon the clinic becomes the second miracle, besides Christian, that my days orbit around. I take the women food I've stolen from my kitchen, show them how to treat their wounds so they don't get infected. I try to tell them—women who believe only in the powers of dead saints and monstrous jinni, in God and not science—what to eat so they have the strength to withstand their ninth or tenth pregnancies. I wipe away their tears when they cry after giving birth to a girl.

"Ten girls," one of the women says to me after a Herculean labor that's left me covered in blood and at least three hours late for dinner. "I don't want her."

She refuses to look at this tiny, squalling child who did nothing other than be born a woman in a world that has no need of women—other than to produce more men.

When I walk home that night, I'm weeping, and I don't even know which injustice I'm mourning.

"Enough clinic work," Edouard says when I walk in the door, having missed dinner and Christian's bedtime, looking nothing like the blond and deliriously stupid eighteen-year-old girl he married.

Just as the city of Rabat is locked up each night, the space I'm locked into is becoming smaller and smaller—and so much harder to break free of.

10

It's Time to Lose Ourselves

Pau, April–May 1941

Navarre gestures to an enormous pile of francs. "Five million," he says, which can't be true. "And a transmitter." He points to a brown leather case with leads, dials, plugs, and sockets spilling from it.

"De Gaulle said no," he goes on, when it becomes apparent that I'm speechless. "I told him our network would transmit all our information to him but had to keep its independence. He told me that whoever was not with him was against him."

I should have known that Navarre and De Gaulle, two men I'd met arguing in a Parisian salon, would never come to terms. It's a blow. Few people knew who Charles de Gaulle was in June 1940, but now that he's in London, with the ear of Churchill and the leadership of the Free French, he's become a rallying point for the small number of French people who want to work against the Nazis.

"Then how . . ." I indicate the goods and money.

Navarre does something I've never seen him do. He beams. "MI6. We're part of the British intelligence services. They're happy to help us without needing to control us. And we have a new name: Alliance."

Now my smile matches Navarre's. A name, money, a wireless transmitter, and a British intelligence service waiting for information isn't just a hole in the swastika of German oppression; it's a rent right through it.

But Navarre brings me back to reality. "The British know nothing. And Dönitz's wolf pack rules the seas. Last month his U-boats sunk seven hundred thousand tons of cargo bound for England. The Brits are about to run out of food, fuel, iron, aluminum. Without supplies, they can't plan an attack on the Nazis."

I frown. It sounds as if it might be months before they can think of anything more than just staying alive.

"They want us to put agents into the submarine bases," Navarre goes on. "If we can tell them the U-boats' movements, then they can blow up those U-boats. If we save their supplies . . ."

"They can use those supplies to build tanks and airplanes and ships."

"Exactly."

"I thought they'd be further ahead with plans to invade Europe."

"That's why they need Alliance." Navarre thumps the table. "For now, we help them understand their enemy and protect their supplies. The rest comes later."

How much later? The occupation began almost a year ago. Will it go on for another? Until mid-1942, perhaps?

"Schaerrer's ex-navy," I say, moving over to my map, because we'll only be ready to fight in mid-1942 if I act, not worry. "He can start on the U-boats. What else?"

Navarre inserts himself between me and the map, expression inscrutable. "Every agent needs a code name. As Alliance's leader, I'm N1. I told them my chief of staff is POZ55. It's time to lose ourselves."

Will we be able to recover ourselves, once the war has ended?

If it ends.

Stop. I make myself focus on Navarre. "Your chief of staff? Who's he?"

"Take a look in the mirror. And say hello to POZ55."

Me? Impossible.

But Navarre just says, "I didn't tell them you're a woman."

I'm once again a lie. Chief of staff for a team of men, led by a man, reporting to men in Britain who don't know I'm a woman.

But Navarre is already moving on, unconcerned by the magnitude of having lied to MI6. "I told them what Faye's up to in North Africa."

Léon Faye. The man with the dark hair and the fire inside him. Will his coup in North Africa set the Nazis ablaze? Or will it set him ablaze instead?

And will the British set *me* ablaze if they find out I'm a woman?

I tune in to Navarre saying, "The British want to speed things up in Algiers. I'll focus on North Africa and leave the French sectors to you. They want answers to these questions."

He passes me pages and pages asking: *Where are the anti-aircraft defenses located? What ships depart from each port? What do they carry? How many U-boats are in the Gironde estuary?*

Rather than being terrified at the amount of information they want, I'm thrilled with its specificity. Now I know exactly where to recruit the go-betweens who will link the British to the answers they need.

Providentially, Couscous arrives shortly after with a prize—a man who's so tall it's hard to take him in at one glance. Even so, his clothes are too big for him, as if his mother made them for a giant who turned out to be refreshingly human instead.

"This is Vallet. He knows all about radios," Coustenoble says.

I point to the transmitter. "Then that's yours," I tell Vallet. "You'll need to find a room where you can discreetly hang the aerial. Your code name is CIR36."

He beams as if a code name is a *Légion d'honneur,* and I blink at the way he's so proud of his illegal radio, trying not to show more emotion than a woman in charge of men should. But how much is too much? Would the people working for me prefer someone indifferent, or someone who's moved by each poignant second that marks her days?

I turn to Schaerrer, remind myself that I have to start being like Navarre. "You'll head up the Occupied Zone," I tell him.

To Couscous I say, "You're my adjutant."

Pride rather than fear is evident on their faces, too. It makes my next words falter, spoken in the voice of Marie-Madeleine rather than POZ55. "We have to go to Paris."

Occupied Paris. Where the Nazis rule.

Coustenoble frowns. "What's our intrepid leader doing?" He points to the questionnaires and pages of coding instructions Navarre dumped into my arms. "You have all the work and all the danger, too."

"Navarre's focusing on North Africa, which is hardly risk-free," I say curtly.

It's redundant for me to ask questions like: *Would I be holding all the paperwork if I were a man?* When millions of lives are at stake, you back your leader. You get people to do the things they're best at. Navarre's a visionary. And I'm chief of staff of a British-sponsored Resistance network, a job I know almost nothing about. But nor does anyone else. So I'll just have to get on with it and try not to get any of us killed.

God help us.

The first time we're due to receive a radio transmission from London, Coustenoble, Schaerrer, Navarre, and I cluster around the box of dials and crystals watching Vallet, our gentle giant. His face lights up, he gets to work with his pencil, and I transpose his scribble into columns so I can decode it using the sign and key number of my own personal code book, Dumas's *La Dame aux Camélias*.

Yesterday we sent our first transmission to London detailing the movements of a U-boat out of its base, intelligence Schaerrer gathered from an informant. What emerges from tonight's decryption is the news that the British have sunk that U-boat with all hands aboard. And a convoy of container ships it was stalking got away with enough supplies to see Britain through another month.

Thanks for your friendship stop we shall avenge them together end, the message concludes.

Vallet picks me up and swings me around. Couscous takes my hand and we spin too, before Schaerrer twirls me halfway across the room.

Navarre raises his fist into the air. "To Alliance."

I'm used to Aprils in Paris when the dawn plays a joyful pizzicato over the sky, plucking away the night, when the boulevards fill with Parisiennes swinging baskets of bread from their arms. But that was back when Paris's heart was red, white, and blue.

Now, near the Louvre, soldiers are gathered around a tank whose guns point along the Rue de Rivoli at housewives queuing for food. One soldier takes out a dagger and cuts off a tranche of butter, smearing it onto a baguette. The French boys nearby whisper their admiration. They want to be that Nazi with his dagger and muscular tank.

I've spent so much time surrounded by people who think the same as I do that I've forgotten our enemy isn't just the Nazis. It's ignorance and passivity, things as hard to battle as a flesh-and-blood foe.

As if to underscore the thought, around the next corner is a poster: *The German military tribunal pronounced a death sentence for Professor Bénédict James of Paris for enacting violence against a soldier in the German army. He was shot this morning.*

The name on the poster blurs and I picture Navarre's name, my name, Coustenoble's name.

God. We're fighting against tanks and bullets with little paper notes.

But as I stand there, I see that a V has been cut through the grime on a neighboring window. V for victory. My eyes attuned, I see more of them. Scratched onto a wall. Carved into the sidewalk beneath my feet.

Somebody knelt down in the dead of night and scraped that mark into the cobblestones so others would know that Paris still has a heart.

So I ignore the poster and walk to my old apartment to see if it can be used as a base. But the concierge shakes her head.

"The Germans were here," she says. "They're looking for you, Madame. They ordered me to tell them when you returned."

I thought the Vichy police were only onto Navarre. But if the Nazis were here . . .

Thank God the false papers I'm carrying, made for me by a crony of Navarre's, say I'm Jeanne Châtel. Nobody knows that Marie-Madeleine is in Paris.

"The SD have set up in one of the finest townhouses on Avenue Foch," the concierge continues. "They take people there . . ." She falters. "They never come back out."

The Sicherheitsdienst, charged with gathering intelligence about Nazi enemies like me. My hand tightens on the doorknob.

"I need five minutes," I say.

"Hurry," she says before slipping out, leaving me alone with my possessions.

My piano, constant friend from childhood, treasure house of sounds that can squeeze your heart until you're breathless from the sheer, fugitive beauty of it all. I can't make myself touch it. Because—when will I ever play it again?

Over there, wrappers from the candies my amah used to buy me and Yvonne in Shanghai. Christian's rattle. Béatrice's red shoes that she loved so much the soles are almost worn away. One glance is enough to put me right back there when she unwrapped them at our first Christmas in Paris, when my children no longer had a father and I thought my mistake of a marriage might ruin them forever. She'd laughed so delightedly that I realized they weren't ruined at all.

I touch the shoes, tiny pieces of the person who used to be Marie-Madeleine Méric. Wife. Mother. Rally driver. Pilot. Journalist. Radio host. The woman I tried so hard to shape after I left Morocco. I don't want to let her go. But . . .

It's time to lose ourselves, Navarre had said. That's when I feel the wrench, as if Marie-Madeleine just stepped out of my skin, leaving behind POZ55, whom I don't know at all.

But she's all I have.

I make myself leave, refuse to look back. Those things are ephemera and their time is done. I can never let myself think of those little red shoes, because then I would drown in the flood of my tears.

When I arrive on Maurice and Marguerite's doorstep, they take one look at my face and pour me a drink.

"The reality of Paris is more shocking than reading about it in notes?" Marguerite asks sympathetically.

They've been sending me information since the beginning, so I should be prepared. But right now I feel like my expertise is chief of nothing.

"I need a bigger hat," I say, pulling off my chic little Schiaparelli madcap.

I choose one of Marguerite's enormous cartwheel hats,

which completely obscures my face, and prepare to go back out there. Before I can, Marguerite passes me a note from my sister.

Ma chère soeur. Bless you.

That's all it says. But I know what it means. Yvonne's husband is no Nazi, but he has many friends in the Vichy government. I can't go near their apartment and put them at risk. But they want me to do what their profile and connections mean they cannot.

God, I want to hug her. All I can do is write her an equally innocuous note in return: *I love you both*.

On the doorstep, Maurice says, "Tell us if we can do more."

He's the ideal person to lead the Paris sector. But he's also a duke and the father of three children. I don't want more families caught up in this battle. So I just kiss his cheeks and stride off, keeping the hat brim low.

For how many months will I walk like this, unable to tip my head up to the sky?

I visit my friends and acquaintances. Some meetings are sweet, others bitter as people talk gaily about Nazis they met at a dinner party. But I'm able to establish enough letterboxes at bars and brasseries where agents can leave information to be collected by couriers who'll bring everything to me at Pau.

One night, as I'm walking back to my rented room, I hear footsteps behind me. I don't know whether to slow down or walk faster. The British have given me a gun, but I only know how to shoot and hope. The Nazis know how to shoot and kill.

When I reach my room, I collapse onto the bed, breathing as fast as if Hitler himself were stalking me.

Schaerrer finds me there some time later. His face is too serious for such a young man.

"A courier came," he says. "You need to go back to Pau right now."

"What happened?" My breath, only just under control, gallops once more.

He shakes his head. "I don't know."

11

My Armor

Rabat, 1932

ask the maid to look after Christian, then I borrow one of her haiks, slip it on, steal out the kitchen door, and work a full day amidst babies and mothers, despite Edouard's forbidding me. Near dusk, one of the midwives approaches, face so solemn I know it can only be a death.

"Who?" I ask.

The woman I'd cared for last week. The one who'd given birth to her tenth daughter. Last night, the midwife says, she committed the gravest of all sins and threw herself from Rabat's walls, unable to bear the guilt of bringing another girl into a world that will shroud her and rule her until death.

I press my forehead to the window. Through the glass, black mountains are silhouetted against a crimson sunset that bleeds into red sand. Standing there, I believe there will never be a place more extraordinary than the one I'm in now—but nor will there ever be a place so cruel. I'm as empty as Marguerite feared I'd become. I want my mother's arms around me, my sister's.

Especially if . . .

My breasts have been sore for at least a fortnight, my hip worse than normal, as if something is softening the ligaments that try to hold it in place. Last night, Edouard snapped, "For

God's sake, stop limping around," and I'd gone to bed early because I couldn't hide the hitch in my gait.

I stumble-run back home, not even thinking to hide from
Edouard, who shouts when I burst through the door, "How dare
you sneak out of my house!"

My diary confirms the most terrible fear I've ever known.

I haven't bled for three months. Out of one of those infre-
quent nightly visits my husband makes to my room, something
has bloomed.

And I know, the same way I know that Christian is toddling
down the hall to see me with his delicious little smile, that this
time it will be a girl—and that watching her grow up here under
Edouard's command will make me feel like a thorn-swallowing
Aïssaoua, torn apart from the inside out by every wretched
spike.

He's still shouting at me, still demanding to know how I
dared, when Christian, sobbing, wraps himself around my leg
like armor.

So I dare because that's what love is—you risk your neck, go
out on a limb, bare your breast, lay yourself open, dance on the
razor's edge, and now I'm limbless and bloodied and split wide
open and yet I will continue to love because it is worth it.

Christian holds on tighter.

God, it's worth it.

"I have to go back to France," I tell Edouard, making my
voice nonchalant because he cannot know how much I love this
child or the one that's coming. "I'm pregnant. You've always said
it isn't as hygienic here as in France. It would be better to have
the baby there."

He laughs. He laughs and he laughs and just when I think
he'll stop, he laughs some more. Then he straightens his tie,
examines himself in the mirror.

"No man in my position gets divorced," he says crisply. "And
you can't divorce me without my consent. So go back to France.

Christian will soon be at school, and many wives return to Paris at that time. Have the baby there. But you are Marie-Madeleine Méric, my dear, until death do us part."

Maurice and Marguerite drive Christian and me to Casablanca. On the way, I try to think about everything I've been given in Morocco—the gift of Maurice's and Marguerite's friendships, one perfect child and the promise of another—rather than what I've lost. A father for my children. My heart. Myself.

Who is Marie-Madeleine Méric? That's the name I'll wear for the rest of my life, Edouard's brand forever upon me. But I don't know that woman at all.

We draw into the Place de France in Casablanca. Cream posters showing a red car speeding up a hill adorn the walls. *Grande Semaine Automobile du Maroc,* the headline reads.

"Is the rally this weekend?" Marguerite asks Maurice, who nods. Then he turns to me, saying, "If you want to go out with a bang . . ."

Marguerite adds, "I'll look after Christian."

"And I'll be *your* navigator this time," Maurice finishes.

My interest in anything besides going home is roused, just a little. "I can drive?"

They both grin.

Memories of the first and only time I raced in a rally crowd in. But rather than seeing the epic sweep of land we drove through, I remember Edouard's taking my purse from me afterward. "What will Edouard say?"

Marguerite asks, very gently, "What does Marie-Madeleine say?"

I look at her, my friend who's adored by her husband, who revels in life. She has so much, and perhaps right now when I have very little, I ought to be jealous. But, *What does Marie-*

Madeleine say, she'd asked. Not, *What does Marie-Madeleine Méric say?*

"She says yes."

Close to Casablanca, I pass another car and wonder how many are still in front of us. Then we're at the top of the very last hill, and once again Maurice and I look at each other and shout, "Full throttle!"

We soar down that hill the same way I've always rushed at life, with my heart wide open and trusting, a wild child choosing her way.

When I pull up into the square, it's full of people and empty of cars.

"*Mon Dieu!*" Maurice cries. "You won!"

Yes, the world is still magnificent and awe-inspiring and full of miracles. Edouard doesn't have the power to change that. I might be tied to him against my will for the rest of my life, prohibited from falling in love ever again, but I, Marie-Madeleine, can still search for one miraculous moment in every day. And I will protect my children, who are the most magnificent of all miracles, with my life.

I turn to Maurice and Marguerite, who's run over to embrace us, my son in her arms. "Thank you both. For everything."

"This isn't goodbye or the end," Maurice tells me. "We'll see you again, Marie-Madeleine. And when we do, you'll be winning at something more important than a rally."

12

It's Time to Be a Warrior

Pau, June 1941

rush into Pension Welcome to find the atmosphere as exuberant as usual and Navarre very much alive and not in jail.
When he sees me, he tells everyone to leave. Dread tangles in
my stomach.

"I'm joining Léon Faye in Algiers," he crows.

"You're joining Léon Faye in Algiers?" I repeat.

"He and I are going to launch a coup."

The charming Léon Faye is about to try to overthrow Vichy
France in North Africa. And Navarre is leaving Alliance so he
can run off on a boy's own adventure.

You fools, I want to cry out. Want to march them both to
Paris to show them all the tanks and soldiers. Want to pull the
future out of time so they can see themselves in Algiers with
the bloodied bodies of their fellow fools all around them. But
the only way to persuade Navarre not to make mincemeat of
himself is to remain calm.

"I've just seen how powerful the Nazis are," I say, voice
steady. "They'll crush you."

"Crush us? The next time you hear from me, I'll have taken
over Algiers."

Nazis who use daggers as butter knives will never let that
happen. So I take on my leader for the first time ever.

"I've just recruited so many people. I've told them you're Alliance's leader," I shout. "You can't run from that. You stand by your people—otherwise, how will they trust you?"

He shrugs. "If this succeeds, Churchill will have a base in the Mediterranean. That's how wars are won."

"No!" I lean across the desk the way men do when they want you to listen. "You taught me that wars are won by men like Rivière finding a piece of information and Vallet radioing it to the British until they have enough intelligence to put together a strategic attack—one that will win, because there are no second chances and we have lives in our hands."

But Navarre has never gifted a man a code name. He's never known one of the agents well enough to bestow a diminutive upon him, never sorted through intelligence looking for gold in the dust.

Now he tumbles from the pedestal I shouldn't have put him on.

"What am I supposed to do?" I ask, voice sharp, a nondiatonic note played against the key of Navarre's recklessness. "Sit here waiting for you to come back? Ask everyone else to wait, too?"

"Keep transmitting to London."

Yes, I'm to sit waiting like Penelope for the hero to return. I thought this wasn't like Morocco, that while I might still be a woman in a man's world, I had some ability, in this supposedly more cultured civilization, to shape that world. But Hitler, Edouard, Navarre, De Gaulle, Léon Faye—they're the composers. I'm just the drum they beat their breasts upon.

At the doorway, Navarre says, "You have an elephant's memory, a snake's caution, a weasel's instinct, a mole's perseverance, and a panther's cunning. You're the pivot around which everything turns. So turn, POZ55. Turn."

If the radio wasn't so valuable I'd throw it at him. I'm a weasel and a mole, a creature who has to face the humiliation of telling the men that what I promised them might never happen. Navarre could well die over there. Then the Alliance we toasted to in this very room will die, too. I'll never walk into my apartment holding my children's hands, ready to unpack boxes containing red shoes we once wore in the time of freedom.

I do what I can to make everyone believe that Navarre hasn't abandoned us. I tell Coustenoble to travel through the free zone and Schaerrer through the Occupied Zone delivering questionnaires and code books. And I tell both of them to be careful.

"Little one, you should be the most careful," Couscous says with uncharacteristic seriousness. "Vichy knows you worked with Navarre before the war. That you left before he could be arrested. If everything goes wrong in North Africa . . ."

"They'll come looking for you," Schaerrer finishes.

"That's why," I say, "Coustenoble is going to pay a visit to General Baston."

The old soldier who helped get us out of Vichy will be the first to hear what happens in Algiers. I've written a note asking him, for Navarre's sake, to tell me the moment any news comes through. Then I leave a skeleton team at Pau and take Vallet and the transmitter to Marseille, because if Navarre and Faye lose, the Germans might discover that Pau was the last place Navarre stayed, and they'll come investigating. I'm not losing our one hard-earned transmitter over a bold idea pursued at the wrong time.

The fruit-and-vegetable shop Rivière purchased is in tiny le Vallon des Auffes, a village clustered around a shimmering blue pocket square of sea embroidered with white sailboats. Houses scramble up the cliffs in shades of cream and gold, accented by turquoise shutters.

Rivière bellows to his wife, another Madeleine, to organize extra beds, then shows us through the shop proper and out the back, where familiar piles of paperwork sit. When Vallet un-packs the transmitter, Rivière has to clap both hands over his mouth to mute his exclamations.

I set up my gramophone to block out the noise of the trans-mitter's Morse key, then carry on interviewing men. Messages come in about ships and explosives; that Schaerrer's found a man who can give him the schedules of all the U-boats in Saint Nazaire.

The British are delighted. I think of that each night, rather than how tired I am. Fatigued by the work, but also, occasion-ally at one in the morning, tired of being alone. I'm thirty-one years old and there are so many more years ahead of me, and the idea that they will all be spent by myself has me pulling back the blackout curtain and staring out the window, searching for a sliver of moon.

It doesn't come. Nor does any word from Navarre. I sew into the early morning hours so I don't jolt awake from nightmares about standing in a room, watching Béatrice and Christian walk right past me, not knowing who I am.

Sew, Marie-Madeleine. Sew.

At breakfast one morning I pass Vallet the product of my stitching. "If I've done it right"—I nod at his too-large shirt—"it should fit better than that one."

He unfolds my gift with Christmas Eve eagerness, running his hand over the cotton, such a delicate movement for such a large man. "My grandmother thinks Vallets are taller than giraffes," he says, voice a little wistful, and I remember that he's nineteen and should be out meeting a girl, falling in love.

"You're more a palm tree than a giraffe," I say, trying to lighten the mood. He is exactly that—a column with a shock of hair that points left, right, and up into the sky.

"She still thinks I'm a kid and has to make my shirts with plenty of growing room." Now his face is a cloud passing over the trunk of his lanky tree.

He *is* a kid. Or he would be, in a normal world.

Rivière stands abruptly, takes out rationed butter, and spreads it thickly over a hunk of bread before putting it on Vallet's plate. These people, giving comfort in butter. They break my heart—and they fill it up, too.

"Where's your grandmother now?" I ask.

"Paris," Vallet replies through a mouthful of bread. "My father and brothers were taken to a prisoner-of-war camp when France surrendered. My mother died bringing me into the world. So my grandmother . . ."

Is all I have left. The unfinished sentence hangs in the air.

"I used to look out for her. Give her money. But now she's alone and . . ." He pauses, chews bread, swallows. "I don't know if that's right."

Navarre would say, *Of course it is.* It's right for Vallet to be here so that his grandmother doesn't have to live out her days in a German-occupied city.

But a lonely grandmother in Paris is someone I've never thought about and should have. Someone needs to take responsibility for her, for all the agents' families—they're part of Alliance, too.

"I'll send her money each month," I tell him, voice husky. "So you don't have to worry quite so much."

"When you're young, they tell you that war is men in trenches shooting and dying," Vallet says contemplatively. "But maybe war is the ones left behind, stuck in trenches of fear. Their only weapon is not giving up hope." He clears his throat. "Thank you. If I know she has money, then I know she can get food. Then I know she can still hope. And I know it's right for me to be here because I have to make her hope come true."

God. I'm going to weep. We all are.

Rivière clutches his wife's hand. Then he reaches over to take mine and I hold on as tightly as if I might fall through the bottom of the earth if I let go.

Three days later, Rivière bursts in, anxiety running off him like seawater. "Get out!"

Dressed in his new shirt, Vallet freezes in front of his transmitter. My hands halt their movements over the coding grid.

"A neighbor told the police he can hear suspicious noises," Rivière tells us.

Despite my gramophone, someone has heard the Morse key tapping.

I've only just pushed myself to my feet when Coustenoble, who's supposed to be distributing questionnaires, hurries in. "General Baston came to find me," he blurts. "Navarre's been arrested."

Breathe. Scoop up papers. *Have I got them all?*

"Hurry," Rivière urges.

We've lost our leader.

We've lost everything.

"Let's go." I hear my words from somewhere outside myself. I see my body running up the crumbling staircase cut into the stone, the three of us racing along the Corniche, the ocean a taunting Marseille blue beside us.

If Navarre's been arrested, I can return to my children.

Except I have treasonous intelligence reports in my valise. The man beside me is carrying an illegal transmitter in his suitcase. The man on my other side has a map showing the entire Alliance network hidden in a rolled-up boat flag.

"Baston said he'd meet you at Pau," Coustenoble puffs.

Pau. All right. We'll go to Pau.

On the veranda of the Pension Welcome, General Baston is waiting, his face as joyless as my mood. "The two of them are an explosive mixture and everything's just blown up," he says, referring to Navarre and Faye, and it only occurs to me now that if Navarre's been arrested, then Léon, the coup's architect, will have been, too.

"Where will you go now?" Baston asks me. "Home to your children?"

"No, here," I say distractedly, meaning I'll stay until I've told the staff. Then what?

I glance at Vallet and Coustenoble and see not worry on their faces, but some strange kind of hope.

"You can't carry on alone." Disbelief trumpets from Baston's words. "You're much too young. And . . ." He stops before he tells me the obvious—that I'm a woman. "You're mistaken if you think you can take over from where Navarre left off."

As if they can feel the first tremors of my wrath, Coustenoble and Vallet usher the Pau team inside.

"Navarre was mistaken to go to Algiers," I retort. "Mistakes aren't only made by young women."

"Preposterous," Baston mutters. He strides to the steps, leaving. As if Alliance really is dead.

Behind him, the Pyrenees rise up over the Nazi-gray sky. And I remember that before Alliance existed, I stood on Navarre's porch and believed that the mountains were like warriors.

There's more than one way to be a warrior. You can be the Herculean figure charging into battle with guns and war cries. Or you can be like the mountains—unyielding. This is the moment when I can charge like a bullish Navarre and tell Baston to take his prejudices back to Vichy and never come here again. Or I can be what Navarre told me I was: the snake and the mole, the panther and the weasel. Watchful. Steadfast. Clever. A person who does what's right for the men she's recruited and promised a future to.

"Wait," I tell Baston, making my voice as strong as the mountains behind him. "Go back to Vichy and run that sector for me. Watch me prove I can do just as good a job—or perhaps better—than Navarre."

It's the most arrogant speech I've ever made in my life. But

Navarre, even Faye, Baston too—these men are all arrogant in different ways. I might be young and a woman, but now it's time to be a warrior, too.

Baston's sigh is profound. "I admire your sangfroid." He studies my face and a deep sadness pours into his eyes. Then he nods. "I await your proof."

I think he just agreed to my proposal.

My legs aren't entirely comfortable with keeping me upright. I sink onto the step.

Around me, Pau is blossoming. White flowers are threaded like pearls onto tree limbs, some of them airborne, tiny parachutes adrift but dancing. A golden eagle's piccolo cries sing out across the sky; the smell of cooked trout fills my nostrils. Josette must be preparing dinner for the agents; I can hear more voices than usual, as if the men have heard about Navarre and come home one last time.

It will be the last time only if I let it be.

The door opens and Coustenoble appears. "Dinner's waiting," he says.

I shake my head and a teardrop lands on my hand. Despite my bravado with Baston, what do I think I'm doing? If I accused Navarre of living a boy's own adventure, aren't I, too? I should be eating dinner with my children, not sitting here.

Rather than running from the tears like men ordinarily do, Coustenoble sits and puts his arm around me.

"Dinner's waiting, little one," he repeats. "A soldier eats with his men. If you don't, they'll feel like they've been left without a leader. And I don't think they have."

I hear what he's telling me. He thinks I can do it. And also that I can cry in front of a select few, but then I must stop and show everyone I'm the leader, because only then will they believe it.

I walk into the dining room and take my seat at the table. I tell everyone about Navarre's arrest. Many of them shrug.

"I don't even know who he is," a boy I recruited last month says.

So many of them have never met Navarre. But I've met them all. They know me. They trust me. Their grandmothers depend on me.

Which means I have no choice but to do the unbelievable—become the provisional female leader of a Resistance network. If I do, I won't hold my children for more than a night or two until Navarre is freed.

The moment I've been running from has caught up to me at last.

I can't choose my children. Not when France is ruled by a man who runs his tanks over every border in Europe, never looking down to see what he's crushed. But if I choose this fight, the nightmare of my children walking past and not recognizing me might well come true. And Hitler might never be defeated.

Then the door to the pension flies open. I drop my knife and fork with a clatter. But it's not the police—it's Schaerrer with a man I haven't met before.

"This is Antoine Hugon," he says to me. "The man I told you about."

I recall the message about someone who knew the movements of U-boats in Saint-Nazaire. Hugon unbuttons his shirt. I stare at Schaerrer, who says, "You'll see."

Hugon unfolds an enormous map from his body.

"All the U-boat pens in Saint-Nazaire," he says, pointing to what I can now see is a drawing, exactly to scale. Every pen. Every shed. Every wolf in Dönitz's pack.

It's exactly what the Allies want—the kind of detail that will show them where to strike from the air so precisely it will be as if the U-boats are sailing atop the ocean, rather than hidden in its depths.

A cheer courses around the table. The men clap me, Schaerrer, and Hugon on the back, some of them poring over the plans, others raiding Josette's wine cellar.

That's when I remember I've always believed in unbelievable things. That I'll one day escape my marriage and fall in love again. That my father travels like a shadow ship beside me. That shooting stars drop miracles into the souls of those who watch them fall.

And I believe with my entire heart that if I do this, I *am* mothering my children. And now I'll care for every man in this network and his family as well.

I walk to the head of the table.

"What time are we transmitting to London?" I ask Vallet.

"In ten minutes," he replies.

"Send this message."

I scribble on a piece of paper: *N1 arrested stop network intact stop everything continuing stop POZ55 end*

A reply comes back: *Who is taking over command end*

I pass Vallet another message: *I am stop surrounded by loyal lieutenants stop POZ55 end*

Coustenoble nods. Schaerrer nods. Vallet does, too.

The British don't need to know that I'm a woman. They just need to know that Alliance will not falter.

From this moment on, I'll do everything in my power to succeed so that my children can have the futures of awe and wonder that I promised them. So that Vallet's grandmother can finally make him some clothes that fit. So that Coustenoble can dye his hair black again. And so that Schaerrer can keep looking up toward the sun.

Part Two

WARRIOR

France, 1941–1943

To this day, historians of the Resistance persist in the belief that no women led Resistance networks, blatantly ignoring the work of [Marie-Madeleine] Fourcade.

J. E. SMYTH, Historian

I'm Going to Madrid

Pau, September–November 1941

"MI6 wants to parachute supplies to us," I announce, leaping up from my chair in the ops room.

Vallet whoops, Coustenoble gapes at me, and Schaerrer whistles and says, *"Incroyable."*

"Then they can send in more transmitters and . . ." I pause theatrically. "Their best radio operator. Which I can't believe I just said. Me, the woman MI6 assumes is a man, is talking about watching money, guns, and a Briton fall from the sky."

My three agents all start laughing.

It's the night shift at Pau, when the busy flow of couriers, agents, and headquarters staff ceases, when Vallet and I take our seats at the wireless receiver, Coustenoble and Schaerrer often there beside us.

I don't laugh with them, not this time. Receiving supplies from the Nazis' enemy in the middle of the night is the most dangerous thing we've done so far. But I suppose it *is* funny that this is ordinary life now.

A smile tugs at my mouth.

"You're still allowed to relax in front of us, little one," Couscous says.

"Because we're . . ." Schaerrer considers. "Not the three musketeers. We're a tricolor."

"I'll be the red stripe," I say. "For as long as Navarre's in prison, I'll need that kind of fire."

But Coustenoble shakes his head and says very gently, "Little one, he means me, himself, and Vallet. You're the flagpole, holding us aloft."

Oh la vache. From laughter to tears in the space of five minutes.

I summon my most commander-like voice. "As Alliance's acting leader until Navarre gets himself out of prison, I'm banning sentimentality."

"So I should stop wearing my shirt?" Vallet teases.

Because yes, I'm as sentimental as anyone here. I didn't know these men nine months ago, but now we're as close as siblings.

Then Vallet, whose ears are as finely tuned as his radio, turns his head. "Car."

We brace, ready to run. That's what the sound of cars does to us now that Navarre's awaiting sentencing for being a traitor. Any noise could be a Nazi boot, a gun shouldered and ready to shoot.

Our lookout bursts in—Josette's son, who's fifteen and follows me around with puppy love in his eyes, which the men of my tricolor find very amusing. "It's General Baston," he announces two seconds before the old general from Vichy enters.

"Thank you, Lucien."

Lucien bows reverently, then rushes back to his post.

It's after ten at night, so I ask Baston warily, "Is something wrong?"

"Not this time," he says. "There's an opportunity instead. Vichy's naval attaché in Madrid needs a man to courier the diplomatic mailbag between Spain and Vichy. Did you know customs officers aren't permitted to search diplomatic mailbags?"

I stare at Baston as my mind leaps from his words to ambitious plans. We urgently need another way, besides the parachute drops, for the British to send us radios, money, and questionnaires, and for us to deliver intelligence to them. This could be our answer.

"You're saying this courier would be able to bring anything into France?"

"Indeed," he says, eyes twinkling as if maybe he's not just doing this for Navarre—as if maybe he's enjoying himself. "Things from the British Embassy in Spain, for example."

I kiss his cheeks. "If our code names weren't letters, I'd call you Santa Claus."

Lucien, who's in that awkward half-man, half-boy phase that reminds me of a downy fledgling, comes in at the same time and stops, agog. "What do you have to do to get a kiss?"

"He found a way to bring in supplies from MI6. If you find a way to bring in military secrets from Germany, I'll kiss you, too."

He looks as if he might charge out and run all the way to Berlin.

Couscous, Vallet, and Schaerrer don't even bother to pretend they're not howling with laughter. Even Baston smiles.

I'm letting Navarre's network devolve into a swashbuckling Dumas story. Or perhaps it's possible to lead with humor and fellowship, too. Even so, I restore us to as much order as ever exists at HQ by saying, "Schaerrer's navy background makes him our strongest candidate."

He returns three days later with the news that he got the job, meaning he'll be working out of Madrid and Vichy from now on. We'll see him every couple of weeks when he passes through Pau, but it won't be the same.

When we step out onto the porch to say goodbye, Coustenoble tells us, "The man I sent to Clermont-Ferrand came back with news."

Clermont-Ferrand is where Navarre and Léon Faye are imprisoned—thankfully by the French police rather than the Nazis—awaiting trial.

"They're fine," Coustenoble reassures me. "In fact, the prison guards are awestruck at looking after two such highly decorated military men. But Navarre said your name is in some of the documents the police found in Algiers."

I cross to the balustrade. Beyond, the Pyrenees are crowned by the sun, lighthouses unbowed by time and storms and history. Not even Nazis can stop them from putting on their glittering afternoon show.

But if my name is in documents found in the possession of the leaders of a coup, then the police know I'm a traitor, too.

I turn back to my tricolor. Their faces are somber. And the knowledge falls down upon me like a dust storm—they might be thrown in jail as well, just because they know me.

Pension Welcome—Josette, the fried trout, the evenings of stories—can no longer be my home.

"I need to stay somewhere else," I say flatly. "I can code intelligence and organize Alliance anywhere. But if the police come looking for me, I can't let them find all of you."

Vallet begins to protest, but Schaerrer says, "She's right. Surveillance has stepped up everywhere. Hugon told me it's worse than ever in Bordeaux."

Hugon, who brought us the map of the Saint-Nazaire U-boat facility that the British consider a crowning achievement, is one of the biggest swashbucklers we have. If he's worried . . .

"I'll tell everyone to be careful," I say. "But you be the most careful. If they catch you smuggling radios across the border—"

Schaerrer shrugs, his eyes that can stare unblinking at the sun refusing to look at me. "No one is irreplaceable."

Dread ices my veins. I almost tell him to return to tracking U-boats. But how is that less dangerous than a Vichy-sanctioned diplomatic position?

"You, Vallet, and Coustenoble are irreplaceable," I tell him. "What's a tricolor with all its colors gone?"

He still won't look at me. Is it premonition I'm feeling, or an ordinary, maternal kind of worry? Do I pay too much heed to my gut, or not enough? But I can't afford, in the sunlit comfort of day, to question every decision I make. I do that enough in the dead terror of night.

I let Schaerrer walk me over to my Citroën and drive away.

Coustenoble and I leave for the station speaking loudly about leaving Pau, hoping to make eavesdroppers believe I've gone. Then we double back to the Hôtel du Lycée, where the owner won't make me fill in registration papers and will bring me meals in my room. I take a moment to look up at the sky, that place of angels and airplanes, of pilots and birds and weather and stars and full moons and heaven. After today, I'll see it only through the window of my room while I work.

I once thought locking the city of Rabat at night was too confining for me. What I wouldn't give now to have the freedom of an entire locked city in which to roam.

On the night of the parachute drop, I smoke and pace my tiny room, which is exactly fifteen steps by twenty, waiting for Coustenoble and imagining a hailstorm of illegal goods and our new British radio operator dropping in a mantle of white silk to the ground. The second I hear scratching at the door, I fling it open.

Coustenoble's grin is gigantic. "You have to come and see this."

My rule is to go to HQ only if absolutely necessary. But if your first Englishman falling from the sky isn't a necessary occasion, I don't know what is.

We creep along laneways, Coustenoble looking back at me like a child taking me to see a unicorn. When we reach the pension, what I find is no mythical creature, but a ludicrous parody of a Frenchman. The man who's meant to train us to use the new transmitters and ciphering system is sporting a goatee beard, pince-nez, waistcoat, and spotted cravat, topped off with the pièce de résistance: a British bowler hat.

We might as well hang out a sign saying we're harboring a British spy.

Vallet's crying with laughter, looking every bit the nineteen-year old boy he is, especially when Couscous plucks the bowler hat from the man's head and executes a jaunty spin. God, I've missed being around them every day.

I swallow a giggle and introduce myself to the agent, whose code name is Bla. He replies in accurate French ruined by a Cockney accent. But, as a mother, you learn on a rainy day to make treasure out of the paper the butcher wraps the meat in, and I'll do the same with him.

"You need to shave off your beard and get a new set of clothes," I tell him.

He strokes his chin. "Really? I was worried I'd look too English without it."

This time, the laugh almost bursts out of me. I turn away and point to our motley crew in their dirty trousers, shirts grayed with age and unbuttoned at the neck. Not a goatee in sight. "This is what the French wear."

I send him off to find some clothes with little Lucien, who somehow grew a head taller while I've been domiciled elsewhere, then turn my attention to what else MI6 sent. Two more transmitters. One for Paris and one for Lyon. Invisible ink. Silky-fine paper that doesn't rustle when hidden in the lining of clothes. False pencils made to conceal notes rolled inside them. Dozens of packets of cigarettes. Coffee, sugar, and tea, my own weakness. Ten million francs to pay the agents and their families. MI6 mightn't be experts in French dress, but they're very good at this.

Soon after, I hear Lucien, who's been feverishly excited at the prospect of hosting an Englishman, asking Bla hundreds of questions about Britain. When Bla asks him, "What's your real name?" I spin around, shocked.

But Lucien says with endearing hauteur, "We don't have names. I'm TOM11."

I send him a smile of congratulations for abiding by the rules and he grows another head taller. I also make a mental note to remind Bla of the rules, which, as an MI6 agent, he should know better than we do. That's when I see what's obvious tonight because everyone's gathered here to celebrate. We're too big as a headquarters. We've been here for months undiscovered. Our luck won't last if we stay.

We need to move again.

One more supply drop, I decide. Then we'll leave what's been as happy a headquarters as the name Pension Welcome suggested.

The sound of Couscous coughing diverts my attention. "You need rest and warm milk," I say, knowing he's been outside for hours in the cold waiting for the airplane.

He shakes his head. "I have to escort you back."

I point to a chair. "I'm ordering Vallet to escort me instead. And I'm ordering you to sit in front of the fire. Right now."

Vallet and Coustenoble blink like I've poked them in the eyes. I never order. I always ask. But it has the effect of making Coustenoble drop into the chair and Vallet leap up from inspecting the new transmitters.

I disappear into the kitchen, where Josette, who's as besotted with Coustenoble as he is with her, has already got the milk warming.

"Thank you, little one," Couscous says to me when I return with the milk. Then his expression shifts. "A note came for you this afternoon. They were sentenced yesterday. Navarre for two years. Faye for five months."

I close my eyes, picturing Navarre at that long-ago party arguing with De Gaulle, who's safe in London. And Léon saying, *I will see you again.* The words had seemed fantastical— and are even more unlikely to come true now. While Léon might be allowed out of prison in five months, the last thing he'll do if he values his life is come anywhere near a Resistance network.

For one second I let myself recall the quick spark of fire in his eyes that he hadn't been able to hide.

Then Coustenoble proffers me a wrapped parcel. "Happy birthday," he says.

And I remember. I'm thirty-two years old today.

"It came down on its very own parachute," Couscous adds.

He makes me smile, which is why he's my adjutant. I smile still more when I find a pair of red shoes with real leather soles, not the wooden soles that rations have made ubiquitous in France.

Then Coustenoble starts to sing. "*Joyeux anniversaire . . .*"

He has bags under his eyes from being out so long in the dark, and he coughs nastily at the end of every line, but still he sings so cheerfully that all my agents join in. I stand there like I'm merely happy when, in fact, my heart is cracking.

Finding Bla a new wardrobe doesn't end my troubles with him.

"Has he been trained in undercover work?" Coustenoble demands when he and Vallet pay me an unscheduled visit the following week.

I'm wearing my new red shoes, which are the one spot of color in this turbid room. "MI6 said he's their best," I reply, barely looking up from decrypting messages.

"Then why is he sitting in the park where anyone can hear him, telling our Marseille radio operator how to work the receiver?" Vallet asks.

"He's told everyone his real name," Coustenoble adds, my imperturbable second in command definitely fired up.

"And the address where he'll stay in Paris," Vallet says.

Now they have my full attention. Transmission lessons in a public park? Telling everyone his very English name? Giving out his address?

"He keeps asking where you're staying," Coustenoble adds, shooting a look at Vallet as if they've debated whether to tell me this.

The realization that I'm only ever one decision away from destroying Navarre's network hits me in the gut. I light a cigarette, take a moment, wishing I was outside where I could see the mountains rising up like storm waves, white-capped with snow. Out there, my instincts blossom. In here, they're wilting like a hothouse rose.

But surely it's illogical not to trust the man hand-selected by MI6?

I stand. "Let's go see Bla. I need to make sure he's stupid, rather than dangerous."

Vallet grumbles, "He's definitely stupid," which makes me smile a little.

Bla is walking away from Lucien when I enter the pension, and a warning clamors. Have I been unwise allowing a boy with no experience of duplicity to join us?

"I need you to follow the rules," I tell Bla.

"I am, Madame." He stares down at me like Edouard used to.

"Then I won't hear any more reports that you've asked an agent for their address." It's a fine line I'm treading. I have no idea what MI6 will do if I show distrust. Nor do I want Bla to storm off before he's finished training everyone.

He inclines his head in a stiff nod. He doesn't like me. I don't like him. But he's a genius with radios and he's been sent to us by the people funding our operation, so all I can do is remind every agent about the rules. If they don't talk, it won't matter if Bla asks questions.

But I tell Coustenoble to make the arrangements to send Bla north next week. He's scheduled to go to Paris briefly, then he'll be based in Normandy, far from us. I'll arrange for him to relay information about U-boat movements directly to London, not via me. Problem solved.

Still, I pull Vallet into the kitchen.

"I need you to go to Paris," I say. "If we're putting MI6's first transmitter into the heart of the Occupied Zone, then the best radio operator should go with it. And we have enough agents there now that I need someone I trust to manage them."

"You want me to keep an eye on Bla."

He doesn't look scared, this boy with the too-large frame who wears the shirt I made for him almost every day. I don't want to send him away. I've already sent Schaerrer, our tricolor's bold stripe of blue, to Madrid. I want to be like King Solomon and cleave them in two, but I know I'd never be happy with just half of either of them.

I squeeze his hand. "Choose whoever you think is the best operator to stay here at HQ to transmit my messages."

"There's a fellow called Frédéric whom I've been training. He'll do."

My last words to Vallet are the same ones I told Schaerrer: "Be careful."

When Bla leaves, escorted by Coustenoble and Vallet, I relax a little, especially when Schaerrer passes through from Madrid with three more radio sets from MI6.

"How's my car?" I ask him.

"Only missing one headlight," he deadpans.

I laugh. "You'll need to bring me at least ten radios if you ever hurt my car. When are you coming back from Vichy?"

"Next Wednesday."

Which means I'll be working all night until then, scribbling

THE MADEMOISELLE ALLIANCE

coded notes for London in invisible ink on the backs of innocent-looking letters, which Schaerrer will take in the diplomatic bags to the British in Madrid.

The radios aren't the only nice surprises. I receive a note from Marguerite, who's managed to get an *Ausweis* and is coming to Pau next week with some information she says I'll be interested in. I can't wait to see her, but my enthusiasm is dampened by the return from Paris of a livid Coustenoble.

"Bla wasn't supposed to speak on the train," Coustenoble fumes. "But he asked stupid questions in his horrible accent at a volume they could probably hear in England. And he kept touching the transmitter, as if he wanted everyone to look at what was hidden in his suitcase."

Navarre would remind Couscous that we're untrained amateurs and Bla is a professional. So I keep my red shoes quiet on the floor. "Once he's in Normandy, if he gives MI6 the information they need, that's all that matters. Maybe they do things differently in England. I mean, they drink beer instead of wine, so . . ." I roll my eyes and Coustenoble manages a smile.

But I hardly sleep until a message comes through from MI6 that Bla's radio is transmitting normally. Still, with our upcoming parachute drop, which requires noise and movement—everything opposite to secrecy—I decide it's time.

"Find another HQ by the end of the week," I tell Coustenoble. "Let's start packing."

Coustenoble shakes his head. "You're the one person we can't afford to lose. Nobody else knows Alliance like you do. So unless you want it to fall apart, stay here. I'll see you tomorrow."

My exhale is frustrated. I want to be like Navarre and throw caution into a hurricane. Go to HQ and help pack up. But I'm the only one who knows what the British want from us, where every agent and sector of Alliance is located, whom to pay and when and how much. Navarre's in prison and I'm caretaker of a network I've promised not to ruin.

"All right. Divide up the equipment. You take four million francs, give Lucien three million, and Audoly can take the rest back to Marseille," I finish, referring to our Marseille radio operator who's been at HQ learning to use the new code.

That night I dream. Of Schaerrer being marched away with a gun at his back. Of Bla announcing to a trainload of people who Vallet really is. Of the police pouring into Pau, brandishing the documents that have my name in them.

I wake up haunted by the sensation that someone hasn't just walked over my grave—they've opened my coffin.

Hours pass. Coustenoble doesn't come. I pace, worry. Smoke.

When night becomes dawn becomes afternoon becomes dusk and the packet of cigarettes is empty and my shoes have cut blisters into my heels, I know I can't stay here any longer. I have to find Couscous.

As I move toward the door, the handle begins to turn.

My scream when it flies open is cinematic.

Thank God it's Marguerite. Yes, she was coming today. But her face is white as bone.

"They've been arrested," she whispers. "Coustenoble. Josette. Everyone at Pau except Frédéric and Lucien. Coustenoble sent them out the back as the police came in and Lucien met me at the crossroads. And before I left Paris, one of our letterboxes was discovered with messages and guns in it. The police arrested Vallet, Hugon, and seven more."

Coustenoble and Vallet. *No.* My tricolor, torn to pieces.

"They're about to start searching Pau," Marguerite finishes. "We need to go."

We hurtle down the stairs and into her car. We've no sooner pulled out onto the road when a police car charges past, followed by another.

I slide onto the floor. "Are they turning around?"

She shakes her head.

I've never seen her without a smile. But we're no longer racing for a trophy. We're racing for our lives.

We make it to a convent on the outskirts of a nearby town. But they turn us away. They've heard of me, they say, and the risk is too great. I'm shocked that my name and reputation as a *résistant* is so widely known and that their faith doesn't extend to mercy.

We return to the car terrified the nuns might turn us in.

"I can't put Marseille or the other sectors at risk by going there," I say. "Not until I can somehow contact the British and find out who's left."

"I know a couple who live in Tarbes," Marguerite says. "They wouldn't be my first choice, but it's close by. And we're almost out of gas."

What choice do we have? I'm clutching not at straws, but at the hems of hope.

"I shouldn't have gotten everyone into this," I say.

"The Nazis got everyone into this," Marguerite says, voice ferocious. "If you didn't have a network, we'd have found someone else who did. We aren't doing this for you."

"You make me sound like an egoist," I say, well and truly scolded for my hubris. But how do you separate hubris from responsibility?

I was the one who let Coustenoble return to HQ. I sent Vallet to Paris. But to seize hold of culpability and wave it around like my own sovereign flag is to reduce their courage to the mere following of orders. They aren't subordinates—they're heroes.

I should do them the justice of not wallowing in my guilt.

"Pull over," I tell Marguerite.

"Why?"

I manage the tiniest smile. "We'll get there faster if I drive."

Marguerite stays in Tarbes only long enough to introduce me to her acquaintances as a friend who's fallen ill on a holiday. "My pilgrimage is calling, otherwise I'd stay with her," Marguerite says with innocent eyes before she drives off, purportedly to go pray in Lourdes.

I keep to myself that she was the one who taught me how to swear in Arabic. I also keep to myself her real destination: Vichy, where she intends to find Schaerrer.

The next day and night are long. Couscous and Josette are in jail. Vallet is, too. Our money, radios, and arms from the parachute drops will have all been taken unless Coustenoble somehow got them away. The British will think I've failed—and I *have*. Failed to keep everyone safe. Failed to caretake Navarre's network.

Instead of sleeping, I write another of those letters I can never send:

> *Mes chéries, remember the summer at Mougins when the pig fell in love with Christian? It bleated when it couldn't see him until one day it charged through the fence, knocked Christian over, and snuffled all over his face, giving him muddy kisses. It was the same summer you learned to swim, Béatrice, and you wanted to be in the water so often I didn't think our skin would ever be smooth. That's how I think of you now—Christian laughing so hard he couldn't push the pig away and Béatrice laughing as she paddled toward the shore.*

I hold the letter for an hour before I make myself burn it in the fire.

Finally Marguerite returns with Schaerrer, whom I embrace as if he were my son.

"There's a warrant out for your arrest," Schaerrer fills me in. "Even though Coustenoble's taken responsibility for Alliance's activities and told the police he's the leader of a handful of malcontents. But he's been mistreated."

"How?"

"Baston told me they've made him balance on his knees on a ruler suspended off the ground for hours. And—"

I drop into a chair. "What?"

"They've burned him with cigarettes."

I push myself out of the chair so forcefully that both Marguerite and Schaerrer must think I'm about to storm into the prison and demand Coustenoble's release, because they take hold of my arms.

What do you do when all your radios might be gone, when you have no way to contact MI6, when your adjutant is balancing on a ruler with burns on his body? When you've broken the network entrusted to you?

You fix it.

It'll be easier to reach the moon than it will be for a woman who's wanted by the police and who has no travel papers to get across a border that's sealed shut by Nazis. But sometimes a leader has to hoist her flag and charge over the barricade.

"I'm going to Madrid," I say. "To meet MI6."

14

Trying to Squeeze a Horse
into a Handbag

France and Spain, December 1941

All night we throw around ideas about how to smuggle me over the border. I can't hide in the trunk of Schaerrer's car; they always check the trunk, the back seats, and the floor. Finally I ask the one thing I've been praying I wouldn't have to. "How big is the diplomatic mailbag?"

Marguerite stares at me as if I've just asked Schaerrer for the size of something far more intimate. "You cannot be serious," she says.

Schaerrer grimaces. "Two feet by four feet. Too small to fit a person inside. Besides, the road over the Pyrenees is closed for winter. To get to Spain, I have to put the Citroën on a flatbed carriage at Urdos. Even if you could somehow fit inside the bag, you'd have to stay in it for the two hours it takes them to hoist the car onto the train and for it to cross the border to Canfranc. When I say it would hurt, I'm making the biggest understatement of the year."

"I imagine being burned with cigarettes hurts, too," I say.

We're all quiet for a moment, then Marguerite shakes her head. "You're mad. But that's why I love you."

It's exactly what I need to hear—a few words of faith to bolster my own.

Schaerrer empties the bag of official correspondence.

I'm five feet six, far from tall, but I might as well be a giant when it comes to trying to cram myself inside. The bag comes up to my breasts when I stand in it. I try to crouch down, but it's too narrow.

Marguerite starts to laugh. "I know it's not funny, but it's like trying to squeeze a horse into a handbag."

We're all laughing by the time I've wriggled into twenty different and increasingly comical positions. After ten more minutes, I say despairingly, "I'm just too big."

Schaerrer's expression becomes concentrated. "Maybe . . ."

He pauses, examines me and the bag. "I once saw a circus performer fit himself inside a bag a bit like this one by pushing his feet into the corners, then squatting right down to the ground. He wrapped his arms around his shins and curled his forehead onto his knees."

"Here goes," I say pessimistically, standing with legs akimbo before squatting down as low as I can. My hip groans.

But I'm almost there.

I press myself lower, hip shrieking, sweat sliding down my nose, my back. I only need to be another centimeter smaller. How?

Marguerite raises an eyebrow at me. I know what she's thinking.

I climb out of the bag. "Nobody is to talk about this. Ever."

I remove my clothes.

Standing there in my underwear, I feel barer than if I were nude. I've had this brassiere for three years. In pre-ration times, when new lingerie could be bought at Galeries Lafayette as easily as bread from the boulangerie, I'd only wear one this old on laundry day. But I'm about to wear it—pink silk faded to almost white, straps frayed, lace torn in two places—across a border guarded by police who want to arrest me.

How do you hold your head high in front of your enemy when you're wearing your wash-day bra?

You don't get caught.

Which means pretending I'm wearing shocking-pink Schiaparelli. It means stepping back into the sack, tucking my feet into the corners, squatting, curving my shoulders around my forlorn bra, ignoring my hip, and praying that my head is inside my mailbag prison.

Schaerrer tugs the top of the sack, then gives it one good, hard wrench. "It closes."

But my windpipe is crushed, my lungs screaming for air. My hip is weeping.

"She's going to die in there after half an hour!" Marguerite protests.

A scraping sound. Then a metal blade appears an inch from my face. Schaerrer cuts three holes near my mouth. It makes only the smallest difference. But Coustenoble is being used as an ashtray, so the least I can do is crouch in a bag for a couple of hours.

"Carry a pair of scissors," Schaerrer says grimly as I climb out gasping, hand pressed to my hip. "In case you start to suffocate."

"Maurice will kill me when he finds out I've let you do this," Marguerite whispers.

"Are you sure?" Schaerrer asks me.

"No," I tell him. "But isn't that the way we live now?"

I stay in the passenger seat of the Citroën until we reach the woods outside Urdos, where I take off my clothes and cram myself into the bag. Once I'm curled as tightly as a hedgehog—and feeling as uncomfortable as if that creature's pins were pressing into my lungs, my hip, and my skull—Schaerrer seals the bag. He piles four spare tires up beside it on the back seat to disguise its strange shape.

I can do this.

My hip shrieks in disagreement. My lungs join in.

But I have the promise of freedom in two hours. Coustenoble and Vallet don't have any such promise. And I'll never be able to see my children again if the police arrest me and the British hear nothing from us and withdraw their support and Alliance becomes something I took over from Navarre and ruined. I owe it to him, but most of all to my dream of walking into my apartment to the sound of feet running toward me, and two sweet voices calling, *Maman!*

I imagine that future so hard the pain settles to a hum. Until one of the tires shifts, pressing the bag's metal seal onto my head. I might be less than five feet tall by the time I get out of the bag—if I can even walk.

Living with congenital hip dysplasia means I've known pain before, the feeling of being devoured by it, that not a single sense works except the receptors that draw each spasm closer. I repeat like a mantra, *Two hours. Two hours.*

The car stops and Schaerrer converses with the stationmaster.

"The morning train just left," the stationmaster says cheerily. "We moved the timetable forward an hour. We'll have coffee while you wait for the next train."

"The next train?" Schaerrer asks, panic in his voice for the first time ever.

"It leaves in eight hours."

Eight hours!

I'm going to die.

The panic is more suffocating than the crush of my windpipe. I haul images of Christian and Béatrice into my head, cradling those pictures in my mind as tenderly as I'd once cradled my children in my arms while the Citroën is hoisted up. It sways precariously in the wind, a pendulum marking the time remaining before I'm asphyxiated, paralyzed, caught. Then it's deposited with a thump onto the carriage bed.

The long wait begins.

Cold December mountain air creeps inside my car. I feel it in my feet first; they numb rapidly, then my hands, too. I don't count the hours because there are always too many left to endure. I breathe in as much air as I can, force my brain to reconnect to each finger and toe. I pretend my hip isn't attached to my body, that the agony is outside me. Most of all I remember—like fever dreams—my family. Mother. Sister. Children. But their outlines blur, and blackness is threatening my vision when I hear Schaerrer arguing with the stationmaster, who won't let him ride in the Citroën once the train departs.

"It's too dangerous," the stationmaster says. "Sometimes the ropes snap on the curves and the cars get thrown off."

Thus another way to die is added to the already long list.

I document them all: hypothermia, suffocation, decapitation from one of the tires on the seat beside me, the crushing of my body as it's flung into the side of the mountain. At least the last two would be quick.

I'm so cold I've stopped shivering. I know it's a bad sign. I try to move a toe. Just one.

I can't.

Then the train starts to move!

Only two hours left. I'm through the worst of it.

Remember my children, ignore my hip. I repeat the words over and over, a mantra to get me through.

But just when I'm so close, my body starts to betray me. My breath slows. My heart rate, too. I can't feel the pain in my back, my hip, or my neck, not anymore.

I don't have another two hours left in me.

As if through water, I hear footsteps. Then the sound of the car door being wrenched open. I'm so far gone I'm hallucinating. But no—the bag is being untied and my head is off my knees and now I'm gulping in freezing air like it's champagne.

"Are you all right?" Schaerrer asks, eyes wild, militarily tidy hair rumpled like Tintin's. "I thought I was going to have to tell everyone I'd murdered you." He grabs a blanket from the trunk and tucks it around me.

"Not yet," I mumble.

He tips Armagnac into my mouth and I want to bathe in its warmth. My eyes adjust and I see that we're in the Col du Somport, the tunnel leading to Spain. I wish we were already at the other end.

"I jumped from carriage to carriage to get back here," Schaerrer says, and I actually manage a half smile.

"So you're practicing for Hollywood and me for the Moulin Rouge," I say thinly, referring to my underclothes.

He laughs, then claps a hand over his mouth. "Sorry."

I shrug. "If I was in your shoes rather than my bare feet, I'd be laughing, too."

"Only an hour to go," he promises.

Sixty minutes. Three thousand, six hundred seconds too many.

I've never wanted to do anything less than curl back up and feel the bag seal behind my neck. After that, I count every single second the way an insomniac tallies sheep—but I do it to *stop* myself from drifting into darkness.

I've reached one thousand when I wonder if I'll be able to walk after this. My hip is a wildfire. But a hip isn't the same as a life. I only have to get out of this with my life.

At last the train slows.

As my car is lifted up and set down on the ground, my hip spasms so much I think I might vomit. The tires shift, curling me into a still tighter ball, my windpipe so squashed the panic crests again. I have the scissors in my hand, the scissors I told myself I wouldn't use because it would mean Schaerrer's being marched off to prison. But right now I want to stab not just the bag but myself.

That's when the car door opens.

A flashlight waves back and forth as the car is inspected by customs officers.

Suddenly I'm glad of the tire on top of me, making me even more invisible.

The flashlight retreats. The car door slams.

"We just need to get out of the station and into the woods, and then you can climb out," I hear Schaerrer say.

"I can't," I whisper. I haven't eaten or drunk for ten hours. My hip is a living beast of agony. I can't remember the last time I was able to move my fingers or my toes.

The whirlpool comes for me and I let myself fall into it.

The sound of water. Then cold, right through to my bones.

Bones. I have bones. That means I'm alive.

Pain, so much pain.

I want the whirlpool again.

But there's a light above me. The moon. Sky. Night glitter, stars. And Schaerrer's face, ravined with worry.

"Thank God," he says. "A decent cigarette and you'll be fine."

Yes, we're an alliance of adventurous optimists, thinking a cigarette will cure all.

I can't move my mouth or my head, so I can't disagree, nor throw a tire at him, which I'd quite like to do. Instead, I swallow more Armagnac. It revives me enough to see that I'm propped against a tree by a stream, blanket thrown around me. "I'm never doing that again."

"At the risk of sounding like I suffered more than you, I don't think I can do it again, either." Schaerrer takes a seat beside me. "I aged a thousand years over that ten hours of imagining you dead. I couldn't decide whether Coustenoble would shoot me or if Navarre would burst out of jail and do it, or if the whole of Alliance would tie me up in the mailbag and throw me into the sea."

Every muscle protests my attempts to make something besides my mouth move. "Well, I still can't walk, so you might yet have some explaining to do."

"Here." Schaerrer puts the cigarette to my lips and it tastes better than Christmas dinner. Then he carries me back to the car, which isn't even an indignity, but a necessity. I could no sooner walk than a newborn could run.

When the car draws up at the British embassy in Spain, I still can't straighten my legs. I try to open the door, but even that small movement makes me want to tear my hip off my body. Schaerrer reaches in and lifts me up again, ever so gently.

"There are at least two flights of stairs," he says matter-of-factly.

"I suppose it means my entrance will forever after be remembered." I offer him a flicker of who I'm meant to be, Marie-Madeleine, intrepid leader. "At least I'm now wearing clothes."

We're both laughing as we enter the embassy.

I have a couple of days to recover the ability to use my limbs before Crane—the man from MI6 whom Navarre met in London—alerted by the British embassy staff of the sudden appearance of POZ55, arrives. I watch the staff send the message, so I know they haven't mentioned my gender; they aren't privy to our clandestine work and don't know it's a secret.

But it soon won't be.

Once in a room with Crane, there'll be no hiding that I'm a woman. I might have almost killed myself for nothing. Because MI6 could easily refuse to work with a woman.

Then it really will be the end for Alliance.

As soon as I can walk, I do something irresponsible. I let the embassy staff take me out to have my hair and nails done; buy me cosmetics, lingerie, a black silk dress, more new shoes, and stockings, too. My sore hip and worsened limp hide, almost forgotten, beneath new and stylish clothes that aren't faded or frayed. I contemplate tossing my old pink bra in the trash. But I can't make myself do it—the Nazis have been in France just a

year and a half, but the habit of keeping everything in case it can
be mended, repurposed, or resewn is already as established as
the orange tree I planted in my courtyard in Paris.

I feed my hip two aspirin, then go outside. It's so quiet, like
Paris when I visited in April, as if all over the world, only the
echo of the grand symphony that was once Europe remains.
Spain is officially neutral, but Franco loves Hitler, so swastikas
drip like blood from buildings that bear the wounds of the Civil
War's gunshots as I make my slow and careful way to the Prado,
ears straining for birdsong that never plays.

At the museum, I avoid crucifixions and Goya, sit on a bench
where I stare at cherubs and gentle nudes. But on the walls
beside them are other paintings, history rendered in oils—stories
of war, of the weak defeating the strong, stories of lovers weeping.

I should have gone to a bar.

It takes longer to walk home. My hip's defeated the aspirin.
I'm moving so slowly I can see myself in detail in the shop windows, and if I look past the limp, the woman in those windows
seems so young. And she is. Just thirty-two years old.

My mother once told me that this decade would be one of
the loveliest. My children would be old enough to sleep through
the night, and I'd fall in love with them as people, rather than
loving them with that more animal instinct to protect them. I'd
have time to go out with my husband, and we'd rediscover romance and tenderness and passion.

I didn't cry in the mailbag, but tears trickle from my eyes
now, because yes, this decade is lovely—and monstrous, too. In
this decade, my soul is different because of an alliance of people
who walk right up to danger and stand there, facing it.

Which means I can no longer avoid thinking about tomorrow's meeting with Crane. I owe it to everyone in Alliance not
only to make sure the British get over the fact that I'm a woman,
but also to show them how deeply I understand this network.
There's been a disaster in Paris and in Pau. But that means we

need to strengthen what we've started so we grow like the arte-
misia plants in Morocco's desert—stealthily, unexpectedly,
leaves nondescript until transformed into green, sparkling ab-
sinthe.

We've been stealthy. But we haven't yet dared to sparkle.

Maybe it's time to tell the British what *I* want.

Do I dare?

I carry the question with me as I make my halting way back,
wishing suddenly and acutely for someone with whom I could
share my worries. Someone who might hold me in a gentle embrace; someone who might take the weight from my hip.

The only person with whom I've shared what truly drives me
is a dark-haired man I met in Vichy, who's now in a prison cell.
A man I hardly know, and who'd probably be less than what I've
made him into if we were ever to meet again.

I have only myself. So I'll just have to dare. The same way I
did when I left Morocco eight years ago.

15

It's All Just Beautiful Risk

Madrid and Marseille,
December 1941–February 1942

put on my new dress and shoes and trademark smile. I have to hide from my enemies every day in France. I don't want to have to hide from my allies, too. I'm a woman, and that's a fact I'm not going to mitigate with a plain dress and a sober face.

When Schaerrer and I walk into the meeting room, MI6 agent Crane holds out a hand to Schaerrer.

Schaerrer gestures to me. "This is POZ55."

Crane stares, waiting for Schaerrer to admit it's a joke, and I plunge into this encounter the same way I've tackled blind corners, clouds enveloping my plane, and gossips at parties—boldly. I'm one individual in the midst of a conflict that's reached global proportions—while I was in the mailbag, America entered the war, too—but I'm temporarily in charge of a Resistance network that deserves MI6's faith in *them*.

"You're disappointed," I say. "But I didn't want you to abandon the agents of Alliance because of something I can't change. I wanted to prove myself first . . ."

But what have I proved? That on my watch, Navarre's network can be torn apart.

My smile vanishes. Navarre's had a thousand strategy meetings with intelligence officers and politicians and military men over his career. This is my first. If I don't make it count, it's going to be my last.

"Hitler's stolen the world," I tell Crane with the same passion and openness Edouard so despised. "I want to take it back."

"You're still going to work with us?" Crane's tone is unmistakably anxious.

My eyes meet Schaerrer's, and in his I see my joy mirrored. Crane is as worried as I am about losing our association. What Navarre said months ago is still true—the British know nothing and Alliance is the only network giving them useful information.

I could be a toad and they'd still want to work with me. Which is bad for my ego but music to my soul.

I take a seat and explain what's happened.

"We know," Crane says. "We also know that your agents in Paris have been handed over to the Abwehr. They're in Fresnes prison."

The Abwehr is the Nazi's military intelligence service. At least if you're taken by the Vichy police, like Coustenoble and Josette, you still have a chance. Being held by the Nazis in Fresnes is the worst thing of all.

I swear on my life that I will never again remain in one place for so long. I swear, too, that I will get them all back—somehow.

"Your Marseille and Nice sectors are still intact," Crane continues. "That's how we heard what happened. And Normandy is transmitting, too."

Rivière and his lovely wife and that beautiful shop on the harbor are safe! And others are safe, too, like Bla in Normandy.
Like Bla in Normandy.

"Was it Bla who betrayed us?" My question is abrupt and I grimace at the way I've blurted out my suspicion without any evidence.

"Bla?" Crane looks understandably puzzled.

I outline my fears about the British radio operative. But Crane shakes his head. "We check our agents' backgrounds so thoroughly we know what they're thinking before they do. It's not Bla."

Maybe I'm just hoping to find another scapegoat besides me. But there isn't one.

Which means—MI6 knows what they're doing in England, but I'm the one who's been standing on the soil of my occupied, shattered, desperate country for the past year and a half. I have to fix this so it will never break again.

"I want enough money to pay the salary of every agent and their families as well," I tell him. "I want scheduled monthly drops of supplies to properly equip each sector. At least six more radios. Another way of getting messages into and out of France. A proper brief about strategy, one that I have input into. If you agree to that, then yes, I'll continue to work with you."

I'm a mother, estranged wife, and notorious nonconformist, and I'm making demands of a British military intelligence expert. But Crane smiles and says, "You can have everything you want. Your network *must* last."

Over the next few days, I receive a master class in intelligence gathering from Crane, who's more respectful and collaborative than I'd imagined. We discuss bold plans to have small planes called Lysanders land in secret fields in France, planes that will use only the moon to guide them. That's how we'll bring more MI6-trained operatives, messages, and supplies into and out of France.

It should be daunting. But I can't wait. Especially when news comes through that Laval—that weasel who came to investigate Navarre's fake illness in Vichy—has been removed from his post as deputy prime minister and Admiral Darlan, who's known to play all sides equally well, is taking over. He's far from lenient, but he does want to appease the old French guard who love their country and are afraid that things are going too far. He might be less vigilant in hunting down Resistance activity in the free zone.

Crane finishes my training with the strategy discussion I wanted. "The Allies will eventually land in France," he says. "I can't tell you when, because I don't know. It depends on how much information you can get us about the Nazis' infrastructure and how many U-boats we can keep blowing out of the water. We're relying on you to help us do those two things."

"Alliance will never let you down," I promise him.

I don't care if an Allied attack is months away. I just care that it's coming. Until then, I'll continue to play cat and mouse with the Nazis—but with the courage and strength of a lion.

Returning to France in the mailbag is survivable because the journey takes the expected two hours rather than ten.

"If only I'd known, when I almost gave Baston the code name Santa Claus, that I should never make jokes about what might be carried in this sack," I grumble when I'm let out in the woods at the foothills of the Pyrenees, revived again by Schaerrer's Armagnac.

"I don't think Santa carries semi-naked women around in his sack, otherwise people would never let him slide down their chimneys," he jokes. "This story is going to keep Alliance going for years."

The only part of me that's capable of movement, besides my mouth, are my eyebrows. I lift one in what I hope is a forbidding way. "We're telling nobody about this."

"We'll see," he says as he passes me my dress.

We've reached Marseille and are weaving through the narrow streets of le Vallon des Auffes when Schaerrer tells me, "I'm going back to tracking U-boats. Like Crane said, we need that intelligence more than ever. And Hugon's in jail, so . . ." He shrugs. "I'll do it."

Vallet and Coustenoble are in jail. I'm not losing Scharrer, too. "Sneaking onto submarine bases is the most dangerous thing of all—"

He cuts me off. "You just did the most dangerous thing of all in that sack. The least I can do is go to Bordeaux and tell you when the wolf packs are setting sail."

He stops the car in front of the fruit and vegetable shop and climbs out as if the conversation is over. And I know that I have to let him do this, no matter if staring up at him is like seeing my son in ten years' time.

Rivière greets me with a hug almost as crushing as the tires in Schaerrer's car. I have to force my still-aching bones not to flinch.

"You're too thin!" he shouts. "Come and eat."

The Marseille sector is humming. Audoly, the radio operator, is hard at work, as are the other recruits I met when I was here with Vallet. When I gave him his shirt.

Is he wearing it in prison?

Stop, I tell myself. When I'm alone tonight, I can think of Vallet and of Schaerrer. Right now, I have to be the charming, in-command Marie-Madeleine because everyone's nerves are chafed by the raids.

We gather at the table. Rivière's wife serves us fresh-caught fish and plenty of vegetables while Schaerrer regales everyone with the story of my journey to Spain. When he gets to the part where he opened the bag and found me looking dead, I can't help laughing at the expressions on everyone's faces.

"Even if I *had* been dead," I say, "his Armagnac could revive a corpse."

Everyone toasts, then they make Schaerrer finish the story, right down to my ordering him not to tell anyone about arriving in the forest in my underwear.

It's late when we hear the sound of scratching at the door.

Everyone freezes, hands slipping into pockets that once carried handkerchiefs and now carry guns. Rivière strides to the door. "Who is it?"

"It's Baston. Open up."

In comes the old general, whom I'd radioed from Madrid with instructions that I hope might get Coustenoble and the others freed. He crosses the room with the pace of a much younger man and clasps me to him. "*Mon Dieu*," he says. "When I found out you'd gone to Spain . . ."

He presses his palms to my cheeks. "I only ever wanted to stop you from having to . . ." He pauses. "There are some things I'd rather you not have to feel. Which is to say—I'm glad you're safe, my dear."

My dear. He says it as if I'm something precious. And his eyes are as shiny as mine when I whisper, "Thank you"—to this man who always knew I'd be trouble, but who's become one of our staunchest troublemakers in Vichy France.

He composes himself beneath his handkerchief, then tells me, "I did what you asked. Got a note to Coustenoble with the address of a house in Pau where I planted some innocent documents and a little bit of money. He confessed the address to his interrogators and they've recovered the evidence, which is so benign that everyone from Pau should be out of prison soon. As for those in Paris . . ." He sighs. "I have no power against the Abwehr."

He picks up Schaerrer's Armagnac flask, pours himself a healthy finger, and stares at the liquid, which looks crimson in the firelight. "It's Le réveillon de la Saint-Sylvestre, the last night of the year, and we should be eating wild boar and oysters and kissing beneath sprigs of mistletoe. So we should toast . . ."

I hold up my glass. "To Vallet. To breaking him out of prison. And to 1942. The year Alliance rules."

One month later, when I approach the vegetable shop from the troglodytic cave Rivière has found for me to live in, I see a tall, dark-haired man waiting beneath the awning. There's the slightest graying at his temples now, but arranging a coup and spending five months in prison would probably change the color of my hair, too—although it doesn't seem to have harmed his muscular frame. He's wearing a half smile as if he's anticipating something wonderful.

I touch a hand to my dress, wishing I'd worn one of the new ones from Spain. But I wasn't expecting to see Léon Faye this morning.

When he looks up, his gaze is like a half-drunk glass of Bordeaux abandoned beside a shucked-off red silk dress.

I quash that thought with a quip. "Is this the soonest you could get here?"

"You're the hardest woman in the country to find," Léon replies with a much too bewitching smile.

I lean against the wall beside him, fixing my eyes on the little harbor where boats knock gently back and forth like xylophones. The movement of the sea beneath the glistering sun makes it look like stars are diving into the waves. Above, the mimosas have just started to flower, yellow blooms of optimism promising that winter is almost done, that we can soon stop wearing blankets over our clothes, and the chilblains that have formed in red patches of discomfort around my nails will fade.

I keep my face turned toward the view as I ask, "What are your plans now?"

"I told Navarre I'd take you somewhere safe. Friends in Algiers are happy to hide you. Last year's coup wasn't a complete disaster—things are still moving in the right direction over there. North Africa will be free of Nazis before France is."

"Do your friends have room for the entire network?"

Our eyes meet again.

Attraction, desire; we have so many names for what makes

two people linger beneath the shadow of an awning, bodies an-gled toward each other, the visceral sensation of proximity head-ier almost than touch. But is there a word to describe the sensation of not yet touching—that moment when it's all just beautiful risk, dancing in the spaces between our bodies?

Léon's reply to my question is slow to come, as if he, too, wants to let the risk dance on and on.

"The network doesn't exist anymore," he says.

"Who told you that?"

"Navarre said everyone had been arrested."

Rather than bridling at the suggestion that I need help to be transported to North Africa and that Alliance is dead, I decide to take this moment to have a little fun.

"Come inside," I tell him. "I have some people to see, then we can talk."

16

Tonight Will Not Be the
Last Time I Weep

Marseille, February 1942

éon and I have only just stepped into the warehouse when Lucien scrambles in, face alight. He's been watching the prison where Coustenoble, his mother, and the Pau team have been jailed.

"They're out!" he shouts, and we grin ridiculously at one another for a minute. I want to rush straight to Pau and embrace my adjutant. But I know I can't risk being seen with Coustenoble and getting him sent back to prison.

Instead I ask Lucien, "How's your mother?"

"She told me my clothes were dirty," he grumbles.

"And Coustenoble?"

"Coughing up his lungs."

I ask Rivière's wife, Madeleine, "Do we have anything other than carrots?"

"Just some spinach. Maybe a few apples."

Late winter on rations is measured by the degrees of emptiness in your stomach. Hungry. Ravenous. Happy to eat shark.

I pull out some of MI6's money and give it to Lucien. "I don't care what black-market shop you have to go to. Buy milk. Eggs. Meat. Tell Coustenoble I'm ordering him to eat it. Josette, too. And find a building to rent. You're in charge of locating and furnishing a new Pau office."

Lucien races out with a worshipful little bow that makes Rivière chuckle.

That one glorious relief gives me the fortitude to ask Audoly a question I've been worrying over for days. "Anything from Schaerrer?"

He shakes his head.

"He's never gone this long without a transmission," I say to Rivière, who looks as somber as I feel.

He drops his broad hands onto my shoulders. "Perhaps things are just too hot right now."

Schaerrer *has* been sending us vital information about U-boat personnel numbers, torpedo stocks, and embarkation dates, so perhaps he does just need to lie low. I can't send anyone to look for him, because if there's a trap waiting, they'll be caught. I should ready another man to take over the sector, just in case. But Schaerrer is irreplaceable.

No one is irreplaceable, he once told me.

I shiver, trying not to think of every premonition I've had that's turned out to be more accurate than a sniper. "I'll wait another week," I tell Rivière.

Then I turn to Léon, who's watching everything with a be-mused expression, studying the maps and their code names: *Bonne Mère* for Marseille, *Restaurant* for Grenoble, *Hangar* in Bordeaux, *Palais* in Pau. Rivière turns to Léon, too, not with the usual buccaneer's glint in his eye, but suspicion.

"It's Commandant Faye," I explain.

Rivière gives Léon a sweeping salute and shouts, "Tell us about the Algiers affair! I wish you'd been able to trounce them all."

"So do I," Léon says wryly.

"Maybe the storytelling can wait until lunch," I tell them, not about to let the point I'm trying to make be derailed by one of those long, mythologizing conversations men have about their exploits.

"Is Siegrist here?" I ask Rivière, who nods. I lead Léon to the room where I interview agents, explaining that Siegrist is a former Paris policeman who fled the city after his network leader betrayed everyone. I've been checking out his story with MI6 and last night they confirmed it was genuine.

I take a seat across from Siegrist. "You must be worried about your family. They're still in Paris?"

Siegrist nods. His ears are the size of saucers and his nose would rival a dolphin's, but the bleakness in his eyes renders his face far from comical. "My daughters are six and nine. They're with my wife."

For one second, my own eyes smart at the thought of those children, who are just a little younger than Béatrice and Christian.

Perhaps a man so obviously distracted by his absent wife and children is someone I should hesitate to employ. But it's his very depth of feeling for his family that makes me say, "I need someone to manage Alliance's security team. As a policeman, you're perfect for the job. It'll involve teaching every sector how to use lookouts and keep their premises secure, as well as forging identity papers and ration coupons. I'll send money to your family each month and I'll pay you a salary, too."

Siegrist grasps my hand. "Thank you, Madame."

Another man joins Alliance, but it's not enough. I need men trained in the military if I'm to do what the British want. Which is what I'm hoping Léon Faye can help me with, once I've proven to him that the network doesn't just exist—it's flourishing.

He watches as my secretary summons me over, frowning at the new invisible ink Crane gave me. If it's too close to a fire, it turns brown. I have Audoly send a message to MI6. A courier arrives with messages about a cargo of arms being sent to the Nazis' Afrika Korps disguised as tins of food. I code the information and Audoly radios it to MI6 so the ship can be blown out of the water. In between, Madeleine brings me cups of *café na-*

tional, the ground-almond murk that now passes for coffee. She's wearing the shoes I bought in Madrid; I have the ones MI6 sent me for my birthday and I don't need two pairs. As she cooks for all of us, she sings and taps her heels against the floor, and I love the sound—the steady pulse of Alliance.

Finally, Léon's impatience reaches a crescendo. "Let's eat," he says, standing up. "We'll try one of the black-market bars on the Canebière."

For a second, I imagine sitting in a bar and drinking wine and eating food with him as if we were just another ordinary couple getting to know each other. I shake my head. "After escaping Pau, I'm lying low. I live in one of the cave dwellings below the Corniche, and I go only from there to here wearing very large hats."

"What about my room at the Hôtel Terminus? I have some clandestine materials there, too, as it turns out." He smiles. "Will a Monbazillac do?"

"In the absence of champagne"—I return the smile—"I'll drink Monbazillac."

Before the war, a woman would only go with a man to a hotel room for one thing. Now, I go to so many strange places with so many men that I don't even think of his suggestion as improper, just practical. I need someone like Léon, who's led squadrons and no doubt has a legion of pilots loyal to him who could help expand the network. And I don't want to talk to him in front of the already curious Gabriel Rivière.

As we're leaving, another courier arrives with a message that I wish had come yesterday when I wasn't trying to show off the network in its best light. I pass it to Rivière, who shouts, "The little bastard! Chasing after money at a time like this?"

"I'm more worried about him giving us up," I say. "If he's caught and has to give up something to free himself, he won't give up his new network."

"What is it?" Léon asks, and I reluctantly explain that Frédéric, our Nice radio operator, has defected to another network that will pay him more. I don't want Léon to think it means I can't command the agents' loyalty.

"He *is* a little bastard," Léon concurs. "What kind of network poaches agents?"

"Trained wireless operators are as rare as good Germans," I explain. "Now that De Gaulle's Free French are starting networks, we're competing for staff. It's the first time it's happened to us, though," I add, hoping that disclaimer is more persuasive than it sounds.

When we reach his room at the Hôtel Terminus, Léon pulls out foie gras, bread, and wine and puts them on the table. "Spoils from a friend with a farm near Sarlat," he says, taking the seat opposite and sipping the wine while I fall on the pâté with gusto.

He lets me eat my fill before saying, "I made a stupid offer to escort you to North Africa and then you set out to prove that you were doing just fine without me." He smiles wryly. "Tell me everything."

I do. I explain that Alliance has been charged with blunting the Nazis so the Allies can make plans for an invasion of France. Léon listens, interrupting only occasionally to ask a perceptive question, and never, despite his experience in war and men, criticizing any of my choices. I wonder if the experience in prison has tamped down some of the fire I saw in him in Vichy so it still burns, but more enduringly.

And more endearingly.

Stop it, I tell myself. I don't know why this man has such an effect on me, just that he does—and also that I can't let myself feel it.

"What do you need most of all?" he asks, refilling my glass with the last of the wine, which tastes like honey and fig and makes the foie gras sing on my palate.

"Two things." I lean back and relax for the first time that day. "We transmit the urgent messages to London twice a day. Everything else goes via the Vichy diplomatic bag to Spain. It takes too long, and Vichy will soon find out the bag is a party to treason. So MI6 wants to land planes here in France by moonlight. I need someone to—"

"Recruit people who know enough about planes to land one in secret in the dead of night," he finishes, standing up, pacing, clearly electrified by the prospect. "What's the second thing?"

"To start up sectors of Alliance right across France. But we need trained leaders to run those sectors, not just eager volunteers." I sigh. "Navarre always said we needed military men, which I suppose I had mixed feelings about. But he's right."

"I can name at least three colonels who are almost sick with the armistice roles they've been forced into," Léon says. "And I know dozens of younger pilots to fill the ranks."

I grin. "Now I'm imagining Alliance as an enormous airfield populated by dashing airmen—and me, back in my plane, flying alongside them."

"You fly?" His face lights up with something different now. Admiration, I think, and the chemical composition of the room changes. Heat and fire.

Léon stops in front of me. "If you'll have me, I'm at your disposal."

I don't know how many meanings are trapped in that sentence, just that there are more than one.

I escape past him to the window embrasure. In my head are the words I thought once before, in Spain: *someone who might hold me in a gentle embrace; someone who might take the weight from my hip.*

But I'm not in Spain. I'm in a hotel room in France with a man who turns all the air around me to turbulence.

"I met your husband in North Africa," Léon says from behind me.

My whole body stiffens. Who was she, that woman who'd wanted a grand adventure in Morocco with a debonair young captain she'd also fallen for on first sight, the woman who'd instead found a life without bars that had imprisoned her all the same?

What if Léon is hiding locks and bolts beneath his charm, too?

"He never mentioned you," Léon continues, voice contemplative. "I wondered why, but now, standing here, I think . . ." He tries again. "You once called me impassioned, but you speak not just with words, but with your eyes and hands and face. With your whole body. Whereas Edouard Méric . . ." Léon shrugs and says only, "was very different."

When I don't speak or turn to face him, he goes on. "I heard other men speak of you too; that they regretted having been able to tempt you into conversation, nothing more. All I could think was—I'd never regret any conversation I was lucky enough to have with you. And that if I was married to you, I don't think I would ever stop speaking about you."

For one second I imagine being so cherished with words. And I have to hold on to the windowsill, because I absolutely cannot let myself turn and look at Léon right now.

"What do you want, Marie-Madeleine?" Léon asks softly, still on the other side of the room.

So many things.

But my reply, when it comes, is almost angry, because that's something I'm allowed to feel, as opposed to every single forbidden feeling I have for Léon Faye. "Will your air force colonels be happy to live on the run, working for an organization that changes shape every day? Will they be happy to report to a woman?"

My hands clench harder on the sill, my wedding ring a scar on one finger, the chilblains around my nails red and ugly—hands so hideous they no longer look like a woman's. I curl my fingers into my palms to hide them. "I never want to have to ask that question again."

I hear Léon walk toward me. Side by side we stare at the dusk stealing blue from the sky, at the absence of lights in this city that was once a golden, blazing thing, lit up to welcome anyone who might cross to its shores. "I'm prepared to take orders from you," he says.

I know, I don't say. *I've known that since we first met.*

But what he says next shocks me. "Navarre isn't coming back. Alliance is *your* network, Marie-Madeleine. That's what I saw today. It's not Navarre's. Not anymore."

Alliance is mine.

Mine.

I let go of the windowsill. My body turns ever so slightly toward Léon, and I wonder how it's possible that I lived with my husband for five years and he didn't know me at all, whereas the man beside me is a virtual stranger and he not only knows me, but he's prepared to show me the things inside me that I can't see. All this time, I've been leading Navarre's network but adding the word *until.*

Until Navarre takes over again.

I've been a commander in words but a subordinate in my heart.

Outside, Marseille is consumed by night. And in the darkness, I whisper, "If I stop believing that Navarre is coming back, then I'm truly saying farewell to my children. The person the Nazis will come after is the network leader. What kind of mother . . ."

I can't finish the sentence. There are tears in my eyes, and if I speak, they'll be in my words, breaking apart the syllables and scattering them onto the floor.

"The kind of mother who taught them to never sit back and accept something that they know is wrong," he says very gently, and now I feel like my heart will break and scatter onto the floor instead. He remembered what I said to him in Vichy more than a year ago.

If I reach up to wipe my cheeks, Léon will forget everything I showed him at the warehouse—that Alliance was alive and hungry for men like him, that I had everything in hand.

But he reaches into his pocket and lays a handkerchief on the sill between us—a white square to wipe away my grief.

He lets me weep, but not alone.

When I can speak, I tell him, "I don't have a chief of staff. I haven't replaced anyone. Replacing Vallet is like saying I don't think he'll come back. Recruiting a chief of staff is like saying everyone must stop thinking Navarre will return."

"It's saying you're *la patronne*. That's what I saw today."

La patronne. Another name to bear.

Back in 1941 in my apartment in Paris, I thought Marie-Madeleine had stepped out through my skin. Now it's time for her to step out of my soul.

My first act as a true leader is to say, "When I was Navarre's chief of staff I never spoke to him about his frailties. I need a chief of staff who tells me mine, like you just did."

Léon rests his hips against the windowsill so his head is a little lower and it's easier for us to see each other. "Loving your children isn't a frailty. It makes you the kind of person the men I saw today follow, because you understand they have families, too. Alliance is a family and that's its strength. And your not realizing you hadn't let go of Navarre—that just means your loyalty is larger than your ego, and I'd say that's a strength, too. One that I, and many others, could probably learn from."

He doesn't move closer, hasn't touched me; not once, but he's told me in every word tonight that he wants to—and that he wanted to understand why I carried my husband's name, and that extramarital affairs didn't suit his honor. Nor do they suit mine. But if marriage is a union, I am not married. The only thing left of my marriage is a piece of paper, easily burned.

So it isn't marriage that prevents me from taking Léon's

hand. It isn't that I don't want to. God, I do. I want to slip my fingers into his, feel the warmth of his palm against mine. I want to slide my hand over his jaw, see how much darker I could make his eyes become.

Do I remember how to kiss?

Yes, I remember. And I'm sure Léon has always known.

"What do you want, Marie-Madeleine?" he asks again, very softly.

My children in my arms. A free France. The safety of my agents.

Three incompatible things. In choosing the first, I'd be turning my back on the rest. By choosing to fight for the second, I'm endangering everyone I love.

I can't let myself long for any more incompatible things.

Besides, a leader doesn't have time for wants.

"I want to go back to HQ."

I don't know if it's hurt or understanding that flickers in Léon's eyes, but he nods and follows me out.

Rivière is waiting at HQ with an expression so uncharacteristic it's frightening. No ebullience, but that same depth of feeling poured into sadness.

"Be brave," he says, grasping my hand between both of his. "A message came in. Schaerrer was caught a week ago at Bordeaux. They . . ." He clears his throat, makes himself say it. "They shot him, chief."

I cross to another window and turn my back on different men, while inside, my bones weep. I know Schaerrer is dead. I've known, somehow, for days. Something else my cowardly heart hasn't wanted to face.

Schaerrer, who gave me Rivière. Schaerrer, who could look straight into the sun. Schaerrer, who told me that the harder it is to see something, the more beautiful it was.

Schaerrer, who christened my first three lieutenants "the tricolor."

Only the flagpole stands. But it is cracked and broken now.

I never knew it would be so terrible—to be the cause of someone's death.

I don't know how it happens, but Schaerrer is suddenly beside me—not his body, but his courage, his ghost breath slipping through me, whispering, *I'm with you. Carry on.* And my mouth is turning up at the corners, the way it always did when Schaerrer was there, tipping Armagnac down my throat, joking about Santa Claus.

What if, in war, the dead are not dead? What if they're allowed to walk among us when we need to believe that the world isn't really as wretched as it seems?

As abruptly as it arrived, Schaerrer's presence is gone and I'm left blinking away tears.

Rivière passes me a tiny piece of paper that was hidden in the corner of an envelope sent from the prison to Schaerrer's uncle. But I know it's meant for me.

I am glad I have preserved my honor, it says.

It means he hasn't betrayed us. That he gave up his life to give us ours.

I could weep as if one of my own children were dead. But I am *la patronne* now, the one who is never allowed to cry.

So I dam up my tears. I steady my voice. I say to everyone gathered there, "From today, we will work harder than ever, for Schaerrer, who cannot. We will uncover the location of every gun emplacement in France, every munitions factory, every airfield. We'll thwart the movements of every plane, ship, and U-boat; we'll wear down the Nazi military machine until it's so weak that an Allied invasion planned around all the information we're about to gather will be so successful, I'll *never* hear the word *Nazi* again."

I pause for breath from the words that have come out as a

battle cry and a prayer. "I'm reorganizing Alliance. As leader, my job is strategy and planning. Faye is my new chief of staff. For all day-to-day matters, see him."

And so the title—*la patronne*—settles over my head like a double-edged sword waiting to fall. For I am both *la patronne* and a murderer. Schaerrer will not be the last man I send out to die.

And tonight will not be the last time I weep.

Part Three

QUEEN

France, 1942–1943

I would not be a queen
For all the world.

— WILLIAM SHAKESPEARE

17

Lingering

Toulouse, February–May 1942

Léon summons his air force colleagues and I'm impressed at how many arrive for a meeting after just one message from their former commanding officer. We meet the first, Colonel Kauffmann, in the lounge of the Hôtel de Paris in Toulouse. He's impossible to miss, wearing a pair of army trousers so old they belong in a museum, and a gray cape—a man who must always fly, even when not in a plane.

"I know he looks a bit like an actor left over from the silent film era," Léon murmurs as we approach.

"I think he looks like a seasoned swashbuckler ready for his next exploit."

Léon laughs. "That's exactly who Kauffmann is."

The colonel slaps Léon on the back with affection before all but shouting, "You need help on the ground this time, Commandant?"

I shoot a look at Léon. Is Kauffmann trying to give us all up?

"I'll book a room upstairs," Léon says, and once his back is to Kauffmann, he whispers to me, "Slight deafness is an occupational hazard for a pilot." He hesitates only a second before adding, "He's not the only one."

Of course. Sitting in a cockpit every day with the roar of an engine hammering your ears is damaging. I like that Léon has handled the situation so he doesn't embarrass his friend, and I like that he's revealed his own vulnerability to me, rather than trying to hide it.

Léon Faye grows more charming by the second.

Upstairs in a room that looks as unloved as everything else in France that hasn't genuflected to Nazis, Kauffmann bellows, "Child's play," when I ask him to lead an Alliance sector in the Dordogne.

"My farm in Sarlat can be our base," Kauffmann goes on. "I know someone who can be our radio operator and another who'd make a good courier."

I smile. The colonel is an even better recruit than Léon promised. Even my soul relaxes. Was this how I made Navarre feel? As if he needn't only rely on me to do things, but to anticipate them as well?

Except . . .

The final hurdle.

"I'm in charge of the network," I tell Kauffmann.

"Fine," Kauffmann says in a manner so unfazed I'm not even sure he's realized I'm a woman, and I'm happy that my appearance has, for once, been so completely disregarded.

The colonel nods toward Léon and says, "I've had enough of reporting to him. Back in Algiers, we renamed the military citations 'the Fayes' because we'd all have to sit there waiting for the endless recitation of his brilliance at dangerous low-flying missions to end so we could finally get a drink."

Léon's cheeks are pink as he says to me, "You can order him to stop."

But I grin and shake my head and Kauffmann leans conspiratorially forward.

"Commandant Faye was the wood we'd knock upon before a mission, the four-leaf clover we'd want beside us. He survived crash landings and enemy fire, even being captured by the enemy. There was a boy named Louis Faye who decided he wanted to be as decorated as the man who shared almost the same name as him. So he asked to take Léon's place in a mission. The kid went out, but he never came back. Mechanical failure in the plane our friend Faye had been meant to fly. He's ruled by the goddess of fortune."

Halfway through this recital, Léon moves over to the sideboard, pouring out three brandies, keeping his back carefully turned toward us until Kauffmann finishes. When he returns with the drinks, the gray in his eyes has clouded over the green, as if he still mourns the boy who'd wanted to be like him and who had died instead.

The sidewalk is crowded on our way back to the station, and Léon and I are constantly moved together and apart by passersby. Léon always maneuvers himself back to my right side—the side with the limp. I'm surprised he's even noticed it; most people don't. I also hate that he's seen my hidden weakness on top of the obvious one everyone points out: that I'm a woman.

The next time the traffic separates us, I maneuver myself to his other side, only to have him steer himself instantly back to my right.

I stop. He must see on my face that I'm aware of what he's doing, because he looks at the ground like a guilty child. "I wasn't trying to patronize you," he says quickly. "I know you don't need my help. I was just trying to make sure you knew help was there, if you ever did."

The truth is, I do sometimes need help. French roads are cobbled and uneven and occasionally I stumble. It's why I usually walk beside walls.

"Léon," I say, and he looks back at me, expression wary. But I'm not angry. The man beside me isn't Edouard. He'll never scold me if I lose my balance. "Thank you."

"Marie-Madeleine . . ." He hesitates, and there's something

about the way he's looking at me that makes me feel like we're standing against a backdrop of Tchaikovsky, silk, and champagne, rather than a street stained with swastikas. "I'm trying to only give you as much as you'll take," he says softly, and his words are the music, the silk, and the heady cocktail, too.

For the very first time, I acknowledge both what is and isn't happening between us. "I wish I could accept more. And I wish . . ."

Not that I hadn't married Edouard, because then I wouldn't have Béatrice and Christian. Not that it wasn't wartime, because then I'd never have met Léon. "I wish I'd met you fifteen years ago," I say at last.

The touch of his finger against my hair is so fast, so light—almost as if he's making sure I'm really there, saying these words to him.

"I thought maybe you were just being kind to a man with a crush, like you are with Lucien. Knowing you feel something, too . . ." He stops.

A beat that neither of us knows what to do with, then he grins and says, "I was a jerk fifteen years ago. Better that you didn't know me then."

His smile is a coup de foudre and I have to make myself turn away from the storm.

Léon and I travel for two months, always in each other's company. It's exhilarating to see the second wave of Alliance taking shape in sectors led by Léon's excellent air force contacts. He might be a better chief of staff than I was, which I admit to him after a successful meeting with a gypsy pilot named Mahout who's promised to help us pull off the aerial magic trick of landing London's new midnight plane service.

Léon laughs. "Only when I've managed to fold myself into a mailbag will I be a better chief of staff than you were."

I make a show of tipping my head right back to take in his six-foot-plus frame and say cheerfully, "Well, it looks like I really am the best, then," and we board the train with smiles on our faces, smiles that widen when we find a blissfully empty carriage.

I toss my red beret onto the rack—the Vichy regime thinks they're a sign of one's *la francité,* so I wear one everywhere—and run a hand through my hair, taking the opportunity of having no eavesdroppers to summarize what we've accomplished so far.

I conclude by saying, "Paris still doesn't have a proper leader. And I need someone to head up Brittany—Lorient is the largest submarine base, and those U-boats are eating up Allied ships like they're croissants. I need someone to take over from Schaerrer." My good mood fades. "Hopefully I won't be gifting the Nazis another agent to murder."

"Your agents are offering themselves," Léon says. "By keeping them inside a network, they're safer than if they were out there committing random acts of sabotage."

It's an optimistic assessment. Which is why he's my chief of staff—to remind me that for every peril of leadership, there are blessings. It *is* safer to be part of a network than to fight on your own. So I decide to be sanguine for the rest of the journey to Pau.

"It'll be good to see Coustenoble again." I smile at the thought of what color his hair might be now.

"You trust him?" Léon asks.

There's fire in my voice when I reply, "He knelt on a ruler for eight hours while they burned his skin with cigarettes, and he told them nothing."

Léon grimaces. "I need to make sure that Alliance's agents are loyal. Especially the ones closest to you."

I hear fear in his voice. Someone is scared for me. Not just for me as *la patronne.* But for me as Marie-Madeleine.

"If the Nazis find out what you're really doing—" He cuts himself off.

I can no longer hold his gaze, the same way I can't hold the hand that rests on his knee—one palm large enough to wrap around both of mine—even as I remember what it's like to let your fingers slide into someone else's, the frisson of claiming each other.

Just the idea of it makes my stomach clench.

"Years ago, before I had children," I say, voice low, "I loved to drive too fast. I'd pause for just a moment at the top of a steep stretch of wildly curving road, then I'd fling myself at it, wanting the feeling of being only a second away from exhilaration or injury. Now . . ." I shake my head, marveling at how much love can change you—at how much you *want* to change because there's nothing more important than the two warm bodies you've been given the honor of mothering.

"Now, when I pause at the top, I think of Béatrice and Christian. Then I take the road, still going fast, but not too fast. For just one moment, I regret being seconds away from the exhilaration, knowing I can never have it again. Then it passes. With every step I take for Alliance, I pause and think of a gun pressed to Coustenoble's temple. To Rivière's. To . . ." I make myself say it: "To yours. I do only as much as I can without bringing those guns close enough to shoot. You don't have to worry about me."

I look at Léon at last. I shouldn't have. In his eyes I can see the most fearsome combination of all—danger, as well as devotion to an ideal. Ideals like honor do not have warm skin and powdery scents and tiny beating hearts. Ideals won't stop you from taking the road too fast—they make you take it without any brakes at all, until the curve in the road is right there and the car is flying into the air and nobody can say it was wrong, but those watching weep just the same.

Léon's a soldier. He'll break my heart if I move even an inch closer. He will never brake, not while there are Frenchmen in prisons and Nazis on streets, not while there's still a line drawn like a scar across the country he's sworn to give his life for. He won't brake even if I'm standing at the top of the hill begging him to stop.

Worst of all, this thing that will break my heart is also why I feel the wobble of standing on the edge of falling in love with him. I thought I'd been a fool the first time I fell in love, but it turns out I'm still just as heedless. To know the person you could love will break your heart and to consider loving them anyway is the most reckless thing of all.

I don't know how much of that Léon sees on my face, but the hand on his knee clenches as if he has to stop it from reaching out. "I'm sorry," he says.

"That's like apologizing because the sun is too hot to touch," I say softly.

As brilliant as the sun is, so too is Léon, and I wouldn't want him any other way.

When Coustenoble opens the door to us in Pau, he snaps, "You shouldn't have come. We've spent weeks protecting you and now you walk right into the lion's den."

It's like being told by my children that they don't want me. I flinch, and Léon's hand touches the small of my back as if he's trying to absorb my shock.

"Are you all right?" I ask Couscous, then flagellate myself. *What a stupid question. Who would be all right after torture?*

"I'm sorry—"

Couscous cuts me off. "Everyone's inside."

I feel like even more of a fraud when I shake the hand of every agent who was imprisoned—embracing Josette—only to have them thank me in return.

Then Lucien hurtles in, exclaiming, "Look what I did!" He waves an arm around at the villa he's set up with everything a sector headquarters needs.

"This is for doing even better than finding a way to cross into Germany." I kiss his cheek.

Lucien gapes at me. The men hoot at his dumbfoundedness and I can't help but smile. When everyone's settled down, I tell them that Léon is Alliance's new chief of staff, an announcement that's met with a thrilled chorus. Léon's reputation as the architect of the Algiers coup has given him a kind of warrior status, and they listen eagerly as he allocates them jobs.

Amid the noise, I want to look across at Coustenoble and search through his brown eyes to see what's troubling him. But I'm afraid I'll find reproach there for the things he had to do for me. So I focus somewhere around his shoulder and indicate that he should follow me into the adjoining room.

Coustenoble shuts the door and, his back turned toward me, says, "You still have confidence in me? I knew something wasn't right, but I still got caught."

At last I understand. When Christian was three, he peed on a new rug and I shouted at him. Afterward, neither of us could meet the other's eyes, both afraid we'd done something unforgivable. As soon as I realized that all we cared about was each other, I pulled him into the tightest hug and said, "I'll love you past forever no matter what you do."

To Couscous, I say, "There's no one in France I'd rather have as my adjutant."

He faces me at last, relief flooding his eyes.

"How's your cough?" I ask. "Take time to rest before you come to Marseille."

"I've been in prison resting for weeks, little one."

So we talk until Léon comes in with an air of impatience and says, "Let's go."

Couscous bristles as if he thinks Léon's ordering me to leave, but I hear again the fear in Léon's voice. He doesn't want me in Pau for long in case it's raided again.

I tell Léon, "Give me a minute." When he's gone, I ask Coustenoble, "Can you go to Fresnes? See what you can find out about Vallet and the others, if it's possible to arrange an escape. And take this"—I pass him a package of money, soap, and a pair of stockings from Spain—"to Vallet's grandmother."

Couscous smiles. "Léon Faye is the kind of man legend gathers around, and we need someone who inspires late-night stories told over campfires. But more than that, we need someone we can revere. People lay down their lives for the things they worship, little one. There's a difference between inspiring and revering—the first we do to someone we think we can be like. The second we do to someone we know we can never be like, because they are extraordinary. That's what I hear when the men speak of you at night. Léon will find good men and he'll furnish them with ideas that make them blaze. But you'll go to Spain in a mailbag and then ask about my cough; you'll know the names of the agents' children. You'll send their grandmothers your own silk stockings. That's why it should always be you in charge, and no one else."

I squeeze Couscous in a quick hug, then escape the villa, chased out by long-ago words from the Bible: *I will destroy your idols and your sacred stones.*

No! I want to tell any agent who thinks he reveres me. I'm nothing more than a false idol, and when people worship those, pillars crash down, chariots burn, and entire cities are buried forever beneath the dust.

Back on the train, I can't shake the foreboding, and I say to Léon, "We need to move. I've been traveling too much. Vichy will notice." I sigh a little wistfully. "I'll miss Madeleine Rivière and her shoes making music while I work."

Léon replies, "I'll find you something just as good."

My new navigator. My spirit lifter.

But there's still a melancholy in me, like a song in D-sharp minor, the key Schubert said ghosts would speak in if they had tongues. My self-doubt is a constant ghost, and I want to wear Léon's confidence instead, stand in the shoes of his military reputation, walk into a room as a known leader.

"When you were first put in charge of men," I ask quietly, "did you doubt yourself?"

Léon thinks for a moment, then moves to the seat beside me. "When you enlist in the military, you're bargaining with your own life. But when you become a lieutenant, a captain, a commandant, you're bargaining with other people's lives. If you don't doubt yourself in those circumstances, then you're a monster."

Through the window are cliffs dropping precipitously to a bruise-colored sea, but the ground Léon's next words move us onto is the most dangerous of all.

"I was more nervous meeting Coustenoble today than I've ever been, even in a lightning storm turned upside down in the clouds," he says. "Because if he didn't want me, I think you would have turned me away. And . . ."

I don't know if he pauses because he doesn't know how to finish the sentence or because he can feel the lightning storm between us, the one that's turning *me* upside down.

For the first time, my body leans ever so slightly into it.

"Why did you decide to fly?" I ask, voice a little huskier than before.

He smiles. "Moroccan skies are so magnificent that I wondered what it would be like to be in that sky. So I learned to fly."

"Do you miss it?"

He nods. "That and Aleppo soap."

I laugh. "And coffee."

"Sitting on a terrace, watching a sunset." Wistfulness now, rather than humor.

"Playing the piano," I say.

"Lingering over breakfast with a newspaper."

"Just . . . lingering."

Suddenly my hand reaches out. Too late I remember my red-raw chilblains. Before I can withdraw it, Léon folds his hand around mine as if he doesn't see the blisters—but as if he's been waiting his whole life for this moment.

And it's just how I thought it would be. Too much and still not enough.

We sit like that for the rest of the journey, lingering over the view of cliffs almost as beautiful as those that lifted Rabat up to the sky, of pink flamingos and startlingly white horses galloping across the Camargue plains. And I wonder how much longer I can hold on to my vow to not fall in love with Léon Faye.

I don't return to HQ with Léon. I need my family; need my mother to tell me I'm not a terrible person for holding a man's hand. I need to not have Léon ask, *What does this mean?*

I don't know.

I know only that as I walk down the path of the house at Mougins, my whole body is alert for the sound of my children. Then Christian flies out of the house and into my arms, hurtling me straight back into the past, when I was a mother.

Now my daughter is making her careful way along the path, wincing from the ache in her hip, determined not to wait on the steps for me. She'll reach me no matter how much it hurts.

I take Christian's hand and we walk toward her, not detracting from her effort, but showing her that we'll do what we can to reward her striving. Her last few steps are faster and they cost her. She's within an arm's reach when she falters, and her face twists as her hip pops. I lift her up, letting her wrap herself around me even though she's too big to be carried. But after so many months of absence, who doesn't want to be enveloped by their child?

"Your hip is worse?" I whisper, and she nods.

I carry her inside, embrace my mother, and sit down with

Béatrice on my lap. My mother makes us a hearty soup of vegetables she must have been saving in the cellar, and even a little meat. We eat like it's ice cream, and I listen to my children's stories of the wily hen who hides her eggs each day in a new place, and the friends they've made at school. The breeze ushers in the scent of lemon, thyme, and honeysuckle summers. Above us, the moon is waxing and hangs incomplete and golden, and my feet press into the ground like roots, anchoring me.

Later, I kneel by the bath and help Béatrice wash her hair. When I braid it, I almost weep because my fingers remember exactly how to do it. Then I tuck my children into bed and curl up in a chair in the corner of their room. They keep opening their eyes, peeking out as if they think I'm just a dream. Their father relinquished them years ago, and I read in those anxious glances a fear that I might abandon them, too.

But no. My daughter needs a doctor. Tomorrow, I'm going to telephone everyone I know until I find someone. And I'll somehow be by her side every step of the way.

My mother slips into the room and puts her arm around me, studying me the way I've just gorged on my children. Finally she whispers, as if the secrets in my heart can be read in my eyes, "If Edouard has seen the things you've seen these past two years, he'll no longer want to hold you to a piece of paper for the sake of pride. Be free, *ma chérie*. Don't be afraid to love."

But I'm not just afraid to love—I'm terrified. I'm fighting to rid France of Nazis, fighting to keep my children's love for me alive, too. Loving Léon will mean fighting a third war. In every decision I make, I'll want to consider whether I can protect him as well.

Except the leader of a Resistance network must protect her agents above all else.

Where does that leave my children? Where does that leave a man I could love?

Late the following afternoon, I walk into HQ and halt when I find everyone in the operations room standing frozen, like a domino chain about to fall.

Then it does fall.

Baston is there, rather than in Vichy, wearing the gravest expression I've ever seen. "My dear," he begins, then Lucien inexplicably bursts through the door, panting, and says, "They have your papers!"

Baston sighs heavily. "Commandant Rollin has ordered you be brought to Vichy to explain yourself."

My stomach drops like I've just fallen off the cliff outside.

18

I Am Hérisson the Hedgehog

Marseille, May–June 1942

left Pau as soon as I got your note," Lucien says to Baston, who pats him on the back. Then Baston tells me, "I sent a courier to Lucien last night in case Vichy arrested me rather than letting me come and collect you."

"Collect me?"

"I found Rollin brandishing a piece of paper yesterday and ranting, *Who is POZ55? Who is COU72?*" Baston explains. "Luckily the papers went to him rather than the Deuxième Bureau, otherwise you'd already be in prison. Luckily he's a friend. He agreed to a forty-eight-hour amnesty as long as you explain what the papers mean. You'll need a very good story. Even then . . ."

The half-moon bruises under Baston's eyes underscore the gravity of his words. "I don't know how you'll get out of this. Not with Laval maneuvering to return as deputy prime minister. If that happens, I'm afraid—"

He cuts himself off, but the unspoken words echo: . . . *you're done for*.

Laval doesn't give amnesties.

I'm frozen in place. I know exactly what piece of paper Rollin, the Vichy head of security, has. One from Pau, before it was raided by police. I thought it had been destroyed. It lists our code names. And it's in my handwriting.

It's enough to condemn me.

But the only way Rollin could have that paper is if someone who's been through Pau took it and gave it to Vichy.

Which, means—one of my agents is a traitor.

It hurts; God, it hurts—that someone I trust is stabbing France in her defenseless back. But this person has also put my loyal agents in peril, so I stand on *la patronne*'s feet and say to Lucien, "Thank you. A true Alliance agent could have done no better."

He crosses his arms. "I'm ready to be a true Alliance agent. If you don't let me, I'll find another network that will."

I can't be responsible for the imprisonment and death of a sixteen-year-old. It's Marie-Madeleine who whispers that. But it's *la patronne* who knows, *I'm the leader of a network, not men's souls. I have no right to refuse their honor.*

The Lucien in front of me is almost as tall as Léon. He looks like he's started to shave; he's almost a man.

So I make myself be the leader France needs me to be. But I also do what I can to keep Josette's son safe. "Commandant Faye needs an adjutant," I tell Lucien. "He'll interview you for the position." Then I turn to Baston. "And I'll go with you to Vichy."

Where I'll need a miracle, not a story.

Léon swears. "There's no way you're going to Vichy." His voice is implacable—a commandant's voice. "It's a trap."

The eyes of my agents swivel from Léon to me and back to Léon. He is not my commandant. I am his. He told me he was prepared to follow me. And I think we're about to put that to the test. Better to do it now, before I've let myself love him.

I keep my voice level. "If I don't go, Marseille will be swarming with police by tomorrow. Then everyone will be arrested instead of just me."

"They'll never let you leave. Then where will Alliance be?" Léon shouts.

"Outside," I snap, stalking out.

Behind the shop, where the bins, roaches, and vermin congregate, we face each other, equally stubborn, equally sure we're right—but also equally afraid, I think. "I have to do this to keep everyone safe," I tell him. "And you have to accept it. It's your job."

He braces one hand against the wall, shakes his head.

My voice softens. "Trust me. Trust that maybe I have a plan that will let me walk out of there."

Léon's eyes fall to my hand, as if he's remembering that one moment of physical intimacy we shared—the way it wasn't just our hands held fast together, but our fears and our worries and our souls, perhaps, too.

He lifts his eyes back up to meet mine. Swears once more, but says, "All right. I'll take the same train to Vichy but ride in another carriage so nobody knows there's any connection between us. Then I can . . ." His mouth twists. "I can warn the others if the worst comes to pass."

I'm not used to sharing things. Since Edouard, I equate it with leaving myself exposed. But I lean against the wall beside Léon, let the back of my hand touch the back of his, knuckle against knuckle. But it's like his hands are in my hair and his lips are on mine and I want to find a way to drink in this hot, hot love and not be burned.

His voice is husky when he speaks. "We need to work out who's betraying you before they give up anything else."

"I'll think about who had access to that list. And Léon?" I look across at him. "You'll interview Lucien? You need an adjutant."

He laughs, the tension slipping from his face. "The Gestapo could be marching in the door and you'd still be talking about the agents, not yourself. So yes, I'll give him the job."

"Thank you."

"I'll miss you," he says very gently.

I can't let myself say it. Not when I'm about to stroll in to see the Vichy chief of state security, whose government I've been plotting against for the last year and a half.

Will I end up in prison like Navarre? Do they torture women? How long would it take for me to crumble?

Will I ever see Béatrice and Christian again?

My thoughts clatter in time to the train's wheels on the tracks. I try to light a cigarette, but my hand is shaking. Baston reaches for the lighter and flicks it, frowning. It's his reputation on the line if my plan doesn't work.

I close my eyes and try to settle into the role I need to play: the silly woman led astray by Navarre. The beautiful blonde with nothing going on in her head.

Maybe it's the lull of the train. Maybe it's naïveté or Schaerrer's ghost or some kind of external grace that makes me relax enough that I dream, even though I think I'm awake. I see animals, hunted animals: prowling, pacing, proud. Coustenoble is a stealthy cat—the Tiger. Rivière is a Wolf—clever and loyal. Siegrist, my head of security, has ears that make him an Elephant.

I know what this dream means. If Vichy has our code names, we need new ones. I'm seeing the future. And in that future I'm not locked in a Vichy prison. I've become a creature nobody thinks much of. *Hérisson—the prickly little Hedgehog,* I think with a smile.

In Shanghai, parents dressed their children in bonnets stitched with white silk dragons' teeth or lions' manes made of wool. They believed that, by pretending to be animals, their children would be safe from the predators of the spirit world.

With animal code names, my agents will be safe from the Nazis.

When I exit the train, Léon steps down from the last carriage, reaching his long, beautiful arms up into the sky. He will be my Eagle, the one who soars above the mountaintops.

My quills are bristling when I walk through the halls of the Hôtel du Parc to Commandant Rollin's office. Whispers follow me like spies, and I hope my optimist adventurer tendencies haven't just caused me to sign my own arrest warrant. But I hide those thoughts under a demure navy-blue dress and a little toque hat adorned with white egret feathers, impeccable *maquillage*, and a charming Marie-Madeleine smile.

At the door to Rollin's office, I fire first. "How dare you!"

Rollin jumps. He's short and graying, a grandfatherly former naval intelligence officer, a fact that made me radio MI6 last night to see if they knew him. They do. Rollin has continued to correspond with MI6's chief since the German Occupation. He isn't providing information, but nor is he turning his back on his friends.

I hope it means his heart won't be in the business of questioning a woman over the suspicion that she might have been agitating against the very people whose views he despises. It's a gamble akin to bluffing with only a pair in hand, but if a Resistance leader can't bluff like a magician, then she doesn't deserve her job.

From my purse, I pull out some letters, letting a hanky, a doll, and a child's book spill out—evidence of my femininity, my *esprit de famille*. The first two or three pages are legitimate letters from doctors about Béatrice's hip surgery. Baston, Lucien, and Léon spent yesterday afternoon traveling to Toulouse, Grenoble—where one of our agents is a doctor—and Nice, collecting them. The others have been forged by Elephant. I don't want Vichy to know which hospital I'm planning to retreat to with Béatrice after this, I just want them to believe in my motherliness.

"You're coming after me while I sit at my daughter's bed-side?" I demand, making sure my voice is hysterical—female. "She needs an operation and I've been summoned here to dis-cuss some ridiculous hieroglyphics?"

I point to the list of code names on the desk. By themselves, they're meaningless. And in the light of my performance, they look like nothing more than scribbles.

"You know Navarre," I go on. "He loves intrigue. I got caught up in it for a while. But I haven't seen him for months, which you know because he's in prison. I've been busy with my daugh-ter, as you can see from these letters."

I slide into a chair, cross my legs, and light a cigarette, mak-ing sure my hands are visibly trembling, demonstrating my weakness.

Baston jumps in and says, "Look at her! That's hardly the face of a criminal mastermind."

I can feel the wink he wants to send my way as he spouts at Rollin the same beliefs he used to share.

Rollin sits heavily in his chair. "But I know it wasn't just Na-varre who was in contact with the British. You were, too."

Merde. They know more than I thought. But I'm not the only one in the room who's in touch with the British; Rollin is, too. He isn't the first Vichy officer to pledge loyalty to Pétain but want the Germans out of France. So I take a shot at the honor I hope he still possesses.

"I left my daughter's bedside to see if there were any French patriots left in Vichy and all I find is a silly list of numbers."

"Patriots in Vichy!" he shouts, and for a second I worry that I've gone too far.

"I despise the Germans, too," he continues, still blazing. "But there's a way to do these things. Leave it to people who know what they're doing. Trained French military officers, not house-wives."

That's when I know I'm safe. He loves France, thinks he can

ease Pétain onto the path of right. I want to tell him that's a dead end. But I've given him a story that will appease his superiors. All I need to do now is shut my mouth and be nothing more than the woman they all think was Navarre's mistress. Rollin will think little of that woman. More importantly, he'll believe her.

I'm fleetingly grateful for what subordination has taught me, even as I hide lies within truths that make me want to cut out my own tongue. My daughter *does* need me. But I've just shamelessly tossed her plight and her pain into the room to get what I want, like the goddess Hera throwing her son off the top of a mountain.

Never did I consider myself immoral before now.

Then a worse thought cannonballs into me. What if this is just the beginning?

I no longer have to fake the tremble in my hands.

Thankfully Rollin does what might be the kindest thing anyone in Vichy will ever do for me. "I've been fielding phone calls about you all day," he says. "Most people want you arrested. If you were in the Occupied Zone, you would be. But here"—he picks up a cigar that's been smoldering throughout our conversation and puffs on it—"I'm in charge. I'll make you a false identity card so you can travel to your daughter's bedside without being arrested. Stay with her. If you do anything out of the ordinary, you'll be brought straight back here and I won't be able to help you again. And watch out. Laval is doing everything he can to get back into power. If that happens, I'll be removed from my position and you'll need more than a false identity card to keep you safe."

He leaves the room to get my papers, an old patriot who's made his one act of resistance. He clearly believes there's no network behind me anymore—that I'm a lone ex-rogue—which means I've just bought Alliance some breathing space to blossom into.

But when I walk out of the Hôtel du Parc, Pierre Laval

walks in. He watches me, malice sparkling like black ice in his eyes.

He looks like a man intent on winning.

The following week, so help me God, I set up Alliance's head-quarters in my daughter's hospital room in Toulouse and hone my talent for duplicity still more when the nurse greets my luggage with a startled, "*Mon Dieu.*"

I'm carrying one small valise for my clothes and two enormous suitcases full of maps, folders, and codes. "I was worried Béatrice would be bored," I say. "I've brought some things to keep her spirits up."

Having passed off MI6's intelligence questionnaires as children's playthings—and once Béatrice is asleep—I hide folders under chair cushions, cover my map with a blanket, and start making a list. Which sectors have strong teams, which sectors need starting up. Where to send the transmitters that were dropped in by parachute last week. Which of our new sectors need wireless operators, how to find a replacement for Frédéric, the operator who defected.

That's when I realize. He was at Pau.

He might have taken the list of code names as insurance. Perhaps he's been captured and is cashing in his bond?

It's actually a relief if it's him. He was with us only a short time and knows nothing of the new recruits we've added to Alliance, so he can't hurt the network's second wave. I write a note to Coustenoble asking him urgently to find out if Frédéric has been arrested, and I explain the new animal code names.

When Dr. Charry comes in the next day to check on Béatrice, I ask him, "Would it be all right if we have a lot of visitors? I have a large family."

The doctor says genially, "Your large family may visit whenever they like."

He turns his attention to my daughter. She's being taken to the operating room tomorrow, he tells us, so I ignore my maps, sit on the bed, and tell Béatrice the stories she most loves to hear—about my childhood in Shanghai with my sister, Yvonne. I describe my English governess who gave me a taste for tea, and our amah, who let us roam through the streets as fearless explorers.

Béatrice nestles into my shoulder.

"Are you frightened?" I ask, stroking her hair.

"Are you?" she asks very seriously, and I pretend to misunderstand.

"Not when I think about you running toward me so fast that you beat Christian."

She laughs delightedly, as if she has a goal to work on in the months after I leave.

"I love you," I tell her. "If you ever think you hate me for even a moment—"

"I would never hate you, *Maman*," she says, shocked.

I sleep in her bed that night, then hold her hand while they anesthetize her, try so hard to keep the tears at bay when her little body goes limp.

Dr. Charry disentangles our fingers, saying, "I'll take good care of her."

I pace Béatrice's room for hours, crossing to the window and back to the door. Late morning, I see a man across the street, a man with graceful arms and the kind of smile that makes your heart hurt because it wishes it could smile right back.

Léon Faye, my Eagle, can't come into the hospital, but he's found a way to be here. And that's when I realize this is no infatuation brought on by war. This is real.

So I leap.

I press my fingertips to my lips, let a kiss drift down to the street below. Léon catches it and tucks it into the pocket of his jacket, the one that sits over his heart.

And I know—there's no going back from this. There will be a next kiss, a proper kiss, and it won't be a subtle, drifting, invisible thing.

Alliance is my family now. Not a husband I haven't seen since 1933.

I am Hérisson the Hedgehog. I belong to no one, carry the name of no man.

I divorce myself from my marriage.

19

If Only I'd Never . . .

Toulouse, June–August 1942

Béatrice wakes in tears. The plaster is brutal, wrapped from the tips of her toes to her armpits, preventing movement and fixing her legs in an awkward, akimbo position. All she can do is lie still, which, for a ten-year-old, is untenable.

I'm trying to console her when Coustenoble strolls in, pulls a stuffed tiger—his new namesake—from behind his back, and growls. Béatrice giggles, tears arrested.

"Where did you get that?" I ask. A stuffed tiger in rationed France?

He looks mock offended. "When have I not been able to get what you need?"

I kiss his cheeks and try not to wince at how thin he still is from prison. "My mother made a tincture for your cough. She'll yell at me if you don't take it, so to save me from an earful . . ."

He takes it with a laugh. "Don't tell me she's more stubborn than you?"

"Where do you think I get it from?"

When Béatrice falls asleep, exhausted, we turn to business.

"So we're going to turn into a menagerie," Couscous says. "No matter how much you bristle, Hedgehog, you'll always be little one to me."

I laugh. "Can you report to Commandant Faye—"

"Eagle," Couscous admonishes, and I can tell that soon we'll truly be a zoo.

Once my instructions are done, Couscous tells me, "Frédéric's still with his new network. He's not in prison trading his life for yours. And I went to Fresnes. It's a fortress. Inescapable. But I found a way to get information out from inside. The prisoners get a sheet of paper once a month to send letters to family. They tear off small squares and hide them in the laundry their relatives are allowed to wash. Vallet's girlfriend has been saving the papers."

"Vallet's girlfriend?" I close my eyes. Will I ever be a true leader? One who can not only think of a way to get Vallet out of a fortress, but who'd also know that he had a girlfriend, and her name as well?

"She's fearless," Coustenoble says, looking awestruck. "She climbed a tree across from the prison and shouted through the windows for them to keep their spirits up."

I want to applaud. But . . . "She'll get herself arrested."

"She told me . . ." Coustenoble hesitates, but my prickles bristle.

"All right, little one," he says. "No hiding anything. She told me Vallet's clothes show the marks of his having been tortured."

Torture? *No.* If only I'd never—

Never what? Never let him be our radio operator? Never met Navarre? Never grown up loving France? When did it start exactly, my resistance? Which moment would have been the right one to change?

I know only that I need to read Vallet's messages. In them, he mentions beatings, brutalities, and traps, and the fact that it's impossible not to let small things slip to the Germans.

I understand. If someone had, with the threat of more pain, asked me a question the moment I'd been released from the mailbag in Madrid, I'm sure a secret would have forced its way from my lips, too.

"The upshot of his messages is that the Nazis know more than we think," I tell Coustenoble. "Which means someone is talking. But if it's not Frédéric, then who?"

"Bla," Couscous says without a moment's hesitation.

The English radio operator whose behavior had worried us enough that I'd asked London to double-check his background.

"MI6 said he'd been fully vetted," I remind him. "He's been sending them regular transmissions from Normandy. It can't be him."

"Then why is he at the prison every week visiting our agents and their families?"

My pen drops to the table. "He's not supposed to be in Paris at all."

Suddenly I don't care about the assurances of the professionals in London. "Find someone who can courier my messages rather than you," I tell Coustenoble. "I need you in Paris keeping an eye on Bla."

He salutes and walks to the door, and one of those haunting presentiments lands in my soul, telling me it won't be long before Vallet walks beside Schaerrer. The blue and the white together again.

"Couscous!" I call. But he's gone.

For how long can I keep the red safe, too?

After breakfast each day, I wheel Béatrice's bed over to the windows. She looks at the sky and tells me she's imagining traveling to all the faraway places. My daughter has the fortitude to lift her spirit out of the prison of her cast. I need to do whatever I can to help the rest of us slip through the Nazi-barricaded windows of France.

I interview the people Léon sends me. Families and towns and entire communities join Alliance hiding behind animal names: Mandrill in Bordeaux, Unicorn in Brest, Dragon in Normandy. I send for General Baston, who needs to leave via the new escape line we've set up over the Pyrenees for agents facing too much Gestapo heat and for downed pilots the British want evacuated. The minute Vichy discovers I'm not the innocent mother they think I am, they'll arrest Baston, the man who sat by my side while I lied.

He refuses to leave France. "I want to lead the Brittany sector for you."

Brittany is where the mammoth Lorient U-boat base is located. I desperately need an experienced agent there. "But that's more dangerous than Vichy," I protest.

"With my hair color, I'll be Sheepdog," he says firmly.

His eyes, a little watery with age, look out at me from a face lined by all the battles he's fought in his years of being a general. And he wants to fight on still.

Yet again, the people of Alliance bring me to my knees. Like Coustenoble, who's more tired than ever from the couriering. But I haven't found anyone to take on that task—until he arrives one day with a woman in a cotton dress and cork-soled shoes. She's blond and petite with a ferocious scowl on her face.

"This is Monique, Vallet's girlfriend," Couscous says. "She's made so much trouble at Fresnes that the Gestapo are looking for her."

"I'm not going into hiding," she says resolutely.

Another optimistic adventurer. So I tell her, "You can be my courier."

"My code name will be Ermine," she announces, and I smile. The little snow-white hunter of the night. It's perfect.

"We need evidence that it's Bla," I tell Coustenoble, who'll now return to Paris. "And we need it—"

"Yesterday," he finishes, before he's gone, another bottle of cough tincture pressed into his hand.

Ermine plays with Béatrice while I read through the messages Coustenoble delivered. The most important one tells me that a British agent is coming in via parachute to train Léon's air force recruit, Mahout, and we'll be landing our first Lysander in August, which is next month!

With planes coming in and out, bringing us supplies and taking out intelligence, an invasion will soon come. Maybe even by the end of 1942, just a few months away. If we work harder than ever, we can make that happen before anyone else dies.

Ermine leaves with a kiss for Béatrice and a wave for me.

"She's my favorite," Béatrice says.

"I thought I was your favorite." I tickle her under her armpit, one of the few places not covered by the cast.

"She's my favorite animal." She giggles. "You're a mommy."

She has no idea that everyone calls me Hérisson now.

"Which animal is your favorite?" she asks.

My favorite is the Eagle, I don't say. The one who writes at the bottom of each message, in code, *I miss you. How's Béatrice?*

My eyes fall on another of MI6's messages. *Want you in London next month.*

A leader can't leave her network. Which means I'll have to send Léon to London. There's no one else I trust to represent us to the British as I would. So the next day, I send a note telling him to be ready for the first Lysander flight. And I pray: *Please God, let me see him at least once before he leaves.*

Too soon, the morning arrives when Dr. Charry says, "Now that Béatrice's cast is off and she's moving around, there's no reason why she can't go home. But I don't want to throw you out."

I understand what he's saying: He'll keep sheltering me. But then I might bring the Nazis to my daughter's door, which would be the vilest thing I could ever do.

So when Ermine arrives, I ask her to tell Léon and my mother that I'll be ready tomorrow. Léon's found a new HQ, and

Ermine has found my mother and Béatrice a cottage near the Pyrenees, far from danger. Christian is safely ensconced in a boarding school in Toulouse. But that afternoon, Coustenoble makes an unscheduled appearance. His face is sheened with sweat. Dr. Charry is with him and he beckons for me to follow, obviously having been drawn into more subterfuge.

Inside an operating room, Léon and Ermine are waiting beside a tray lined with scalpels and catgut sutures.

My hip pops and I only just catch hold of the wall in time.

"Laval's been reappointed Pétain's second in command," Léon says, voice grim. "The Nazis want Vichy to do something about Resistance activity in the free zone, and Laval is their man. He's going to let the Gestapo take radio detection vans into the free zone to hunt down Resistance networks. And—"

Coustenoble thrusts out a note. "From Vallet. Bla just had the entire Normandy sector arrested. And Bla must have told Vichy that you lied because Laval's issued a warrant for your arrest." He whispers the next part. "Vichy said you were another Mata Hari. You've been declared a spy and an enemy. And they've put a price on your head."

"Which means it won't just be the Vichy police and the Gestapo looking for you," Léon breaks in. "Every thief and pirate in France will be on the hunt, too. And they won't stop until they find you."

Mata Hari. She was a mother of two.

They shot her dead.

On our first night here, Béatrice had asked me if I was frightened. *I'm terrified, my darling,* are words I can't say to anyone.

"What's my price?" I ask lightly, hiding the fear—always hiding something.

"It isn't funny," Léon retorts.

I take Vallet's note from Couscous and the deciphering grid from Léon.

Last interrogation made me certain. Bla traitor. Gestapo showed
me OCK set delivered to him after my arrest.

I swear, using one of the most colorful phrases I've picked up
from my agents, then pass the decrypted message to Léon. His
curse is worse than mine.

Vallet is saying that the guards have shown him a transmitter
I'd sent to Bla as a backup. The only way the Germans could
have gotten hold of it was from him.

He's had our whole Normandy sector thrown in jail. He's
responsible for last year's Pau and Paris arrests. For Vallet's imprisonment. And a terrible part of me wishes it had been anyone
other than Vallet, who has a grandmother to care for and a girlfriend, Ermine, who's standing somberly at my side because she
knows as well as I do what it means.

If the Gestapo have shown Vallet that they have one of our
radio sets, it's their final play. If he doesn't talk now, they'll have
no more use for him.

And the white will join the blue in heaven.

It's lucky that London is impossible to travel to—otherwise
I'd be halfway there, storming into the offices of the men who
sent Bla to us. The men who've caused me to so badly let down
the people I asked to trust me.

For the first time I realize what I'm up against. Not just
Vichy. Not just Nazis. But the enemy within.

People will make me trust them, and then they'll betray me.

To fight them I have to tamp down the incandescent grief
and the fear, but I can still feel it burning away the perimeter of
my heart. What if every grief I smother makes my heart smaller?

"Thank God for Vallet," I say, voice so compressed I hardly
recognize it. "The Germans don't know he's getting messages out.
So they don't know that we know about Bla. Take this," I instruct
Léon, scribbling out a message to be transmitted to MI6 inform-
ing them that Bla's a traitor. "We'll wait for their instructions."

"Let's go," Léon says.

I shake my head, holding up a leader's hand—or perhaps a mother's hand—to silence everyone's protests about arrest warrants and danger. "Send someone to fetch me in two hours. I need to say goodbye to my daughter."

I walk away from them, close the door, stop in the corridor, press the flat of my hand against my mouth. *If Vallet dies, then I'm once again a murderer.*

But I'm still not stopping, not leaving to go to the Pyrenees with my daughter.

Which means I'll keep on murdering.

Marguerite's last note told me the Germans had rounded up more than ten thousand Jews in the middle of the night. Ten thousand people vanished in the span of one moonrise. More people will vanish if the Nazis aren't stopped.

My heart, not yet ash, cries out: *What kind of justification is that?* Not an eye for an eye, but Vallet and Schaerrer for some possibly futile hope that, one day, the violence will end.

If I look at history, I know—the violence never ends.

Béatrice holds on and holds on and won't let me go. "*Maman,*" she weeps, arms and legs clinging to me like a monkey.

To make her let go, I'd have to hurt her, and I can't do that—can't fight against love, because isn't love what I'm fighting for?

So I stand there with my daughter wrapped around my body, both of us sobbing, until my mother comes in and does what I'm not brave enough to do—she unpeels Béatrice and it feels like being skinned.

I have no idea, standing there saying goodbye, that Béatrice won't hold me again for two long years.

Sometime later, a man appears in the doorway. No, not a man. A magnificent eagle.

We watch each other for a moment before Léon says, "No reply from MI6. Meanwhile, Bla is probably telling the Nazis everything he knows about you."

"At least he doesn't know you," I say, needing to find a glint of silver in the cloud. "Or most of the second wave. And he doesn't know we're onto him. So, I'm safe until—"

"Until he finds out," Léon finishes, jaw rigid with tension.

I push myself up from the chair, watch him physically brace against the argument he's terrified is coming. But it's Marie-Madeleine who speaks, not Hérisson. "I can't talk about Bla tonight. Today has been . . ." I pause, permit myself one understated word. "Awful. And the problem of Bla will be the same tomorrow whether we argue about it now or not."

His exhale is frustrated. But he nods, then smiles. "All right. There's something else I need to debate with you, though. Shouldn't Alliance's leader be named after something fiercer than a hedgehog?"

I laugh. "Who else but a ball of prickles could escape the lions?"

Léon laughs too, both of us still on opposite sides of the room. But the awareness of the kiss I blew to him, the one he caught with his hand but not his lips, lives in our eyes, in the gaze we can't shift from each other. On Léon's face, there's an extra crease beside his mouth carved by all the things he wants to tell me but hasn't. In the curl of his hand, I can see the symphony his fingers want to play through my hair, if only I'd let him. And I can feel the need, like saxophone and flesh, that we have for one another.

Léon says very softly, "I've heard more stories than I've flown planes about the fabulously beautiful Marie-Madeleine, whom every Alliance agent is in love with. But I've never heard anyone describe you as prickly."

My words fall out into the dusk like stars. "There's only one man in Alliance who I wish was in love with me."

"I guarantee you he is."

Far away in Venezuela, there lives an everlasting lightning storm, where forks of fire endlessly spark. Now, that place is here.

I pick up my suitcase and walk toward him.

But first we must drive along the clifftops of the Riviera to our new HQ.

On the way, Léon asks me, "Are you okay? Leaving your daughter—"

"I'm okay."

"It's not the same, but I have one brother and five sisters," Léon tells me. "When I left home at seventeen, my baby sister was only one. She cried like she knew I was going to war. And I remember thinking that if I was lucky enough to come back alive, she'd be a kid, not a baby. And she probably wouldn't recognize me. But when I got off the train, she was the first person to come scampering over."

I picture a seventeen-year-old Léon going off to war and then committing his life to fighting for France, and I'm reminded of the difference in our ages—twelve years. But he's never once imposed his experience on me. So he isn't just made up of passion and idealism, but of some quality I don't have a name for— that of happily subordinating himself to a much younger woman because the larger picture is all that matters.

"I wish I could meet your sister," I say.

"You might," he tells me. "I recruited her."

"You can't let people you love do this!" I cry.

And he says, "There are already people I love doing this."

That's when I reach out and touch his jaw. When the pulse in his throat thrums, I stroke that, too.

"Will it make me sound like a schoolboy if I say that I don't think I can bear your doing that until I know I can do it to you?" he whispers.

There's no road shoulder to pull onto. If there was, I don't think either of us would be able to resist.

For now, I have to content myself with imagining the moment when we're finally together and every time I touch him, he reciprocates.

20

Don't Regret This

Le Lavandou, September 1942

The house Léon has found in Le Lavandou is one of only a few built on the sea side of a headland that juts out into a tranquil, Monet-esque bay. It's whitewashed, scrubbed clean of the filth of our time, shutters painted a soft verdigris. Flower boxes filled with silvery lavender scent the air, and midnight hangs above us like a velvet curtain waiting to be drawn so we can shut out the world. I want, so badly, four walls that are mine and Léon's, and my children's as well. There we would stay, imprisoned in happiness.

These are the kinds of thoughts I would once have poured into the piano, letting the simple progression from a major 1 chord to a minor iii weep for me. Now, I don't know what to do except to feel it—but it hurts so much.

Léon takes my hand and some of my heartache slides out through my fingers and into his, his grip telling me that whenever things become too heavy to lift, he'll be there beside me, the white flag I can surrender myself to.

"I'm here with you until I'm dead, Minerva," he whispers. "And that's all I'm going to say about it."

"Minerva," I repeat. The goddess of war.

I'm not a hedgehog tonight.

The door of the cottage opens and a woman and two lanky youths greet us.

"This is Bee," Léon says, introducing the lady. "She's a pilot, too."

Another woman who's joined the menagerie. I wonder if, after it's all over and we've won—*please God, let us win*—these women will continue to do all the things war has allowed them to do. Lead. Climb mountains.

Inside the house, pale oak floors are dressed with rugs in shades of cream and blue. Huge urns filled with fresh-cut white bougainvillea mass like clouds in every corner. On the wooden table, a dinner is laid out that, in ration times, is like a feast. There's wine, too, and all of the best glassware. It's as if Bee knew, somehow, that tonight was special.

I catch Léon's eye and there's a hunger lurking there that isn't for the food.

The two boys are firing questions at him, so I step out into the yard, which extends back toward the road. It's edged with wooden frames holding up even more bougainvillea flowers that grow profusely, in defiance of war. They're glorious. And the wood beneath doesn't break or bend, as if it's trying to tell me that sometimes it's better to twine your stems around another.

When I step back inside, Bee points to a building in the distance. "We'll be in the smaller cottage if you need anything."

"You can't leave your home to shelter me," I protest.

She takes my hands in hers. "You can never ask enough of me. Or my sons." Then she disappears out the door.

From the opposite side of the room, Léon says, "One thing I'm learning is that there are more different kinds of love than I'd known. Love for a family member. Love for an idea. Love for a country. Love for someone you don't even know—but knowing they're alive and fighting is enough to make you hope. You need to let people give you their homes, Minerva. You need to smile

and thank them. They believe it's their small role in the something greater you're going to make happen."

God. I want to slide my back down the wall, wrap my arms
around my knees and cry for what I've done—for what I didn't
know I was doing. I can't be the hope or the metaphor. What if
I let them all down?

I glance desperately across at Léon and it's like he understands how frightened I am, because he crosses the room in two
long strides. At last I pull his mouth to mine.

Everything we've been holding back is finally unleashed.

I step back against the wall, drag the heat of his body against
the length of mine. I want bare skin and he does too, because
we're both tugging at buttons, pushing fabric aside until his fingers splay over my spine.

In all my years of coaxing music from the body of a piano, I
never once wondered what it would be like to be the piano—
two hands playing hot jazz all over my body. Now I know.

"Léon," I gasp, and he buries his face in my neck, murmurs,
"Sorry . . ."

I laugh and throw his shirt on the ground. "I don't want apol-
ogies, Léon. What I want is a bed."

Afterward, Léon pulls up the blankets, cocooning us together,
the intensity of everything that just happened still trapped between us. "You're definitely not a hedgehog," he says, and I laugh
once more.

"You're going to make fun of my name until we see the last
German leave France, aren't you?"

He grins, reaches out for his cigarettes, and I touch a finger-
tip to the bicep on the long, muscular arm that once made me
think of an eagle's wings, determined to memorize every part of
him in case—

I cut off the thought and accept the cigarette, watching his eyes as the lighter flares. It's so dark here in the blackout that I can't see much, and I almost wish I hadn't seen what that one spark of light just showed me. What we've done has deepened everything. Which is what I wanted—and what I was afraid of, too.

He cups my jaw. "Don't regret this."

"I don't," I tell him. "I only regret how much it will hurt."

In the dark, where he thinks I can't see, I know his eyes are blinking back tears. The deputy chief of l'Armée de l'air, someone who's seen men die—who's been inside a prison—has been brought to tears by the thought of us.

Dear God, why did we let ourselves become so vulnerable?

He burst into my life like a star, so beautiful I couldn't turn away. But you don't fall in love in wartime, unless you're prepared to lose the beautiful things that you love. France. My children. Léon.

My darlings, precious and rare.

How many of them will still be here when it ends?

I lay my head on Léon's chest and his fingers make vows over my cheek. *We'll all be here. I promise.*

You were right stop Bla a traitor stop working for the Gestapo stop secure everything he knows stop we are issuing execution order end

"Execution order," Léon repeats after I pass him the transmission from MI6.

It's the morning after the glorious night we spent together. But today, there is no glory. Just more horror. In a war zone, execution is justified for traitors. But can I really kill a man?

That brutal voice inside me spits back: *You already have. Schaerrer is dead. And Vallet might soon be, too.*

In Pau last year I told myself it was time to be a warrior. I had no idea what that meant. Now, I think I do. Or . . . will I look back at this moment in another year's time, on the cusp of doing something even more terrible, and realize I was an innocent still?

Gathered in front of me in my new ops room by the sea are Léon, Bee, Couscous, Ermine, my radio operator, and Lucien. So I focus on finding Bla. Not on whether I can pull the trigger.

"A couple of months ago, Bla was complaining to MI6 about being cut off from Alliance HQ," I say, thinking fast. "I'll radio him, tell him I want to renew contact and arrange to meet."

"You're not—" Léon only just cuts himself off before he orders me not to go anywhere near Bla.

Couscous actually smiles at Léon. "On this, we agree. Hérisson is not going anywhere near Bla."

I exhale a long, frustrated breath. I know MI6 will say the same. You don't send the network leader out to meet a known traitor. Being a leader means letting other people do everything that's dangerous so the network never completely falls—because the network is more important than anything or anyone.

I shouldn't have taken the crown of thorns if I couldn't bear the pain.

"I'll ask Wolf," I say quietly. "It needs to be someone Bla knows, not someone from our second wave. Elephant can follow and move in when it's time to trap him."

Does it make it worse or better to ask something dangerous of someone who'd never refuse the task? I know that Rivière, Alliance's loyal Wolf, will say, *Of course I'll do it.*

I send a transmission to Bla. He replies; he'll see me in Lyon in two weeks' time.

Two weeks to relax—as much as you can when you're a woman with a price on her head. That's something I don't let myself think about, just like I've shut the door on the memory of Béatrice's cauterizing sobs, the feel of her little body wrapped around mine. But that night in the bath, when I rest my forehead on my knees, it isn't only the bathwater that wets my skin.

What if I never see my daughter again? I can't even remember what she was wearing the last time I saw her, carry only the impression of her weight, but not her warmth. I don't think I even told her that I loved her—what if that's all she remembers, the lack of those three words?

Then a thought stops me cold: What if Bla has children, too?

Homer taught us that war was Agamemnon, shining like the sun with the goddess Athena, golden too, at his side. But no—war is a woman with red eyes sitting in a cold bathtub, wondering if the man she's been ordered to execute has a daughter, too.

21

The Time Has Come to Kill

South of France, August–December 1942

transform the house at Le Lavandou into a headquarters focused on two tasks: tracking U-boats and finding out where the Nazi war machine's cogs are made. In the hospital, I'd hoped that invasion would come by the end of this year, but if it was coming that soon, we'd have been asked to collect more specific information about the place where the invasion fleet would land. But we haven't. Which means another Christmas with Nazis. Another winter. But, I pray, not another summer. Surely we'll start the New Year with an invasion to actively plan for.

Bee and her sons live in the small cottage. Lucien and the two radio operators stay in another outbuilding. In the main house, Léon, Ermine, and I have rooms. The operations room, the radio room, Elephant's identity card operation, and a cabinet full of guns from the British take up the ground floor. Léon's office and mine are on the first floor. We find time most mornings to walk along the beach, holding hands like a normal couple, trousers rolled up, arms bare, skin tanned. After a few days, a package from Bee appears on my bed—one of her swimsuits for me, one of her sons' for Léon. From then on we swim, Léon grinning as he flicks water at me, saying, "If we can't fly, this is the next best thing."

And it is; it's France reminding us why we're fighting. If the Nazis take over Europe, I won't be allowed to play in the ocean in a swimsuit that shows off my body, wouldn't be allowed to love Léon. A Nazi woman has no private needs. She serves only the whims of her husband and the state. She can't stand on a bed of bone-white seashells holding her lover's hand; can't be *la patronne* of her own soul.

So I swim above buried treasure and dolphins, wild and free, taking a half hour each day to be human. Léon swims beside until his arms twine around my torso, my legs around his waist. After a sultry expanse of minutes he says, "We always say we're going for a walk, but we never seem to do much walking."

I wade into the shallows and start to stroll. "We can walk if you prefer."

He catches up to me, spinning me around and kissing me so deeply my heart triples in size.

This is love. It's the most exquisite thing I've ever known.

When we return to the house, I pretend to Bee that the flush on my cheeks is from the sun, and the sand in my hair is from the wind. Léon tries to catch my eye and I do my best to ignore him, whispering, "You're a rogue."

He grins. "Always."

I try not to question it, try not to ask if we're the rip in the ocean—a place to be drowned. Or if we're the distant horizon, an untouchable space no Nazi will ever reach.

The day before Rivière is due to meet Bla, Léon wakes me, telling me we haven't time for our walk.

"But . . ." I protest. He's leaving for London at the end of the week, the first passenger on our moonlight airplane service, and I want every one of those morning half hours with him before he's gone.

He shushes me with a kiss, grinning like a kid trying not to blurt out a secret. "You'll want to wear something special for what I have planned."

So I slip into the black silk dress from Madrid, guessing he's come up with something to distract me from Bla. But I shoot him a nervous glance when he drives to the station at Saint-Raphael. I'm supposed to be in hiding.

"You'll be safe," he says, leading me to the gleaming gilt and blue carriages of *Le Train Bleu*.

I have no idea what we could possibly be doing on the luxury train that travels overnight from Paris to Nice, but I'm delighted at the ordinariness of being surprised by a lover, and the extraordinariness of being outside and about to step into something that looks like fun.

Léon opens the door of compartment number seven. Inside are Maurice and Marguerite!

To say that we fling ourselves on one another and weep and laugh in equal measure is an understatement. "Why are you here?" I cry.

Maurice and Marguerite exchange what can only be described as guilty looks with Léon. And I know. I've been trying to solve the problem of Paris, where we've had no proper leader since Vallet was imprisoned. I'm not solving it with my two dearest friends.

"Before you get mad," Léon says, "let's have breakfast."

I'm about to say that I'd prefer to yell at him in a private compartment, but the three conspirators have slipped into the corridor. I follow them to the blue-upholstered dining car, my arms folded like a stubborn child. The minute we sit down I say, "You can't."

"*Ma chérie*," Maurice says. "You would never let anyone decide for you what you could and couldn't do."

It lands like a hard truth in my soul. He and Marguerite know better than anyone how much my spirit suffers when someone tries to take away my right to decide. Which means I have to do one more thing that three years ago I could never have countenanced—involve my friends properly in something I know might kill them.

That question gnaws at me again, a leech burrowing into an always-open wound. What is the most terrible thing I'll do in the disguise of *la patronne*? Will I even know it at the time? Or will I one day be so terrible that I'll forget to ask this question at all?

I want to get off the train, go back to the beach, swim away. But the waiter intrudes, bringing over a Beaujolais. Léon pushes his glass across to me and says, "Have mine, too. You need to drink enough that, by the time we get home, you'll forget you're mad at me."

He looks as if he really doesn't know whether I'll forgive him for what's an act of love—doing something necessary that I couldn't make myself do.

I push his glass back toward him, lift mine, and say, "Then you won't be able to toast to Alliance's new Paris chiefs."

The duke bows his head. "It would be an honor."

The next hour passes like a prewar time. Léon and I don't pretend to be partners in resistance only, which we do in front of everyone else. We hold hands as if, in this carriage, time is frozen and life is filled with love and friends and food and wine.

Near the end of the meal, Léon asks the duke with amusement in his voice, "Which creature will you be?"

"Saluki," Maurice says without hesitation.

"You can be Firefly," I tell Marguerite, who's still as radiantly golden as when I met her in Morocco almost fifteen years ago.

And so the final sector of Alliance falls into place.

The Nazis might know that I'm up to something, but they don't know that Alliance now has sectors all over France. And that tomorrow, Rivière will catch a traitor.

We're winning this secret war.

The next day proves it.

Baston arrives at HQ, having come himself because what he's carrying is so important: a folder of papers listing precisely the number of U-boats at Lorient, the biggest base in France, as well as the schedule for each ship, and its identifying sign.

"How sure are you that it's real?" I ask, because it looks too good to be true. If I'm awestruck, MI6 will be astonished. There's no better way to blow up U-boats than to have their sailing schedules.

"Jacques Stosskopf gave it to me," Baston says.

"Stosskopf?" I whisper, shocked. Stosskopf is the French head of naval construction for the Nazis, a man regarded throughout France as a filthy collaborator.

"He's a spy for us, not a collaborator," Baston reveals.

"Then he needs to be very careful." I take Baston's hand. "So do you."

This isn't just playing with fire—this is standing in the middle of the bonfire and hoping the flames don't burn you alive.

We radio everything to the British, and their reply is a fanfare ending with the words, *This is how we win a war*.

I hug Ermine and Bee, and the operations room bursts into a cheer.

It's only an hour later when Rivière and Elephant race in. "Leave," Rivière shouts. "Bla wasn't at Lyon. But the Abwehr were. It was a trap set for you."

I don't think I've ever stood quite so still. There isn't just a price on my head. The Abwehr are hunting me.

And Bla's still out there, trying to annihilate Alliance.

Until this moment, I'm not sure I truly believed that Bla, who'd seen what we were fighting for, could betray us. There's so much love in Alliance that I thought it was a shield. But it's a weakness, too. It's made me blind when I need to be a prophet-

ess, reading a man's eyes to see if his heart is as black as a swastika.

"Hérisson." Someone is saying my name above the sound of
Rivière's anxious breath. "You need to decrypt this." The radio
operator holds out a piece of paper.

Decrypt. Yes, I know how to do that. But what emerges is so
awful I do it again and again, trying to make the code have a different meaning.

Eventually, Léon takes the decryption from my hand. "*Putain
de merde.*"

The message is from Marguerite. It says that my sister and
brother-in-law have been arrested by the Gestapo. Every acquaintance of mine in Paris has been interrogated.

Each time I think I've found hope, I discover that it has
fangs—and the Nazis' breath is hot against my neck.

If someone had told me even last year that I wouldn't stop
doing the thing that had put my sister in danger, I would have
torn open my chest and shown them all the love for her that sits
inside it. But listen to me now issuing orders like a machine
gun:

Dismantle the radio.
See if Saluki can free Yvonne and Georges.
Everyone is to take different trains.
Meet at La Pinède.

I'm racing out the door when Lucien stops me cold by saying,
with a nod at Léon and prescience beyond his years, "Make sure
the Gestapo never find out." Hastily, he adds, "I think I'm the
only one who's guessed. Maybe Ermine, too. Neither of us
would ever say anything."

But I'm fixed on his first sentence. Because yes—that's exactly how the Nazis would get me to talk. Or Léon. By threatening the thing we each love beyond reason.

I'm in the free zone, I tell myself as the train chugs along. Under the terms of the Vichy–German armistice, the Gestapo and the Abwehr can't actually arrest anyone in the free zone. The Vichy police have to make the arrests—and then they turn you over to the Gestapo. Bla doesn't know where I am—yet.

Yet. I might. It's possible. Hope, and fangs.

I arrive at La Pinède, the house high in the hills that I've been renting in case of an emergency, to some good news. Maurice used his police contacts to arrange a paperwork mix-up resulting in my sister and brother-in-law being mistakenly freed. They've been spirited out of Paris and will soon cross into Switzerland, to freedom.

But it's made the Gestapo even more furious.

Rivière tells me that one of his informants believes a Gestapo radio-finding van is about to zero in on a transmitter in Marseille. It might be one of Alliance's.

"Tell all radio operators to keep transmission time to twenty minutes," I say, knowing it takes the direction-finding equipment that long to pinpoint a location.

It's all I can do except hope our new British radio operator, who's coming from MI6 on the plane that's taking Léon to London, has a few more tricks for us.

London. I'd forgotten; Léon is leaving tomorrow.

"That's enough for today," I tell everyone. When my office clears, I sink into a chair, exhausted from a sleepless three-day train journey. I don't know what my face says, but it's enough that Léon strides across the room, kneels before me, places his hands on my thighs, and says, voice fierce, "The Gestapo won't stop until they find you. I've never been more scared in all my life."

In reply, I do something I've never done before. I kiss him right there in the office. But it's not possible to just kiss Léon when his hands and eyes are so passionate with fear for me. I have to pull away before the sound in my throat escapes.

His voice is fiercer still when he says, "I will only go to London if you stay right here. No leaving this house."

I make him that promise, and that night we lie awake in my bed, the back of my body stretched along the front of his, passing a cigarette back and forth, not speaking, just holding on, both of us thinking about how precarious life is—but how wonderful it is, too.

The day after Léon leaves, I do very little work until it's time for the BBC radio's French service—the segment where odd messages are played for Resistance groups across France. Finally comes the one I'm waiting for: *Birds of prey fly far today*.

It means Léon arrived safely in London. I hug Bee and Monique, whom I'm becoming so close to that I mostly think of her by her real name, rather than Ermine.

"Didn't you say his air force colleagues thought he was a four-leaf clover?" she says, smiling, my new spirit booster now that Couscous is hunting Bla. "He'll be back safe in a month. And in the meantime, you don't have to worry about him. Nothing bad can happen to him in London."

She's right. There's no Gestapo there.

I don't go anywhere for the next month. Monique couriers my messages indefatigably, and there are plenty. The Allies are asking for so much information about cargoes and squadrons headed for North Africa that I'm certain they'll attack there soon. It's not mainland France, but it's something. I'm also occupied with briefing the new chief radio operator, code name Magpie, who MI6 have sent in from London on the same airplane that took Léon out. His demeanor is very British, but he speaks French without any trace of an accent and isn't wearing a bowler hat like Bla.

Bla. Whose trail has gone cold.

Is he regrouping, getting ready to strike? But where?

The night Léon is due back from London arrives sooner than I imagined. I sit in front of the transmitter, Bee and Magpie by my side, and as I talk to our new recruit, I discover another Vallet. Magpie's not as tall, but he's just as gentle.

"The Nazis won't come out in the rain," he reassures me as we wait to hear from Mahout, our agent in isolated Thalamy who's in charge of the Lysander operations.

Even so, all I can think is how unsafe it is to land in a field in Occupied France using only the light of the fickle moon as a guide. I watch the clock and the transmitter, wanting the first to hurry up and the second to spring to life, and I whirl around when the door opens, but it's Monique, who should have been back hours ago from delivering Vallet's grandmother her monthly paycheck and some chocolate from MI6.

"I had to deliver a note from Josette to Coustenoble," she explains. "And then one from him to her. I knew you wouldn't mind." She smiles irrepressibly, a staunch believer in asking forgiveness, not permission.

"You're an incurable romantic," I say, managing a smile, too.

But she shakes her head adamantly. "Romantics just believe. I'm more like . . . Aphrodite. I'll do anything to make sure love survives the Nazis."

She stands there wearing her emotions as obviously as I'd once worn mine, an impetuous young woman fighting for love the same way crusaders once fought for religion. Magpie watches her with a bemused expression, eyes flickering to me, probably wondering if I'll admonish her for delivering love notes rather than intelligence. But Monique loves Vallet so much that she climbed the trees outside a Nazi prison to shout messages of hope. Loving is in her nature. I can't reprimand her for that.

"How's Couscous?" I ask.

"He said to tell you, *Little one, stop worrying about me.*"

It makes me laugh, which I'm sure is what he intended.

But I don't laugh when two o'clock becomes three o'clock becomes dawn and no messages arrive.

What if Bla found out about the airplanes? What if Léon is in Fresnes, too?

"The weather was bad," Magpie says, voice matter-of-fact. "They probably couldn't land."

There are so many ways to die when flying clandestinely into Nazi-occupied France.

Then the transmitter springs into life. Magpie passes me the message.

Vesta a no-show. Mahout.

It means Léon's plane didn't arrive. But I don't know if he's safe or dead.

That day is one of the most tense I've ever known. The night is worse, bringing no news. Bee makes me food I don't eat. She brings me cups of tea, and Magpie stares at them like they're chocolate.

"A Frenchwoman with taste," he says before giving me an exaggeratedly formal bow. "I salute you. All I have to do now is get you to swap your Gauloises for Pall Malls, and then we can be friends."

To which Monique and I both react with an impassioned, "Never!"

Monique grins at Magpie. I still can't smile, so I give him my cup of tea instead.

After that, Monique and Magpie talk to each other. I smoke. The soundtrack of worry—cups chinked against saucers, voices murmuring, my lighter going *click-click*—plays all night.

Again, the clock ticks past seven in the morning. If we haven't heard anything by eight, I'm going to break my promise and drive to Thalamy.

Eight o'clock chimes. I stand.

Then Magpie spins around, headphones on, and nods.

I'm desperate to know what the transmission says. But ignorance is also bliss. Right now, I can believe Léon is fine. After I read that message, everything might change.

Magpie pushes it across to me.

Vesta's landed. Eagle's on his way to Marseille.

I only just manage not to burst into tears.

A month after my glorious reunion with Léon, MI6 tells us that the Allies will be landing in North Africa soon, an attack that's been planned using the intelligence we provided. The end is about to start, and that thought has me smiling every day. But my smile falls off my face the morning Léon bursts into the villa, even though he's meant to be on his way to Toulouse with Magpie.

"Bla was at Saint-Charles station," he gasps.

Bla's tracked me to Marseille.

The entire headquarters staff is frozen, listening to Léon's words. "He recognized Magpie. They were at the same training course in London. Magpie signaled to me before he walked off with him and I followed them to a bar. When Magpie excused himself to the bathroom, he filled me in. Bla's told Magpie a fairytale about having escaped the Gestapo and wanting to join Magpie's network."

We are issuing execution order, MI6 had said.

The time has come to kill.

22

The Animals Are Ill With the Plague

Marseille, December 1942

Léon delivers a note to Magpie telling him to take Bla to an empty building on the Corniche where Léon, Rivière, and Lucien will be waiting. Monique fetches me as soon as Bla's secured.

"He thinks Eagle and Wolf are from the Vichy police," she says flatly. "He keeps giving them a number to telephone, saying they'll be ordered to free him. The number . . ." Her mouth twists. "The number is for Gestapo HQ in Paris."

Bla carries the telephone number for the Gestapo in his pocket. A cold, hard rage that I want to train on Bla like a gun pours through me.

I sit by Monique's side on the trolley car even though I have a rule that Alliance agents aren't to travel in the same carriage. But she's weeping for Vallet. The young woman who wants to keep romance alive is about to come face-to-face with the man who destroyed hers. All I have to give her is my hand, which is small and weak, where Vallet's is large and strong. But she takes it.

Tonight, the sky is punctured not with stars, but with sharp, white teeth. I can't smell the sea even though it's right beside us, can't taste cinnamon and cumin; can only scent the flayed bones of rotting fish and the garbage that's stacked in skyscrapers along the street.

Marseille is the city of my birth, but it holds a traitor within its walls.

When I push open the door, there is Bla's clean-shaven face. There is his mouth, smiling at Léon as if he thinks he'll win again.

I clear my throat. Bla turns.

Terror floods his eyes.

"You haven't been arrested by Vichy police." I pull off my gloves and advance into the room, which, bare of furniture and lit by one bare bulb, looks like a gangster-noir set piece.

The place where men come to die.

I toss my hat onto a chair and stand in front of our first traitor.

Almost worse than being in the room with Bla is thinking that word: *first*. As if I know there will be more. That I'll stand in another room like this one.

But will I be the interrogator or the one under arrest?

Tonight my skin is made of tin, and a hundred cats are scraping their claws on it. But I will not shiver in front of this man.

"You're the person I was looking for," Bla says with a shrug. "You've won."

He's so cavalier, as if he thinks I haven't the *couilles* to bring this to an end.

Léon's clenching his fists, Rivière, too. But nobody will touch this man until he tells me exactly how far he's tried to ruin us.

"Stand up," I tell him. "And start talking."

"I'm working for Mosley's British Fascists," he says, perhaps having realized there's nothing to gain from staying silent. "I worked my way into British Intelligence, then won the confidence of your agents, and had them arrested. Except you," he says, regret so obvious that Léon takes a step forward and I hold up my hand, not sure if even that will stop him from punching Bla in the face.

Léon curses but halts.

"Where's your radio set?" I ask.

"At the Abwehr headquarters in Paris."

My inhale is audible. "And the transmissions it's been sending to London?"

"I sent them," Bla says cheerfully. "London can tell if a different operator is using a radio. So I sent information MI6 already had, along with a little bit of false information. That was fun," he says with a sigh, as if the only thing he rues is that he'll no longer be able to mislead the Allies into wasted operations. As if Vallet and the others in prison are things he's played with and disposed of as casually as cigarettes.

I want to be sick.

Bla talks and talks until his body is swaying from standing. I think he's so exhausted he'll give me the names of his London handlers so MI6 can arrest them, but every time I ask, he says, "Nobody."

Eventually I leave the room and brace my arms on the kitchen counter. They're shaking, so I fold them across my chest. "I need to tell London we have him," I say to Léon, Lucien, and Rivière.

Léon accompanies me to headquarters, where a reply comes straight back.

Confirm execution order

"Stay here," Léon says. "What happens now doesn't concern you."

I shake my head. "I have to be there, for Vallet."

"If Bla is in Marseille," Léon says grimly, "it means the Gestapo know you're here. I can walk the streets, but you can't. Don't make a mockery of Vallet's silence and sacrifice by getting yourself arrested."

Is it cowardice or the formidable weight of responsibility to the network that keeps me at HQ, prowling the rooms, ears straining for the slightest sounds until finally the first trolley car of the morning clatters up the hill? When Léon enters, he collapses on the sofa, as if the air is so heavy it's crushing him.

This is what it does to a man to kill someone.

"We put one of the cyanide capsules from London in his soup," he says, voice stripped of emotion. "Three hours later he was still alive. We put the next one in his tea. Two more hours and nothing. He's still *alive*."

I slide to the floor, back leaning against the sofa. Eagle has shot down men's planes in the thick of battle. But cold-bloodedly executing a man is something his honor chafes against. A man like that is someone I want to spend the rest of my life with.

It's not something we ever discuss. After the war. What will happen. I don't know if he'll ever meet my children, give me his last name, grow old by my side.

But I know that I am *la patronne*. I know that Bla must die. It's my job to encourage Léon to kill.

Help me, God.

"This is our battlefield," I say into the dawn darkness. "Temporary houses and landing fields, letterboxes and bars. Manning those battlefields are people who haven't seen their families for months, who might die because of what they're doing. Bla is standing on a battlefield and he's an enemy who'll never lie on a sofa and let his conscience talk him out of killing any one of us."

Léon reaches for my hand and we hold on, hold on, hold on.

When Léon returns, I know it's done and that he will never tell. He'll carry it in the deepening creases in his forehead, in the faint shadow in the backs of his eyes. All he says is, "He had some last words."

Premonition, like a Locrian scale of lunatic shadows, plays over my bones. "What?"

"He said the Germans are invading the free zone on November 11."

"No." I reject the very idea. "No."

If the Nazis occupy the free zone, then there'll no longer be a part of France where the French police are still technically in charge. Instead, the Gestapo will be on every street corner slicing butter and throats with their daggers.

Today was supposed to be a good day. The Allies are landing on German-occupied territory, near Rabat, Casablanca, and Algiers. The battle for France has begun, but now . . .

"Do you believe him?" I ask.

"I think I do."

In front of me, Léon looks so tired. He's been awake for two days. And he's dealt with Bla. So I'll deal with this.

"Go take a shower," I tell him. "Rest before you throw yourself back into everything."

He squeezes my hand gratefully.

I go into the operations room. If Bla's right, we need to move HQ. Tonight. Soon we'll be like Moroccan nomads carrying tents on our backs.

I code a message to MI6 about the Nazis invading the free zone and Magpie begins transmission.

"No response," he says after ten minutes. For the first time ever, I hear something other than calm in his voice.

I keep my eye on the clock. We have to stop transmitting within twenty minutes; otherwise, we risk being tracked by the Nazis' detector vans. And if the Allies have landed in North Africa, the Germans are going to be more gimlet-eyed than ever. "Change frequencies," I tell him.

Monique, who's just come in from buying supplies, interrupts. "There are men walking up and down the avenue out there."

My prickles rise. It's so quiet today, the mistral absent, the city slumberous. I cross to the windows. The sun is ghostly bright, the kind only Schaerrer could look at.

"Got them!" Magpie calls.

Morse tap-dances into the air. Then an earthquake tears HQ apart.

"Police!"

We leap like the animals we are.

Magpie grabs a lighter and burns the last message. A man with a revolver hurls himself on Magpie, so I hurl myself on the man, shouting every insult I've learned over the past two years. I sound like a hellcat and I fight like one, too. The policeman or *gestapiste*—I have no idea if he's French or German—picks up a chair and holds it in front of him like a terrified schoolboy. It gives me the break I need to dart into my office, take out the tiny paper balls I scribble my messages on, and stuff them into my mouth, wishing to God I'd used MI6's dissolving paper.

I'm gagging when the man who'd tackled Magpie appears and shouts, "She's swallowing papers!"

He must be the leader of this pack.

Another man rushes in and grabs me by the throat. It's impossible to breathe, let alone swallow. I claw at his hand, shouting, "Dirty Boche!" and hoping Léon will hear and escape through a window.

"Get them out of her mouth," the leader snaps at his lieutenant before he returns to the ops room.

The minute he's gone, my attacker's grip slackens. "I'm French," he whispers. "On your side. Keep shouting."

I have no idea whether to believe him, but my choices right now aren't even limited—they're nonexistent.

"I hate you!" I scream, playing my part for all it's worth, searching this man's face to see if it's just a trick to make me talk.

"They're only allowed to detect radio signals," he says urgently. "They're not allowed to touch papers or people until we hand you over. I'm Goubil and my friend Pierre is on your side, too. Tell me what I can do. And hurry." He holds out a handkerchief.

If I spit the papers into the handkerchief and he takes them to his leader, we're done for. But if the Gestapo are here, we're probably done for anyway.

I spit, braced for treachery. Goubil tears the papers up.

"Hide the folders on my desk," I tell him. "And there are more people arriving soon. Can you warn them?"

Goubil flings the documents on top of a cupboard. He summons Pierre and tells him to go down to the gate and warn away anyone who tries to enter. Then he tucks my arms loosely behind my back and leads me into the operations room.

Magpie, no longer a British gentleman, is facing off against the *gestapiste,* who's holding a piece of paper that lists the locations and call signs of all our transmitters. It's the one piece of paper that will cripple our network if it falls into German hands. Heedless of the Nazi's revolver, I lunge.

The *gestapiste's* gun lifts.

I'm one second away from being shot.

Thankfully Goubil, my guardian angel, says to the Nazi, "Calm down. I'll put it in a sealed envelope."

Into an envelope it goes, thankfully in Goubil's hands.

Once the Nazi's gun is re-holstered and his back turned, I indicate with my head that I want to see what's happening on the next floor. I'm desperately hoping my Eagle has somehow flown.

Goubil pushes me upstairs.

But there in the bathroom is Léon surrounded by young French policemen. Inexplicably, he's shaving. Hanging on the hook behind him, in all its glory, is his air force commandant's uniform. On the jacket are his two Croix de Guerre, one from the Great War, one from Morocco. Arrayed beside are the rest of his medals, a glittering parade of courage, honor, and service to France.

Standing there, Léon has never looked more like the man

who's fought for years for his country, a man the French police officers don't want to arrest. Indeed, one of them is weeping.

Léon gives me a shrug at his small piece of necessary theater.

Somehow, in the middle of being arrested, I mouth, *I love you*. If men like him ruled the world, what a world it would be.

Thank God the name on my identity card is Claire de Bacqueville. The police don't know who I am—yet. My only other relief as we pass through the gates of La Pinède is that I see Elephant lurking in the shadows, meaning he's still free and can get the British to transmit the message: *In the south of France the animals are ill with the plague.*

It's the signal to all our sectors to go into hiding.

Monique, Léon, Magpie, Bee, Lucien, and I are taken to l'Évêché, a living cliché of a prison. There are rats scampering over the floors. It's colder inside than a Nazi's smile, but the warden advises me to take off my goatskin coat unless I want it to walk out by itself, carried away on the backs of lice.

"Lice or frostbite; which to choose?" I joke, trying to keep up everyone's spirits, trying not to think that Josette is going to kill me when she finds out her son is in prison.

At least we're in a French prison in the free zone. But if Bla told the truth, this zone is free for only three more days. If we're still here when the Nazis occupy the entire country, we're as good as dead.

It's time to escape from prison.

We're split up, placed in separate cells. Mine contains only a plank attached to the wall, barred windows ten feet off the ground, and a toilet that sputters like a tubercular cough. The only way out is through the locked door or down the drain, and I swear loudly, the sound echoing back at me.

All night I smoke and think.

When Goubil unlocks the door in the morning, he tells me that the Allies have just landed in North Africa. Despite being in jail, I can't contain my smile. I know the Germans' military might in Morocco and Algiers is less than it could have been because Alliance has warned the Allies about the ships and airplanes headed there, and they've been blown up before they could reach their destination. I know the Allies have detailed information about the concentration and location of the troops they're facing because we gathered that intelligence for them. I know—the same way I know we need to get out of here before November 11, just two days away—that the Allies will win over there.

And they'll land in France next.

"The Vichy government wishes to see your commandant friend," Goubil says, and my smile disappears.

The police might think I'm Claire de Bacqueville, but they know exactly who Léon is. And of course Laval wants to see Léon Faye, the air force commander who once launched a coup in North Africa and who's now been found consorting with rebels.

"Don't let him go," I plead.

"I can't prevent it, Madame. Monsieur Faye believes that because of the Allies' landing in North Africa, Vichy might now take some action against the Germans. Especially after he tells *le maréchal* Pétain . . ."—he eyes me questioningly—"that the Germans will invade the free zone."

"Léon is too honorable for his own good!" I cry. "Yes, the Germans are going to invade the free zone. But Pétain won't care if the Nazis break every promise in the armistice agreement. He'll never stop them. And he'll kill Léon if you let him go to Vichy."

Along the corridor come two policemen marching Léon before them. His face shows an implacable calm as he stops in front of my cell.

"For once," I beg him, "care more for yourself than you do for France."

"Pétain is French," Léon insists. "He won't want the Germans taking over the whole country. It's my duty to tell him. I swore an oath to France, Minerva. That's a sacred thing."

Despite the fact I'm in prison and the man I love is preparing to go willingly to see the people who've locked us up, I laugh. Hysterically.

Why is it that the things we love are the things we come to fear in the end? My husband adored me. He adored me so much it was like a spell, bewitching me into not thinking about what lay on the other side of adoration. I've always known that Léon's sense of honor is like his heart—essential to keeping him alive. But now it's the thing that's going to get him killed.

He sees so far into wrong, but he still believes that right will win.

My laughter turns into shaking, convulsive sobs.

"We'll meet again, Minerva," Léon whispers. "In the safe house in the Dordogne. I promise."

Then he's dragged away by the police, off to plead for France's soul with the men who gave it to the Nazis.

The night is long and terrible. My chilblains ache. And my ears are attuned to the distant echo of menace, the dies irae I can feel coming for us all. Pétain will throw Léon into a worse prison than this—if he isn't already dead—and in the early hours of tomorrow morning, the Germans will take over the free zone. Then the Gestapo will be in charge of this prison and my life. Lucien's life. Bee's and Monique's and Magpie's, too.

Dawn is breaking the sky apart when Goubil comes into my

cell, solemn-faced. "Pétain arrested Commandant Faye," he says.

"Is he still alive?" My voice is so thin.

Goubil nods. "The Nazis want all of you and the documents I took into custody."

"If you do that," I say furiously, "you'll be responsible for murdering dozens of people. By tomorrow morning, the Nazis will have occupied the free zone and you'll be made to arrest more French men and women. Is that why you dreamed of becoming a police officer? To serve Nazis?" I practically spit the last words at him, terrible things to say to someone who's helped us. But if Léon's going to be a blazing warrior for right, so will I.

"They want you moved to Castres," he says before walking out.

Castres is a stopping station en route to being deported to Germany.

I have ten cigarettes left in my pack. I've smoked eight of them, all in a row, before Goubil returns, saying, "I radioed Lyon and Vichy. If the Germans were going to take over the free zone, they'd need to bring in troops. There's no evidence of troop concentrations coming this way. I've done what I can."

"Unless you're behind a locked prison door or dead, then you haven't done everything you can," I say coldly, thinking of dear Lucien, a boy who's never even had a girlfriend—and who will die in Castres or Germany before he can.

Goubil storms out.

Hours pass. Hours ticking down to November 11 and Gestapo everywhere.

I have no cigarettes left. No more ideas. But so much anger. It drives me, almost maniacally, to keep my head high and meet the gaze of every officer who passes until Goubil returns, looking weary as he says, "We heard from Moulins. German troops are massed at the demarcation line. You were right."

"Where's Léon?"

"Already in Castres."

My hip wants to cast me onto the floor. I will not let it, not in front of my jailer.

Then Goubil says to me, "I destroyed the documents they took from your headquarters. And I warned your men of the route our van will take to Castres. They'll ambush it. I won't work for Nazis."

I take his cheeks in my hands and kiss them.

23

The Most Terrible Year of All

The Dordogne, December 1942

Rivière, Elephant, and half a dozen agents ambush the prison van, as Goubil promised. It's almost too easy.

Stop, I tell myself. Since when did I become the kind of person who sees only the darkness between the stars?

We travel separately and via different routes to the Dordogne. I'm with Rivière, who's uncharacteristically silent as we chug past Nazi convoys setting themselves up everywhere, having stopped pretending that part of France is free. We aren't questioned; I suppose they think fugitives have more sense than to travel when there are so many Germans on the march.

"I need to go via Toulouse," I tell him.

Rivière's known me long enough that he just sighs.

Josette, whom I moved to Toulouse HQ months ago, greets me by waving one sharp finger in the air. "If you apologize for Lucien's arrest, I'll shoot you like I once promised to shoot the Boche. The ones doing unforgivable things are the Nazis, not you."

I kiss her cheeks, and in her arms I ask, "Any news of Eagle?"

"Still in Castres."

I'm too fatigued to hide my distress. "Can you send someone—"

She cuts me off. "Lucien left an hour ago for Castres with two others."

"But—"

She interrupts again. "An adjutant would never let his commanding officer rot in prison. I hugged my son a half hour ago. Go and hug yours. I'll keep watch while you do."

From one mother to another, the only gift that matters.

We walk to the Jesuit school where Christian's boarding. One of the priests was a member of the Dame Blanche network in the Great War. A man who knows how to evade Germans and protect people—I could think of no one better to keep my son safe.

Ten minutes later, I'm in a room with the boy, whom I haven't seen for a year.

It breaks my heart that he doesn't run to me, but treads warily, like someone yoked. "It's you?" he asks.

"Come here, darling," I say, and at last he dashes forward and doesn't let go.

When we finally separate, he talks for one glorious hour about the books he's read, the histories he's learned, the science he's studied. "Everyone thinks lions are the deadliest animals in the world," he enthuses at one point. "But it's mosquitoes that kill the most people every year. Teeny, tiny mosquitoes."

He shakes his head in wonder that something so small and so ordinary could be so dangerous.

"I didn't know," I force myself to say. "But tell me what you've been learning in math." And he begins to talk about the angles in a lovely, safe triangle while the deadly mosquito buzzes in the drums of my ear.

I leave the school carrying a heart and a head so full of my son that I can hardly climb into the car. But a leader's pain is like the one I've carried in my hip since I was a child—invisible, but almost enough to cripple you, so you brace yourself against the air.

Rivière gives me the gift of five minutes' silence, then says, "Vichy is furious. Luckily the Germans still haven't worked out who you are and what Alliance is. But they want everyone re-arrested. There's a price on the head of Claire de Bacqueville—a significant price. Elephant's made you new identity papers."

"At least they haven't connected Claire and Marie-Madeleine."

"But a description of you has been circulated everywhere. You thought you were in danger before," Rivière says grimly. "Now you're treasure for anyone who wants to make a killing. MI6 wants you to take the Lysander to London next week."

If I went to London, I'd be keeping my promise to my children. I'd be in no danger at all.

But last week, a courier arrived at HQ with photographs that had been smuggled out of a prisoner-of-war camp in Mauthausen, Austria, by a doctor. They showed prisoners so thin we thought someone had dressed skeletons in clothes. The last two images were of the river in Mauthausen, its water colored red with the blood of the dead. That was when I understood that Nazis don't just kill. They're the kings of slaughter.

I can't leave my country to men who'll let her rivers run red with blood.

So I re-dress myself in the costume of *la patronne* in time to greet my agents, calm their fears, and reignite their hopes, because what if *I'm* the mosquito, and the Nazis are the ones who get bitten eventually?

In the heart of France, where Colonel Kauffmann, the partly deaf pilot with a penchant for capes, leads a sector of Alliance, the forests are silent, the winds fierce, the mountains impenetrable, and the paths twist like secrets. This land will hide us like fairytale children in a mythical forest, I think as Kauffmann—

who's taken the code name Cricket—greets me with a warm handshake, saying, "I've found you a new HQ."

"Where are the animals being caged this time?"

"A castle fit for a queen."

In keeping with his antediluvian appearance, Kauffmann's procured the empty Chateau Malfonds near the town of Sarlat, which looks as antique but debonair as him. My HQ staff will work there, separate from his sector, so any attention directed at us won't compromise them.

Monique and Magpie are already in the ops room, setting things up with an endearing combination of his orderliness and her spirit. She locates chairs and other necessary items from all over the chateau, and Magpie places them in functional working spaces. Goubil and Pierre, whom I'll put on next week's Lysander, are there too—they can't stay in France now that they've helped us escape.

"Do I smell truffles?" I ask as I walk into the kitchen and find Bee buzzing around.

Then I hear a cough, and I almost don't recognize Coustenoble, who's been helping the duke of Magenta make Paris into a stronghold. His face is pale, eyes glassy.

"Damn Boche," he says. "I nearly got caught."

"What happened?" I ask, instead of saying, *You're ill. Come and rest,* because I know he doesn't want me to say that in front of his comrades.

"I ran across the border with bullets flying past my ears," he complains. "I don't know why they keep the demarcation line if they've occupied the whole country. I thought for sure they'd get me this time."

"Can everyone give me a minute?" I say, and in thirty seconds there's no one in the kitchen except Couscous and me.

He embraces me. "Jail, little one," he says, as if his being shot at is a minor inconvenience.

His handkerchief is streaked with blood.

"I'm ordering you to rest," I tell him.

"I'll rest when we've won."

I don't have a chance to say more, because my arrest and escape have made every sector leader from across the country descend upon us to make sure I really am alive. In they come, exclaiming, smiling, embracing. Bee brings tea, coffee, and whiskey, and soon the kitchen is alive with voices.

I heat a pan of milk for Coustenoble, who tells me how well things are going in the north. He finishes by saying, "Now that Paris is on its feet, we need someone to focus on the forbidden zone."

It's the most dangerous job of all. The forbidden zone is off limits to anyone without a pass and is heavily patrolled by Nazis who shoot first and don't ask questions. My whole body rebels against what I think he's about to say.

"It has to be me, little one."

The last free stripe in my tricolor. "But you're ill," I protest.

"The whole country is ill," he says. "But here in this room, everyone is well."

He looks around at the animals of Alliance as proudly as if he'd take on every forbidden zone in the world.

Every time I think I've seen true courage, I realize I've witnessed only a little bit of mettle. True courage is a man with bleeding lungs sending himself into hell.

All I can do is pass him the milk and show him the message that just arrived on Magpie's transmitter.

Blockade an astonishing success. Twenty-eight voyages attempted, fourteen ships destroyed.

It means Baston's intelligence from Stosskopf, the man playing a double game with the Nazis, has been so good that of the last twenty-eight U-boat voyages attempted, fourteen have been blown out of the water. Because of Alliance.

"That's half!" Coustenoble cries, and he already looks better, as if warm milk and success can mend just about anything.

It's Baston himself who arrives next. He lets me hug him, but he firmly refuses to listen to thanks or praise. "I have another strategy I hope you'll approve," he tells me.

"Go on."

"My agent in Brittany, Mandrill, has befriended a seamstress who repairs the Nazi submariners' life vests," he says. "When the Germans demand that she repairs their vests quickly, she knows a submarine is due to go out. She's agreed to tell Mandrill when that happens. Then we can radio the information straight to the British."

"You're worried about something," I say, studying his face.

The old general nods. "The seamstress is just seventeen. A child. How can she know what she's getting herself into?"

I understand why he's come. He doesn't, not really—just knows that his guts are filled with discomfort when they should be replete with viands and vittles. So I take the responsibility from him for this young girl's life. "Her code name can be Scallop."

Baston studies my face now. I hold my gaze steady and indicate Monique, Bee, think of Josette and all the other women in Alliance's ranks as I say in my leader's voice, a dagger I use to slice through doubt, "These women will set the world ablaze. And from their courage, a better one will rise. We have to let them."

Navarre, MI6, Léon—none of these men would ignore such a powerful weapon against the Nazis because of mere youth. But as I turn away, I think, *I hope to God she has a large enough shell to hide in.*

A note arrives from Josette to tell us that Léon is out of prison already and on his way here with Lucien. I allow myself to smile only as much as you should if your chief of staff is rescued, rather than your lover—the man I'll hardly have a chance to speak to because he'll be leaving on the Lysander tomorrow. If MI6 wants me in London, I'll have to placate them by sending Léon again and hope they aren't furious with me.

That night, in a bed with the softest eiderdown and a roaring fire beside it, I dream of Léon. Then I hear his voice so near that I sit up, toss a sweater on over the shirt and trousers I've slept in, and go down to the kitchen where, yes: Léon is alive and safe with a crowd of people gathered around him.

"Lucien smuggled me a handsaw via a sympathetic guard, and I cut through the bar on the lavatory window a little every time I visited the facilities," he's saying with a mischievous grin. "They thought the prison food disagreed with me, hence my frequent need to use the facilities. The night Lucien's team was ready for me, I picked the lock on my cell, crept past the gen-darmes, who were snoring away"—he does an exaggerated im-pression of a sleeping policeman and I laugh like the others.

Léon hears and looks over at me. When he smiles, everyone turns their heads to see why his face is so transformed and I worry we might have given ourselves away.

He keeps talking, making them focus on him. "I climbed out the bathroom window and slid down eighty feet of rope. As you can see"—he holds up his hands, which are raw—"the rope got the better of me."

Bee, bless her, gets out salves and bandages.

While Léon's being ministered to, I approach Lucien. He's become a man, I see, in this past month. And it's to the man that I say, "Thank you."

He beams and blushes and is suddenly a child again for just a second until I say, "Tell them your side of the story," and he takes his seat at the table and describes how he got the rope and handsaw to Léon with the kind of swashbuckling exaggeration Navarre once reveled in.

I slip in next to Léon.

"I hear you have another price on your pretty head," he says, words teasing, tone serious. "You know your head is priceless."

"You've gotten out of prison twice. Me only once. I have some catching up to do."

Before Léon can argue with that shaky logic, another visitor arrives.

"Hérisson!" the duke of Magenta shouts, picking me up and twirling me around. "The north is operating like a countrywoman's sewing machine. You're sending people out to safety on airplanes; we're taking them to London on fishing boats."

I laugh. The spirit of competition among my animals is fierce. No sooner has someone perfected one tactic than another finds a way to trump it.

"I came to deliver these." He hands over the last week's worth of intelligence that's accrued while I've been breaking out of prison.

I open the folder, remembering there's something I have to tell Léon.

"Look," I say, showing him tiny photographs gathered by our agents of the system of bunkers, guns, and artillery that are being built along the French coastline. "Take these with you when you go to London. Tonight," I add, as casually as I can manage.

"Tonight?" Léon repeats. Then, "They want you there, don't they?"

Before he can tell me I should be the one to go, I pick up another report. "The Nazis are moving so many troops toward Russia. It might make invading France easier for the Allies. That news should make them happy, so I expect twice as much money, whiskey, and cigarettes from London."

Having sensed I'm not to be budged, he jokes, "You're trading me for Woodbines?"

"The Woodbines would give me less trouble."

He whispers in my ear, "But not as much satisfaction, I hope."

My face turns a shade of pink I can't blame on the fire.

But the jokes fade when Magpie comes in from the ops room with a transmission from Paris. I take it, still smiling, not knowing what the decryption will reveal until the scratchings of my pen become the first desolate notes of a requiem. Everyone in Fresnes has been shot. Hugon. Vallet. And seven more.

"A courier came, too." Magpie nods to the young woman hovering behind him.

I stretch out my hand and take from her what turns out to be Vallet's last letter.

> *I think I have done my duty to my country and my comrades, you will never need to blush on my account. Be courageous, all of you. Farewell . . .*

"Monique," I say hoarsely, forgetting in this terrible moment to use her code name in front of the others.

She reads it and gives one sharp nod, too stubborn to cry in front of everyone. Then she passes the letter around the table, so everyone can read that Vallet was a man who thought of his country and of what was right more than his own pain and his own life.

Mahout, our gypsy pilot in charge of the landing field, is next to arrive. Not knowing what's happened, he says, "We need to get moving."

Maurice starts to say that we can't be thinking of flights to London now, but Monique gives me another, sharper nod. So I force myself to ignore the new hole in my heart beside the one

Schaerrer left and say, "Vallet didn't die so we'd cancel our missions."

We go out into the storm. I'm not supposed to be present for Lysander flights because they're the riskiest thing we do. But Léon is leaving, like Bellerophon riding his winged horse across the sky, even though he's only just gotten out of prison and I haven't embraced him, let alone lain my head on his shoulder and wept for Vallet and eight others.

Wind and rain lash at us. Clouds dress the sky. The night is an E-minor scale, fathomless; rain the only thing that glitters. I stand under Eagle's wing in the hailstorm for hours, but the plane doesn't arrive.

We eventually leave, freezing and exhausted, and Magpie greets us at the chateau with the words, "Transmission just came in. The weather's set to last all week. They won't be coming this moon. Merry Christmas."

Yes, it's Christmas Eve tomorrow. But none of us looks especially merry.

As everyone unpeels their coats, I remember that we started the year with one hundred men. Now, in Alliance, there are almost one thousand.

That is no small thing.

"Christmas dinner tomorrow," I announce. "For Vallet. And for hope."

We sit around the chateau table and eat like kings. Kauffmann's brought food from his farm: a ham, real butter and bread, and dozens of eggs that Bee makes into tiny soufflés. There are English chocolates, vegetables that taste like roasted French earth, chestnuts, and a dozen bottles of burgundy, smoky sweet with a palate of wood fires and cherries.

We eat and laugh, and I try to enjoy what I have and not

think about my mother and Yvonne, of Christian and Béatrice eating bûche de Noël without me. *Next year,* I plead with the Fates, *spin out a future that puts me at home with my family for Christmas 1943.*

With North Africa having been invaded by the Allies, surely France is next. By summer. August 1943 at the latest.

Yes.

But tonight is for my agents, not my fears. I dress my face in a smile and reminisce with Maurice about Morocco, listen for Coustenoble's cough and convince myself it sounds better, watch Magpie talking to Monique with such a compassionate look in his eyes that I hope her heart might be healed by time and tenderness. I ask Kauffmann about his wartime exploits with Léon, who's at the opposite end of the table. Every time my eyes catch his, I can hear his thoughts murmuring against my ear, saying very private things.

Then the duke of Magenta stands. "To the queen of the animals," he says, raising his glass. "Bless you for what you are doing. You alone make it possible for old soldiers like me to serve my country. May your prickles never be dulled and your smile continue to make grown men blush."

The cheering is thunderous and now I *am* blushing, so I stand before he can say anything more and raise my glass. "To Vallet. To Hugon and all the rest. And to an Alliance that will never be broken."

More cheering; damp eyes and cheeks. We hide them beneath celebrations that continue until midnight. Coustenoble falls asleep in his chair, others break away to talk in smaller groups. Léon whispers in my ear, breath hot against my skin, "Don't come upstairs for fifteen minutes. I have a gift for you that I need to get ready."

Anticipation means it's only ten minutes later when I push open the door to my room. The fire is blazing and the air is scented with lavender and rose. Léon is standing in the doorway of the bathroom. "For your present, you need to be naked," he says.

I laugh, the burgundy, the warmth, and the proximity of the man I love almost too much. I slide out of my clothes, watching him watch me, the pulse in his throat beating against his skin. Then I see what my present is: a bathtub full of heavenly hot water, scattered with dried rose petals and lavender.

"It's the best present I've ever had," I tell him. "But only if you share it with me."

He grins. "That was definitely my plan."

We slide into the tub as if we have all the time in the world. I lean my back against Léon's chest and he wraps his arms around me. My eyes almost close, but I don't want to miss anything of the scent, the touch, and the taste of Léon Faye; my Eagle, my love.

"How are you?" he murmurs, trailing the washcloth along my arm.

"I should be asking you that," I say, more lightly than I feel. Always trying to pretend, to never say, *I spend every minute thinking you're going to die and knowing, if that happened, that I would die, too.* "Didn't you just escape prison and leave half your skin behind?"

He laughs. "Serves me right for being cocky. I actually believed my experience in aerial maneuvers would see me down that rope without any consequences."

I stroke my finger across one damaged palm and feel Léon's muscles relax, as if we will, for just a few hours, pretend we're two people who've never seen the inside of a prison, whose friends haven't died, and who don't have intelligence that the Nazis would kill for hidden in a room downstairs.

"I already miss you," I say, thinking of London.

"Me too," he whispers, voice husky, lifting my red, chilblained fingertips to his lips and kissing them as if they were the loveliest hands in the world.

I turn my head, needing to catch his lips against mine, but it isn't enough, so I shift my body, straddling him, his hands gripping my hips, mine tangled in his hair until the kiss becomes too urgent, too unequal at expressing everything we're trying to say.

We climb out of the bath inelegantly and hurriedly. Léon tosses me a towel before he steps me back into the bedroom and I'm on my back on the bed, him above me, his hands as undisciplined as the weather outside, and I can't believe this is all we have—words and mouths and bodies—when this thing between us stretches beyond horizons, fills every ocean, paints dawns red and sunsets gold, gifts the sky its moon and the stars their glittering particles of dust.

When I wake, it's still dark outside. In the firelight, I creep out of bed and search for the present I had London send over on last month's midnight flight. I stare at it for a moment, wondering and worrying, but also stupidly, ridiculously happy.

I wrap the necktie around my waist like a belt and walk back to the bed.

Léon stirs. When his eyes flicker open and he realizes I'm not lying beside him, terror rouses him fully.

"I'm here," I whisper. "Safe."

He shutters the fear instantly, the fear that sometimes becomes too much even for him and soaks the sheets with sweat at three in the morning.

He raises himself to his elbow, looks quizzically at the silk around my waist, moves his lips to my stomach, then along my hipbone to the top of my thigh.

"I have two presents for you," I murmur, needing him to not have his lips on me, not yet. "You'll have to unwrap the first to find the second."

A faint smile lifts the corners of his mouth, and I see something else I love about him—the man who runs at life like it's all a game he's certain to win, and his only job is to enjoy it.

He undoes the tie with one tug of his fingers. It unrolls like the perfect . . .

"Moroccan sky," he says, and I smile.

I'd sent the most detailed and possibly ridiculous instructions to London and they excelled. The tie is the same breathtaking hue that's painted over Rabat when the red sands of the desert reflect the light back up into the sky.

I almost can't say the next thing because I know it will knock the smile off Léon's face.

I pick up his hand. "When I first met you in Vichy in 1940, I told you there were two things I was fighting for. Now . . ." I pause and the seconds march past, so many of them that Léon tries to catch my tear-filled eyes in his worried ones, but the only thing I can look at is the floor.

"Now there are four," I whisper.

"Four?"

"Béatrice, Christian, you. And . . ." I touch my stomach, already in love despite the fact that it's too dangerous and I can't be *la patronne* of the largest Resistance network in France, a woman on the run with a price on her head, and be pregnant, too.

"And our son," I finish. I know it's a boy. And that he'll be a warrior like his father.

"Our son?" Léon repeats, two words that aren't meant for a world tearing itself apart, and he covers his face with his hands, jaw working furiously as he tries to control his emotions.

I gently peel his hands away. "It's okay," I say softly. "It's okay."

He gathers me to him like I'm the very air he needs to fly. "I should have noticed," he says, voice hoarse. "Rations and running have made you so thin that it doesn't make sense that your stomach is a tiny bit curved."

"What will they say?" I blurt. Because it will soon be obvious to those who work closely with me—Monique, Magpie, Lucien, Bee—that I'm pregnant.

He hesitates and I brace myself for him to say, *I'll have to take over. You need to go back to your children.*

All those things are true.

All those things are impossible.

But he smiles. "Minerva, do you ever feel like our lives have been divided into two halves? The half when I didn't know you, and the half where I do?"

Of everything, that's what makes me cry. That he didn't say, *The half where I was an air force commandant, and the half where my role was recognized by only a scraggly band of people and the shadows of British Intelligence.* That he considers his whole life as orbiting, like a moon to its earth, around me.

His fingertips trace over the child we've made, the child we love—the child that might make us behave with more or less courage than we need to. "I'm trying to say that, in 1938, could you ever have imagined a future when there'd be hundreds of men in France who'd unquestioningly do whatever you asked?"

"Well, I do have that kind of face," I joke.

Léon doesn't laugh. He holds my face in his hands and says fiercely, "What's happened in Alliance is extraordinary. I don't know if ever again in history there'll be another woman like you, Marie-Madeleine. One who commands legions with grace and courage and humility and flair."

"Léon," I whisper. Suddenly I can feel, and I think he can too, that same sense of disaster that follows me everywhere—that what we have won't survive the war.

But is it because he'll be captured, or I will? Or both of us?

As one of my arms stretches over my head, his hand caught in mine, I shut my eyes against every second but this one. *Now* is all that exists in wartime. The future is just a mirage made of hope, or a chasm carved away by tears.

I wake so late there's sunlight in the room. Refreshed and ready for 1943, I go downstairs, listening for the sound of Tiger's cough. I don't hear it, and I think, *Ah, he's better.*

But when I enter the kitchen, there are fewer faces than the night before.

"Where is he?" I ask Léon and Magpie, who both look guilty.

"Gone. To the forbidden zone," Léon says.

"We couldn't stop him," Magpie adds quietly. "He wanted to leave like a man. Saying goodbye to you . . ." He shrugs, as if in just a couple of months he's gleaned whatever it was that Léon was trying to explain last night. My leadership. This strange quality that makes men do the bravest things they've ever done, but also run from taking leave lest it make them cry.

I remember Coustenoble's face two nights ago, the way he looked around at his friends, and now I see it for what it was: a prince farewelling his most trusted lords.

I will never see Couscous again.

I stumble outside, let the mistral claw at me. Winter is angry, its teeth keen.

And premonition presses like the cold barrel of a gun against my neck, whispering, *1943 will be the most terrible year of all.*

Part Four

PREY

France, 1943

If there had been any bridle on the terror before 1943, it was swept away now.

— PIERRE DE VOMÉCOURT,

Resistance leader

24

No One Believes a Piece of
Paper Can Be a Noose

The Dordogne, January 1943

id-January, MI6 thinks there's enough moonlight to take Léon to London. After a too-short farewell, he, Magpie, Mahout, and the crew go out to meet the airplane.

Back at the chateau, the rooms gape like mouths waiting to swallow me. Dust chokes my lungs. The spirit of Christmas past is pistol cold against my neck. Even my bones shiver, no matter how much wood I put on the fire.

Time moves like decay in a slow, invisible creep.

Are the Gestapo waiting? Will Léon be shot out of the sky?

Tires crunch over the gravel outside. It's too soon for Magpie to be back.

I snap off the light, take out my revolver. Hide behind the door.

Footsteps mount the stairs. Advance along the hall.

I slide the safety catch off.

The doorknob rattles.

Thankfully I look before I shoot. It's Magpie.

"I knew you'd be half dead with anxiety," he says, "so I took a car to get here more quickly. The moon was full, Eagle is safe, our two policemen are on their way to England, and we have cigarettes. Pall Malls, though. We'll need to make a pot of tea to wash them down."

Thank God for Magpie. I take the proffered cigarette, light it with hands still trembling.

"Lucien's downstairs with money, guns, and messages," he adds.

"I'll start on them now."

It's two in the morning, but Magpie says, "We'll help."

He, Monique, Lucien, and I sit at the kitchen table, fueled by Bee. Magpie and I decode; Lucien and Monique repackage London's supplies of guns, shoes, and warm clothes for each sector. Come morning, the couriers arrive, ready to transport the packages to Alliance's sectors.

I jump every time the door opens. I think it's because I'm waiting for the message to come through telling us that Léon arrived safely, but hours after that message has arrived, I'm still a relentless staccato beat jarring the rhythm of headquarters.

When I look up, I see why. We're too good at this now.

The Nazis aren't stupid. Every win must signal to them that we aren't just a few people. That we're large, organized, successful.

I turn to Colonel Kauffmann, who's come in to see if Léon got away, and say, "Find us a new headquarters by tomorrow."

He lifts his brows. Three weeks ago, we were happily eating Christmas ham. Now I can't wait to get out of here. I don't know why. Know only that I've left every other HQ too late and people have suffered. Presentiment is crawling like a spider through my gut.

Kauffmann nods, cape swirling behind him as he slips out.

I don't sleep. I consume cigarettes instead of food. When dawn breaks in shades of ominous gray all over the sky, the spider becomes frantic.

I send Bee to Paris, Elephant to Toulouse. I'll go with Monique, Magpie, Lucien, and our equipment to the new HQ Kauffmann has found for us.

"Let's go," I tell Magpie, who's still transmitting to London.

"I want to send all your messages first," he says.

But doom is pressing its hands on my shoulders, trying to hold me here just a little longer.

"Now," I snap.

The look on Magpie's face says plainly that I'm losing my nerve or my mind or both.

We load the cars. It takes five too-long minutes.

Above us, hanging like a metaphor, is a huge, dark cloud.

I feel as if I've escaped so narrowly I've left my shadow behind.

My new den is the cathedral in Tulle, a town clinging tenaciously to the sides of the narrow Corrèze valley. We're welcomed by the Abbé Lair, who sets out mats for us in one of the crypts, and I almost ask if we're sleeping there because he knows our futures—and prayer isn't enough to save us.

But I'm too exhausted. We sleep like the dead interred around us.

When I wake, Magpie's already gone back to the chateau to collect the spare transmitter we couldn't fit in the car. He returns a few hours later and the instant I see his face, I ask, "What happened?"

When will I stop asking that question? When will I anticipate good, rather than only knowing bad?

"Two farmers stopped me before I got there," he says. "They said the dust hadn't even settled from our cars pulling out yesterday when the Gestapo arrived. They tore the place apart searching for a Mrs. Harrison?" He shakes his head. "If I'd gone on transmitting for five more minutes . . . *Mon Dieu.* Next time you tell me to leave, I'll be the first one out."

Relief, panic, worry—those are the emotions I ought to feel. But laughter spills out. "Mrs. Harrison," I giggle, and they all stare at me in bewilderment. "Hérisson, my code name. The Gestapo think my name is Mrs. Harrison."

I don't know why it's funny. But if I don't laugh, then I'll have to think about the fact that even a week is too long to stay somewhere now, and I'm carrying a baby whose life so far has been made up of prison escapes and close shaves with the Gestapo.

I stop laughing as abruptly as I started. "Radio London," I tell Magpie. "Find out if the other sectors have called in. Because if the Gestapo found Malfonds—" I cut off the words. "Where can we hang the aerial?"

Abbé Lair points to the belfry, which ordinarily carols the jubilant march of every quarter hour, weddings, Sundays, and devotion.

But it's not a day for joy.

London tells us the Nice, Marseille, Pau, and Monaco radios have all gone silent.

I stand beneath a statue of Mary Magdalene—whose name I bear—patron saint of women and penitent sinners, my conscience aching. There's no way the Gestapo just happened upon the chateau. They knew where to look. But how?

Because we invent the idea of resistance every day and, in so doing, we make mistakes.

At Malfonds, I saw an agent write out the address of his HQ for another agent. I ordered them to burn the paper—addresses are never to be written down. That's been my rule since 1940 when Alliance had just two people, not one thousand like it does now, because we're dominoes in a chain that leads to prison. One person's strip search at a railway station with an address in their pocket leads the Gestapo to a house where more people will be found with things in their pockets, and down we all fall.

Until it happens, no one believes a piece of paper can be a noose.

So many couriers came in and out of Malfonds after the Lysander operation. One of them must have carried the Malfonds address in their pocket.

"Radio every sector," I tell Magpie. "Tell them not to carry anything in writing, not to visit other HQs. They should meet in a bar or a café, always a different one. And . . ."

I scan my list. The duke moved Paris HQ when he returned from Sarlat. Lyon, where I sent Rivière, is in a new location. My finger stops at Toulouse. Josette and the team have been in the same place since I left Béatrice's hospital.

"Tell them to clear out," I say to Magpie.

"I'll see what I can find out about the rest." Lucien leaves before I can shout *No!*

Magpie, Monique, the abbé, and I sit in a silence interrupted only by the scrape of matches, the quick blaze of fire, the inhale and exhale of smoke.

Perhaps the radios have just stopped working? Perhaps the London operator didn't pick up the signals? Perhaps . . . perhaps . . . The word and its attendant fantasies buzz like the deadly mosquitoes Christian warned me about, tempting me to believe.

It's morning when Lucien returns. He stands before me like Vallet and Schaerrer used to, young and with his future truncated because of me.

"Pau, Nice, Marseille, Monaco, and Toulouse have all been raided," he says quietly. "Basset"—our Toulouse leader—"was beaten to death. The Boche are driving stakes into our landing field at Thalamy. They found that, too."

"Your mother?" My voice is hoarse.

"Luckily she was out with Elephant. She's on her way to Paris to join Coustenoble."

Thank God. "And Marseille . . . Rivière's wife?"

Lucien shakes his head.

The Arabs in Morocco beat their breasts with their grief and I want to hit myself so hard that I black out. Madeleine, with the tap-dancing shoes, is in the hands of the Nazis. And the Gestapo will ask every captured agent for the whereabouts of Mrs. Harrison, Claire de Bacqueville, and Marie-Madeleine.

They won't ask nicely. They'll commit every kind of violence against my agents in their attempts to track me down.

I can't let them beat Madeleine Rivière.

I scribble a message to London asking them to alert all transmitters still operating and to send Léon back at the next full moon. "Have them send this out on the BBC," I tell Magpie. The sentence reads: *Marie-Madeleine has arrived safely in London and sends you her affectionate greetings.*

"You're going to London?" Magpie asks. The look on his face states plainly that I have, at last, gone mad—there are no Lysander operations scheduled until February.

Monique answers for me. "No. We just want the Germans to think she has."

I nod. "They'll stop torturing agents for my location. It'll buy us some time to run."

But where?

Only Bordeaux, Paris, Brittany, and Normandy are still sending messages. And London replies that Léon is in Algiers meeting with General Giraud, head of the French armed forces, and won't be back until the March moon. I curse. Alliance needs its chief of staff. We have to rebuild, find new agents.

London's final words are: *If you persist undoubtedly arrested stop take the February Lysander stop awaiting you impatiently end*

I crumple the paper in my hand. "The Nazis know I've previously been in Pau, Marseille, the Dordogne, Toulouse. They'll be waiting for me in all of those places. What's happening in Lyon?"

"Their transmitter is operating irregularly," Magpie tells me.

"Lyon?" Monique repeats, my brave friend as goggle-eyed as if I'd suggested Berlin. "That's like . . ."

"Walking into the lion's den," I finish.

Lyon is the center of Resistance activity in France. Because of that, the Gestapo and the Abwehr outnumber the churches, and *résistants* are tortured by Klaus Barbie with the frequency of Nazi goose steps.

But Rivière is there and the sector is still operating. I have no connection to the city. Perhaps the Gestapo will overlook it.

My newfound courage is almost shattered by the arrival of Colonel Kauffmann.

"My wife," he says, and then he starts to cry in front of us. "My brothers," he goes on. "My radio operator. My couriers. Everyone. Taken by the Gestapo."

My God. How many more will we lose in the first month of 1943?

"The Gestapo said they'll release my wife if I give myself up." Kauffmann's voice thunders through the crypt.

Food I haven't eaten presses up into my throat. I swallow, can't be sick, not now; it's not my turn. Who bargains with human lives?

Monsters.

I drop to my knees, take Kauffmann's hands in mine. How can anyone agree to leave their wife in the hands of torturers? But how can someone as senior as Kauffmann give himself up? It would be the same as marching almost everyone in Alliance into Gestapo headquarters.

Perhaps his wife is worth that much. Who am I to judge?

We're in a holy place, but I don't pray. Prayers are useless words that have never once stopped a bullet that has you in its sights. I speak the truth and leave the rest to the colonel— knowing I'll hate myself for it later.

"I need a chief of staff until Eagle is back," I tell him. "Someone to help me rebuild. I'd hoped it would be you."

I look up at him like a repentant daughter on her knees before her father. No daughter has ever repented like I do.

After a beat, the colonel nods. "Very good, Madame. We'll go to Lyon."

I hope his wife knows how brave her husband is.

Until the message goes out on the BBC tonight, the Germans will still be looking for me. So I send Kauffmann, Monique, and Lucien to take the train to Montpellier and then on to Lyon. Magpie and I will take the train going north, which leaves an hour later. We're readying to depart when Lucien returns.

My stomach contracts as if I'm about to have the baby. "Why are you back?"

"The train passed a German convoy," he tells me. "So I jumped out and came back to warn you. They've surrounded Tulle, put up roadblocks, and are checking everyone going to the station."

We're trapped.

"You shouldn't have come," I tell Lucien furiously.

He looks almost offended. "Eagle told me my most important job while he was gone was to take care of you."

It's a promise that might get Lucien killed, the boy who, two years ago, couldn't speak to me without blushing. Today, he's saved my life—for now.

My heart is racing and so is my breath, and it's bad for the baby but I can't think of anything except the terror I feel in this room in Tulle with a priest, a boy, and an Englishman, with Nazis outside everywhere, and me, the sheep whose throat they want to slit.

"I'll get the doctor," the Abbé says.

At first I think I must look as ill as I feel. But the doctor is one of our agents. So yes, maybe he can help.

Lucien, Magpie, and I wait, white-faced. We can hear Nazis shouting not far away.

Footsteps. As always, we brace, but it's the Abbé and the doctor. He takes one look at me and says, "My *Ausweis* lets me transport patients day and night, Madame. Magpie can be your worried husband. You won't have to act at all to play the part of a patient."

"And Lucien? Just as you promised Commandant Faye," I say, turning to Lucien, "so I promised your mother."

I didn't—Josette would never let me make that kind of vow. But I'll happily lie to keep this boy alive.

"He can stay in my rooms until they've taken down the road-blocks," the doctor says. "A bandaged leg and notes about gangrene ought to keep the Germans away."

I hug Lucien and the Abbé, tell him to leave Tulle, too, and off we go. By the time we reach the checkpoint, perspiration bathes my face and my whole body is trembling. But the doctor is calm—another of those moments of bravery I'll never forget.

The Nazis shine their flashlights into the car.

Magpie is sitting on the transmitter. They'll see it. They'll ask him to step out.

They'll recognize me.

"I might faint," I whisper.

Magpie begins to exclaim that I'm about to die in an extravagant manner that proves our British gentleman has many sides to him. Our performance must work, because the Nazis wave us through. Nobody breathes as the barricades are pulled away.

Above us, the moon is a guillotine blade ready to fall.

25

This Will Only Be a Tragedy
if I Sit Here Weeping

Lyon, February–April 1943

We all make it to Lyon. My friend Madame Berne-Churchill, a journalist for *Marie Claire* whom I met in the thirties, takes us in. Magpie and Kauffmann sleep on the floor. Monique, Madame Berne-Churchill, and I sleep in the bed together like children—and children are what we look like. We each have the same too-slim figure most Frenchwomen now possess, fed on rations, cigarettes, and anxiety. I touch a hand to my stomach, trying not to worry. But it's my third child and it should be obvious that I'm pregnant by now.

Monique places her hand beside mine and says fiercely, "No child of yours would dare do anything other than survive."

I try to believe her.

The next day, Kauffmann leaves the apartment to find Rivière. I pace and smoke, trying to enumerate my blessings rather than my losses.

"Sit down, Hérisson," Magpie says.

I ignore him, walk back and forth, counting.

"Hérisson," he repeats, and I whirl around, my eyes daring him to scold me so I can lash out at something.

"Help me clean this." He points to the radio, passes me a cloth, dismantles parts, and polishes them, and my urge to throw his cloth right back at him dies. None of this is his fault.

The fault is mine. I'm a mess, but it's my job to calm down so I can soothe my agents.

"Your leg needs rest," Magpie says, his eyes so kind, and it makes me realize how bad my limp must be if even he's noticed it.

I sit in the chair he draws over for me and polish.

Kauffmann returns with Lucien and Rivière. I'm shocked when I see the buccaneer from Marseille who's always had a visible energetic force surrounding him. Now he looks like a vagrant, eyes so red and swollen with fatigue and sorrow for his wife that I fear they might fall out.

"My radio operator was arrested yesterday," he says. "And Madeleine Crozet and Michelle Goldschmidt were taken to the Hôtel Terminus."

Madeleine and Michelle are two of his Lyon agents. The Terminus is the headquarters of the Gestapo, run by Klaus Barbie, the Butcher of Lyon.

"I met the prison chaplain this morning and he told me . . ." Rivière's voice is barely audible, his ebullience deceased. "They've been beaten with riding crops. Stripped naked and given electric shocks. Barbie and his mistress burned their breasts with cigarettes. But they've said nothing."

Would I be that brave? My body, which I once used to think of with pride, stripped naked before a butcher, burned and shocked and struck. There are tears in my eyes. Magpie's and Monique's, too. Lucien's jaw is a hard line of anger.

"They know," Rivière goes on, voice hoarse. "The Gestapo know there's a network led by Marie-Madeleine, with Léon Faye as second in command. They know we have animal code names. They're calling us Noah's Ark. And they want us destroyed."

First the Nazis wanted Navarre. Then they wanted me. Now they want anyone who's so much as looked at me.

I told myself I could do this until summer, that invasion

would come by then. But what if I can't last until summer? What if invasion never comes? Why would I bring a child into that world? How many more agents will I let die for this crusade?

A pit opens and I stand on its edge, ready to fall.

"Are you thinking of letting London know you're alive? They must be going mad," Magpie interrupts.

His words make me look at the people in the room with me. Magpie. Monique. Kauffmann. Rivière. Lucien. Joined now, like the five fingers of my hand.

Our first wave of agents was smashed. Our second wave, too.

But the hand is not yet broken. If I stop now, why is Michelle Goldschmidt standing silent before a butcher?

I dig down very deep inside myself to find a shred of the young woman who'd once conquered drawing rooms. "Magpie, radio London. Find out which sectors are still transmitting. But"— I frown—"the detection vans must be prowling Lyon like lions at a waterhole. You need to transmit from the outskirts of the city, not here."

Madame Berne-Churchill takes care of everything as if she's been training her whole life to be a spy. "We'll put the transmitter in my picnic basket. I like to paint, and the hills are the perfect place for painting—and for transmitting. I'll get the doctor to see you, Hérisson. And I'll cut your hair and dye it red. With your complexion, anything dark would be obviously false. My code name can be Ladybug."

I'm too awed to argue with her.

I send Lucien, Rivière, and Kauffmann out on a reconnaissance mission of the sectors in the north. Ladybug and Magpie leave with the transmitter. I plan and strategize. A few days later, we crowd into the tiny living room, which is thick with cigarette smoke, my maps pasted to the walls and folders of intelligence sitting in a pile on the dining table, ready to be carved and served.

I stand at the head of the table, remembering that the Nazis have called us Noah's Ark—a miraculous vessel of creatures trying to start the world anew.

"Mahout and the landing crew are safe," I announce. "When Mahout finds another field, we can still land planes from London. Elephant hasn't been arrested, so we can still make identity papers. Lucien's put them both in a safe house nearby. Paris under Saluki, Normandy under Sheepdog, and Brittany under Mandrill are operating as usual. It's only the south that's crippled. So we have enough to start again. Our first priority is security. We need a team to watch every sector's HQ and to accompany our senior lieutenants when they're on the move. Cricket," I say to Kauffmann, using his animal name, as I try to do in front of others, "can you recruit men for that team?"

Just as when I asked him to take on Dordogne, then to be my chief of staff, he draws his cape around him and booms, "Of course, Madame."

"I've been liaising with MI6 for the past forty-eight hours about our second priority," I go on, making sure my eyes meet those of everyone in the room. "This is the most important thing we've done so far."

They sit forward, waiting. Ready as always to do what they're asked; ready to do even more.

"The Allies need a full and detailed map of the coastline from Saint-Nazaire to Calais." I don't say what I think it means. I'm not allowed to conjecture. But there's only one reason why they've requested a complete and exhaustive picture of every cove and rip, every rock and run, every cliff and tide, every fortification and reef along such a large stretch of coastline—because they plan to invade that coastline.

Soon.

Just thinking about it makes me shiver.

"Coustenoble's up there already and can work from one end," I continue. "I've radioed Baston and asked him to nominate an agent to work from the other end. He's chosen Dragon. I need to courier them the details."

Ladybug says, "My children are fifteen and sixteen, old enough to courier messages."

"No." My voice is firm.

But Rivière, whose wife is in prison, interrupts. "We gave Alliance our hearts long ago. Our families are our hearts, so we give them, too."

In Brest alone, our agent Unicorn has nine family members working for him. Sisters, wives, children.

Kauffmann, whose wife is also in Gestapo hands, nods.

If my children were old enough, would I give them, too?

As if in reply, the baby kicks. What is he saying? That by running and worrying and making myself a target, I've already given him over to this cause?

I nod at Ladybug.

An invasion is the only way out for all of us here—and that will happen only if Alliance does its job.

So I continue our council of war. "Our second wave didn't need much training because they were mostly military men. We need men like that for our third wave."

Lucien jumps in. "Before he left, Eagle found out that the Compagnons de France was about to be dissolved. Now there are a lot of young men out there with not much to do. They hate Pétain. I've befriended some and I can get them ready to join us."

The Compagnons were a Vichy organization that recruited young men, ostensibly for construction and cultural activities, but really to keep them loyal to Pétain. Thankfully that objective seems to have failed. And they've had military training, which we can use.

I'm suddenly conscious of how much Lucien looks like Léon when he's in the thick of planning—energized, confident—and of how wonderful Léon will be as a father. Josette has been Lucien's brilliant mother, but Léon has equally fathered this boy into manhood over the past year.

Nobody ever tells you that leadership is more often about letting people go, rather than holding them close. You can't train warriors and then tell them not to fight.

And so I leap—not into the pit that opened before me a few days ago, but into Alliance's future.

"I'm creating a subnetwork of Alliance," I announce, thinking on my feet. "I'll be in contact only with its leader. I won't know anyone else in that subnetwork."

Every time there's a leak, so many sectors go down—everyone knows everything and everyone and that information is tortured out of them. But if Alliance creates a subnetwork that we fund, give intelligence priorities to, and provide the equipment for—but that we don't recruit agents for—then the agents in that subnetwork aren't implicated when one sector falls, and vice versa.

Everyone stares because it's a serious change—letting go of control, but maybe taking back safety.

"Who's leading it?" Lucien asks, a frown creasing his brow as if he's considering the merits of every man he's dealt with as Léon's adjutant.

"You," I say, hoping my voice won't waver. "You've been trained by the best."

And this boy who would once have been satisfied with a kiss on the cheek doesn't hesitate. "I won't let you down," he vows.

I'm so tired. I don't know when I last slept for more than an hour. I pass mirrors and see a woman with cropped red hair, and it makes me start every time. Because she's me, but I don't recognize her. She's the woman who, over the next two months, allocates Nice, Toulon, Marseille, Vichy, Clermont-Ferrand, and Toulouse to Lucien's new subnetwork. She's the woman who nods when Kauffmann tells her that to distinguish the security team from the regular agents, he hasn't given them animal names, but has named them Lanky, Bumpkin, Buccaneer, and Convict. She's the one who sends Coustenoble and Dragon messages when their reports about the coastline come in, telling them, *No. I need more detail. Precise measurements. Drawings. Photographs. Find a surveyor. An architect. Try harder.* She's the one who weeps when she hears that the Abbé Lair refused to leave his cathedral and was arrested by the Nazis. She's the one who reads Lucien's report with some early intelligence from one of his agents who believes the Nazis are making a new type of bomb, one deadlier than anything used by mankind before.

She's the one whose every hair stands on end at the very thought of that bomb, the one who tells Lucien to ask this agent—Amniarix is her code name—to work only on finding out more. And she's the one who rejoices when word comes through from Léon that the Allies have recognized Alliance as a military organization and made Léon a lieutenant colonel. She's the one who thinks: *If they're militarizing networks, then the invasion of France is getting closer.*

Summer 1943. Please let it be summer 1943. That's only a few months away.

But she's not the one who dreams in short pulses of sleep about a field surrounded by pink heather. It's Marie-Madeleine who does that.

It's such a glorious scene. Until a Lysander lands and Magpie and Léon step off the plane. Mahout greets them. Then, from out of the heather come the Gestapo. They press guns into Léon's back, Magpie's back, Mahout's back. A Nazi crows, *We have arrested Faye!*

I wake with a scream, my body soaked in sweat, the baby

hammering against my stomach, to find Ladybug standing over me with her arms folded, a man beside her.

"The doctor," she says crisply.

I'm too sleep-hazed to demur. Léon is flying home next week. What if my dream is premonition rather than nightmare?

"What symptoms are you having?" the doctor inquires.

"I have nightmares," I whisper. "My stomach hurts when I eat."

"How long have you been doing this?"

"Almost two and a half years."

He sighs. "My diagnosis is," he says, and I brace for dreadful news—that I've harmed the baby, that I need an operation that will take me away from Alliance—"that you've put your whole heart and soul into this. But your body needs your heart and soul. As does the baby. If you want to keep going, you need more sleep. And quiet."

But the minute he leaves the room, I call Mahout.

"You don't use any landing fields with pink heather, do you?"

"Pink heather," he repeats. "No."

"Are you sure?" I press.

"Absolutely. Why?"

I can't tell him. I'll sound like I'm losing my mind. Perhaps I am. Perhaps that's what two and a half years of fighting Nazis does to you.

"Promise you'll never use a landing field with pink heather," I say.

"All right." His tone is placatory, as if he, too, suspects I'm crazy, but I know our trusted gypsy will do what I ask.

The night Léon is due back, I don't know whether to cry with joy or weep with despair. I don't sleep. Ladybug, who's eager to meet Léon, sits up with me and doesn't complain about the cigarette smoke that chases the oxygen from the room. In the early hours, she begins making him a delicious breakfast of sausage and pâté that she's procured from somewhere.

What if the plane crashes?

What if my nightmare comes true?

What if Léon never meets his child?

Footsteps outside. I run to the door, can't risk flinging it open until I hear the password. Then I do, but . . .

It's Mahout.

I sag against the doorframe. If Mahout is here without Léon . . .

Pink heather, each bloom a lethal gun.

Monique materializes at one side, Ladybug the other.

"It was just the weather," Mahout says quickly. "They'll try again tonight."

Mahout eats Ladybug's fine breakfast. I drink coffee and smoke, smoke, smoke.

I should remember that bad news comes in avalanches. The fact that Léon's been delayed is just a light snowfall.

The unscheduled appearance of Kauffmann, Alliance's indefatigable Cricket, heralds the avalanche. He passes me a piece of paper with ink scratched over it in a shade that makes my stomach roil. "Is that . . . ?"

He nods, and for the first time ever, his voice is very quiet when he says, "Blood. A courier from Paris brought it."

It's happening again. Our Paris radio operator has been captured, has used a pin dipped in his own blood to write this note. Only one of the agents caught in the decimation of our sectors in January had his address. He's the one talking to the Gestapo.

In some ways it's a relief to know this. To not be wondering— did the Gestapo get lucky or is someone betraying us? This arrest in Paris is down to an agent who can't withstand torture. Alliance is solid. No other leaks or betrayals.

Yet.

"They broke down Saluki's door," Kauffmann tells me. "He got away. He's in a safe house with his wife."

Before I can exhale with relief at the news that Maurice and

Marguerite managed to escape the Gestapo, Kauffmann falls to his knees before me, the reverse of our positions two months ago. He looks so pitying that Monique and Lucien, who'd come in earlier with a report, each take one of my hands.

"Your children have been placed on the Gestapo's most-wanted list," Kauffmann says heavily. "They want them as bait to reel you in."

Béatrice running through fields with her newly strong hip; Christian learning how to race in a rally. Me, racing beside them.

I'm falling into that lovely world when Ladybug orders, "Get her some water."

The splash of water on my face makes my dream recede and now I'm being buried alive beneath my own hubris. Once upon a time, before Alliance existed, I thought I could give my children a future of airplanes and music and freedom and awe. But now Edouard could accuse me of being a worse parent than him, and he'd be right. The one thing I was good at—being Christian and Béatrice's mother—I stopped being good at the moment I told myself I could keep everyone safe.

In Shanghai, my English governess read *Macbeth* with me and she explained the concept of hamartia—that it was Macbeth's ambition that led to his beheading. *Ambition was his tragic flaw,* she said.

But this will be a tragedy only if I sit here weeping.

The ferocity particular to a mother pushes me to my feet. The Nazis have made my quest as personal as it can possibly be. So I will call on the courage of every hero mother throughout history to give me strength—like Jochebed, who put her son Moses into a basket in a stream and pushed him away from her empty arms to keep him safe. I will remember my daughter wincing as she made her way down the steps to me at Mougins, a girl who put love before pain. What a magnificent place a girl like that could make the world into if she was free.

So, in a voice akin to a snarl I say, "If the Nazis are going to burn my women, then I will watch those Nazis go up in flames. If they're going to hunt for my children, I will chase them all to hell. From this moment on, we will do everything we can to deliver the Allies such a detailed map of the beaches in Normandy that there won't be a single Nazi left standing after the Allies invade."

L'Amitié Chrétienne, who've saved hundreds of Jewish children, using convents to hide them until they can be taken over the border from Lyon to Switzerland, agree to help with Béatrice and Christian. My mother has a chalet in Switzerland. I think Yvonne and her husband are there, although it's impossible to get letters across the border. The children can join them once they're smuggled out of France.

Monique leaves to fetch Béatrice, Lucien to get Christian. Ladybug accompanies me out of the house with one of Kauffmann's new security agents, Bumpkin, following us. I need to live elsewhere—I can't let our new HQ fall again if the Nazis find me. And Ladybug has used her considerable organizational skills to find a nurse friend to shelter me at the Clinique des Cedres until the baby comes.

I try not to cry when Ladybug leaves. Léon's plane is due tonight and I won't be at headquarters when he arrives.

If he arrives.

"Try not to worry," she tells me. "The skies are clear. He'll come."

But all night I dream of pink heather.

26

My Court Is a Brothel

Lyon, May–June 1943

"Marie-Madeleine," I hear a voice say. "Minerva."

I bolt upright in bed, terrified, then realize it's Léon. His inhale is even more shocked than mine. "There's nothing left of you," he says, crossing the room in two strides and wrapping me in his arms.

That's when I cry. I cry and I cry and I cry like I've never cried before.

I don't know how many minutes pass before I realize I haven't even said hello, have done nothing other than sob. At last I look up, and laughter—strange, wild, incredible laughter—spills out.

Léon is an old man with white hair, a hunchback, and spectacles. I push my own hideous disguise—red wefts of hair—out of my face and Léon smiles.

"What a pair we make," he says wryly.

"Who made you up like this?" I ask through still-violent fits of giggles.

"The chief makeup man at MI6," he tells me, shrugging off the hunchback, which I can see now is a device fitted into a coat. He pulls off the gray wig and the spectacles and unfurls to his usual height.

"Does that make me Esmeralda?" I ask, trying to keep the lightness here with us.

Léon shakes his head vehemently. "Our story will have a happier ending than a Victor Hugo novel, Minerva."

Now I'm crying again, and maybe he is too, because the words have come out with such certainty I almost believe them.

Béatrice and Christian are with the Amitié Chrétienne. Tomorrow, go to Ladybug's house at midday. Stay by the window. Ermine.

I'm lost in the clouds, barely know where the ground is, or the sky, as I leave the clinic—per Monique's note—for the first time in weeks. My focus narrows to Ladybug's window and I ignore the tea she sets beside me. Luckily she refrains from ordering me to drink it; I can't keep anything down.

Then, on the street below, a familiar blond head. Monique, holding the hands of two children. One is a boy. The other a girl. Both have worried looks on their faces, but when Monique says something, they smile.

She doesn't look up. If someone is watching, the slightest gesture in my direction is like hanging a sign with my name on it over the door for the Gestapo to see. All I can do is hope they can feel what's pouring out through the glass: a love so expressive that if all the instruments in the world came together to play, it still wouldn't be enough.

Mes chéris. My darlings.

Sometime this week, they'll be smuggled into Switzerland by the peasant guides who live near the border and who now convey people for a living. There they'll stay for a length of time so uncertain it's like time has become meaningless. It won't be weeks or even months. If the Allies were invading that soon, I would know.

It won't be this summer.

I'm not even certain it will be this year.

I slide onto the nearest chair. Invasion has always hung before me like the sun teasing an airplane into believing it's possible to land on its surface. But it's still a mirage.

What I can see on the street right now is no mirage, though. So I press my forehead to the glass and take in every detail.

Christian is almost as tall as Monique. And Béatrice's stride looks so comfortable, as if she has no pain at all. There's still the faintest trace of a dimple in her cheek, and I memorize that because it will be gone the next time I see her.

What if this is the last time?

There isn't enough air. My lungs pump, but the enormity of what my children are about to do stops the breath from getting in. For the first time I wonder—can I really save them all? Léon. Béatrice. Christian. The baby. France. And if I have to choose between them, whom should I save?

How can anyone make such a choice?

I pound the glass. "Look up!" I scream. "Look at me!"

The words die as they hit the double-glazed window.

Monique moves on, the children's hands tucked in hers. I can no longer see their profiles. I can no longer see their hair. All I have left is an impression of height, a stride, and a dimple.

The words Léon is saying are impossible. That cannot, can never, have happened. There's no ground beneath my feet, only a void, and I fall down in a dead faint to a place that's dark and cold, where the ground is covered in the tiny jagged pieces of my broken heart.

"Minerva! Wake up!"

No.

"La patronne!"

The void draws away. Yes, Léon knows exactly the words to

use to rouse me. I blink back to consciousness to find him whispering my name, kneeling on the floor beside me—a pillar to rest my desolation upon.

Everything he said five minutes ago echoes appallingly in my mind.

A message came though. The border was overrun with Nazi patrols. The guides refused to cross. So . . .

Léon has no children except the one in my belly, but even he could hardly bring himself to finish: *They pointed Béatrice and Christian in the direction of Switzerland,* he'd said. *And they . . . they told them to go on alone.*

To go on alone. Across no-man's-land. Past the guns. Through the barbed wire.

A dimple in a cheek. A little girl's stride. A young boy's height.

Léon is saying two words over and over. My ears cling to them, finally process them into meaning.

"They're alive," he's saying. "They're alive. They're in a Swiss refugee camp."

The void almost opens up again, but Léon takes hold of my cheeks and says, "Don't you dare," and I realize I've frightened him more than he's ever been scared, even in a trench facing a gun.

How did two unaccompanied children make it through a patrolled border zone and into a refugee camp?

"They're ten and twelve," I whisper. "Just ten and twelve."

"They are their mother's children," he says.

Which is appallingly true. If they weren't my children, they'd never have had to face such danger in the first place. Yet face it they did. So how dare I lie down on a floor when my children did not lie down and let horror overwhelm them.

I push myself up yet again, hope that I can get a message to Yvonne so she can find my children, take them out of the camp and on to the house in Switzerland.

More than one hundred Nazi U-boats are patrolling the seas now, and London's appetite for intelligence about them is insatiable: *We can only send the Allied armada if we can get the supplies safely to Britain to build the armada,* Crane writes from London. So we surround our man Stosskopf and the seamstress Scallop with an entirely new network peopled by Triton, Cod, and Lobster, and our sea creatures deliver and deliver and deliver.

Until . . .

Monique doesn't arrive at the clinic at her scheduled time. In a prewar life, a friend's lateness meant you'd just order another coffee. Now, it's a warning.

Something is wrong.

Something is always wrong.

I'm so pregnant I can hardly move. I look like a twelve-year-old with a distended belly and have a limp so pronounced that everyone comments on it now. But I limp and pace until the telephone rings.

Monique whispers, "I've hurt my foot. I won't be able to come out."

Then she hangs up.

It's our code phrase. Someone's been arrested.

But who?

I want to scream. I'm so useless, can't run to the house—I can barely walk. I can only pace, limp, worry.

God bless the fearless women in my network. It's only about two hours later before Monique appears, gasping for air.

"Eagle, Cricket, and Magpie have been arrested," she says between each rapid inhale. "By Vichy, though, not the Gestapo. The police kept me at the house because they didn't think I was a threat. I slipped out the back when I told them I needed to use the bathroom."

Thank God we're women. Thank God the world believes us to be nothing.

But three of the people who know the most about Alliance, besides me, have been arrested. The father of my child has been arrested.

Monique's face says it all. "You need to leave Lyon. If you're caught as well, it'll be the end of Alliance."

I shake my head ferociously, remember my vow: *If the Nazis are going to burn my women, then I will watch those Nazis go up in flames.*

"Find Ladybug," I say, voice as sharp as a military tattoo. "Tell her to warn everyone in Lyon to move to a safe house or leave the city. I'll go somewhere the Nazis will never think to look." I pause for only a second. "Like a brothel. At least two madams in the city give us information. Ask if they'll house me."

So Monique leaves to find me a bed in a brothel.

I check my watch. *Where are you, Léon?* How long does it take to escape prison? And how ridiculous that I actually consider there might be an average time span for such a thing. If it was anyone other than Léon, I'd be thinking of numbers—this is his third time in prison. The number three, he once told me, is cursed. If three men lit their cigarettes from the same match in the Great War, it gave the enemy time to see the flame and shoot.

But Eagle is the fourth leaf of the clover. Perennially, ridiculously lucky.

More hours pass. Hours of my heavy belly, too many cigarettes; my uneven footsteps clicking like rosaries at a prayer vigil. Light moves in shades of white-yellow-gold over the sky. Then sienna, gray. Now black.

Night falls.

A burst of running footsteps. My God, is it my turn now?

I flee to the window. Will my belly fit through? I'll have to make it fit, make my limping, aching hip stretch enough to fling my leg up to the sill.

Before I can, the door crashes open and my heart almost bursts apart.

Léon!

He collapses on the bed, face awash with sweat, lungs sucking air, desperate to speak but utterly unable to.

So I swallow my fears, pretend I'm not the Nazis' most-wanted woman in the entire country, and lie down next to him, my stomach between us the size of the moon. I rest my hand on his chest, feel how fast his heart beats as he lifts one arm above his head, exhales, and manages to say, "I escaped."

"Shhh," I say, stroking his face.

Two minutes of his breath slowing, my hand soothing.

"We were having lunch," he finally says. "The police broke in—Vichy, thank Christ, not the Gestapo. We told them we were with Vichy Intelligence and were outraged by our arrests. The inspector began to doubt that he'd arrested the right people. While he waited for orders to come from the Germans, we realized the main door of the police station was wide open. The minute he left the room to make a call, we walked to the door, told the guard we were just going out to get some food—he had no idea who we were—and once we reached the corner, we ran like the devil."

"Thank God for bureaucratic incompetence."

The baby kicks as if it shares the same sentiment, and I laugh, taking Léon's hand and placing it on my stomach.

"And thank God for this little one," he says.

"You'll have to think of a few embellishments for that story when you tell it to everyone. That you walked out of prison to get some lunch is hardly the stuff of legend."

He laughs, too, and while he's momentarily joyful, I say, "You and the others have to leave Lyon. When the Nazis find out that you escaped again, they'll blockade the city."

"I know."

"I can't travel," I whisper. "It's only a week before the baby comes."

He moves his hand from my stomach and cups the back of my neck, drawing me in as close as my belly will allow.

Moments later, there's a light tap on the door, a signal from my nurse, whose code name is Cat.

"Bonjour, Monsieur," she says to Léon, as if it's perfectly normal for a fugitive to be lying on a bed next to a very pregnant Resistance leader in a women's clinic. "I'll get you some food."

Food. Water. The army of people who succor you. Nobody ever thinks about those things when they think of war. They think of guns and ammunition, but if nobody's fed you, you can't hold a gun.

When Cat returns, Léon devours everything as fast as he can. Then Cat tells me, "Your friend is ready for you, Madame."

Monique is back. We're off to a brothel.

Léon and I have time for one quick embrace. I pack a clean dress, underwear, my gun—I've long ago stopped thinking about lipstick—before Monique and I slip away. Outside, the night is unpopulated by stars and hides an army of hostile shadows.

A flurry of notes passes between Ladybug, Monique, and me. The Gestapo have barricaded the city, having finally worked out that I'm not in London, but Lyon.

They're tearing the city apart, furious that Noah's Ark has once again sailed off into hiding. They've tortured and deported the police inspector who let Léon slip through his fingers. They've captured Ladybug's daughter. But Ladybug is indomitable and throws herself into contacting her Red Cross friends and asking if we can use their ambulances, which are rarely searched by the Germans, to spirit Kauffmann, Magpie, Léon, and herself to Paris. I don't have the chance to say goodbye.

But Ladybug didn't say goodbye to her daughter, either.

The new HQ it's taken me five months to build has been

destroyed. It's summer 1943, the juncture I convinced myself I needed to make it to. But the invasion isn't here. And Monique and I are alone in Lyon under the protection of the ladies of the night.

Aren't we all ladies of the night now?

I don't know why the baby wants to come into this world, but he does, determinedly so. The prostitutes, who've been forced to service Germans every day for years, put on an epic performance the night my labor begins, screaming their pleasure at the top of their lungs to hide the noises I can't keep in. I'm biting the cleanest sheet Monique could find, but childbirth is all-consuming, especially when you're an anxious ruin and too thin besides.

"Oh, yes!" I hear screamed through the walls and I scream too, but my scream is curse rather than fulfillment.

Soon my cries aren't even from the pain, but from the exhaustion and the doubt that I have the strength to do this.

"You can," Monique says stubbornly, letting me crush her hand in mine.

The easiest thing would be to lie back and close my eyes and finally go to sleep. To sleep so deeply that I don't dream of pink heather—that I don't dream at all.

Instead I pace, hip hitching and popping—another pain to distract me—until I can't move, and then I stand with my forehead leaning against the bedpost, arms wrapped around it, letting it hold me up as the waves of pain push the baby down and down and finally into Monique's waiting hands.

"It's a boy!" she says, beaming.

He howls, protesting the world he's burst into. Every woman in the house lets loose too, and suddenly I find myself smiling at the ridiculousness of it all.

I've just given birth in a brothel. There's a price on my head. My lover, the father of this gorgeous boy, isn't here with me. And yet I'm so happy I want to fling open the windows and shout my joy into the night.

Monique attends to the afterbirth, having helped four older sisters deliver babies in years past. Then she slips out of the room, leaving me alone with my son.

He's so beautiful.

He has a scattering of hair, dark like his father's. He has a devilish set to his countenance, like his father's. And he has passion like his father. Listen to those lungs! I bring him to my breast and he quiets, lids closing over bright blue eyes the color of Moroccan afternoon skies.

Will Léon and I ever travel back to those skies with the son we've made together? Will he know his half-brother and half-sister?

For too many nights I've shivered in my bed from fear and doubt. Tonight, I cling to belief the same way my son clings to my finger for safety, my breast for food, my body for comfort. I believe in everything. I see it all as if it were real.

Béatrice's dimple. Christian's height. Léon's smile when he sees the baby's eyes. All of us standing, astonished, in the red dirt of Morocco beneath a sky whose color can't be named because it's one part sapphire, another part smalt, with a wash of liberty blue.

I let myself have that one night with my son. I let him sleep, wake, feed, and make tiny baby sounds beside me until dawn pushes the sun up into the sky.

Then I weep.

How many tears live inside me? Seven oceans' worth and more. They come out now, drowning Marie-Madeleine the mother. She slips below the surface, the waves closing over her as I tell Monique the god-awful truth.

"I can't keep him with me. I can't run from city to city with a baby in my arms."

"I'll take him to a safe house in the south," Monique says. "I'll look after him."

"I can't ask you to do that—"

She holds up one adamant hand. "I told you I'd do whatever it takes to make sure love survives the Nazis. This is what it takes."

The queen of the animals, the duke of Magenta called me. My subjects have teeth and talons, my court is a brothel, but my God, I've never known love like this—my animals are all blue whales, their hearts the largest that exist on earth.

My breasts are aching as the train draws into Paris. Today I will lead a Resistance network and tonight I will pump milk from my breasts because I cannot feed my son. I'm bleeding, milk-heavy yet empty, and nobody can know about any of it. Nobody can know that every time my eyes close, I see my son's tiny fist wrapped around my finger as if he knew from the day he was born that I would leave him.

The train draws into the Gare de Lyon in Paris with a defeated exhale and I leave behind the mother who has no children and become, once more, Hérisson.

27

I Named Him Achille

Paris, July 1943

scan the platform for Tiger's face, thankful I was wrong at Malfonds all those months ago—I will see Couscous again. I know Léon won't be there; it's too risky. But Couscous would never miss the chance, now that we're in the same part of the country, to escort me to headquarters.

But when I step down, it's Magpie who greets me.

"He has tuberculosis," Magpie says, reaching for my hand.

Another thing I've known but pretended not to: that I've given Couscous to this war, too.

Couscous had also known, and it was why he wouldn't rest or seek help.

"Where is he?" I ask.

"In a hospital in the Massif Central. Josette is with him."

I'm so glad they have each other—another couple forged by war. I can't risk ending his life earlier than the tuberculosis will by appearing at the hospital and bringing the Gestapo with me.

What do you say when you once would pray *Please, God* but no longer have faith in any higher power bringing mercy to those who deserve it?

You let your heart whisper *I love you, Couscous* and hope that his gut, always as highly strung as my own, can feel it.

Paris is like another Shanghai, bicycles everywhere—bicycles and poverty. Magpie and I make our way through my once-shining city to visit his orchestra: six transmitters hidden in different locations.

"I thought Tuba should have some friends. So this"—he gestures to the transmitter in the corner—"is Harp. I also have Flute, Flageolet, Ocarina, and Banjo."

"Ocarina?" I say, smiling. "So there is a sentimental soul hiding beneath the pragmatism—a man who makes orchestras out of Morse."

"Just doing my bit to keep the romance alive," he says quietly, then blurts, "How's Ermine?"

"She misses you," I say, because I want at least one moment to belong to Monique and Magpie and the thing between them that they're scared of. Monique hadn't said specifically that she missed Magpie, but she talked about him every day of the two weeks we spent together.

His smile is the absent light Paris needs, but it fades as he turns to the practicalities, explaining how his system works. The sets are located equidistant around Paris—I've made sure each operator in our major sectors has been given two, three, or four transmitters to do the same. The operators carry around only their microphotographed operating schedules and the crystals they need to work their sets.

The Gestapo has perfected its method of tracking and capture, and wireless operators now have the shortest lives of anyone in the Resistance. A transmission longer than twenty minutes gives the Gestapo the general coordinates of the radio. A second transmission of the same length from the same location allows them to track it to the exact street. The third has them sending in three detector cars, which are placed in a triangle on the street to zero in on the precise building.

We know to be on the lookout for wires traveling down the necks of men because those wires signal a Nazi operating the portable detector that will bring the Gestapo to the apartment door. Then the radio operator is captured and tortured, more arrests are made, and finally, they're put to death.

It's a chillingly efficient system for murder.

Magpie starts cursing—he rarely swears and I'm immediately on edge.

"It's taken me ten minutes to rouse London," he says, face sheened with sweat. Meaning he has only ten minutes left to transmit everything. But our stack of messages will take twice that long.

I can't operate a radio. But I can keep time. After nine more minutes, I tell him to stop. We take a vélo taxi to the next house and resume the process. As he taps the Morse, I think about the other sets around France—Adagio at Rennes, Harmonium at Carentan, Clarinet at Nantes, Scherzo at Autun, and the sets in Caen and Cherbourg, Louviers and Brittany, Bordeaux and La Rochelle. Together, they make music every day, a carefully timed symphony of coded letters played for freedom.

But if they play for just one minute longer than their twenty minutes of grace, our enemy will always win.

Headquarters is now a luxury apartment on Rue François 1er that's been loaned to us by a friend. Silk carpets adorn the floors and Aubusson tapestries and Renaissance art hang on the walls. After having lived in a brothel for a fortnight, this feels like a palace.

"Marie-Madeleine!" Maurice—who's refused to stay in his safe house—shouts when he sees me.

I throw my arms around the duke. "You should take the Lysander to London—"

He cuts me off. "So should you."

All I can do is shake my head. "Is it true that you got away because of your tattoo?"

He throws back his head and laughs, and Marguerite takes up the tale. "We escaped out the back when the Gestapo raided us, but we ran straight into a den of thieves. Luckily they were thieves who hated Nazis. When they saw the tiger on his forearm, they thought he was an underworld figure who should be looked after lest he toss them into the Seine. They hid us somewhere revolting but very safe."

Well, I gave birth in a brothel . . . I can't make the joke. I don't even know how many people beyond the tight circle of Monique, Magpie, Léon, Lucien, and Ladybug knew I was expecting. And if I even think of my son, let alone speak of him, I'm terrified of what might break.

So I wrap my arms again around two people who should be taking one of our escape routes to safety but who are still running Paris HQ. And I hear myself say, "Let's go out for dinner."

"Dinner?" Maurice stares as if I've said I want to go to prison.

"Choose one of the blackest of all black-market restaurants. Somewhere packed with Germans. They'd never think I'd dare to dine among them."

"Dinner," the duke repeats, eyes fixed on me, and I wonder what he sees. The red hair that Monique cut into a bob. The frame that's ten kilos lighter than it used to be.

The pain in my eyes.

"Let's go out for dinner," he agrees.

We walk along the footpaths of a Paris whose vanished statues and silent bells and lopped trees are interposed with women whose hats are decorated with a red ribbon, a white flower, and a blue feather—pride and spirit stitched with a couturier's thread.

Outside the brasserie, there's a man waiting. He has gray hair and a monstrously stooped back. We cannot clutch each other out here on a public sidewalk and I cannot tell him the name of his son nor the color of his eyes, because then Léon's legs will buckle—hearts can take only so much pain before they toss you on the ground. So we just smile, and our eyes promise, *later,* and in we go—the hunchback, the redhead, the Englishman, the tattooed former flying ace, and his wife.

"Am I supposed to be your arthritic grandfather?" Léon murmurs, the back of his hand brushing mine.

"What does that make him?" I indicate Magpie. "My father?"

Magpie, who's six years younger than me, rolls his eyes, and suddenly it's like one of those carefree nights from before the war that we thought would unspool forever. Music, laughter, and tables crowd this restaurant that's exactly as I requested: steak, chips, and caviar, with a side of Nazis.

The waiter brings us two bottles of Beaujolais, and Léon lifts his glass and calls out to the Germans at the next table, "Your health, gentlemen!"

A laugh escapes me. What are we doing? Just what we need to, perhaps. My eyes catch Léon's and in them I see exactly what sits at the back of mine—shame, marbled with pain.

We've left our child to be raised by others for an unknowable period of time.

But here in this room filled with a hundred Nazis, men who've killed my friends, I know I can't keep recalling the tiny fist wrapped around my finger and fight the Germans, too. A moment's inattention from me and three thousand people will die—because that's how big Alliance is now. And as surely as I know that I love my newborn son, I know that the Allies' invasion plans will be delayed without the information we send them—and then thousands more will die in those extra months or years that the Germans are allowed to rule over France.

So I pick up the menu and say, with just the faintest trace of a quiver in my voice, "I haven't eaten caviar in three years."

"Then we'll order caviar," Marguerite says.

So we eat caviar and drink Beaujolais and the night is full of humor and warmth and love until right near the end, when we all fall silent at the same time and I feel the ghosts of our dead or captured comrades take a seat beside us, place their hands on our shoulders, and say, *Gather your strength. The worst is still to come.*

Léon walks me to my new lair where, as soon as the door is closed behind us, he wraps his arms around me. Caught between us is the ghost of our child.

Léon's shoulders are shaking through the awful hunchback coat as if he's imagining a teenage boy hurling words at him: *You weren't there when I was born. You didn't meet me for months.* So I don't cry, not now.

"Come and lie down," I whisper.

I slide off his coat and slip off my dress. I'm still bleeding from the birth, but I need my ankles to wind around his, our elbows to lock together, our torsos to touch. Just like the scent and warmth of skin calms a baby, I want my soul to tell Léon's that everything will be all right.

I trace my fingertips over his chest like I did the first time I lay in a bed in Le Lavandou and drew the tattoos of my love onto his skin. "I named him Achille," I whisper. "It's one of Christian's middle names, and anyone born in war needs the name of a warrior. He's so like you. I don't think there's much of me in him at all. It's like—"

I halt, paralyzed by what I'd been about to say. *It's like he's the future Léon.* Which would mean the man beside me now is only the past or the present, but I have to believe he's my future, too.

Despite every effort, a tear slides down my cheek. Léon raises himself to his elbow and threads his hand into mine, eyes the same as they were when I met him in Vichy three years ago, glittering with stars.

"Marry me," he says urgently. "Whatever Méric thought

about divorce before the war, he won't think now. He's fighting in North Africa on our side. He never joined the Germans. War will have shown him how petty grudges are."

It's perhaps just another dream to imagine that I truly can engage myself to Léon, but there's still so much space inside me to hold on to dreams. It's how I was raised—to believe in more than seems possible.

It's why I'm still here beyond the time I thought I could endure.

I pull Léon's head down to mine and kiss him like I've never kissed him before. When he draws back, he says huskily, "I'm looking forward to when you're recovered. But in the meantime . . ." He looks uncertain. "I don't know if that was a no or a yes."

"Marie-Madeleine Faye," I say, grinning.

Léon kisses my neck so hard that it tickles, and I laugh, head tipped back, the sound accompanying the symphony of radios tapping out optimism all over France.

28

He's Either a Fool or a Traitor

Paris, July 1943

E ven though Paris is the most Gestapo-infested city in France, the days pass in exuberant peace compared to the chaos of Lyon. My new set of identity papers declare that I'm Pamela Trotaing, yet another name in a life full of them. Under that guise, I run Alliance HQ from one office while the duke of Magenta runs Paris HQ from the office beside. I stand in front of my maps with my hands on my hips, daring France to try to get the better of me. And I get things done.

I have Mahout find a new landing field for the Lysander pickups, one that's closer to Paris. I assign Ladybug to manage the addresses we use for letterboxes and safe houses, tell Kauffmann to get his security team to retrieve some papers Léon left in Lyon and to evacuate Elephant, who's still trapped in a safe house there. I look at microphotographs of sections of a map that Dragon sends me from Normandy, the map he was working on with Couscous until Couscous became too ill, a map that makes me smile. This is exactly what the Allies need. I send him more men so he can document everything faster, tell MI6 to get ready because soon we'll have everything they require.

It's all going so well until the agents from Kauffmann's security team come back from Lyon with only the films Monique had hidden the day the police arrested everyone.

"Where are Léon's reports?" I ask Kauffmann.

"Bumpkin and Lanky said that's all there was," he replies, his cape looking threadbare today, and I make a note to ask Ladybug to find some fabric to have it mended, because that cape is emblematic of the noble spirit of Alliance.

But first, the missing documents. I confer with Léon, who looks similarly worried.

"I've worked with Kauffmann long enough to know he's telling the truth," Léon says. "But if those documents are in the wrong hands . . ."

I ask a terrible question. "Is it possible an Alliance agent took them?"

Léon doesn't ask, *To do what?* We both know I'm talking about traitors again. The Gestapo would pay someone a lot of money for those papers.

"Go to London," Léon says suddenly. "MI6 is ordering you to go. They know as well as you do that the Gestapo's most-wanted woman in the country shouldn't be in Paris, especially if someone's trading those papers with the Nazis."

"Not now. Now when I've only just gotten everything working smoothly again."

Léon's exhale is frustrated. "Then will you at least go everywhere with a bodyguard? Please?"

I acquiesce so he feels he's had a win of sorts.

From then on I'm accompanied everywhere by Pierre Dayné, a family friend who's been working for Alliance since my first trip to Paris in 1941, and who also works with the French secret police. He can pretend I'm a prisoner under arrest if there's any sign of trouble, which will get us through roadblocks and identity checks.

Not long after, Bertie Albrecht, the woman who helped start the Combat resistance network, is arrested. The news causes a council of war at HQ.

"It's rumored she was beheaded," Léon says to me in a voice

so abrupt I'm silenced. His hands are shaking when he adds, "My God, that must never happen to you."

Kauffmann, Elephant, Magpie, Lucien, and Rivière all nod in furious agreement.

I press my hand to my mouth. "They wouldn't . . ." I imagine Béatrice and Christian finding out later that their mother had had her head put to the sword. "Excuse me."

I lock myself in the bathroom.

Léon doesn't even wait a minute before he raps on the door. "You need to go to London," he says through the wood.

"No," I say. "An absent figurehead is—"

"Better than a dead one," he cuts in with quiet fury. "Minerva, I know you decide everything with your heart, and I love you for that, but this time, please decide with your head. Because I want you to keep it."

I open the door because his voice is too loud. I know he's scared. Or maybe he's angry. But not at me.

"Not yet," I say, fixing my eyes on him.

"Promise me," he says in an urgent whisper, "that if one more thing happens, you'll go."

"I'll go if anything more happens to the network," I say, which isn't exactly the same thing, and he exhales with both frustration that I didn't promise more and relief that I promised something.

I should know by now that these things don't come in trickles, but in floods. Jean Moulin, De Gaulle's head of Resistance activities in France, is the next to be arrested. Not just arrested, but tortured and killed by Klaus Barbie in Lyon. And I thank God that I left Lyon when I did, that the baby hadn't come a month later.

Hérisson, you're needed in London, the message comes through from MI6 again. Léon watches me as I crumple it in my fist.

The next day, Bumpkin arrives at HQ with the news that Elephant was caught on his way to Marseille with all our forging equipment.

"How the hell did you let that happen?" Léon barks.

"I thought it was a simple job," Bumpkin says miserably. "So I gave it to Buccaneer and Lanky. Lanky was the lookout, and on his way to the meeting place, he saw the Gestapo nearby. So he ran to the tram stop to warn Elephant—"

I explode. "The tram stop! He thought Elephant was coming by trolley car with three transmitting sets, stacks of identity forms, explosives, and guns? Was Lanky really trying to warn him or was he running away like a coward? Lookouts never leave their post. Because this is what happens when they do!"

"He's a smart kid," Bumpkin says. "He panicked. He wants to apologize to you in person."

"Not a chance," Léon snaps.

I agree. Nobody except Alliance's top lieutenants and most trusted couriers know the address of HQ.

"Then he's either a fool or a traitor," I tell Bumpkin. "You're forbidden to bring him anywhere near headquarters. And you're forbidden to ever delegate a security job involving an Alliance lieutenant again."

Bumpkin's trembling. These boys are all so young. They don't understand consequence. But when Bumpkin's gone, Léon confesses the biggest consequence of all.

"Elephant had my duplicate notebook," he tells me. "He took it before I left Lyon in case I was caught on the way to Paris. It's in code, but it lists addresses of safe houses and HQs and letterboxes." He pauses. "They'll torture him for the key to the code. And he won't tell them anything."

Which means the torture will be worse than anything that's happened before.

Elephant has two daughters here in Paris.

"Everyone's still talking to everyone else, delegating when they ought to be doing," I say despairingly, stopping when Kauffmann hurries in.

"They're very sorry, Madame," he says to me, clearly having just spoken to Bumpkin. "Give them a chance."

He looks so much like a liege on bended knee that my anger dissipates a little. "I'll give them one more chance," I tell him. "Confine them to Lyon for now. They can run Rivière's security, get more experience."

As soon as Kauffmann's gone, Léon pounces. "You told me that if one more thing happened to the network, you'd go to London."

"Let me sleep on it," I say, and he growls in frustration.

But I don't sleep. My mind is a hornet's nest. I can't abandon Alliance. But nor can I let myself be caught. If that happens— and it isn't egotistical to say it—Alliance won't survive. *A goddess and her worshippers,* Léon had said to me at Christmas. I'm no goddess, but I know I'm Alliance's heart. You cut out a creature's heart and it dies.

It's already thrashing.

The following afternoon, Lucien appears at HQ even though he should be in the south. He tells us the Gestapo surrounded the house he was staying in. He just managed to escape out the back.

"They knew my code name," he tells me.

The creature flails.

Is someone talking? Are these things just accidents? Or—are we the kill, cornered by the mistakes we didn't know we were making?

"You're going to London on the next Lysander," I tell Lucien. "MI6 wants to give you more training. After a month of looking, the Gestapo will give up. Then you can return."

"London?" He whoops the way we all used to, back when we had a headquarters in Pau and nobody had died and Coustenoble and Schaerrer and Vallet were a tricolor and Lucien just a fifteen-year-old boy nursing a harmless crush. "I've always wanted to see London."

Dayné, my bodyguard, appears, ready to escort me back to my secret apartment. I escape with him, Léon's eyes drilling into my back. Two things have happened now, not just one. And I'm still not leaving.

We take our seats on the Métro. At the next station, a man sits opposite, and it takes only a moment for me to realize I know him. An officer acquaintance of Navarre's, one who snubbed me in Vichy and who's since been working for Laval.

He blinks and, despite the red hair, recognition crosses his face.

I'm seconds away from being caught.

Dayné yanks me to my feet and we make it out through the train doors a millisecond before they close and we're chopped in two.

"He'll pull the emergency brake," Dayné yells. "Run!"

Métro stations have more stairs than the Eiffel Tower, and my strength isn't what it should be. But I throw myself at each step in a frenzy.

We make it back to headquarters, where I collapse into a chair. Before Léon can say anything, I tell him, "I'm going to London."

July 18 is the date set for me to fly out. On the night of July 16, I dream of pink heather: Léon and Magpie stepping out of a Lysander into a field profuse with pink heather, the faceless men closing in, one of them crowing, "We've arrested Faye! We are delighted."

I wake with the word *No!* caught in my mouth. In my dream, my cries were loud; in reality, I'm making no more sound than a star in the night.

I lie perfectly still and force myself to replay everything. Perhaps from one tiny detail—a signpost, a church—Mahout will be able to identify the landing field and we'll never use it again.

Perhaps if I remember what the Nazis were wearing, I'll know the time of year. But I finish that horror movie drenched in sweat and with no idea where the field might be.

I call Mahout. "You're sure there are no fields with pink heather? Masses of heather. Not just a bush or two?"

"You asked me never to use a field with pink heather. And I never will." Mahout's sincerity is unmistakable.

"I'm sorry," I tell him.

"Don't be," he replies. "Our instincts are all we have left in war. I'd be more sorry if you didn't trust your own."

The day before I leave, Monique arrives at my apartment, and before I even have to ask, she says, "Achille is healthy and happy. Cat has him in hand." Cat, my nurse from Lyon, will share the care of my son with Monique, swapping places every fortnight.

"Does he cry a lot?" I whisper.

She beams. "He just learned to smile."

My son smiles. But not for me.

I disappear into the bathroom, brace my hands on the sink.

First smile, first laugh, first food, first word. First wave, first tooth, first hug, first step. Someone else will delight in all those firsts. The memories of those moments will live in rooms not my own. All I will possess is the ache . . . and the longing.

My breasts let down, my milk not quite gone. All that food I'm making but will never feed my son.

The cry that tries to escape is like a baby's—unfettered, violent. I shove my knuckles against my mouth, double over until my breasts stop weeping, too.

Then I haul myself up. In the mirror, my eyes are two stark orbs of blue in the thin face of a woman swaying on an edge too narrow to balance on. Dreaming of disaster. Crying almost every day.

There are so many reasons to go to London—to request guns

to arm the groups we're readying to fight, to plan for the invasion that must soon be coming. But now I see what Léon has perhaps already seen; I need to go for my own sanity. I need one month where I don't have to run and hide, study every face, every shadow, every step.

If I'm to see the end of this fight, I need to take a moment to heal.

"Why are there so many people here?" I ask Léon when I arrive at HQ.

"They've come to honor you," he says. "To say goodbye."

He points to the adjoining room, where Marguerite is holding up a blue silk dress of the kind I used to wear before I understood that gowns and parties were the province of people who took being alive for granted.

"To represent France to the British," Marguerite scolds me, "you need to be the Marie-Madeleine who once raced cars across deserts. Wear this one tonight, and I've laid out three more to be packed."

"Remember when I used to write about couture?" I say. "Maybe our lives were silly and meaningless before. But there's something to be said for making people pause and look at beautiful things for just a minute or two, isn't there?"

So I let her style my hair and make up my face. I put on the dress and twirl for Léon with a mischievous smile. The bodice emphasizes the inward curve of my waist, and the skirt is cut seductively to mid-thigh on one side. On the other, it tumbles in an orgy of silk to the floor, and I feel like the most beautiful woman in the world, because that's how potent Léon's smile is.

He holds out his hand. "You've surpassed gorgeous and claimed a brand-new word—*magnisquise.*"

"*Magnisquise?*"

"Half *magnifique,* half *exquise,* and wholly and completely *magnisquise.*"

I reach up onto my toes and brush my lips against his. "I love you."

"Me too, Marie-Madeleine Magnisquise," he says with a smile that wraps so entirely around my heart it's hard to breathe.

The bar we use as a letterbox is closed to the public for our party, and we eat food that the proprietor must have sold half his soul to commandeer. We drink wines that have been in the cellar for years. We talk about what we love.

"Bouillabaisse!" Rivière declares. "On a Marseille terrace with my wife beside me and the sun making the city glow like fire. And never mixing the broth with the fish." He smiles at me, recalling that long-ago first meeting when he shouted, *Good God, it's a woman!*

"My mother's chicken pie," Lucien says. "In the kitchen of the pension in Pau on a winter's night with the fire blazing and the pie almost too hot to eat. But it smells too good, so you can't wait, and it burns your tongue and warms you up—not just your stomach, but your life."

Beneath the table, Léon reaches for my hand and I hold on in lieu of weeping.

Across the table, Monique and Magpie are holding hands too, as if Vallet, while never forgotten, will hurt her heart a little less as she makes room for another. Only Magpie could ever be good enough.

I want this night to last forever.

We wait until almost curfew before we leave and Léon murmurs in my ear, "We still have a half hour. Let's walk."

I haven't strolled along a street for years, let alone a street in Paris. As a woman wanted by the Gestapo, I shouldn't stroll now. But I'm leaving tomorrow, and that makes me rash because fate wouldn't be so cruel as to let me be captured when I'm only hours from safety. So I slip my arm around Léon's waist and we walk along the Champs-Élysées, the constellations above us bright and numerous in the blackout. The streets are untroubled by traffic, the leaves of the horse chestnuts a brilliant chartreuse, and I can smell the last summer flowers—precious gifts that endure despite the very worst of times.

And memory turns a kaleidoscope that re-forms *ma patrie et ma vie* with each click. There I am in a Vichy square, staring at my first-ever Nazi. There I am on the porch of the Pension Welcome in Pau, the scent of Josette's trout tickling my nostrils. Walking along the Corniche in Marseille, the spires of boats beckoning the faithful down to the water and the Notre Dame de la Garde standing like a lighthouse of hope above it all. The Dordogne, place of elves and magic and airplanes guided in by the silent moon where, in a bed in a chateau, I told Léon about our son. Lyon, where the Saône and the Rhone were two rivers of silk circling the city in brilliant blue as I gave birth to that son. Paris, where my cheeks are pink-tinged from the Bordeaux, the taste of *tarte Tatin* lingers on my tongue, and the reminiscences of heroes have filled my night.

Then Léon picks up my left hand and slides something onto my ring finger. I look down and see that it's no grand jewel, just a simple band of gold with letters inscribed over its surface. I trace over the words, see they're written in my code. Unreadable to anyone except us.

Marie-Madeleine Faye and Léon Faye.

I look up into the face I've kissed and loved, the face that still makes me shiver whenever I see it, and I know—it will make me shiver until the end of time. Not until the end of our time, but beyond that. For as long as I have thoughts, Léon Faye will make me shiver.

"I don't have any legitimate powers," Léon says, voice fierce, "but I have the power of honor and right and resolve and they are no small things. So by those powers, I now declare us man and wife."

"I definitely prefer," I say, voice wobbling a little, "being Marie-Madeleine Faye to being a hedgehog."

Léon's smile is the same mix of devil-may-care and charm he first turned on me in Vichy in 1940. "And I prefer being Marie-Madeleine Faye's husband to being Eagle."

"I love thinking of you as an eagle. Soaring above all of this. Safe."

"Safe," he repeats. "God, that's all I want. Do you think . . ." He hesitates, blinks, tries again, "Will I ever . . ."

Now my heart is cracking open. I know what he's asking: *Will I ever meet my son?*

"Yes," I say, ferocious now, too. "You'll hold him. You'll love him. You have to, because . . ."

I falter, don't know how to explain that even the love we have for each other does not reach the limits of love. There is another kind entirely—the love of a parent for a child, which is the largest thing in the world, and it's the only gift I want to give him.

"You will," I repeat, and standing there on that Paris night, I believe in that promise like I believe that we are such a stronghold of hope nothing can ever tear us down. Not the swastika flags cracking like whips around us or the scowl Paris wears under the rule of a despot. My promise will stand because promises made by hearts in blacked-out cities on wedding nights are like the aqueducts and amphitheaters that remain in France from Roman times: monuments that have outlasted civilizations and flags and despots. They may be damaged and broken, but they are never destroyed.

At 4:55 the following afternoon, I walk, hat brim pulled low, suitcase in hand, to the corner of Rue François 1er. I climb into the vélo taxi beside Dayné and we pedal away.

As we turn onto the Champs-Élysées, I see an old hunch-back smoking a cigarette and pacing back and forth. And I thank God for the vélo taxi, which ambles rather than speeds, and in those precious, ambling seconds, the hunchback turns to face me, and his damp, glittering eyes betray the fact that the smile on his face is riven with tears.

But seconds do not last forever and soon the man is gone and all I have left is the memory and the pain.

Always the pain.

29

You Matter

Paris and London, July 1943

t the Gare de l'Est, I'm very aware that I'm in the open with a price on my head that makes me a lucrative investment for any Nazi, criminal, or desperate Frenchman. My hat is pulled so low I can barely see Lucien waiting farther along the platform.

We take separate carriages to Nanteuil-le-Haudouin, where Mahout meets us and leads us to a roadside ditch that we all climb into. There, I finally embrace Lucien.

"Any word from Amniarix about the new weapon?" I ask.

"It'll come on the next Lysander," Lucien says, face grave, and my gut recoils, unable to imagine what further horror the Nazis have in store for us.

"Tell her to be careful," I say. "MI6 needs that intelligence, but she needs to stay alive."

We're interrupted by the sound of an arthritic car driven by the doctor who helped me escape from Tulle. "Mahout tells me you never accept anything," I say once we're on our way. "Not even money for fuel. There must be something I can give you."

The doctor considers, then says, "I'd love a good bar of soap. There's nothing worse than visiting the sick without really clean hands."

So I add soap to the list of gifts I'll buy in London. A robe for

Coustenoble. A rattle for Achille. Books for Béatrice and Christian. Underwear for Monique and Marguerite. And something perfect for Léon.

At 10:00 P.M., the doctor parks beside a corn rick. On the field before us, Mahout's team is engaged in a strange kind of dance, marking out the shape of an L where the plane will land.

"It's so peaceful," Lucien says.

Yes, the moon is a benevolent eye keeping watch over us, redirecting the clouds to other skies. The air is as soft as a lullaby.

But the longer we wait, the more the moon starts to seem too bright. It's casting our silhouettes onto the ground, beckoning the Nazis toward us. A breeze carries every sound: the rustle of a shirt; our thoughts, which are a too-loud coalescing of worry. *Will the Germans come? Will the plane find the field? Will the weather change?*

I try to think of the baby.

Then, figures glide onto the field. Mahout and his team, who've heard the distant thrum of a plane. They fire up their flashlights, one positioned at the head of the L, another at the heel, and the last at the toe. Mahout flashes the Morse letter *M* into the sky; the Lysander replies.

And everything is beautiful again. Mahout looks like a sorcerer, hands sweeping elegantly through the night, summoning the plane to him.

It deposits itself precisely at the head of the strip, then taxis toward Mahout. He keeps the Lysander steady as I haul myself up the ladder, Lucien following. No more than two minutes pass by before the plane taxis away and we're in the air and on to London, a land that isn't ruled by Nazis.

A driver takes us from Tangmere Airfield in the south of England to a delightful cottage surrounded by flowers. "It's like a fairytale,"

I whisper to Lucien, who's so stunned by all this careless beauty that he can't speak.

I step out of the car and a voice cries, "You must be Marie-Madeleine. I'm Barbara. And this is my husband, Major Bertram."

Barbara ushers us inside, explaining that they use their cottage to look after travelers who've just arrived from France.

Crane, whom I met in Madrid, is waiting for us. "Golly, we've been worried about you," he says. "You look like you need a good supper. Luckily we have that in hand."

That's when I see something even more spectacular than the cottage. A dining table laden with eggs and bacon and bread and butter and a strange yellow fish and tomatoes and beans.

I hear myself swear softly in French, then clap a hand to my mouth. "*Pardon*. I've spent the last three years surrounded by men—"

Barbara smiles. "I'd be more surprised if you'd never uttered a curse living beside those damn Germans."

I laugh. Then I eat. And at last, I sleep.

Bang! Bang, bang!

My eyes fly open. Someone is pounding on the door. Gestapo. I'm on my feet instantly. Why did I sleep? I never sleep.

"Marie, it's time to go to London," a voice calls.

Who's Marie? London?

I blink and remember—I'm in England. There's no Gestapo here.

I open the door to find Crane smiling brightly. It's too much. Too much joy. Too much food. Too many flowers. Not enough agents and family and friends.

I should never have left them.

Desolation lands in my stomach alongside all the food from

hours ago. I want to throw up. The tears come in such a rush I have no chance of stopping them.

"Oh dear," Crane says.

There's nothing to cry about. And I don't want Crane to think I'm a weak woman who shouldn't be left in charge of MI6's most important Resistance network. But I can't stop. I don't even know where the tears are coming from, just that they won't be brooked.

I'm fraying, like an old dress whose threads have been tugged one too many times. Would a man fray, too?

But a man will never know what it's like to watch a baby slide out of his body, all the while knowing he can only hold that child for one short week.

I don't even realize Crane has left the room until he returns with another man. A doctor, who gives me a similar prescription to the one I was given in France. Rest. Peace.

He also hands me vitamins. A little pill for my body. But nobody has a prescription for my soul.

I've left that behind me in France.

"So this is the terrible woman who had us all scared," Claude Dansey, the head of MI6, says to me one day later in the luxurious hotel room I've been given to live in. It's so grand I hardly dare sit on the chairs.

Dansey takes my hands. He's balding, with round glasses that make him look like a discontented pig, which is an uncharitable thought, especially as his next words are, "It's good to have you safely here."

"Just for a month," I say, something weeping inside me still—a strange need to get back to the place most people want to run from.

"We'll see," he says in that way men have of pretending to listen to a woman. "Averages tell us a Resistance leader can't last more than six months. You've lasted over two and a half years. It's sheer witchcraft."

Before I can respond, he launches into a profusion of gratitude. "We're indebted to you and to Alliance. We wouldn't be planning an invasion without everything you've told us. Thank you."

I relax a little. Stress and anxiety have misaligned my gut's compass. This man is on my side, a fact proven when he says, "What can I do for you in return?"

"I want to write to my children in Switzerland."

I don't say, *And my baby*. Nobody in England can know that I've had a child. An illegitimate baby is a sin so colossal they might throw me out of my own network. I also don't want them to think of me as a woman. Because *woman* still equals *weakness* in the eyes of most military men. *Especially the one in front of you,* my gut whispers, still mistrustful.

Dansey concludes our meeting by saying, "In the meantime, relax. I shall be very angry if I hear that you're working."

"I'm here to work until the Nazis are gone."

It seems impossible that I can sit and put uncoded words into a letter that Béatrice and Christian will soon receive. I fill pages and pages, trying to picture their faces, but the faces I see are the ones from a couple of years before, not the faces they must wear now. But I know their hearts, and it's to those two strong hearts that I write, hoping they don't imagine me wallowing in a London hotel room while they've been in a Swiss refugee camp for months before finally being found and taken by Yvonne to my mother's chalet.

When I've finished, I walk to the MI6 offices and begin the work I need to do, despite what Dansey said. I start in the building—a whole building!—dedicated to radio transmissions, the Tower of Babel come to life. Into it flow coded messages in all languages. Hundreds of men and women seated at desks listen and decode. I tell the head of this operation that Magpie wants the British to call us first, rather than the other way around.

"Out of the question," he says.

I grit my teeth. I bet he goes home to the same house each night, doesn't scramble to six different addresses like Magpie does.

I try again. "I'm tired of listening to radio operators pleading, *Come on, pick up,* risking their lives because you aren't answering. Last month, ten minutes went by before Magpie could rouse anyone. That's half the time he has to spare. If you call us at the agreed time, we'll pick up straightaway. Then we can use the entire twenty minutes to transmit messages. It makes perfect sense."

"Tell them to change frequency. That's how they'll avoid detection," the obstinate little man replies.

"Have you ever seen a Gestapo detection-finding van?" I ask coolly, and he blinks, offended by my persistence, and I want to strangle him for insisting on these laws that someone who's never been in France has made.

London might be a world where I'm meant to bow down to maleness and might, but my hip's too stiff for bowing.

I march to Dansey's office and tell him I want Magpie brought over at the next moon. If anyone can show that idiot exactly what a radio operator is risking, he can.

"All right," he says pleasantly. "But—"

I cut him off with a feminine little smile. "I'm going shopping," I say before he can tell me to relax again.

I meet Lucien on Oxford Street. He's doing a training course to land heavy bombers in his sectors, and the responsibility has made him grow about another foot taller, almost matching Vallet's height. And here, without the threat of Nazis, the memory doesn't ache. It makes me smile to think of how lucky I am to have been granted the privilege of working with men like these.

"Shall we?" I say, holding out my arm. He takes it with a grin, and we set off for Selfridge's, which is full of glorious things.

I locate the men's robes and it's my turn to grin as I tell Lucien, "You'll have to model it. Coustenoble deserves the best."

He can't argue with that so, beneath the saleslady's bewildered eye, I have Lucien try on about a dozen different robes, rejecting black, red, and green in quick succession.

"Would your . . . er . . . your . . ." She looks back and forth between Lucien and me, hoping for a clue as to how we're connected. She tries again. "Would the gentleman like it in navy?"

"What do you think, dear wife?" Lucien says. "Does navy suit me?"

An actual giggle escapes me. I don't think I've giggled for years. "You always look dashing in navy, *mon cher*."

The saleslady darts off to get navy and I erupt into laughter.

"You've learned too much devilry from Léon," I tell Lucien. "I'm ten years too old to be your wife."

"Commandant Faye is about ten years older than you," Lucien counters, and I shake my head, still laughing, unable to believe that Lucien can now flirt with the best of them.

I settle on the grandest and most English of all the robes. When I picture Coustenoble opening it and laughing, it makes me smile, as does the sight of Lucien purchasing the navy robe for himself.

"Have you already met a nice English girl you want to impress?" I ask, and he blushes redder than the pillar boxes outside.

"Aha!" I cry. "Bring her over for dinner."

He rolls his eyes but looks happy as I help him choose shoes for Josette and a lovely brooch for his English *amie*. "I'll probably never see her again after I leave," he says as the saleslady wraps the gift. "But sometimes when you can't sleep, it helps to think that maybe someone is remembering you. That you mattered, just a little."

Oh, *mon Dieu*. I want to wrap a bandage around his heart. All I can do is reach for his hand and tell him, in the sparkling jewelry department of a store full of dreams, "You matter. To me. To Alliance. To the world. Whenever your friend looks at that brooch, she'll know she was lucky to have met one of the best men in the world."

He tips his head back and stares at the ceiling, blinks, exhales. Then he says to me, "Forged by one of the best women."

I do my best to stand dry-eyed beside my lieutenant. There have been enough tears already.

So I slip my arm into his again and we walk away from the sentiment but take with us the affection as we set ourselves to purchasing a dozen cases of soap for the doctor; stockings and underwear for Monique, Marguerite, Bee, and Ladybug; and gifts for my children.

In one of the shops, a pair of cuff links catches my eye. Two eagles.

I ask the sales assistant, "I don't suppose you have a hedgehog?"

"We could have one made if you wish."

The eagle and the hedgehog cast in silver: real, solid, sparkling.

30

A Cunning Little Shit

London, August 1943

éon transmits messages to me daily, each with plans more daring and elaborate to prepare an army of Frenchmen to support the Allied invasion. Crane and I pore over them, considering which are most feasible and least dangerous—until Crane disappears. He's replaced by Tom, who's so British his upper lip doesn't move when he speaks. His body and personality resemble a stiff little plank.

"Dansey and I don't agree with that," he says almost every time I put a proposal in front of him.

I remind myself to use my head—to not wear my emotions like a bright red dress. "I think you should listen to the people who are actually *in* France."

"And I think," he says very coolly, "you should remember your place."

It's all I can do not to throw a paperweight at him. I'm wearing trousers, have a revolver and a packet of cigarettes in my purse rather than a compact, but I still have breasts and longish hair and dainty features, and that's enough to make me inferior.

I press my hands onto his desk and say in a voice so crisp you could snap it, "I remember my place every night when I'm lying in my comfortable bed here in London. I remember my place because normally my place is a burrow, a cave I might spend a day in—or a week if I'm lucky—before the Gestapo find it and I'm once again placeless, relying on friends who value freedom more than their lives to give me a different burrow for another day or week. My place is the air, the void, the very edges of existence. And from that place, I manage three thousand agents, the only network that covers the whole of France. So I think the only person here who needs to remember his place is you."

His face mottles purple like a turnip.

I stalk out onto the street, then slow, still unused to being able to walk freely. The sky here in England has never made acquaintance with a van Gogh paint box. Its palette is like those mordant Whistler oils, and in the gloom, the questions pile up. How can Dansey say he's indebted to Alliance but then send Crane away? What's the best way to manage these men and still get what France desperately needs: a successful Allied invasion as soon as possible?

The British need Alliance. But I need the British, too.

I cross to St. James's Park, bypass the air-raid shelters and the flowerbeds given over to vegetables, and sit on an empty bench. The vista is of rubble and rain. Even the people are gray. No tricolor feathers adorn their hats. I wish for a moment that I hadn't recolored my hair to its natural blond—a redhead here would be like a shocking pink flamingo against a backdrop of snow, and wouldn't it be nice to be that visible, just for once, rather than always trying to be the night, the shadow, the eclipse, but never the sun.

Someone takes the seat beside me and I stiffen. I don't turn—you never turn to see who's taken the next seat unless you want to be arrested.

But Crane's very welcome voice says, "I've debated whether or not I should tell you this. When Dansey found out that the person who ran our most successful network was a woman, he was . . ." Crane chooses the next word carefully. "Horrified."

So my gut's initial assessment—that Dansey was a discontented pig—was right.

"He's a cunning little shit," Crane goes on, "but—and I mean this in a positive way—so are you. You've survived longer than any other Resistance leader. Your cunning is a force to be reckoned with; his is a meanness. But recognize in him those qualities that you also have, and you can win. Also, Tom isn't showing you half the messages that are coming in from Alliance. He's only showing you the ones he knows you're expecting."

I'm so stunned I can't speak. These people are my allies? Why are they hiding things from me? Then I remember something Navarre once told me: *All men want is power and glory.* These men see Alliance as the path to their glory; they want something they can beat their chests about for years to come.

They can have the glory—I have no intention of beating my breast. But they can't have Alliance. My network isn't a tool. It's a fifteen-year-old boy who's now a man who risks everything and yet still isn't sure he matters.

Then Crane whispers, "Dansey's the one who sent in Bla. He makes mistakes and he doesn't admit to them."

Crane walks away, and I'm left with bile and rage.

Dansey is the one who got Vallet killed.

I make myself not storm into his office. I make myself sit. I have the lives of people I love in my hands, and I need to sift through the politics to protect those lives.

That's when I realize—Crane said Dansey was horrified when he found out I was a woman. Every time I've mentioned going back to France, he's stalled. He controls the planes. He has the power to keep me here.

But like so many others, he sees the woman rather than the hedgehog who lives beneath my skin. My quills are sharp—and they sting.

I've outwitted the Nazis for three years. I can outwit a discontented pig, too.

Gibbet has Ant and Caviar. Restaurant down.

The message comes in Léon's daily dispatch. Gibbet is the Gestapo. Caviar is an agent from our Paris HQ and Ant is Dayné, my trusted bodyguard. Restaurant is our Grenoble sector.

It's happening again. How? A small mistake? A deliberate error? A traitor?

The next transmission is worse: *Firefly and Saluki on run from Gibbet.*

No. Not the duke of Magenta and Marguerite.

Another message tells me that Léon's notebook, which was found on Elephant when he was arrested, has been partially decoded by the Gestapo. That's what yielded up Ant's and Caviar's names. As for Maurice and Marguerite, they were already wanted by the Nazis, so it could be coincidence. But the timing is troubling.

I make frantic arrangements to get Marguerite and her children to the Amitié Chrétienne, where I pull in one final favor to get them over the border to Switzerland. Then I order Maurice to escape to London on the next Lysander. His reply is exactly what I thought it would be: He'll come at the September moon, once Marguerite and the children are safe.

I go to see Dansey. If the Gestapo have Léon's code book, I need to make some changes.

"Eagle needs to come back with Magpie at the August moon," I tell him. "I have to decentralize the network completely. Make each sector independent, like Lucien's. They'll get money, questionnaires, and intelligence priorities from me, but they'll recruit their own agents. Then there'll never be another code book full of every agent's name, and we won't have to rebuild from scratch every time one person is arrested."

Even Dansey sees the sense in my request. As for me, I'll see Léon very soon, and while that's exhilarating enough, I'm hoping that this time, we'll make Alliance strong enough to see us into the promised, but still undated, Allied invasion of France.

August arrives and I watch the moon grow bigger every night—crescent, quarter, gibbous—until it's as big and round as Coustenoble's eyes the first time I met him. Lucien is going back to France with all my gifts, questionnaires for the network, and one very special item: Alliance's first military medal, awarded to Coustenoble. I picture him sitting in bed in his robe, medal pinned to it, Josette beaming at his side, and my smile is a *demi-lune,* too.

"Kiss Josette's cheeks for me," I tell Lucien at the Bertrams' cottage before he departs for the airfield. "And stay alive so you can wear your robe for your English friend."

He grins. "Maybe I already have."

I laugh, hoping it's a sign—that such a joyous parting will end in happiness, not loss.

I'm scared of a pink heather nightmare, so I don't sleep that night as Lucien and Léon swap places on a landing field in France. I wait up with Barbara Bertram, who talks easily and quietly, a steady stream of nothing in particular that's soothing all the same, until the telephone shrills and I jump, spilling tea into my saucer.

She listens to the phone, then smiles. "Time to put the kettle on for tea."

I hug Barbara so hard I'm surprised she doesn't protest. Then I watch the door, willing it to open.

Finally, it does.

Léon and Magpie have both flown to London before, so they know Barbara. Minutes pass while they kiss her cheeks and press gifts upon her. She laughs and accepts their affectionate greetings. Then it's my turn.

I embrace Magpie and try to give Léon, in front of an audience, only the same companionable greeting. But his hand slips briefly under my hair and strokes the back of my neck, and I turn my face in to his chest for the merest second, inhaling France and Gauloises and the laurel of Aleppo soap. Thank God Magpie is still entertaining Barbara with an out-of-tune version of "Home Sweet Home," because I'm unable to stop a quiet gasp as everything inside me catches fire at the feel of this man.

Léon's eyes fall to a gold chain I'm wearing around my neck, tucked into my dress. I bring my hand up to touch the place on my breastbone where my wedding ring lives.

He smiles, eyes blazing like my insides.

But I won't be alone with him for hours yet.

The driver takes us to my office in London, where Léon says, "When Lucien stepped off the plane, he asked me if one notebook he was expecting had come in. When I said it had, he told me to give it to you first."

Clipped to the front of the book is a note hastily scribbled by Lucien: *I saw half of this material before we left for England. I know it looks preposterous, but I have total faith in Amniarix. She got the information directly from an officer who works at the site where these things are being built.*

I know this notebook is going to tell me about the terrible new weapon Lucien warned me the Nazis were making. My hand moves very, very slowly to open the covers. Because— what if I read that this weapon is powerful enough to stop an Allied invasion?

The first page reads:

Kampfgruppe KG 100 is reported to be experimenting with bombs that could be guided by the bomb aimer from such a distance that the plane can remain out of anti-aircraft firing range. Accuracy is said to be perfect . . .

As if that wasn't chilling enough—an aircraft armed with bombs that can be fired from so far away we won't even know they're coming—the next part is worse.

The final stage in the development of a stratospheric bomb is said to have been reached. This bomb is reported to be 10 cubic meters in volume and is launched vertically into the stratosphere before traveling a horizontal range of almost 500 kilometers. Trials are reported to have begun, with excellent results as regards accuracy. An expert estimated that just 50–100 of these bombs would suffice to destroy London.

A long-range stratospheric bomb, just fifty to one hundred of which could destroy the entire city I'm living in now—the city that holds all the plans and money and expertise we need to defeat the Nazis.

"This could change the face of warfare entirely." Léon's face is pale. "Unless the Allies can destroy it first."

"Thank God for Lucien," I breathe. "Now we might be able to do just that."

"Thank God you trusted him enough to give him his head," Léon says soberly. "I don't know any other Resistance leader who'd let a young man start up an independent sector of their network."

I shake my head. "I can't take any credit for this."

A touch of rose is starting to brighten the gray sunrise as I walk to MI6, where I tell Tom, "I'm not leaving until you pass this information on to someone who understands bombs and physics."

"You don't need to worry so much," he says condescendingly, as if I'm concerned about seating plans for a party rather than the destruction of London.

"I think you ought to worry more." I sit down at his desk, take out a Gitanes, light it, and close my eyes. "What a comfortable chair. I could sit here all day."

"Bloody French women." But he finds me a physicist who reads the reports and says just one word: "Extraordinary." Then he looks across at me. "Who is the source?"

I tell him the truth. "The most remarkable girl of her generation."

Of all the intelligence Alliance has gathered over the years,
this is our crowning achievement. And I hope that one day soon
I can meet Amniarix and tell her how remarkable she is.

It's Crane who sends me a coded note to tell me that Amniarix's
report landed on Churchill's desk the very next day and that
plans are being drawn up to bomb the base where the weapons
are being developed.

On August 17, nearly six hundred RAF bombers take to the
sky. Léon and I imagine it in our bed together the following
night, each airplane the beacon of a life the Gestapo took from
my network. Schaerrer. Vallet. Madeleine Rivière. The women
in Klaus Barbie's prison in Lyon. Because of them, the network
grew and survived, and now the Peenemünde base where the
stratospheric bombs are being built has almost been destroyed.

Crane's note reads, *We still expect to see some bombs manu-
factured and launched, but the air raid will have delayed German
production enough that it won't wreak havoc with our invasion
preparations. Thanks to Alliance.*

"I wish I was at HQ with Monique and Lucien and Maurice," I tell Léon. "I wish I was saying to them: *Thanks to Alliance.*"

Léon rolls on top of me. "You'll have to make do with celebrating with me."

So I do.

31

The Fight We Have to Have Is Here

London, August–September 1943

With English friends or French friends now in Britain, several nights a week Magpie, Léon, and I go out. I rediscover the pleasure of dancing, of being held in Léon's arms for hours, our bodies moving to the music of "A Nightingale Sang in Berkeley Square," a song about two lovers who meet in a town paved with stars.

September, the month when they're returning to France, arrives too soon. As the moon swells from half to gibbous, the nightmares begin. Pink heather. Léon and Magpie, the landing field, the glorious flowers. The Nazi gloating, *We've arrested Faye.*

I sit up in bed too quickly, head spinning like a hangover. The phone is ringing. Dansey's coming to see me.

My nausea climbs into my throat.

"We're moving you to a cottage for security reasons," Dansey tells me as soon as he's seated. "Somehow everyone in England knows that both the head of Alliance and its chief of staff are here. I can't risk some kind of attack."

"If you're moving me into a cottage," I reply, voice flat, "it means you're not planning to let me go back to France any time soon."

"You can't go now," he says with absolute finality. "By remaining here, you can get the overall view essential for organizing the network. This winter is going to be terribly tough. The Nazis are stepping up their drive against the Resistance. Reserve yourself for the future. The moment will come when your return will be imperative. But it isn't that moment now."

"Will the invasion take place in autumn?" I ask.

Please say yes. Please let it happen before the end of 1943.

Dansey's face clouds over. "We're not ready. Which is why we need you here. Until then," he says and smiles benignly, "just follow this old fox's advice."

Old fox is about right. But I'm no rabbit waiting to be snared in his jaws.

It's easier to be angry at Dansey than it is to imagine surviving into yet another year, a fifth year of Nazis and Gestapo and running and dying.

But his next words are "My dear," and his tone is kind. "Eagle mustn't go back to France."

I want to hug him. If MI6 makes Léon stay in London, he'll never be arrested by the Gestapo. Every field in France can grow pink heather and it won't matter.

But Léon would kill me if he found out I didn't fight for him.

Invisible hands reach out of my heart and grab at the words I'm about to say, trying to stuff them back inside me. But the part of me that knows I have to be able to tell Léon that I protested wins—just.

"Have you sworn to cloister us up one by one?" I ask coolly.

Dansey crosses one knee over the other, opens a packet of cigarettes, and offers one to me. I accept a little too eagerly.

"I ought not to indulge your vices," he says, and I want to poke the cigarette in his eyes. Every man in MI6 smokes. Every man in Alliance smokes. Anyone would smoke when they've been trapped in a brothel for weeks with the Gestapo hunting them.

I inhale with the utmost pleasure.

But Dansey wipes my satisfaction away. "Over the last three

years, I've seen Resistance fighters arrive and depart, never to return. Eagle is going to be arrested again. I've been through his file. Three arrests. Two escapes. Three two-way Lysander trips. He's survived for too long. His time is up."

All of a sudden, I'm back in the fortune-teller's room in Vichy, sitting before a different man, this one telling me I would make it to the end of everything. I want to go back there, to the question I didn't know I should ask: *But will everyone else? Will Léon?*

Léon *is* my everything, so for me to make it through, he must, too.

But if Léon is my everything, why don't I steal away with him to a cottage and turn my back on war? If my children are my everything, why is it that all I have is the white-hot wreckage of months not spent with them?

Snow is white. Gardenia flowers and bones, the dome of the Sacré-Coeur. The lies I tell myself are not. No, my lies are a night so dark you can't see through them to the truth that lurks, Sphinx-like, within.

So I tell one truth at last. "There's something more than statistics. There's premonition. I feel it, Léon's arrest. No." I shake my head, speak three bare, uncoded words, "I've seen it."

And Dansey, this man I don't especially like, shudders as if premonition has shown him a crystal ball depicting a bloodied future, too. Perhaps beneath the distaste of women in war and the possessive circling of Alliance, there is a man who feels a thing or two for the people taking risks for him.

"In different ways, we foresee the same thing," he says soberly.

The relief that MI6 is on my side, that they'll help me keep Léon alive, is so enormous that I have to restrain every muscle in my body so I don't let Dansey see that Léon is much more to me than just my chief of staff. I grind out my cigarette, make sure Dansey understands fully the problem. "Eagle won't agree to stay. He's a soldier. He's sworn to give his life for France."

"If you order him not to return, we won't provide him with a Lysander. I'm putting his fate in your hands."

Oh yes, Dansey understands. And now, so do I—I *am* the rabbit, writhing in the jaws of a trap I've walked right into. The job of ordering Léon is mine.

I stand, turn my back to Dansey. God, when can I scream? When will there ever be a moment when I can howl like an animal and pick up all the papers on the table and sweep them to the ground and set fire to them all?

If I order Léon to stay in London, he'll obey because he's a military man and Alliance is a militarized organization and I am his commander.

But I'll lose him. He could never love a woman who took France from him.

But if I let him return to France, my gut and Dansey's, too, say it will be the end. He'll still love me—but what does that matter if he's dead?

My things are moved to the cottage by a team of secret service personnel. I leave them to it. I don't care where my things go when I have Léon's life in my hands and my choices are to pull the trigger on him or on love.

I walk through the city for hours, searching not for answers, which don't exist, but for solace. But the facades don't shine white in the afternoon sun like in Paris. People speak with hard consonant sounds; there are no silent letters. There are voids where there once were buildings, a sky that's too listless to ever be set aflame by the sun.

I try to parse out the facts, leave the emotions behind. But Léon isn't a fact. He's the father of my child, the man who gave me a ring with our names written on it in a code only he and I understand.

I return to the cottage exhausted.

Léon is there, holding his arms open for me to walk into, his smile devastatingly charming. "Shall we go out tonight?" he asks. "Just the two of us. No one else."

He studies my face and I know he can see I'm struggling with something. He frowns when I say nothing. In every struggle, he's been my lieutenant. But not this time.

So that I don't have to speak to him, not now before I'm ready—*will I ever be ready?*—I bathe and slide into the blue silk Maggy Rouff dress that I wore on my last night in Paris. I put on makeup and comb my hair, and for one fleeting second in the mirror, I see her. The young girl who tore around mountain passes, who searched for adventure in the cockpit of an airplane; the one who thought adventure equaled joy.

But it is loss and agony, too.

Léon comes up behind me, slips his arms around my waist. "I'll have to come up with a better word than *magnisquise*," he says, kissing my neck.

"Alive," I say. "That's the best word of all."

He frowns again, but before he can ask, I take his hand and we go to the Ritz, heading belowground to what was once the Grill Room and is now a nightclub. We sit at one of the tables lit by a candle stuffed into the neck of a wine bottle. All around us, similar flames flicker, breaking apart the darkness. A chandelier made from more wine bottles sends a delicate halo over the dance floor so you can't see the sandbags lining the walls or the cheap utility tablecloths. But you can see a large caricature of Hitler and Göring. I turn my back on them and talk to Léon about everything other than war. Flying. Morocco. Our families.

"They were so in love," I tell him after I've described my trailblazing mother, who gave birth to my older sister in Shanghai and only returned to France for a few short months under duress to birth me. "She couldn't bear not to be with my father."

"I don't know whether it's the romanticized imaginings of a man who's never had to raise seven children." Léon smiles briefly. "But I think my parents were the same. They needed so little. They had so little. One tiny town. No travel to faraway places. Just fierce pride in France, in their children, and in love and honor. They didn't ever seem to want anything else."

He looks pensive, as if he's trying to figure out if his memories are right or if he's rewriting the past to suit the narrative he wants to believe in. All night we've been using only one hand to sip from our wineglasses, our other hands entwined, but I untangle my fingers now to stroke his beautiful cheek. "I can tell by the man you are that their pride was well-founded."

He smiles. "I'm sure there were moments when they thought the better of it."

I'm about to ask him to tell me about his youthful escapades when I realize: Léon didn't have a youth. He was in the trenches at age seventeen. By age twenty, he'd been awarded his first Croix de Guerre. His life has been war, and training for war. He was made, built, lives for, this fight.

What if that's his destiny? Not me. Not our son.

God.

Léon senses my shift in mood. He leads me onto the dance floor as the music changes to "Silver Wings in the Moonlight," and I know I won't get through this song—about a woman who shares her pilot lover with the moon and who prays to the moon to keep him safe—without weeping.

The moon is the thing we set our schedules by. It's our only way to get supplies, to get to London and return to France. Everything turns on the light of the moon, something easily extinguished by just one cloud.

Léon lets me have one silent, struggling minute. Then he murmurs, "You look so beautiful tonight. But so sad."

My inhale is sharp and loud—the sound you make before you sob. Then I do sob, all over his jacket. Léon responds by holding me close until the song is finished, then he reaches into his pocket for a handkerchief, pressing it to the waterlogged crescents beneath my eyes. "Please tell me," he says.

"What if this is all there is?" I blurt, arm sweeping the room. "A few stolen nights? A dance or two? What if this is all there *is*?" I repeat and, unbelievably, he smiles.

"Then we'd better make the most of it."

"I've had enough of that!" I cry. "Of romanticizing the absences and the longing. Of being so grateful to be alive that just waking up feels like a bonus. It should be our right, Léon. It should be our damn right."

The noise of the band makes it impossible for anyone else to hear me roar, but Léon hears, and now his eyes are turned away, glittering with pain or tears or a matching fury. While he's not looking at me, I say, voice resolute, "Dansey wants you to stay in London. To not return to France."

His whole body stiffens. "What did you say?"

We're waltzing still, such a gentle dance, but each of my words is a bullet. "You've lost all your lives and then some. Dansey says the law of averages—"

"Damn their law of averages," he breaks in.

And now the fight we have to have is here.

"I agree with Dansey," I say.

Léon stands very still and waits for me to look at him.

A true leader would look her lieutenant in the eye when she tells him to do something he abhors. So I lift my eyes up very slowly.

Around us, couples swirl, taking advantage of proximity and wine and darkness to extract a little pleasure in a hopeless world. Léon and I stand, bodies apart, eyes locked together, both quivering with anger.

If I'm mad, I won't cry.

"I'll *never* stay here." His words are violent. "I'll *never* agree to fall down on my job."

A lesser man, someone I could never love, would have breathed a sigh of relief and said, *Okay. I'll stay in London, where we can dance and worry only at a far remove about the people who believe in us.*

My anger dissipates, only a truth as cruel as man remaining. "I know."

But Léon is so furious he doesn't hear me. "Tell them I've got fifty bombing missions to my credit," he blazes. "According to their calculations, I should have been dead long ago. This ghost is going to France!"

I dig down into the villainous murk in my gut and unsheathe the largest weapon of all. My power. "You can only go if I say you can."

There's a beat. Then another. A drum fills one, a violin the next. Then the other instruments break in and couples move elegantly around us and the candles flicker and everything is the same as it was—but the things that matter are all different.

"You can't do that to me." There's fear in his eyes now, fear of me. "I can't let down all the airmen I've recruited, can't let them be caught in place of me."

Damn him for showing me this isn't about personal glory. That it's about his men. But just as he's a leader of every pilot he's brought into Alliance, so, too, am I *his* leader.

"Come outside," I say. "I have something to tell you."

I see his heart break right in front of me.

He sets his jaw into the face of a man who'll do what every atom of his soul tells him he shouldn't, if I order him. Because that's how military structures work.

But it's not how hearts work. Hearts never do what will hurt the least.

They always do the thing that will break them, and I've known this since I first met Léon in 1940.

I lead us along Piccadilly, turn in to St. James's Square. In the middle is a statue of a man on a horse charging off into battle. It's what men have done since the beginning of time, men like Hitler, who's ridden over the bodies of so many dead that the soil of France may grow only the skeletons of heroes from now on.

My back turned to Léon, I speak to the waxing moon. "This is why I tried for so long not to let myself love you. I knew I'd have to choose between a decision I'd want to make because I love you, versus the one I should make for the good of the network."

Behind me, I can feel anger rippling from Léon like the concussion of a bomb as I prepare to do the one thing I swore I never would.

I choose Léon over France.

"Alliance needs for you to stay here in London, alive, doing the job that nobody can do better than you. *France* needs you here." My voice cracks and I swear, a cry as useless as a prayer. "But because I love you, I'll let you go."

I can't stop the sound that follows those words, not a sob, but a wail, like a beast, like a person dying, the kind of anguish that makes you lock your doors and hide under the bed and pray you never come face-to-face with its kind. If crying is the limit of what we have as humans to express pain, then my God, how inadequate it is.

Léon is in front of me now, cupping my jaw in his hands, trying to hold still my flailing arms, his words urgent. "Minerva, if anything happens to me, know that I'll be the one washing the sunsets for you so your world still shines. I'll be the one giving you Moroccan blue afternoons—"

I shove him away. "Stop it! Dying isn't romantic. When I think of Romeo and Juliet, I don't press a hand to my heart and smile. I think, *You stupid fools.*"

"What about Joan of Arc?" Léon pleads, holding my face again as if he wants to make me see the world the way he does.

"She saved France because she kept on fighting. Do you think she was a fool, too?"

"Yes." My voice is savage. "Because what did it change? Five hundred years on, and men are still tearing the world apart. There is no honor. Just war and death. And I'm tired of pretending any of it is heroic."

"It isn't heroic," Léon whispers. "It's right."

Putain! I want to shout, a word I've never said aloud, let alone screamed at the man I love. Instead, I pull him back to the cottage and up to my room and into my bed, and we make a warlike kind of love—the only kind you have left when you know the one you love might die tomorrow. Our lips and our limbs clash, his mouth barely landing on my skin before it moves away to claim some other territory, my hand barely touching his jaw before I find something else to hold on to, chasing that moment of being so tangled together, it's as if we'll never let go.

But you always have to let go.

Of course I dream of pink heather—unrelenting, calamitous pink heather. I dream of the plane landing, the Gestapo, the voice. I can't even close my eyes without seeing neon pink outlines beneath my lids.

Eventually I climb out of bed and creep down the stairs and into the music room, and I remember that once upon a time I was a girl who played the piano for eight hours a day, who wanted to be a pianist, making music for the pleasure of crowds.

What a life that would have been.

Chopin's "Revolutionary Étude" pours out of me, that piece about patriotism and rage and heroes. It takes a few attempts at the opening bars before the fingers on my left hand move as neatly as they used to, and then I have it—and I let the music cry for me with every broken semiquaver.

"Minerva."

There in the doorway is Léon summoning the goddess of war.

He walks over to me wearing a pair of pajama pants, torso muscular and strong. He drops to his knees, resting his forearms on my thighs, hands holding mine. And I say what perhaps the music has just told him. "I'm going back, too. We'll fly back and forth to France on alternate moons so that one of us is always here doing the invasion planning and one of us is always there."

He shakes his head furiously and I whisper, "Just as I can't ask you to stay here, neither can you ask it of me."

"We all think it will be me, but—" He swears, eyes glittering, angry—not at me, but at the world. "What if it's *you* who's caught? You being—" He cuts himself off and I don't know what, specifically, he was about to say—*tortured, burned, beheaded*—but it doesn't matter. It all ends the same way.

"I can't even bear thinking about it," he finishes, voice hoarse.

"But you ask me to bear it for you."

"*God,*" is all he says, and now his head is in my lap, the music having unleashed something in him I didn't mean to loosen.

When I met Edouard, I thought it was the kind of love I would sacrifice everything for. But here I am with the man I love more than any other, and we aren't choosing each other.

We each break and are broken. We each love—but we are warriors, too.

"If it is me," I say, my voice cracking, "will you tell Achille about me?"

Léon's voice is fierce. "I'll never read him myths about Greek heroes. I'll tell him the story of his mother, because she's the world's only true hero."

Then we're on the rug on the floor, and Léon is kissing the side of my hip where the pain sometimes lives and whispering, "I love you." He whispers it again as he kisses the inner and outer bones of my ankles, and then again as his lips find the inside of my elbow, the lobes of my ears, the tip of my pinky finger.

We say those words to each other just before the end, and then again at the end, and also after the final moment has passed and we're lying in each other's arms as the dawn breaks like our hearts over the sky, weeping gold.

In the morning I tell Dansey that Léon is going back to France, that I've given him strict conditions: The minute he lands, he won't stay with the reception committee but will make his own way to Paris. He won't roam around the country until he's looked into the arrests. Then he'll start the process of decentralizing the network. In October, he'll return to London and I'll go back to France and we'll divide the job between us, back and forth each month until the invasion finally happens.

"You've made a very grave decision," Dansey says.

I hang up the phone and weep.

32

Forever

London, September 1943

The night before Léon leaves on Operation Ingres, the moonlight flight that will take him to France and bring the duke of Magenta to London, we eat, we dance, we make love. We do ordinary things, even though we are not ordinary.

In the afternoon, the driver takes Léon, Magpie, and me to the Bertrams' cottage. English countryside rolls past. Narrow roads, green hedges, redbrick houses. The rubble of bombings, left to decompose like animal droppings. Then . . .

Pink heather. Pink heather in a vast field backdropped by an extraordinary sky.

My lunch is in my mouth.

I swallow, breathe, stare, try to scream, *Stop!* But my voice doesn't work. Nor does my mind. Even my heart isn't beating— it's like I'm already dead, right here in this moment of watching the future that's been showing itself to me for months finally step into the present.

Then the heather is gone and I whip my head back to see if it was just a hallucination. Why didn't I pay more attention to the details? Look for all the ways it wasn't the same as my dream?

Because I *haven't* dreamed this. There's no Gestapo in Britain. No planes land in the field we just passed. Léon isn't going to step into it. The only thing the same was the heather, incandescent behind us, like fresh skin before the knife falls.

I search wildly for Schaerrer's ghost or Vallet's, one last remaining angel, to tell me what to do. If I tell the driver to go back to London, Léon and Magpie will think I've gone mad. They haven't even looked at the heather.

If I tell Léon he can't go to France because I just saw pink heather and I've been dreaming he'll be captured in a field of pink heather, he'll just ask me how many other things I dream of every night and pay no attention to. And Magpie, our pragmatist, will scoff.

I've probably seen pink heather many times while I've been here, maybe even this same field the day after Léon arrived and we drove to London. No rational person believes that dreams are real.

But I hardly say a word for the rest of the drive.

Barbara welcomes us warmly, saying, "Come and have dinner," as if she thinks food will cure our worries. But food is not magic.

She puts bacon and eggs on our plates. We push them sideways, in circles. Even Magpie hardly eats.

It is 9:58 P.M.

9:59.

Ten o'clock.

"Time to go," the major says.

The Bertrams and Magpie leave the room. I have thirty seconds, the most important seconds of my life. I don't know what to do with them. *I love you?* Léon knows that. *I'm scared?* He knows that, too. *I miss you.*

More things I don't need to say.

We stare at each other. Then he reaches for the chain around my neck, letting the ring spill into his hand.

"My wife," he says simply.

I pull off the chain, put it around his neck, tuck the ring into his shirt. "My husband," I say. "Forever."

The waiting begins.

Barbara talks about her knitting, about her childhood, and then, gradually, she asks me questions about Léon. At first my answers are brief. One word, two at most. But then I tell her about when I first saw him, a head taller than all the others, striding into a room, making me stare. I tell her he was the only person in the world to ever ask me why I was doing this, that he wants to wash sunsets golden for me, but that I would rather there were no more sunsets and he was alive.

One o'clock strikes.

My fingers twist against the backs of my hands, trying to tear a hole through my skin. It's too early for news. But still I expect it. I expect the phone to ring and the major to answer and for him to tell his wife to make tea for one guest, Maurice.

One-thirty ticks past.

Barbara holds my terrified eyes in her calm ones.

1:45 A.M.

1:50.

If I could give my life to make the phone ring, I would.

1:59.

The phone shrills.

The major listens, then hangs up.

"Tea for the same two guests," he says.

My exclamation of shock fills the room.

A few minutes later, Magpie and Eagle arrive, starving, tired, and cross. Léon hurls whiskey down his throat. Magpie tears a bite off one of Barbara's cream buns.

"The moon was as bright as the damn sun," Léon says furiously. "Sorry," he apologizes to Barbara, who waves off the language. "We flew over the landing field three times but nobody was there."

I don't care. I care only that the pink heather has no power.

But then I realize—we have to go through all of this again tomorrow.

33

The Noose of Pink Heather

London, September 1943

*W*hale fishing is a dangerous occupation, is the coded message the BBC plays the next morning to tell Mahout to come out again with his team for Operation Ingres.

All day I think, *I'd rather go whale fishing than say goodbye.*

In my last moment with Léon, I try one final time. "Even the plane refuses to take you back. What if it was a warning?"

Léon touches a hand to our wedding ring, hiding beneath his shirt. "It was just the moon, Minerva," he says. "I love you."

Then he and Magpie leave once more.

Barbara's knitting needles click. The clock ticks. My heart tears itself to pieces: one piece for the soap I didn't accept. One piece for the pâté we shared in his hotel room when we realized we were talking to kindred spirits. One piece for our first Christmas, when I told him I was pregnant.

One piece for our son.

Tick tick. Click click. Rip. Rip.

A clock. A needle. A heart.

It's only one o'clock when the phone rings.

"Tea for our new friend," Major Bertram says.

It means Léon and Magpie are in France.

Minutes later, Maurice walks in.

I throw my arms around the duke's neck and he holds me as if he knows how much I need comfort.

But his words don't bring comfort.

"It was chaos at the landing field," he says. "The old airman's intuition told me we were being watched."

The headache that's been threatening all day starts to pound. "Eagle . . . ?" I whisper.

"I told him to leave as fast as he could." He gives me one last squeeze. "Don't worry. He always gets away."

Barbara summons us over to the table. I think food goes into my mouth. Certainly whiskey does. But all I can think about is Magpie's first message, due to come in at one o'clock tomorrow. Only when it says that Magpie and Léon both made it to Paris will I finally let go of the noose of pink heather that's tied around my neck.

Part Five

OUTLAW

France, 1943–1945

Who were the men and women who, at the cost of their lives, resisted Nazi domination? They were the members of a military intelligence network, which fought without cease in France from 1940 to 1945. Soon, nobody will know what they did, nor why they did it, nor whether it was necessary to do it; you may even pity them for dying for nothing. I want to know that they will not be forgotten and, above all, that you understand the divine flame that burned in their hearts.

—MARIE-MADELEINE FOURCADE

(translated by Natasha Lester)

34

The Very Last Station Before Paris

Bouillancy, France, September 1943

As the Lysander banks to the left, Léon can see Caen on the north coast. A smile soars over his face. He's back in France, ready to help prepare Alliance for an invasion sometime next year and to prove to both MI6 and Minerva that he can survive for at least a month.

Below, lights flash as the reception committee signals the Morse letter A. The plane banks again, descends, then touches down in the thirty feet of space it's allowed. Léon climbs out, feet coming to rest on the soil of the country whose soul he's fighting for.

He claps Mahout on the back, then the duke of Magenta, who whispers, "Don't stay here a second longer. This stinks."

Léon scans the field. There are more people here than there should be.

Go straight to Paris. Don't linger. The rules Marie-Madeleine had set, rules that seemed overdramatic and put in place only because he was the man who loved her and not just her lieutenant, come rushing back. Suddenly, he believes them. He needs to get out of there.

A second plane lands and Magpie darts over, worry etched on his brow, too.

"Why are there so many agents here?" Léon asks Mahout as

they drive to the farmhouse, where they'll store the supplies that came in with them.

"The Gestapo are busier than usual," Mahout explains, his gypsy ease relaxing Léon a little. "I thought we might need re-inforcements."

It makes sense. But something feels wrong—the air is too crisp for September, as though a hailstorm lurks, waiting to fall.

At the farmhouse, Léon's hackles rise still more when he sees two men from Alliance's security team who have no links to this sector. One of them is Lanky, whose errors were responsible for Elephant's capture a few months ago. Léon doesn't want his life in that man's hands, and besides, they're breaking all of Marie-Madeleine's rules about not mixing different teams, which is how multiple sectors fall, rather than just one.

"Why are they here?" he demands, not just curt now, but angry.

"You've been away for some time, Commandant," Mahout replies, face trustworthy as always. "There are more Gestapo out there than leaves of grass. If I let Alliance's Eagle be captured, nobody will forgive me. I wanted more security."

Again, it makes sense. Mahout lives by his instincts, and they've proven sound for the past two years. "Let's get to Paris," Léon tells him.

"The Gestapo know that Noah's Ark moves at night. We'll go at first light."

Does he want to take his chances out there alone in an area crawling with Gestapo who all have the name Léon Faye tat-tooed onto their bullets? Even Minerva wouldn't want him to do that.

So he stays at the farmhouse. But he doesn't sleep. He stares at the ceiling, recalling what Marie-Madeleine told him. *You've used all your lives—and then some.*

One more, he thinks. He needs only one more: one that ends with him and Marie-Madeleine together.

"What do you think?" he asks Magpie.

"I don't like it."

They rise from their beds. Léon takes the front of the house, Magpie the back, and they watch for those glacial shadows they can both feel until dawn breaks.

But nothing happens.

They leave the farmhouse just after five and walk to the station at Nanteuil-le-Haudouin; all of them spaced out in small groups along the road. At the station, Lanky, who seems to think he's in charge, bustles them all into the same carriage, saying, "We can protect you more easily if we stay together."

I don't need protection, Léon almost growls. He's always protected himself. And never before has he broken so many of Marie-Madeleine's rules: that he should go straight to Paris, travel alone. That he should not sit in a goddamn compartment with eleven other Alliance agents.

His hand aches to touch their wedding ring, but he won't do that in a public place. That's a private devotion he'll resume when he's alone.

But then it happens.

At Aulnay-sous-Bois, the very last station before Paris, the carriage doors burst open. And the Gestapo rush in.

35

Did You Do What I Asked?

London, September 1943

One o'clock arrives and there is only silence.

"Check again," I tell the radio operator at MI6.

"There's nothing, ma'am," he tells me.

Where are you, Léon?

Maurice reminds me, "Sometimes radios fail. Just because Magpie hasn't been in contact . . ." He stops, as if even he's afraid of the end of that sentence.

"Then why hasn't Mahout messaged?" I demand. "He has a radio. Paris has four operators. They don't need Magpie to send a message."

The afternoon turns into evening turns into morning. All around me, radio operators tap and annotate, a sound I used to believe was a jubilant symphony, but all I can see now are messages meeting fire as they fly out the window, echoes turning to ash.

It's two days before a message finally arrives from Ladybug via Le Mans.

Three passengers from Operation Ingres arrested by Gibbet, plus Mahout, Lanky, Bumpkin stop all Paris radio operators arrested stop seven more sectors taken stop Barricade team all escaped stop Dragon and Lucien studying ways to repair damage end

Why was Lanky at Operation Ingres? He's supposed to be on minor security duties in Lyon. And why does it say three passengers were arrested by the Gestapo—or Gibbet—when there were only two passengers on the airplane: Léon and Magpie? At least the Barricade agents—Paris HQ—are all safe. But Mahout and the others . . .

Arrested. Seven sectors. All the Paris radio operators taken. *No.*

I scribble out a reply asking Ladybug, who's taken over Paris in the duke's absence, to tell me urgently the code names of the passengers who were arrested and to direct all sectors to go into hiding. I finish by asking, *Where are Eagle and Magpie?*

Then I flee to my cottage and shut myself in the bathroom.

The face in the mirror is as wild-eyed as a *fakir*—those men who have nothing, who give up everything, who perform outlandish tricks.

Where are you, Léon?

My eye falls on the sedative the doctor prescribed for me weeks ago. I rip off the cap and drink straight from the bottle.

The phone rings, fades, crescendos. My hand lies immobile on the bed. I can't lift it up. But the phone shrills again. I peel my eyelids open, stare at my hand, concentrate on getting it to wrap around the receiver, to lift it to my ear.

Dansey barks down the line. "We were about to break down your door. I'll be there in five minutes."

He hangs up before I can tell him to leave me alone.

I hate being a leader. I hate it more than I've ever hated anything. I want to follow, to give every agent to someone whose hands are better able to form a carapace around the three thousand souls who are urging me onto my unwilling feet.

But there is no one else. I am the one they call *la patronne*.

It takes me the entire five minutes to get to the door.

"The London air doesn't suit you, my dear child," Dansey says after one glance at my face.

"I need French air," I snap. "I have to go back."

"I will never agree to let you set foot in that hornet's nest."

"Do you think he's been arrested?" I whisper.

"Not if he obeyed you and left the landing ground straight away," Dansey says almost gently.

Did you, Léon? Did you do what I asked? Or did you fly down the hill without once thinking about using the brakes?

Then Dansey looks me in the eye. "You know how fond I am of Eagle. I should regard his arrest as a personal loss. We'll avenge him, I promise."

Now I know for certain—he thinks Léon is in the hands of the Gestapo.

36

Someone Must Be Talking

84 Avenue Foch, Paris, September 1943

Léon knows where he is as soon as he wakes. The Gestapo didn't allow him the dignity of being conscious while they transported him, but he hopes he gave at least one of them a sore head to match his own.

His hands move slowly, assessing the extent of the damage. Definitely a couple of cracked ribs. Broken nose. Otherwise, just deep cuts and bruises. They want him alive. They want to smile as he bites his tongue through the torture but eventually submits to the pain and says things that will betray everyone in Alliance.

The last place he inspects is his breastbone, and the relief he feels is almost as painful as his wounds. The wedding ring is gone, and he remembers pulling it off his neck and dropping it on the ground before the Gestapo pounced. They have no way of knowing that Marie-Madeleine is both his weakness and his strength, and that by striking against his love, they could undo him more easily than a shoelace.

He pushes himself up gingerly. Three seconds of stars. The room whirls. Then a Gestapo officer enters; he must have been listening outside. He takes a seat on the single chair, crosses his legs, lights a cigarette that he plucks from a jewel-encrusted case, and offers one to Léon.

Even though he's desperate for the comfort of smoke in his lungs, Léon declines.

"Radio operator Pie," the Gestapo officer says. "Mahout, head of your clandestine airplane service. Colonel Kauffmann, or Cricket. Gabriel Rivière, or Wolf. I'm holding two hundred and ninety-seven more animals from Noah's Ark in jails across France."

The blow is so shocking that Léon almost wishes the words had been accompanied by another fist to the head, because then he'd have an excuse to vomit. Three hundred of Alliance's agents have been caught—that's ten percent. How were so many taken all at once?

He tilts his head back as much as he dares, inspecting the room. The ceiling slopes, indicating he's at the top of the building, probably in what was once a maid's room. There are no windows, but there's a skylight between him and freedom. It's covered by a ventilation shaft that intrudes about six feet into the room. The base of the shaft is blocked by iron bars.

"You can't escape through it," the officer says faux helpfully. "Perhaps if we hadn't added the bars. Now it's impossible."

But I could rip the sheets off my bed and hang myself on those bars, Léon thinks grimly. They've taken his cyanide. If he's going to end it all to escape the torture, the bars are his best bet.

Except he can't die without meeting his child.

"You might as well talk," the Gestapo officer continues. "The others are. Why let yourself be tortured to death or insanity when the outcome will be the same? The only question is: How long will it take?"

"I'll talk," Léon says pleasantly, before taking three steps toward the *gestapiste.* He stands militarily straight, swallowing down the nausea from his pounding head. "Alliance is a military organization and I'm one of its commandants. That makes me a prisoner of war. You can't try us or execute us until the war ends. You know the Geneva Convention as well as I do."

The *gestapiste*'s smile spreads right across his face. "You're negotiating with me? How about I tell you the code name for your Paris headquarters. That's Barricade. Lyon is Villa. The duke of Magenta, code name Saluki, is running your Paris sector. Shall I continue to prove that I wasn't joking when I said we already know enough to wipe Alliance out?"

Léon really does almost lose his stomach then—and all of his dignity. For the Boche to know so much, someone must be talking.

Wrath propels him two more steps forward. "Germany is about to be defeated. No," he growls. "Pulverized. Rendered so useless that the shame of your subjugation will be inherited not just by your children, but your children's children. The German army would be better advised to reverse its allegiances and join the Allies. There's still time."

He smiles at the end, like a man unworried.

The officer strides to the door, slams it shut, and Léon's grin widens. He made it through one interrogation without being beaten. It's a win and he'll take it. And if his jailer can be provoked, it means he still has feelings. Léon can work with feelings.

And—there are so many ways to escape prison. He's done it three times before.

It's time to add a fourth to the list.

37

A Queen Ruling over a Palace of Bones

London, October 1943

think about my agents, my Alliance, the people France owes so much to, rather than what Dansey believes. I send one message of hope to all sectors: *Do not try to contact anyone stop am investigating ways of parachuting supplies stop you will be given all assistance and help stop love end.*

Not long after, I discover that the Bordeaux, Brest, Rennes, and Nantes transmitters are still operating. Hope flickers. Perhaps Alliance will lick its wounds, will stagger back onto its feet.

But after that, it's like watching stars fall from the sky, leaving a wound of black over France.

The next message confirms that Magpie was arrested.

My dear, swashbuckling Rivière, who's been there almost from the very start.

Cricket, the caped Colonel Kauffmann.

Bee.

Amniarix, whom I'd believed I'd one day thank in person.

General Baston.

So many names: Unicorn, Triton, Urus, Bat, Siren, Scallop.

Dordogne falls.

Autun.

Then Brest. Eight members from the one family.

Rennes.

Paris.

Brittany.

And one more name, foretold to me by a dazzling pink field of heather.

My magnificent Eagle has fallen. And with him, perhaps, three hundred more.

The executioner's axe rests solely in my hands. I'm a queen, ruling over a palace of bones.

38

Climb to Freedom

84 Avenue Foch, Paris, September 1943

Two weeks of seeing nobody besides his guard, whose name is Kieffer, pass. Léon uses that time to let his bruises recover and his bones heal, and he manages to not get beaten again. He examines his cell and discovers that if he had some sort of tool, he could chisel away the cement around the bars at the bottom of the skylight shaft. Then he could climb to freedom. But how to get a tool?

The question becomes a possibility in the early hours one morning when he hears the percussion of Morse. When you've spent two years listening to the Morse key on the radio, you speak it like your mother tongue. He's immediately on his feet, searching for where the sound is the most audible.

Anyone there? Anyone there?

It could be a Gestapo trap. But the Gestapo are more likely to batter Morse onto his body than tap it onto the walls at midnight.

Yes, he replies.

In the small hours, he learns that he's talking to a British agent named Inayat, who's in the room next to his. She says that another British agent, named Bob, whom she believes is trustworthy and whom she's been communicating with via notes in the communal lavatory, is on the same floor.

She tells Léon where to find the notes. That she's tried to escape once before. That she wants to try again. That Bob is allowed out of his room to work for the Nazis as a draftsman.

By morning, Léon's ribs are still bruised and he hasn't slept, but none of that matters because, with the combined knowledge of three secret agents, he'll find a way out of this inescapable torture center and back to Marie-Madeleine. If Bob is a draftsman familiar with the building they're locked in, he might know where the skylight leads. He might have access to tools, to rope.

Access to hope.

39

If You Get in My Way, I'll Watch You Burn

London, November 1943–May 1944

Weeks pass in a stasis of nothing except the constant question in my heart: *Where are you, Léon?* I dream of Kauffmann in his ancient cape, shouting as if he didn't understand that clandestine work was secret. I see Rivière eating bouillabaisse, Bee burying tables beneath food to nourish us. They aren't the ones talking to the Gestapo. They will never tell.

But someone is. For so many agents and so many sectors to fall at once, someone is betraying us.

I ask Dansey for a plane to take me back to France. He refuses, says the weather is too bad to even send supplies to the remaining agents. But I understand subtext—he thinks Alliance is dead.

Dansey is killing me, too.

Furious messages come through from my remaining agents. *We need money and transmitters and new codes*, they urge me.

Maurice, who's trapped in London too, stares soberly at me. We've asked and we've begged, but Marie-Madeleine and the once-brash flying ace have no idea what to do.

"Perhaps I should shut it all down," I say to him one night in my cottage, which I hate for its vast windows, chintzy sofas, and state of order. I want my cheeky radio operators, tiny balls of paper, secret rooms with drawn curtains . . . an address nobody knows.

"You can't," the duke says, but even his head is bowed.

I stride over to the windows, throw the drapes across the glass. When I withdraw my hand, I can see there's blood around my fingertips and that I've stained the curtains with the blistering mess of chilblains that have marred my hands every winter of the war. They ache, God they ache, but I ignore the pain and instead tell Maurice a hard and painful truth. "Alliance is like the gray wolf, hunted to extinction—only the taxidermized carcasses of you and me remaining."

"You don't believe that," Maurice says.

My laugh is wild. "Believe? All I did was believe. I believed in too much when instead I should have been a tyrant like Dansey. I should have ordered Léon to stay. What Alliance needs at its head is a stone."

And I write a message with my stony hand: *If I do not succeed in normalizing the situation I will give everyone their freedom of action on January 1.*

"Unless a Christmas miracle happens this week," I tell Maurice in a voice like Navarre's once was, made of flint and steel, "I'm sending this message. Then Alliance's remaining men and women will no longer be beholden to a slaughtered network whose leader is trapped in London—a leader who's been fighting for so long, she has nothing left to give."

The duke of Magenta gives me two days. On Christmas Eve, the night when we should be celebrating, he pounces.

Last year, he called me the queen of the animals. This year, he passes me a glass of cognac and says, "Queens can't give up. They can't resign or stand down. They can only be overthrown. Nobody else has stepped in to lead Alliance. So you're still our queen."

I hold up a hand to silence him.

But he won't be quiet. "Everyone in Alliance will choose you, every time. You have me in the north—I know you'll find a way to get me back to France—and Lucien in the south. Dragon is still out there mapping the northern coastline, the thing you told us was our top priority. We can rebuild from that. We can deliver that map. And you also told me you think there's a traitor. It's your job, Queen Hérisson, to find out who that is and slit his throat. I once told you that, one day, you'd be winning at something more important than a rally. But here you are, thinking of walking away before the final victory."

"We aren't winning," I say in my new voice of granite.

Maurice just picks up his jacket and tells me he's going to a party.

I rush after him, but by the time I get to the door, I can't see him anymore. Fog has landed like incendiary smoke, rendering London invisible.

I step out into it.

It's the kind of fog that makes people ride their bicycles into lampposts. It reduces all the larger sounds and magnifies the small ones. I can hear a cloud move, a spider's footsteps, a web spinning.

Perhaps I'm dead, and this is hell.

The loudest sound of all makes me stop. *If you are dead, Minerva, would you be proud?*

Léon's voice.

My whole body turns. Where is he? If I can hear him, he must be alive.

And if he's alive, then how can I stop before the prisons are emptied and my agents freed?

When I arrive at MI6, I look so completely unlike the wreck I've been over the past weeks that Dansey does a double take. I look like the beautiful spy, which I know is what they call me. Black gloves hide my hands and my lipstick is red, too-fast jet-engine red, emergency-light red, no-man's-land red, the red of brandy drunk straight from the bottle. It's the kind of red that says I'm no longer the ash, and if you get in my way, I'll watch you burn.

I don't let him speak. "I won't accept Tom as my MI6 liaison anymore."

"My dear—"

I want to shove his *my dear*s down his throat. But I keep my temper in check because I will leave here winning today, rather than losing. "Tom is to go," I repeat. "You owe me this. For Bla."

I look not just into his eyes, but into his soul, and I use my own eyes to say that I no longer believe I can win if I lead like a woman. I no longer believe I can win if I lead like a man. To fight against animals, you have to become one. And that is what I am.

Dansey nods.

The next day, Crane is back by my side, as is the duke. We rebuild Noah's Ark once more. As the duke said, Lucien's southern region is operating as if nothing has happened. Stosskopf, our inside man in the submarine base, remains free. As is Dragon, who's mapping the coastal defenses. Mandrill, who's in charge of operations in the vital Bordeaux sector, hasn't been captured, either. Messages are trickling in. I gather them into one comprehensive intelligence report, reapply my armor, stride back into Dansey's office, and place a folder of transmissions on his desk.

Toulon bombing a success stop 1,500 Germans killed.

14 submarines currently in Saint-Nazaire stop consider bombing.

Have microphotos of bunkers housing long-range missiles pointed at London.

"Do you want to blow up these submarines, keep killing fifteen hundred Germans, get hold of those photos of the bombs pointing straight at you?" I ask Dansey. "Or would you like those submarines to blow up your invasion plans instead?"

I thrust out one more message, from Dragon. *Map nearly finished. Need Lysander to deliver it to you.*

Dansey almost smiles. "I'll have the team draw up new questionnaires for your agents. One step at a time."

Alliance rises up again.

Crane, who was once a navy officer, helps me navigate the ban on Lysanders by finding a launch that can creep in close to the French coastline. The duke returns to France with money, questionnaires, transmitters, and instructions. Once Dansey hears that we now have nine transmitters operating in the north again, he agrees to our first Lysander landing since the arrests six months ago.

The quantity of information that comes back on the airplane is astounding. But there's also a letter from the duke telling me of Coustenoble's death.

My dear Couscous was being ferried by ambulance to hospital to escape the Gestapo. He died of tuberculosis seconds before the Nazis surrounded the ambulance, fulfilling the vow he'd once made: *The Boches shall never get me alive.*

The letter also says he received his medal and his robe. They were his greatest joys.

Once upon a time, a man named Navarre invited me on a crusade. I recruited a first wave of agents, among them Schaerrer, who got me to Spain; Vallet, whose clothes were too big; and Coustenoble, who called me *little one.*

All dead now.

And Josette has been arrested, too.

Three months ago, Couscous's death would have felled me. But I need to be able to tell the world that he died for freedom.

And I have to tell Lucien the news of his mother in person. Because he's my son now.

So I prepare to meet Dansey, to demand another airplane. But Crane appears, saying, "Someone came in on the Lysander."

Dragon steps forward, a fierce Norman who looks as if he was descended from Vikings. "For you, Madame," he says proudly.

Out of his suitcase bursts a fifty-five-foot-long map of the Cotentin Peninsula, the entire northwest coast of France. On it are marked, in minute, perfect, beautiful detail, every anti-tank trench and access path, every coastal battery and gun emplacement, every piece of artillery and barbed wire, every minefield and observation tower.

"My God," Crane says as he stares in utter astonishment. "It's the most complete and detailed picture of the landing sites for—"

He cuts himself off.

But I know what he was about to say: *of the landing sites for the Allied invasion.*

Which means it's coming. And with this map in hand, the Allies will win. No one else will die.

Alliance has stumbled, but it has never fallen.

It is indispensable.

With every win, there are losses. Stosskopf is arrested. So are the twenty people who worked with Dragon gathering the information for his map. As soon as he returns to France, Dragon is arrested, too.

From Paris, Maurice transmits messages telling me of the capture of new agents I've barely had time to give code names to and have never even met.

On the credenza at my cottage I keep a row of candles. I light one for every agent taken. The credenza looks as if it's made of wax now, not wood.

I let each blow land on the tough skin of my hide and I keep going until . . .

A Frenchman who works in London at the archives of De Gaulle's Free French intelligence organization, the same organization that rejected Navarre's help when he offered it back in 1940, brings me a piece of paper.

"This was sent to the Free French by one of our agents back in October and flagged to be filed," he says. "But I knew you'd want to see it."

The transmission says: *Eagle was arrested along with Mahout and a British radio operator after landing in France. One of the landing crew, a Jean-Paul, was also arrested but is a Gestapo informer and was released by the Boches.*

There is only one Jean-Paul in my network. Lanky. He was at the field when Léon landed in France. He was responsible for Elephant's arrest. After that, I remember I'd said, *He's either a fool or a traitor.*

I'd spoken in anger about what I thought was incompetence. But this note tells me it was evil.

"Why didn't they send it to me in October?" My voice is a whisper. I've been desperate for evidence of who the traitor is, and our so-called French allies have been holding that evidence in their hands for months. Every arrest since October has been because of Lanky leading the Nazis straight to us, again and again and again.

The man in front of me looks pained. It's not his fault, and he's risking De Gaulle's wrath by even being here, let alone showing me this transmission. It's an open secret that the Free French hate the fact that we send our information to the British, rather than to them. But Navarre offered himself to De Gaulle and was rejected. The British accepted us. Is withholding this evidence an act of revenge by our supposed allies? Or was the import of the note just not understood?

I'll never know.

But I know that I have to get back to France.

I give Dansey one last chance. "I need to go now," I tell him.

"You won't last six days," he tells me in that smooth, patronizing voice.

So I do something I would never have considered a year ago. But there are no limits now to what I will do to achieve my goals: Resurrect Alliance. Throw Lanky in jail. Free Léon and all the rest. I don't even care if Navarre, who's been moved from a French prison to a German concentration camp, kills me when he finds out.

I go to see De Gaulle's chief intelligence officer and make a deal with the devil who kept the note about Lanky from me.

"Alliance will become part of the Free French," I tell him, offering no pleasantries or small talk, no smiles or obfuscations. "I'll remain in control of my network, but you'll get my information. De Gaulle wants to be the one in charge when France is finally free, and you know that having Alliance's support gives him power. In exchange, you'll use one of the airplanes you're in control of to get me back to France. But I'll also keep sending our information to MI6 and will keep supporting them, too. I won't be budged on that."

A shocked laugh escapes him. "You're very forward," he says.

I pass him a legal document that outlines the terms by which Alliance will become part of the Free French and fix my eyes on him. "Politicians keep secrets. I'm a commandant. We keep moving forward until we win."

He accepts the papers. He knows De Gaulle is far stronger with Alliance than without it.

My final stop that day is to visit Dansey, to tell him what I've done. He sets his pipe down and says, "You've turned into quite the wildcat."

"I was trained by the best."

Crane gets me new identity papers. I become Germaine Pezet, French peasant, the last identity I hope to possess before I can reclaim my true name. An officer who's an expert in disguise transforms me, using a net to lower my hairline, a dental prosthetic to give me bucked, yellow teeth. My hair is dyed black, spectacles are added, and I look so hideous that Crane bursts out laughing when he sees me.

"Nobody would mistake you for the beautiful spy," he says.

I laugh, then say, "Thank you. For everything."

And he replies, "Thank you for so much more than everything."

I don't weep. A drought now lives where I once possessed tears. But I smile. Because, at last, I am proud.

I'm coming, Léon. Hold on just a little bit longer.

On the morning I'm due to leave, I run over everything in my mind. Of our once three-thousand-strong network, there are still left seventy-five principal agents along with eight hundred foot soldiers and their helpers. Seventeen transmitters.

We need only hold on through the invasion and into the history that must surely follow.

Into a false-bottomed valise go crystals for the radio sets, new codes, money, and the cyanide capsules that announce my two stark choices if I'm caught: Betray my network or kill myself.

There is, of course, a third option: Don't get caught.

I dress in a gray wool suit, a felt hat, and a navy-blue coat. I put in my prosthetic.

A knock sounds on the door. I open it, expecting Crane. But it's Dansey. His expression is dour, and for a moment I think he's going to stop me, and I wonder if I could ever use a gun on this man.

"We're sending you into the wolf's mouth," he says starkly. "So near the end. It's madness."

I say what I always have. "I must go back."

Outside, anti-aircraft fire sounds. Then comes the distant whiz of a V1 rocket, which have been falling on Britain for weeks. The rockets my network told the British about. The rockets that have wreaked havoc, yes, but not utter destruction because so many of the launchers and facilities were blown up due to Alliance's intelligence.

Dansey picks up my hand. "I'm ashamed of seeing you all these years doing things I couldn't do myself."

And in his soul I see something I hadn't understood. It's not that he hates that I'm a woman. He hates that sometimes when he looks at me, he feels as if his own role has been nothing and mine, everything.

And it is.

Then he's gone, and in my hand remains a rabbit's foot, a blessing from someone I never thought would care.

It's time to go home to my family.

40

The Start of the End

84 Avenue Foch, Paris, October 1943

NOTES IN LAVATORY

Bob said you can reach Rue Pergolèse from roofs of adjoining houses. Someone escaped that way a year ago, then they put bars across the shafts. Inayat.

Tell Bob I can get him on a plane to London if he helps. Léon.

He said okay! Inayat.

We need a screwdriver to chisel away bricks around bars. Léon.

Screwdriver hidden in crevice under S-bend. Bob.

Use screwdriver for one day, then leave it for next person. Disguise hole around bar with crumbs from rations. Bob to get flashlight, rope, map of the route to Rue Pergolèse. Léon.

Confirm flashlight, rope, map. Bob.

Everyone make extra rope from bedsheets to rappel off roof. Léon.

Sorry, I took screwdriver on wrong day. But slow going. Needed more time. Inayat.

One hundred push-ups in the morning. One hundred at midday, or as near as he can tell by the angle of the sun through the skylight. One hundred after dinner, which is gruel with a little bread.

Léon hasn't eaten meat since he left London. He can feel his physical strength, which has always been immense, trying to ebb away. But he won't let it. He has three tasks: to exercise, to plan with Inayat and Bob, and to work on Kieffer, the guard who comes every second day and who hasn't beaten him again. Müller, the alternate guard, hits Léon for merely breathing, and Léon knows not to waste time on him.

From their interrogations so far, Léon has gleaned that Kieffer is religious, that he has a wife and a son about the same age as Léon's. Kieffer has seen his child twice. Léon has never seen his. That he even has a son is a fact he hasn't shared with Kieffer, who opens the door now, as Léon knew he would. Kieffer's chief attribute is that he's prompt, meaning Léon's ready to fire before Kieffer can.

"How many people have you killed?" he demands.

Kieffer startles.

"Don't know? Don't remember? Don't care?" Léon continues. "I can tell you exactly how many I've killed, from those I bayoneted or shot in the Great War to those I've gunned down in a plane. I think of them often—perhaps not every night, but at least every week. You know why? Because when you become a soldier, you accept that your job involves killing people. And you have two choices: to become a murderer or to be an assassin. An assassin is given a task and kills only those necessary to that task. A murderer kills because it pleases him. He doesn't remember his count of souls because once the kill is done, he's already looking for the next victim. Some people might call him a devil. But devils don't hide in human clothes and pretend to have souls. So"—Léon sits in Kieffer's chair—"I ask you: How many people have you killed?"

Kieffer's face is white. Léon braces for the punch.

But Kieffer says, "We'll recognize Alliance as part of the French army. You're prisoners of war and won't be tried or executed until the war ends."

Kieffer's words almost turn Léon's knees to water. He's been granted what he asked for, a concession he hardly believed the Nazis would make. It means Magpie and Rivière and all the others won't be killed—not yet. They just have to stay alive until the Allies invade France.

Léon stands and walks four careful paces away, trying to think. *What's going on?*

When he turns back to Kieffer, he sees what he's hoped to find since their first encounter: the flicker of a soul.

"You say the Germans are losing," Kieffer says sharply. "I want to know more."

So Léon tells Kieffer that the Germans have been routed in Russia. That every night bombers fly out from London and drop their payloads all over Germany. That this is the start of the end, which is very near.

In truth, Léon knows the Allies won't invade France until 1944, that there are at least months to go. But he knows that Germany will lose. And most people want to save their skins when it looks like they're about to be flayed.

At the end of Léon's recitation, Kieffer stands. "We are the same," he says.

Léon laughs.

But Kieffer insists, "We're fighting for the same thing. Our country. Honor. *La patrie,* as the French say. So, I tell you." Kieffer walks to the door. "We are the same."

We're completely different! The words die on Léon's tongue. The Nazis fight for lust and for power. But not everyone is a Napoléon.

Léon's war is holy, but he's not stupid enough to think it bloodless. And he's never tortured anyone for fun. He's never lusted for a kill—except perhaps now. Now he prays for the death of Alliance's traitor, whoever that is.

That's when he sees that Kieffer has left behind a folder titled *Noah's Ark. Interrogations 1942–1943.*

Inside are the records of every interrogation of every Alliance agent captured.

Léon exhales. This will tell him exactly what the Gestapo know, so that when Müller comes in to interrogate and thrash Léon tomorrow, Léon will know if he's lying. And if Kieffer has left these papers for him, then Kieffer is open to negotiations.

Léon will promise him a one-way ticket out of France on a Lysander. But to reach that Lysander, Kieffer will have to take Léon—and maybe Inayat and Bob—out of Avenue Foch and set them free.

Minerva, he thinks, throwing himself on the bed, knowing their thoughts are connected like Morse messages on radio waves. *I'm alive and I almost have a safe way out of here. I won't have to take the riskier route onto the roof and down a rope made of bedsheets in the middle of the night. I'm coming home. To you and Achille. It won't be long now.*

41

The Last Road Remaining

84 Avenue Foch, Paris, October 1943

NOTES IN LAVATORY

Close to securing safer route out. Will make sure you're included. Léon.

Chiseling not going well, so hope your plan is successful. Inayat.

Departure set for 22:30 hours, Thursday night. Be ready. Léon.

I've been ready for months. Inayat.

It's Thursday. Müller will never again break one of Léon's ribs, because Léon will never see Müller again, except to hand him to the Allies whenever they finally land in France.

The morning passes in the usual way. Gruel. Push-ups. Grinding stone away from the bars of the ventilation shaft in case something goes wrong tonight, which it won't. The lavatory. Finding Inayat's note.

Thank you, it says. *I know you could have gone alone.*

Only after much persuasion had Kieffer relented to another prisoner's coming. Léon chose the woman; he'd want someone to choose Marie-Madeleine over him. And taking no one with him would make him like Müller, breaking a hope instead of a rib.

Hopes are harder to heal than ribs.

They're also impossible to subdue. His are surging like adrenaline, making it hard to play the role of prisoner. Luckily he's always been such an insubordinate asshole that the Nazis shouldn't notice much difference.

He lowers himself to the floor after push-up one hundred, waiting for the door to open. But it doesn't.

Kieffer should be arriving for the daily interrogation, which has lately turned to planning. Léon and Inayat are to feign illness. Kieffer's physician will say they must be taken to hospital by ambulance, with Kieffer as guard. The ambulance will drive them to what Léon hopes is still an Alliance safe house, from where he'll begin the task of tracking down whoever is left so Kieffer can be taken out by a Lysander, not to freedom as promised, but into the hands of the Allies. And Léon can reunite with Minerva.

What a reunion that will be.

His smile is wide now. But one thought makes it dim: Kieffer is never late.

Fear tries to course through him.

Then he hears it. Footsteps. Kieffer's coming.

Time to double over, to pretend his appendix is about to burst out of his body, like the joy at finally getting out of here alive.

But it isn't Kieffer who enters.

It's a Gestapo officer Léon has never met. By way of greeting, he strikes Léon across the head with his stick.

Goddamn it. At least Léon won't have to act as if he's in pain when Kieffer appears.

For an hour Léon remains silent while each unanswered

question about Alliance and Marie-Madeleine is met with a blow. Then he asks, trying to smile through lips swollen to twice their usual size, "To what do I owe the pleasure of this treatment?"

The next blow is the most shocking of all—and it isn't even physical. "Resistance scum shot Sturmbannführer Kieffer last night," the officer snarls.

The club flies harder and faster and Léon doesn't even try to dodge the blows. This is the moment when you give up at last. When you know you're done, and this is the place where you'll die.

How many times can one man escape prison after all?

You've lost all of your lives and then some, Marie-Madeleine had said to him that night in London when she told him MI6 didn't want him returning to France.

He should have listened to her.

And the thought slips in past the ringing in his ears: Was he too arrogant? Is his patriotism just selfishness dressed up in fine clothes? Who chooses a cell, a thrashing, and likely death over their infant son?

Will his son think his father died for hubris or for glory?

But his son shouldn't have to think of his father. He should *know* his father.

Which means listening to the distant echo of Marie-Madeleine's voice telling him that yes, Léon Faye is the one man who *can* escape from prison four times.

So he waits, curled up in a ball, for the officer's fury to dim. Then he hauls himself to his feet, vomits into the bucket, takes out his bedsheet, tears it to pieces, and wraps the worst wounds, ignoring the violent whirl in his head. He removes the screwdriver from its hiding place, scoops out the breadcrumbs packed in to conceal the widening hole, and chisels away at that passage to freedom through the ventilation shaft—the last road remaining between him and the end.

42

Operation Freedom

84 Avenue Foch, Paris, November 1943

NOTES IN LAVATORY

Escaping via roof too risky. Should reconsider. Bob.

Have courage, man. With your map, we'll be off the roof before they even know we've escaped. Léon.

Please, Bob. You promised. Inayat.

Okay. Bob.

Operation Freedom set for November 23. Léon and Inayat to roof at 22:30 hours. Bob to roof at 1:30 hours with flashlight and rope. Léon

At half past ten, Léon ties the bedsheet rope around his body. That's all he'll take, besides bruises and badly healed bones. He hopes his face isn't so hideous that Marie-Madeleine will recoil, hopes she'll still look at him as if he's the one glass of water in a bone-dry desert.

Without making a sound, he stands on the chair, removes the breadcrumbs from around the bar, places the bar on the bed, climbs onto the chair, and grasps the remaining bar, pulling himself up into the skylight with every granule of his strength. Then he balances atop the bar and considers, now that he's inside the shaft, how to climb it.

It'll be like scrambling up a glacier without a pick. There isn't a single foot- or handhold.

He arrests his doubts before they bludgeon him. Inayat said someone had done this before. So it's possible. What isn't possible is for him to come up with another escape plan.

He braces one foot against the side of the shaft, then the other, splays his hands against the sides, too. He'll have to use the pressure of his limbs against the walls, and he absolutely cannot slip and fall onto the bar below, because that will not only be excruciating, but also noisy enough to rouse every guard.

He starts to climb.

He's only a quarter of the way up when sweat drips from every pore, despite it being November. His legs want to shake and so do his arms, but he won't let them. He thinks of Minerva trapped in a mailbag for ten hours with a damaged hip, and he presses himself up a little higher. Only when he's been in this shaft for ten hours does he have a right to complain.

The sweat is making his hands slip. But he trained in the military for this—the moments when your mind wants to convince your body that it has limits. Tonight, for his son, Léon is illimitable.

There! He's reached the top. Legs shaking like an airplane in a hurricane, he pushes the skylight cover aside, and then he's on the roof, and the stars are above him, and even though Moroccan skies have always been his favorite, right now Paris night skies gulped in at the end of the impossible are the most magnificent of all.

He's just hours away from holding Marie-Madeleine in his arms and then, finally, meeting his son.

Once he's inhaled Paris fully, Léon looks around. Bob's map showed it was possible to cross the roof to a neighboring building that exits onto Rue Pergolèse. But nothing out here matches Bob's map. There's a frantic scraping sound coming from his left that the Nazis will hear, and if they come to investigate, they'll find him up here instead of in his cell.

He moves toward the sound, counts the number of skylights, and realizes it's coming from Inayat's cell. He removes the skylight cover and whispers, "Are you coming?"

"My bar isn't free. But it will be," she says determinedly.

"It's too loud. You won't have time."

"Please." She starts to cry. Beseeches him. And all he can think of is Minerva, that he'd want anyone she begged something of to listen.

Bob's voice echoes from inside the prison. He's never locked in until later; he must have heard the noise and is talking to the guards to cover it. Perhaps with his help, Inayat will make it.

"All right," Léon concedes. "I'll wait until Bob gets here. In the meantime, I'm going to reconnoiter, because it seems like Bob's map is worthless."

"I'll be out soon," she tells him.

She's crazy, but aren't they all?

Like all Parisian roofs, this one slants precipitously down to an internal courtyard, which is patrolled by dogs. He needs to get to the edge, then he can reach the neighboring building, from where he hopes to be able to see a road. He'll have to wriggle like a snake and hope—take the hill without the brakes. But in this situation, Marie-Madeleine would do the same, because the only certainty waiting for him inside Avenue Foch is death.

He slithers down, but the slope is too much. He's going to go right off the edge and into the mouths of the dogs. Of all the ways to die, not that.

Somehow he comes to a halt just in time, thankful that the only heart condition he has is that of being utterly in love.

At the top of the next building, he still can't see any roads. But there's a terrace on the next building across, which they'll be able to reach with Bob's rope. From there, surely they'll be able to get down to the street.

But will it be a street lined with Nazis or an ordinary pedestrian one?

He hauls himself back up to the attic roof, grateful he's had only minor beatings lately and these physical hijinks don't hurt too much.

Inayat's still scraping away. He could leave now, not wait for her, not wait for Bob, who drew a map they can't even use. But when you've been trained all your life to never leave your team, it's impossible to do it now. These two unmet people have been his companions in Morse code and hidden notes since September, and their presence has made each day a little easier. So he makes himself wait, even though his feet want to run.

Finally, Bob appears through the skylight in his own cell. Léon takes him to the edge of the roof and points. "Do you think that house is occupied by the Gestapo?"

"I don't know." Bob's brow is covered with sweat. His hands are shaking and now Léon wants to swear. Thankfully, Inayat interrupts, calling up that she's ready.

Dieu merci.

Léon pulls her out of the shaft and they set off across the roof. He has to admonish Inayat to step quietly. *Where the hell do they train these people?* An elephant would be better at stealth.

They use Léon's bedsheet rope to get down to the next floor, rather than attempt the scramble that almost turned him into dog food. Once there, he asks Bob for the rope—and that's when Bob reveals that he doesn't have any of the items he promised, just another bedsheet.

"Give it here," Léon says, trying not to sound as pissed off as he feels. He takes out the razor blades he's brought with him and cuts the sheet into lengths, twists them together, and down they go to the terrace.

Suddenly, the night around them explodes.

Squadron after squadron of bombers roar overhead, chased by the anti-aircraft guns. Léon recognizes the planes: American Flying Fortresses, most likely on their way back to England after unleashing their payloads on Germany. He's cheered at the sight, but Bob lets out a terrified wail.

"Be quiet, man," Léon admonishes.

These two British agents are just like Bla—dangerous. If they don't get onto the street soon, there's no telling what Bob will do. And Léon can't bear to contemplate that, after having made it out of his cell, he'll be recaptured because he decided to bring two incompetents with him.

That's when he sees Inayat's watch. It has a luminous dial, for Christ's sake. In the pitch-dark of the terrace, it's shining as brightly as the moon.

A German voice pierces the night. Then a flashlight lights up the terrace.

"Put your watch in your pocket," Léon tells Inayat, pushing them all deep into a corner, where he hopes they're hidden.

Bob's entire body is shaking now. Every woman in Alliance has more courage than this British agent, and Léon wishes for one terrible moment that he could push Bob off the roof.

Above them, the Flying Fortresses dodge bullets; tracer shells arc, boom, and explode; and despair clutches Léon like a devil, begging for his spirit and his self-belief, the only things you have that are worth a damn when you're locked in a Nazi prison. But he's held on to those things for two and a half months. He can't relinquish them now, not when he can see a street below—a street that leads to freedom.

"All right," he whispers to Inayat and Bob, who's still quivering. "We stay here until the air raid ends and the Nazis relax. If they saw us, they'd have come after us. I'm guessing it's around four in the morning. The guards won't check our cells until six. Curfew ends at five, so that's when we go. We're so close now."

He says the words in the soothing tones he might one day be lucky enough to use with his son.

But another explosion has Bob jumping to his feet, his hold on sanity finally unloosed. "I'm leaving," he mutters.

Léon should just let him be shot. But his morals force him to drag Bob back into the darkness. And dammit if Inayat doesn't leap up, too.

This time, the flashlight catches them all in its beam.

"Jump!" Léon shouts. "Just jump."

43

Vanquished

éon leaps, wishing he really was an eagle and could soar away. He lands on the terrace below with a bone-jarring thud. No time to see if Bob's groans mean he's cracked a bone—a sentry appears and shines his flashlight up at them.

Léon smashes the window by his elbow. He has no idea what's inside. But if they can make it to a back entrance and out onto a different street, they might have a chance.

"Go," he urges his companions, and they climb through, Bob thankfully following orders, Inayat paler than the moon.

Léon feels his way in the dark, aware of the panicked breaths of the others behind him. But luck finds them at last. There's a set of service stairs at the end of the corridor. They hurtle down as fast as the darkness allows.

At the bottom there's a door. A door that leads onto a street.

He reaches out a hand and turns the knob.

In the blackout dark beyond, he can hear the sound of a sentry's footsteps.

"Be very quiet," Léon whispers to Bob and Inayat. If he ever needed the fabled luck his fellow officers believed followed him like a loyal hound, it's right now.

So he closes his eyes and wishes that tonight, rather than stars, there were ladybugs and horseshoes, silver fish and an elephant's tusk dotted in the sky above. If he holds out his hand, he'll catch the sweet drops of good fortune.

There. He's ready.

As soon as the sentry's footsteps recede to the south, Léon runs into the street. He runs and he runs, has never felt more like his Eagle namesake than he does right now, flying to freedom. He runs for two hundred meters—when he's brought up short by a wall. A damn wall!

He almost roars in disbelief. It's as if he's never done one good thing in his life. Except he *has* done good, he knows he has. He's been risking his life for his country since he was seventeen years old, and he deserves one damn break.

But those are the thoughts that make you lose your mind like Bob. So he sprints back the way he came, can hear the sentry returning from his march. He makes it just in time to where Bob and Inayat are still hiding.

The only thing left to do is to put blind trust in fate and run the same way the sentry has gone, pray that the sentry's back is turned and he can get away down a side street before he's seen. He can't think about Bob and Inayat anymore.

He slips off his shoes so he can run silently. Then he races out.

An explosion of sound meets him. He throws himself to the ground and counts. Ten seconds later, an entire magazine of bullets has been discharged, but Léon can't feel any pain. Dame Fortune is, despite all appearances to the contrary, on his side—it's so dark out here that the sentry missed. Léon needs to take advantage of the few seconds he has while the sentry reloads.

He jumps to his feet, ready to run again.

But from out of the dark come more SS officers. So many of them, when he is only one man. They all have revolvers. They don't shoot, not this time.

They want Léon Faye alive.

They hit him over and over with the butts of their revolvers. He feels his nose break first, then his jaw. After that, everything is dark.

Alliance's Eagle sinks to the ground, vanquished.

For now.

44

I Forget to Push the Bolt Across

Aix-en-Provence, May–July 1944

It takes eleven modes of transport, including a Hudson bomber, a wagon, and a coal truck, to cross France. My palms are brown, rubbed all over with the soil of my country, when I arrive at an apartment on Rue Granet in Aix-en-Provence, my rendezvous with Lucien.

Once inside my new lair, I let myself think about my family. Léon. Béatrice. Christian. Achille. I know the invasion is a day or at most a week behind me, that the Germans are hearing those rumors, too, and will step up every manhunt and trap, every torture and interrogation. So I need this final fight to be quick and over.

Alliance must get to work.

Half an hour later, Lucien scratches at the door.

"Hérisson!" he cries, and we embrace and weep and are ridiculously sentimental for at least five minutes until I step back, wipe my face, take out cigarettes for us, and say, "Update me."

"I have boxes of documents for you," he says. "Dragon managed to escape, and he's with the duke in Paris."

Just like that, it's as if I never left.

He tells me that little has been discovered about the agents behind bars, except that all around France, trainloads of prisoners are being sent somewhere beyond the Rhine.

"Léon?" I ask, forgetting I'm supposed to say *Eagle*.

"Nothing."

But nor have we heard that he's dead. My gut would know if he was.

"You should have ordered him to stay in London." Lucien's words are sharp.

That blow is one that finally pierces my hide. I flinch. "I couldn't."

Lucien stands and, my God, he looks like a blazing, passionate Léon when he says, "That's a lie. But I know why you have to tell it to yourself."

I reach out my hand and take his, our fingers equally smeared with dirt. "I didn't mean it like that. I meant that I couldn't make myself do it, not that it was impossible to make him stay."

"Eagle would have ordered you if he'd been in your position."

Very gently, I tell him, "No, he wouldn't. In that situation, he would have been weak, too."

"Dammit!" Lucien's frustration echoes loudly and he walks over to the ceiling beam, raises both his hands, and presses them against it. His shoulders move up and down in time to his breath, and I press one foot painfully hard on top of the other to stop myself from holding him like his mother would. I let him pretend to be just breathing, when I'm certain he's weeping for Josette and Léon and Amniarix, and every man and woman he's sent out into the field who hasn't returned, and maybe also the girl in London whom he'll never show the hard scars he's had to grow around his heart.

When he turns around, he says, "You can't be weak again."

"I know."

Never in my life did I think that if Léon was in jail, I

wouldn't rush straight out to find him. But never in my life did I imagine that Lucien would one day become my chief lieutenant and I'd watch him try not to cry over the deaths he blames himself for.

In the animal kingdom, lionesses lead their prides, female elephants rule their herds, and the lady hyena takes charge of her pack. It's with the elephant's strength, the hyena's determination, and the lioness's fierceness that I tell Lucien, "Every decision I make now is for one end. Victory. Which is why I won't send an agent to search every prison in France. It's why I can't send anyone to look for Lanky. Because we need everyone we have left to gather the intelligence that leads to victory. That's how the prisons get opened and the traitors caught. I know I'm condemning people to die. But if I make any other decision, I'm condemning even more."

"We'll never be the same after this, will we?" Lucien says bleakly.

Last year I would have lied to him. Now I whisper, "No. And we'll have to learn to live with a desert inside us instead of a soul."

After Lucien has gone to the farmhouse, where he keeps the transmitter, I lie in the bath with my eyes closed. Perhaps I fall asleep; perhaps the dirt on my hands connects me to the smudged dirt on my love's fingertips, but suddenly I can feel Léon in the bathtub, too. It isn't him exactly, nor his ghost. It isn't memory, either. It's as if the water has taken on his shape and the air has carried in his voice. "Look at how beautiful we are," he whispers.

And I know for certain—he's alive. I need to help the Allies win before that changes.

Operation Overlord lands the Allies on the beaches we mapped for them. From there, they take control of entire towns. Across the south of France, music and celebrations play, and I wonder what France looks like that night from the air. A firework, perhaps.

The Nazis will lose. The only thing I can't see is how long it will take. But, as Lucien toasts with the Beaujolais he found somewhere, "Soon. It will be soon."

If you've been stranded on an island for ten years, a year might be soon. If you've been locked in a prison for one hundred years, perhaps ten might feel like soon.

Soon is too far away.

The Germans retaliate. Violence rules. American and British soldiers leave their bodies behind in Normandy. And London demands more intelligence than ever.

I restart sectors, find new agents to man those sectors, answer questionnaires, make my way through reports that come in from the new generation of Alliance. Lucien collects transmissions from me and his operator sends them. The days go on into July, which brings a heavy, blanketing humidity, perfuming the air with roses that still bloom despite it being the fifth year of German occupation.

There's a scrape at the door and Lucien tells me, "The subprefect let me know that the Germans are planning to search Aix-en-Provence tomorrow afternoon. They know the maquis are expecting supplies."

"I'll pack up," I tell him. "Come back for me at seven in the morning."

As I close the door behind him, I forget to push the bolt across.

Five minutes later, it happens. German voices shouting in the stairwell. I race to the door, but there are too many of them.

"Where's the man?" they shout as they break in.

I put on a show. Use my disguise to the best of my ability.

I almost make it.

Almost is a word as bad as *soon*. There's no such thing as being almost free.

I'm taken to a prison cell in an army barracks.

45

The Freedom Bar

Aix-en-Provence, July 1944

Hours later, I'm standing on an upturned bucket on a cot in a cell in a military barracks, the air around me fetid with bedbugs and body odor. The little I've eaten in the last twenty-four hours sits in a disgorged pile in the corner, along with the contents of the slop bucket I'm balancing on. I'm naked besides my underwear and I'm gripping my dress in my teeth the same way a lioness carries her cub. A Gestapo commandant is on his way to interrogate me, and a hysterical bubble of laughter rises up in me at this ridiculous scene.

What am I doing? Thinking I can squeeze through the bars? Surely it's rule number one of building a prison: Make sure the bars are close enough together that no one can fit through.

The laughter vanishes as quickly as it appeared. I want to retch again, vomit up stupid hope. I'm not a Shanghai robber with a slickly oiled body. I'm a thirty-four-year-old mother of three children whom I can't leave motherless.

So I stretch up my arms, take hold of the top of the board covering the window, and haul myself up, feet scrabbling spider-like against the wall. When I'm high enough, I wedge the board under my armpits and throw one leg over, take a moment to catch my breath, then throw the other leg over. Now my whole body is hanging between the board and the bars, hands gripping the top like I'm a cat and it's my ninth life. I have to let go, drop feetfirst onto what I hope will be a sill wide enough to stand on.

What if there isn't a sill and I fall into an opening in the wall? What if it's full of rats? *What if* . . .

Nobody in a war zone asks *what if* questions.

I let go.

I land with a jolt on a stone ledge, pressed between the board and the bars. There are no rats. Just the sight of freedom beyond. I want to linger in the beautiful moment of imagining that yes, the stonemason was incompetent enough not to know how far apart to space the prison bars.

But at the edges of the sky, black is softening to charcoal. I don't have any moments left to linger in the folds of a dream.

I push my head against the space between the first two bars. There's no way it will fit. I try the next two bars. Also impossible. Then the third set.

I gasp. My head almost fits. If I push very hard, I might be able to force it through.

I shut my mind off from imagining what might happen: my skull crushed, ears torn off. That will be a far lesser agony than what awaits me in the hands of the Gestapo.

I shove my head into the gap.

It hurts more than childbirth, more than being folded double in a mailbag for ten hours. But I keep pushing, and the sudden shock of my head popping through the bars almost unbalances me.

I stand there panting, sweat streaming off me, every part of me from my neck down still inside the cell. But my head is liberated.

I steel myself for the rest.

Then a convoy of cars draws up just opposite my window, and I silently swear every shocking word I've ever heard. They'll see my head sticking out!

There are some moments when you think through what you

need to do and others when you know that thinking will undo you.

I yank my head back through the bars so brutally I'm sure my ears are gone.

I stand there, limp and sobbing from the pain. The Gestapo commander has arrived. In a few minutes he'll walk through the door and find me here, naked and pressed between the bars and the board like a butterfly pinned to a display. And he'll pierce me with the final pin—a bullet from his gun, a bayonet from his rifle.

And Noah's Ark will sink to its grave.

The act of breathing is harder than believing in God in wartime. Blackness doesn't just hover at the edges of my vision, but right in front of me as German words punctuate the night. I realize someone in the convoy is talking to a sentry in the courtyard, who's positioned exactly where I'd planned to run.

Merde. I hadn't counted on there being a guard outside. Not that it'll matter when the Gestapo pile out of their cars and into my cell.

Listen, I tell myself. *Translate. Find out how much time you have.*

As I unravel the meaning of their words, I almost collapse again, this time with relief. It isn't the Gestapo. Just soldiers asking for directions.

At last the trucks move off. As they pass, I see it's a military unit that I warned London about—going to Normandy to reinforce troops. How strange to see something I perceived yesterday as a threat but that I now vastly prefer to a Gestapo convoy.

The sentry marches away, back to his post in the courtyard.

I stare at the bars. Everything rebels at the idea of pushing my head *back* through. But this is the moment for true resistance. I've just sweated enough to fill an ocean. Perhaps it'll be easier this time.

Before the devil in my mind can mock my ridiculous optimism, I push. If I thought that pulling my head back in through the bars was the worst pain I'd ever experienced, I grossly underestimated how much pain it was possible to feel. This is torture I don't have a word for. My skin weeps sweat and finally my head passes through.

I stand there filling my lungs with oxygen until I'm ready to tackle my shoulders, which thankfully escape the bars easily, as does my right leg up to my thigh.

Which means it's time for my hips.

I'm stuck half in and half out of a window. There's no going back. So I concentrate on what must be fact—if my head could fit through, so can my hips.

I turn sideways and my God I want to scream. What kind of wreckage am I making of my already damaged hip? I bite my tongue so hard to stop myself from making a sound that my mouth pools with blood. But it's better to hurt now in my own hands than in the hands of the Gestapo.

One second later, I'm on the outside of the window.

I jump onto the pavement below.

"*Wer ist da?*" the sentry shouts.

The beam of a flashlight opens the darkness. I have to move before he sees the woman most wanted by the Gestapo on her hands and knees in the dirt.

Does my hip still work? It has to.

On all fours, I crawl to the edge of the square. Then I stand and run into the open, almost losing my balance in the potholes I can't see in the dark, branches ripping my skin, every muscle braced for a bullet to slam right through me.

I run and run for several minutes but don't feel any bullets, can't hear any sounds behind me. I stop to pull on my dress, then I run again, because if the sentry saw me he'll be readying the dogs.

There'll be no escaping the dogs.

Farther down the road, I come to a cemetery. Safety, perhaps. I could hide in one of the monuments and when the priest arrives in the morning, he might help. But—the dogs. Even if I hide in a chapel, the dogs will sniff me out.

Think, I tell myself, trying desperately to find a way through the pain and the panic when something trickles down the side of my face. Blood. Dogs will certainly smell that. I need to wash.

There's a stream to the east of Aix-en-Provence. I've been running east already, so I run a little farther and then, tearing more of my skin to ribbons, scramble down a stony incline, tug off my dress, and scrub, paying special attention to the bleeding skin on my feet, arms, hips, and head.

Calmer now, my mind begins to work. *Which way is Lucien's farmhouse?*

That's when I realize it's back past the barracks I've just run from.

No.

But there's no other road. And Lucien will arrive at my apartment soon. The Gestapo will be waiting for him. I have to reach him before he walks into a trap.

I've done one impossible thing already. Which means it's time for a second impossible thing—otherwise known as a miracle.

As I hurry back the way I came, dawn rushes over the sky the way it does in Provence: golden and glorious. Birdsong strikes up, a morning symphony completely at odds with my trembling body.

The barracks is just ten feet away. There's a sentry outside.

Do I look dirty and suspicious?

Everyone's dirty after four years of war.

I move forward.

Eight feet to go.

Five feet.

Three feet.

The sentry looks up.

His stare is blank, as if he's dreaming, not really seeing me. I keep my head high. My gaze straight ahead. I'm a proud Parisienne off to market to get the best of whatever vegetables the Germans haven't already taken.

I pass in front of him.

Then he's behind me and I have no idea what he's doing, can't turn to look. I keep my cool until I reach the corner, where I gallop to the next street and hide behind a stand of hollyhocks. Maybe I'm crossing the line between madness and hope again, but the barracks seemed calm. There are no dogs baying. Perhaps nobody knows I'm gone.

Yet.

Soon the reveille will sound. I have perhaps ten minutes before the Nazis open my cell door.

I have to get to Lucien's house.

A woman in mourning clothes, perhaps on her way to mass, is passing through the Cours Mirabeau. I approach and say very quietly, "Madame, I need to find the Vauvenargues Road."

"I'm going that way, too," she says. "You look as if you're in pain. Lean on me."

Perhaps she's an angel.

The second I take her arm, the dogs begin to bark, ready to tear apart the woman whose scent they're sniffing in my cell. A minute later, armored cars pour through the square. But the widow beside me walks calmly on, not commenting on the trembling she must feel in my body.

On the outskirts of town, she points. "It's that way."

I have nothing to give her. Nothing except words. "You've just done me the greatest service anyone has ever done me in my life."

She nods as if it were nothing when, in fact, it was everything.

I hurry away, a new worry besetting me. I have to cross the bridge over the Torse. But the Germans have posted guards there and are stopping everyone, checking papers.

My luck is ebbing away.

I search for a solution. Right near the bridge is a field where a handful of peasant women are stooped over their work of gleaning, gathering up corn ears and dandelion. So I slip into the field, too, and bend my body double. I sift the detritus, pick out ears of corn. The Germans never glance our way.

I continue to glean, moving farther and farther across the field, until finally I'm able to emerge on the road at a point far past the soldiers who are hunting me.

At last I reach Lucien's house. I push open the door and call out, "They're looking for you!"

The minute the words are spoken, my body slides onto the floor.

When I rouse, Lucien is sitting on the end of the bed watching me as if he's charged with caring for me, rather than the other way around. "The Gestapo are hunting for a naked woman"—he raises one eyebrow—"which is a story you'll have to save for later. They even shot their own guard for losing you."

It means they've finally figured out that the leader of Noah's Ark has slipped through their fingers.

"It's time to join the maquis," I say. We've been supplying the maquis in the foothills of the Montagne Sainte-Victoire for some time, so they'll be happy to take us.

"We have to take the weapons with us," Lucien says, eyeing the submachine guns and other arms stacked in piles. "It's twenty kilometers uphill."

I inspect the damage done to my feet from running barefoot from prison. They're shredded, covered in blisters and blood. But I find a smile, because I have to.

A woman who commands legions with grace and courage and humility and flair, Léon once told me. My legions need me. And I need this war to end next week so I can find Léon, arrest Lanky, free France, see my children. It isn't the time to complain about sore feet.

"After last night's adventure," I say, "if it was just an easy downhill stroll I might die of boredom."

Lucien laughs.

We wait until nightfall, then we set off—Lucien, the radio operator, and me—like loaded mules, one almost lame. Every time we hear the hum of an engine, we throw ourselves into bushes or ditches, lie on our faces in dirt and brambles. We walk, dive, cower, wait, stand, lift the packs. I bite my well-bitten lip and walk some more. Sometimes it's only a few minutes between dives; occasionally we have a full half hour.

We're only halfway there when I can no longer walk without support. Lucien props up one side of me, his radio operator the other.

"Go on ahead," I tell them. "Otherwise we'll all be caught. I'll hide until tomorrow night, let my feet heal a little."

"No." Lucien's tone is more stubborn than mine. "You've been shouldering Alliance for four years. It's time for us to shoulder you for a few hours."

So we go on. My reward is a Cézannesque dawn unfurling in delicate pink, silhouetting the turrets of the Vauvenargues Chateau and the regal Sainte-Victoire mountain, which beckons us on. I try to make my feet as strong as the spirits of my companions, but bodies are weaker than souls, and Alliance is peopled with the strongest of all. In the hamlet of Claps, beside ancestral stones that have stood in French soil for centuries, my feet give up and I sink to the ground.

A password whispered by Lucien brings us a mule and cart to take us the last few kilometers to the encampment, where the maquis welcome us and our weapons.

"It's an honor to have you here, Hérisson," their leader tells me.

"It's an honor to be here," I say truthfully.

The maquis are dispersed in groups throughout the forest. There's one house near the encampment and Lucien tells me to sleep there but I say, "I don't think I'll ever be able to sleep inside again. If I sleep out here, I'll be ready if anything happens. Put the radio in the house."

I make myself a nest in a bush, a true animal now, and I wonder what other wild habits I'll form over the coming days, weeks, months—*please God, not years*—it will take for the Allies to move through France.

The radio operator sets up his equipment inside and succeeds in making contact with London. I tell them I'm safe and can almost hear the relief in Crane's reply. Of course he tells me he's sending a Lysander to take back me to England and of course I tell him no, I'm not leaving. So he agrees to send supplies by parachute. The maquis whoop.

I spend the next few hours beside the radio, passing on the intelligence I'd meant to send the night before: what reinforcements are being made to the coastal defenses, which overnight bombing raids found their targets. And so it goes, the minutiae of resistance, be it blistered feet or coded words or tiny miracles.

In the evening, the maquis join me in my clearing around

the fire. They want me to tell them the story, which has already become legend, of how I escaped from a prison with my dress in my teeth and my heart in my mouth.

"I don't know why the gap in one set of bars was bigger than the rest," I finish. "If it hadn't been . . ."

A man stirs the fire, which is embers only, the perfect invisible warmth, and I wonder how long he must have been living out in these woods to be able to make a fire so comforting and yet so discreet. He says to me, "In my real life, I'm a mason. When we put bars into prison windows, after the officers have come in to measure the gaps, we nudge one bar just a little with our thumb. You'll find a bar like that in most prisons built by masons with a heart. We call it the freedom bar."

The freedom bar.

That night, as the maquis slip off to their lairs, I climb into a pile of blankets. Above, the sky is the richest black, like Léon's hair, a magnificence you want to climb right into. Stars gild the night, a soul caught and shining in each one: Schaerrer, Vallet, Coustenoble. In the darkness between each constellation, I picture every vanished man and woman: Rivière, Bee, Magpie, Baston, Léon. And I pray that all of them find a freedom bar, too.

46

The One Who Did Not Die

Bruchsal Fortress, Germany, December 1943

As Léon rouses, flashes of the past day or so drift into his consciousness: standing on a rooftop in Paris and seeing the stars for the first time in two and a half months, believing that all his nights would be starry from then on. Trying to do the honorable thing—which Marie-Madeleine has always said will be his downfall—by bringing Bob and Inayat with him.

If only he'd left as soon as he reached the roof. He'd be in Minerva's arms right now and his face wouldn't hurt like a lion was sinking its teeth into his bones.

No *if onlys*. The path to hell is paved with them, mortared with regrets.

Bruchsal, he'd heard his guards say when he was lying in the back of the van in that twilight state between waking and falling back into blackness. Which means he's in Germany. While escape is a possibility in France, in Germany, it's a mad dream. Especially after he caught a glimpse of what Bruchsal is: a fortress.

He also heard the guards tell the jailer at the drawbridge, *"Ein wichtiger Terrorist, ein Specialist des Entfliehens."*

An important terrorist. An expert in escape.

Not Léon Faye anymore. Not Eagle, either.

God, he wants to vomit. Wants to curl up and try to keep all

his broken bones together. But his ankles and wrists are mana-
cled to an iron bedstead. He's lying on a floor that isn't just
damp, but wet, as if he's so far below ground he'll never see the
sun again.

For the first time in his life, he wonders: *Did I love France too
much?*

The latch in the door clatters, a bowl is pushed through the
hatch. "Half rations," the guard says. "To teach you a lesson."

What lesson could that possibly teach? He already knows
the Nazis are so cruel that no myth or story, no painting or
sculpted hell has ever captured what a real monster is.

Which means he can't let them win. Especially now that his
mind has begun to work and he remembers what the guard at
Avenue Foch had whispered, grinning, into Léon's ear in the
thirty seconds before he'd slipped into unconsciousness: *One of
your agents is working for us. The one who escorted you onto the
train right before we caught you. A tall fellow . . .*

Lanky.

The man who shouldn't have been at the landing ground; the
man who insisted all the Alliance agents stay together on the
train. Léon has to get to Lanky before Lanky gets to Minerva.

Despite being chained to a bed, fed almost nothing, locked
in a room he's told he will never leave, he will do something that
will take more courage than he's ever found inside him before.

Bruchsal is the place where you die—unless you make yourself live.

He'll recall Marie-Madeleine, he decides, centimeter by
centimeter, starting with her ankles. He just has to do that until
the Allies invade; has to be like Hecuba in Euripides's great
play—the one who did not die, even though he's living inside
hell.

47

We Were So Young

Aix-en-Provence, July–September 1944

T he parachute drop arrives with supplies, questionnaires, and instructions: I need to send people into Bordeaux urgently, La Rochelle, too. There are trains to blow up, explosives to send into the field, and I make all of that happen until my feet are healed enough that I can go back to Paris and put the last nails in the Nazis' coffins. The Allies have finally broken out beyond the Normandy beaches and are fighting their way across France, and they want me in the capital to help them conquer the north.

In order to travel eight hundred kilometers across territory occupied by Germans who still have me at the top of their most-wanted list, the maquis find me a disguise: full mourning gear, including a waist-length veil. Lucien can't stop laughing when he sees me.

"After the war," he chortles, "you're going to walk into a room with your real hair and normal clothes and I won't have a clue who you are."

"Ha ha," I say, smiling, too. Because yes, after the war Lucien will still be alive, and I will have blond hair and three children and a husband named Léon Faye.

Lucien holds me tightly—he's staying to keep running things in the south—but we can't cry in front of everyone. So I pull myself away and stride over to the ancient motorbike that's waiting. Sitting astride it is Maurice, who's arrived to accompany me to Paris.

"Full throttle?" I say to him, like I once did in Morocco.

"God, we were so young, weren't we?" the duke says, voice catching. He reaches for my hand. "They mustn't catch you."

"I'm just one small and unremarkable woman," I protest. "Whereas all of you—"

"Would be nothing without you," he finishes. "We can't lose you now."

Because I'm a symbol, not a woman. The end is so tantalizingly near and we can reach it only if we all still believe.

So we set off down the mountain, freewheeling to liberation.

And to Léon.

When the motorbike dies, we're forced to board the train, where I play the part of the widow as if I'm auditioning for my life. I howl and weep on Maurice's shoulder and the Germans leave me alone, believing that the terrible traitor Hérisson would never draw so much attention to herself. Three days later, the train stops, too—the railway tracks have been blown up by an Allied airstrike. So we climb onto a truck and sit atop bags of coal before we finally arrive at Paris headquarters, where Dragon and Ladybug welcome us.

I spend the day catching up on messages. London is ordering me to return. I burn the message. Because they also want an agent in Nancy and one in Strasbourg to act as advance scouts to prepare for the Allied push into Paris and then—*please God*—into Germany, where we think Léon and the other imprisoned agents must be.

Everything I've seen in Paris tells me that, contrary to rumor, the Nazis aren't preparing for a last stand here. They're retreating. The path is clear for General Patton to march in, which is information I need to get to the Allies as soon as possible. But how? We aren't due to transmit to MI6 until late this evening.

"I'll take it to Patton," Dragon says with the zeal of his Viking ancestors.

I smile. "Mapping the D-Day beaches, being imprisoned, and escaping haven't been enough of a challenge for you? You want to cross the front lines, too?"

"Anything to get this damn war over with."

"Come and find me in Strasbourg when you're done," I tell him.

"Strasbourg?" The duke of Magenta frowns.

"I can't ask new people to take risks when the end is so close," I say. "If London wants someone in Strasbourg, it has to be me."

He sighs and points to Ladybug. "She runs Paris better than I did. So let's go to Strasbourg. You know London will kill you," he adds with a grin.

"At least they won't torture me first."

And so, with gallows humor, we set off into the Nazi-occupied eastern sector of France, into what I hope is the final act of war. Then the curtain can finally descend and all the players—*all* of them—can step onto the stage and take their bows.

Getting through a retreating German front line is about as easy as squeezing through prison bars. It requires stealth, cunning, and every other unsavory habit we've learned over the past four years. We travel in a Red Cross ambulance—the only symbol the Germans still somehow respect, especially when we tell them we're Nazi collaborators, picking up injured Germans and taking them to camp hospitals.

If there's one thing the war has gifted me, it's the ability to lie like Odysseus.

We set up camp in the forest near Verdun. The locals join us, bringing their families and friends, eager to be part of the fighting force now that they can scent liberation.

Dragon soon returns, face aglow with the news that Patton is pushing on into Paris because of what we told him. Not long after, the Nazis are driven out of the capital.

But we don't celebrate. I'm worried that if the Allies don't press on, the Nazis will regroup and retaliate. Right now, Verdun is protected by just one scraggly band of German soldiers who look as if they'd rather sleep than shoot. And all the bridges are still intact, ready for an Allied advance.

I write it all down and say to Maurice, "If Patton acts on this, he could sweep through and take the whole of France this week."

"Then it would finally be over," he says, and I hear how tired he is, and I know that while this is just the start of Patton's charge across Europe, we are almost at our end.

Dragon sets out with the parcel of messages and returns two days later, shouting, "They're coming! They want to know if it's safe to march through the Argonne Forest."

The Argonne Forest is just a day or two from here.

Maurice's eyes meet mine and I can see he wants to smile, but he's as scared as I am of celebrating prematurely.

"Let's scout the forest," I say.

I use every animal sense I've acquired to help me steal silently through trees just meters away from retreating Nazi regiments. At the end of each day, Maurice and I return to camp and I curl up in my den of leaves, not even bothering to wash the dirt from my hands.

I send Dragon off with another update. While he's gone, a rumbling sounds, like a million pebbles rolling down a hill. That rumbling soon becomes the helter-skelter rush of German soldiers through the forest, so close that we hear their footsteps and their curses all day long.

Then Dragon returns, wearing the palest face I've ever seen. The duke of Magenta takes hold of my hand.

Please God, let it not be Léon.

"Patton's at Verdun," Dragon says. "France is liberated."

France is liberated.

I cover my face with my hands and weep.

"It's victory," Dragon insists. "You shouldn't cry."

All the villagers are raising their tricolors, opening wine bottles. They sing and laugh and dance, joy pouring out as excessively as my tears.

Maurice pulls me into his arms and whispers, "What is victory to us when those who won it are missing?"

Yes. I had no idea that victory would hurt so much.

48

King of Courage

Paris, September 1944

We return to Paris and, rather than searching for a cave, we're allowed to requisition any building we like for our HQ. For the agents' sake, I choose a luxurious apartment on the Champs-Élysées. We hang a sign right out in the open on the front door that proclaims, *Alliance Intelligence Service*.

But while France might largely be free, the rest of Europe isn't. My agents are still in prison in enemy territory, and they'll be released only when Hitler is dead. So I keep liaising with London and with Patton, answering their questions about mines on bridges lying in wait for our troops, considering their request to send a team of agents to scout ahead of the Allies, right into Germany.

I look up when I hear a familiar voice behind me.

"Lucien!" I cry, kissing his cheeks. "Ready to wear your robe and put your feet up?"

He laughs, but there's something in his eyes . . .

My smile falls away. *Not you,* I want to plead. *You've done enough.*

"I want to set up our first sector across the Rhine," he says. "If Eagle was here, he'd push on into Germany. You know he would."

Yes, he'd be at the head of the Allied advance in a silver airplane, a navigational star guiding our troops.

Of course the man Léon trained won't stop before the fight is over. Once again I see that the things we love in people are also the things that will hurt us the most in the end. Lucien's honor is a mirror of Léon's, and his mother wouldn't have had it any other way. As leader of Alliance, nor would I.

It's only the woman in me who cries out, *No!*

"Send a message once you have a base. I'll arrange a supply drop for you," I tell him, trying to keep my voice steady. "And, Lucien . . ." My voice cracks. "Find them."

Léon. Josette, Lucien's mother. The remarkable girl Amniarix. And all the rest.

"I'll find as many as I can," he swears.

He shoulders his pack and sets off, sunlight glinting on his golden hair, crowning him King of Courage.

The minute the note I've been waiting for arrives at HQ, I run back to my apartment, only just able to make myself stop and scratch at the door instead of bursting in, because I know how terrifying a suddenly opened door still is to everyone in Alliance.

It opens cautiously. "Ermine," I start to say, then stop. I can call her Monique now, openly. "What a habit to break," I whisper. "To not use animal names."

"This will make you feel better," she says, stepping aside to show me the person waiting behind her.

My son. Mine and Léon's. He hasn't seen me for fourteen months. If I rush at him, I might make him cry and I won't be able to bear it.

I crouch down in the doorway. *"Bonjour Achille."*

He holds on to Monique's leg and peeks out at me.

I proffer a khaki-colored bear that I made out in the field

near Verdun from scraps of uniforms. It's stuffed with fleece from inside another bear, one handed to me by a woman who told me that her child had died earlier that year. She'd seen me sewing and had recognized a mother's pain.

"This is . . ." I pause and turn the bear toward me. The one animal we never had in our ark was a bear. He could just be Bear. But instead I hear myself say, "Lion." In French, the word sounds almost like one man's name—Léon.

"Lelelelelelele," Achille chants.

He pokes a finger into the bear's belly and giggles—and my heart finally breaks.

In Paris, the swastikas are burned, German street signs crash to the ground, and the very idea that anyone ever supported Pétain's 1940 armistice is buried beneath voices shouting De Gaulle's name. At Alliance headquarters, surviving agents enter with smiles and hugs and euphoria and tears. Soon, Crane arrives from England on a plane that flies during the day and doesn't have to land by moonlight on an L-shaped runway lit only by flashlights.

We embrace and of course we cry. Into our opulent head-quarters come people from the British Embassy, as well as naval officers, RAF officers, even men in kilts: a veritable parade of uniforms and boots and buttons and brass. I hover at the edges of my own party until Crane steps into the middle of a great circle and reads a speech about extraordinary and heroic achievements. He attaches words to my name like *fighter, strategist, leader, warrior.*

"And brave to the point of making everyone at MI6 tear their hair out," he finishes with a smile, indicating his own balding pate. Then he pins on me a cross imprinted with the profiles of a king and queen, encircled by a pink ribbon.

The Order of the British Empire.

There are so many sobs stuck in my throat that I have to stand with my lips pressed together and just stare, hoping he sees in my eyes everything I cannot say.

When the cheers ring out, I cower; I'm still not used to so much noise. Still can't quite remember that the Gestapo aren't about to charge in.

"What can we do for you now?" Crane asks after the champagne is poured and I've composed myself.

"I need a parachute drop sent to Lucien. Men to search for Lanky. And"—I inhale shakily—"I need you to help me find Léon. And get my children back from Switzerland."

Not long after, in the little apartment I'm living in with Monique and Achille, another gift arrives. It's a gift I both long for and am terrified of—the gift of a fourteen-year-old boy named Christian and a twelve-year-old girl named Béatrice.

They haven't seen me since 1942.

The door opens. My mother and sister stand there. Beside them is a boy who's taller than they are and a girl who's about the same height. I brace for the children to stare, to wonder who I am. I brace for them to walk right past me.

But all of a sudden, there are two people in my arms and I'm holding my children and, my God, they still smell the same and it's the scent that does it, making me burst into tears. We're all crying and laughing and hugging and trying to look at one another all at the same time when suddenly there's a third person in the middle of our embrace, holding my leg and looking up at me with a worried face, as if he cares that I'm crying and wants to help. That third person, little Achille, who's only ever called me Mee-Mad, baby shorthand for Marie-Madeleine, howls, "*Maman!*"

And I wrap him in my arms and squeeze him as hard as if we'll never embrace again.

It's almost too much happiness. Especially when Béatrice says to Monique with a grin, "You're still my favorite animal," and Monique beams like the young woman who joined us in Béatrice's hospital room in Toulouse in 1942.

If tears aren't enough to express true sorrow, then smiles aren't enough to embody the quantity of my joy. But I smile and I laugh knowing that, here at home, I don't have to lead. I just have to love, which is so very easy to do.

And with Achille in my arms, I send an order to his father: *Stay alive, Léon. We're coming. It's time you held your son.*

49

One Year in Prison

Schwäbisch Hall, Germany, September 1944

Léon once thought he'd recall Marie-Madeleine in sections: her feet, her legs, her hands, her arms, her torso. Although, he admits to himself with his only smile of the month, he would probably have divided her torso into more discrete parts. Belly, breasts, the perfect prism of her sacrum. That was back when he thought the Nazis captured you, tortured you, and killed you—and that the Allies were coming and he just had to put off the killing part until they arrived. That was before he understood that to keep someone alive for months on end is the worst thing of all. Or perhaps it's been more than months, perhaps even a year. He doesn't really know; time is as useless a word as freedom.

He's been officially condemned to death now. He stood in a room and argued for every jailed man in Alliance: that they were prisoners of war and couldn't be executed. He argued beyond the point of feeling like he might faint from hunger and, at the end, when his words had been ignored and his sentence passed, he shouted, "Long live France!"

But is France still living? He doesn't know. Knows only that his body is as skeletal as the Russian prisoners he and Marie-Madeleine were sent photographs of, that he's more corpse than man. But humans are truly miraculous, he supposes—they endure even when nourished only on memory.

On the day after his sham trial, when he'd understood this imprisonment was infinite, he'd begun again with his recollection of her body, remembering smaller bones and precise details: the almost indiscernible difference between the contours of her left hip and her right, the fine blond hairs near her navel, the freckle beside her ear. Now it's her eyelashes he's reached on this slow and meticulous journey that began at the third phalanx of her littlest toe.

But today, when it's the same freezing temperature as every other day, when he can't see the sun or the moon or the stars, when he knows that tomorrow he'll again see nothing, he almost cries out, *What happens when I reach the air above her head?*
What then?

That he will still be here, doing this, when he reaches the end of Marie-Madeleine is a kind of desolation he cannot contemplate. So he returns to the memory of the long, black sweep of her eyelashes when she falls asleep on his chest.

It's either that or give up.

50

The Story of the Eagle

France, September 1944–January 1945

My mother stays with the children during the day and Monique returns to HQ as my courier. I know my family is deeply curious about Achille, but I can't speak of Léon, not yet. Not until I know more. Meanwhile, Crane checks every prison and barracks in France and tells me what I already know—that Léon must be in Germany.

"Then we need the Nazis out of Germany yesterday," I tell him. "I'm going back to Verdun."

"Isn't it time to stop?" he says, but he's smiling as if he knows I won't change my mind. "I'll come with you," he adds. "If I know how a parachute drop works, I can persuade MI6 to send more. That's how we get rid of the Nazis."

I leave the duke and Ladybug to manage HQ and we go to Verdun. I'm in the field when the plane flies over, and I help my agents unpack. Crane is very quiet throughout, and so am I—my mind on another parachute drop, the one going to Lucien that night to help him press farther forward into enemy territory than anyone has yet gone.

In the midst of that, Dragon comes to find me, back from a day's scouting through the Moselle.

"They're not moving," he says.

"Who isn't?" I ask distractedly, wiping the packing resin off a gun.

Crane clears his throat. "Let's talk," he says, and at the look on his face, I say, "Perhaps I should put the gun down. Sounds like you're about to tell me something that might make me want to shoot you."

Nobody laughs.

We move closer to the pine trees, which point upward like bayonets ready to break open the sky. Once they would have reminded me of Christmas. But my analogies are contorted by war.

"We've only got one port available to bring supplies in," Crane says, staring up at the tallest pine. "The farther we move away from that port, the harder it is to get the supplies out to the troops. We've run out of fuel. The advance has stopped."

"But you're only forty kilometers from the German border!" I cry. "If you stop, the Nazis will regroup."

"I know."

I curse wildly. Maybe I can cross into Germany. But where would I go? I have no idea where Léon is, or any of my missing agents.

Crane shakes his head as violently as I just swore. "You can best help Léon Faye stay alive by keeping Alliance going until the war ends. Not by waltzing off into Germany and getting killed. We still need information."

"You want to know where the Germans are and how many troops they have at each location?" I say, words heavy as stone.

So I send out two agents: one to scout the border region to the north, the other to the south.

Only one returns.

Crane's frown deepens to a crevasse as the hours tick past. In the end I say, my voice like a blade because otherwise it would be a bottomless ocean of tears, "You wanted to see us at work in the field. This is what it's like. I send out agents. Only some of them come back."

As if to compound the lesson, a courier arrives from HQ with a message from London. It tells us that the plane circled above Lucien's landing field last night. But all the pilot saw was a village in flames.

Lucien's transmitter has gone silent.

I know what it means. Not just another hero lost. But a dear, darling boy.

I push away from Crane, stumble into the forest. The sky is the color of soot, the earth is slush, the trees are ash. All that's left are cinders; the world is scorched of color, of joy, of hope.

Do I still believe in the mission I've clung to for more than four long years? In twenty, fifty, eighty years' time, will anyone remember the men and women of Alliance who gave their whole selves to this war? Or will their graves be forgotten, visited only by weeds, because our murders are too countless to be remembered?

All I know is that being an alliance of optimistic adventurers was not enough—we must become martyrs, too.

Through December, a desperate kind of fury propels me as I think about what this delay will cost. How many more imprisoned men and women will die because we've stopped our advance and given the Germans time to kill them?

What must Léon think? That we've abandoned him. That the country he gave everything to isn't fighting hard enough to bring him home.

I go to Luxembourg with my agents, where we discover there isn't a single piece of artillery east of the Moselle. We tell the Allies, but it's not enough. They want more evidence, and we're the mules going out to get it, because we have more than skin in this game—we have the bodies and souls of our friends.

I go to the German frontier, ignoring Crane's order to stay in Paris.

"You'll have to throw me in jail first," I tell him.

I'm standing on the banks of the Moselle in the freezing dark of night, chilblains back with a vengeance and marking time in painful seconds along with my hip, when four agents pile into a dinghy with a radio and cross the frontier under fire. I'm there when that radio crackles to life, and I know they've made it. I've landed agents in Germany.

Over the next two days, fifty-four critical messages pour in with all the information Patton needs about the strength of German troops near Thionville. I dispatch Dragon posthaste, along with an urgent appeal for action.

Finally, near Christmas, Patton uses that information and makes an advance. But it *still* isn't the end. The Germans fight on.

One afternoon when I return to Paris, bone weary from yet another expedition to the German border, desperate for cold cream for my hands and a chair to sit in, I find someone sitting by Monique's side, his hand held in hers—someone who makes my hopes soar. Magpie!

I fling myself on him. He's thinner than it's possible for a human to be. His wrists are scarred and scabbed from the manacles he wore for fifteen months.

Fifteen months in chains. Nobody would do that to an animal.

He tells me that the British managed to exchange him for a German prisoner the Nazis wanted set free. And then he says, "I saw Léon."

My heart stills.

"Just after the New Year. He's alive. We were transferred to Sonnenberg together and put in dungeons side by side. If we're to save him, we need to act now."

It's what I've been hoping to hear since Léon was arrested back in September 1943.

Now to work out a plan to free him.

As if the Fates have rewound the thread of pain and loss they've been unspooling for me since 1940, two more miracles happen. Magpie finds Lanky, the traitor, parading through Paris in an FFI captain's uniform as if he's on the Allies' side. Luckily the street is busy with true freedom fighters, and just a few shouted words puts Lanky at the bottom of a pile of men. He's locked up in prison, awaiting trial. I don't go to see him. Not yet. Not until I can take Léon with me and show Lanky that we are more powerful than evil.

The second miracle is that my radio operator rushes into my office hollering, "It's just been announced on German radio! The Nazis want to exchange Commandant Faye for a prisoner the Allies are holding."

Magpie and I erupt into laughter, weeping—hysteria.

The Allies will certainly make an exchange for a man like Léon—Dansey told me he'd do anything he could.

It's time for him to keep his promise.

That night, I gather my children around me by the fire and I tell them the story of the Eagle, Léon Faye.

51

Sixteen Months in Prison

Schwäbisch Hall Prison, Germany, January 3, 1945

Never did Léon think it would take this long for the Allies to come. Never did he imagine it was possible for a human being to stay alive for so long when shackled and starved and frozen and beaten and damp and sleepless and broken.

He can feel insanity beckoning every morning when the sun trickles in through the cracks in the masonry. He's been able to ward it off with his slow progress over Marie-Madeleine's body, but the ends of each strand of her hair mark a point past the time he'd believed he would still be here.

He could picture his son, he supposes, the child he's never seen. How old would he be now?

Léon doesn't know, because he doesn't know what month it is, what day, what year. Just that he's been in prison for hundreds of days. And that picturing the child he's terrified he'll never meet hurts worse than the howl of hunger in his gut.

All he can see is a small boy who'll one day ask his mother, *Did my father ever hold me?*

Will she lie and say, *Yes. Yes he did*?

Léon's forehead drops to his knees. His will has always been the strongest part of him, stronger even than his body. But he can feel it dying now.

Please come, Minerva. Please come . . .

He's jolted awake by his jailer, pushed out of his cell. Maybe they're carrying out his death sentence. He wants to care more about this, but they've long since murdered his soul; all that's left is the casing.

He's shoved into a room that holds dozens of creatures who are just armatures of bone draped with skin. Everyone's hair is as white as their teeth would be, if they had any left. Léon raises a hand to his own stubbled scalp. Is he white, too? That won't do; Minerva always loved his dark hair.

That's when he realizes—he still thinks he'll see her again. And he still has vanity. So perhaps there are embers still alight somewhere.

But for how long will they continue to glow?

"Commandant!"

There's a skeleton in front of him calling him commandant. The skeleton's voice is familiar, and Léon feels his face shift, incredibly, into a smile. The skeleton is Magpie!

For a second, he sees in Magpie's eyes the shock at how terrible he looks, which must be bad if it's worse than the other cadavers here. But then the shock is gone and there's only the joy of clasping the hands of a friend, of pressing their cheeks together, their chains making an embrace impossible. But he still feels the relief of knowing he isn't alone and that, with a friend by his side, perhaps he can live for a hundred days more.

Before they can speak, they're herded onto a train and Léon loses Magpie in the shuffle. Then he wonders—was Magpie even real?

The train crawls away and Léon tries to make himself move to search for Magpie, but his legs are unused to activity and refuse to cooperate. Then Magpie, who *is* truly, wonderfully real, finds Léon and they sit side by side on the floor, and Léon discovers it's been sixteen months since he was captured.

More than four hundred and fifty days.

The Allies landed in June. Magpie says that it's January 1945, six months later. His son, Léon realizes with a sharp shock, is more than one and a half years old.

Bon sang.

Soon they arrive at their new hell, Sonnenberg Fortress, north of Berlin, deep into Germany. Astonishingly, he and Magpie are placed in cells side by side. They're allowed to talk whenever they want. It's almost possible to feel happy, to hope—even to believe that, nourished by companionship and conversation, they'll both be able to stay alive until the Allies finally come.

52

Armageddon

Paris, January 1945

efore the war, I thought politics meant the Senate conven-
ing at the Palais du Luxembourg or the National Assembly
gathering at the Palais Bourbon. Men in palaces debating
laws whose effects they'd often never have to experience themselves. But *politics* is just another word for murder. It was because of politics that the message about Lanky being a Gestapo
informant was never given to me by De Gaulle's intelligence
service. And now I discover that the man the Germans want
freed in exchange for Léon is in the custody of the French. He's
in De Gaulle's hands, not Dansey's.

De Gaulle gets to decide what happens to the prisoners
whose cell keys he holds.

He says no to the exchange.

He says no.

He says no.

"De Gaulle's ordered the execution of the prisoner the Germans want," Crane finishes gravely.

Monique yelps. Magpie shouts.

I lie down on the floor and cannot make myself move.

Perhaps De Gaulle is right. Perhaps you should never allow
one Nazi to go free in exchange for a hero.

But aren't heroes worth any price?

"The only thing left to do now is wait until Germany falls," Crane says, crouched beside me on the floor. "Then you must go straight there and find him."

He says it as if he believes that, of everyone, Léon Faye—my Eagle, my love—will be strong enough to survive Armageddon.

Part Six

WOMAN

France, May–November 1945

I ask you to serve our unhappy country so that it may enjoy peace again, and happiness; songs, flowers and flower-covered inns. Close the prisons. Drive out the executioners . . .

— LÉON FAYE

(Taken from his final will and testament, hidden behind a radiator at Bruchsal Fortress for Marie-Madeleine)

53

At Last, the Sky

Sonnenberg, Germany, January 30, 1945

éon writes about flowers and flower-covered inns, about closing down prisons and stopping wars, about forgiveness; about happiness. It's a utopia he describes in his journal, or perhaps it's foolishness. But it's an honorable dream—there's that word again, *honor*, the one that's been his North Star and has guided him to this end.

"*Raus!*" the guard calls, pushing him out of his cell.

He hasn't been outside since that brief moment on a train with Magpie, who's now gone—flown free, exchanged by the Nazis.

Perhaps it's his turn to be exchanged. Perhaps he's on his way to Achille and Marie-Madeleine. Although a small part of him hopes not. He'd frighten the eyelids off a child, the way he looks now. He wants Achille to see a father, not a nightmare.

He concentrates on walking, something he isn't good at anymore—right foot, then left—thinking of the words in his journal. Is it too much to believe that because of people like him, those who would otherwise have died will be saved? That freedom will reign once more? Or are madness and honor one and the same, driving a man to believe that there's something beyond himself, something so precious that, without it, only beasts and monsters will be left to walk the earth, because the thing that makes us human will have died?

The guard pushes him into the center of a long line of men.

Léon closes his eyes and, so that he doesn't feel the bullet slam into what's left of his body, lets his mind linger over the things he'll miss.

The smile his son will never turn toward him.

The sky, the endlessness of it all; the way it made you believe that you were endless, too.

The way Marie-Madeleine looked at him, so that in her eyes he could see a different world from this one—a world where this was the last battle and, after the victory, war would never come again.

A bullet. Then fire.

At last, the sky.

54

We Were Just Paper Airplanes

Germany, May 1945

The end of war is finally declared on May 8. Magpie accompanies me into Germany to find our men and our women. We take guns and safe conducts—but do we take hope? I don't know, know only that I carry the weight of my son's lips on my cheeks as he farewelled me that morning, waving his stuffed lion and saying, *Lelelelelele*.

I want that sound to be the birdsong that summons his father to our nest.

But there is no birdsong once we cross the Rhine. There is only rubble and ruin. So many corpses that the odor permeates the air and we breathe in souls.

Magpie holds my hand, giving me the better part of whatever strength he has left and, God help me, I take it. Because we're not visiting prisons; we're traversing the underworld.

In Kehl, we find the bodies of Urus and eight other men from the Nantes region. Executed in pairs and thrown in the Rhine.

Rastatt: twelve of Colonel Kauffmann's men shot. Their bodies drowned in the river.

Pforzheim: twenty-six agents, including dear Dayné, my bodyguard, shot in the back of the neck and submerged in a pit filled with water. Eight of them were women, the youngest just seventeen.

Gaggenau: nine men, including seven from Bordeaux who'd given the British so much intelligence about the U-boats.

Ludwigsburg: sixteen agents, including the Abbé Lair, who sheltered us in his church. A minister takes us to their graves and tells us they each cried out *À bientôt au ciel* when they were tied to their death posts.

Until we meet again in heaven.

Here, where I most need to, I do not believe in heaven.

General Baston's name is on the prison register. But his body is not accounted for. "Try Ebrach," the minister tells us.

There we discover that the general who called me *My dear,* who took risks long after his age had excused him from serving his country—a defenseless seventy-five-year-old man—was made to stand naked in the snow for hours until at last he died, too.

Heilbronn Barracks: shot on the rifle range as if they were sporting targets, twenty-five agents, including Mahout. Elephant. Rivière. Bumpkin, who thought Lanky was his friend and died for it.

Camp Schirmeck: more than one hundred Alliance agents kept in conditions no living thing should ever have to know, let alone endure. Fifteen of them were women. Once the Nazis understood the Allies were marching through France, they took some of them to Struthof concentration camp and shot them there, including Bee, who gave me her house in Le Lavandou, the place where I fell in love. Others they took to the Black Forest, where Obersturmführer Gehrum presided over a *semaine sanglante,* murdering Colonel Kauffmann. Mandrill. Stosskopf.

This, I understand at last, is war. The rest was just skirmishes.

All along, the Nazis and I were fighting for the same thing:

France. I used to believe we didn't fight the same way; that my way was honorable. But I no longer believe that when, in one of the prisons, I see the names of so many of my agents scratched into the walls alongside the words, *Long live the Alliance*. They are all dead now.

Alliance is dead, too. It dies in the place where I'm standing when I find the remnants of Lucien's backpack in a scorched field. Tucked inside are the burned threads of the robe I bought for him in London, back when he told me he wanted to matter to someone, just a little.

He mattered. Dear God, he mattered.

But I sent him to his death all the same.

In Schwabisch Hall, I'm shown the suitcases that belonged to my agents. Inside are blood-stained clothes. Wrinkled wallets. Photographs of wives and children. Tokens of love and remembrance in a world where there is no love and too little remembrance.

Then Léon's cell.

The chains are still there, lashed to the foot of the iron bed, chains that bound the man I married with a ring and a promise one beautiful Paris night when I lied to myself that we were such a stronghold of hope, nothing could tear us down. We were just paper airplanes tossed into the world by an indifferent hand, always meant to plunge headlong to the ground.

The Americans tell us we can't go to Sonnenberg Fortress, where Léon was last known to have been held, in the cell next to Magpie's. The British forbid us, too. It's in the Russian zone, and the only way we'll get in there, where the Russians now rule, is with a bullet in our backs.

My mind has fled so close to the edge of reason that I'm almost tempted to try.

An officer tells me, "There's a warder here who was at Sonnenberg. He might know something."

The warder, when he enters, bows.

"I know of you," he says. He tells me that he and a few other guards, after being told to kill everyone at Sonnenberg before the Red Army arrived, helped some prisoners escape.

"About five hundred got away. The SS executioners murdered the rest," he continues, enunciating the words as if they hurt his mouth to say. "Eight hundred men lined up. Shot. And then . . ."

He starts to pray, as if that might help.

Prayers are for those with faith. My faith is gone. Where did I leave it? In Marseille, when I learned that our first man, Schaerrer, had been killed? In London, when I heard that Léon had been captured? In Paris, in Toulouse, in the Dordogne, in Verdun? So many places all over France and now Germany where I've learned of things too terrible to understand.

"Their bodies were burned with flamethrowers," he finishes.

Which means there will be nothing left to bury.

And the truth seeps in, like a raindrop in a desert cracking the earth open as it lands.

Leadership means becoming a less moral person, not a better one. To wrest freedom from the hands of murderers, you must sacrifice those you love.

In the end, it seems that I, too, chose France over everyone I loved.

How can anybody call that honor?

But I'll have to pretend to the survivors, to Magpie sitting at my side, that I still believe it was honorable, because otherwise how will they go on? I will live, unable to mourn, because, apparently—we won.

"Perhaps Commandant Faye escaped to Russia," Magpie says as if he's now the idealist, not the pragmatist.

I let him have his hope. But I look across at the warder, who gives the smallest shake of his head.

And I know—by insisting on returning to France on September 15, 1943, Commandant Faye, my Eagle, my love, died in my stead.

That is my masterwork, a violent opus played on keys of bone.

55

I Will Ride with Him Again

Paris, November 30, 1945

In la Basilique du Sacré-Coeur de Montmartre, I listen to the prayers offered up in *La Messe Solennelle* for the soldiers of Alliance who fell. My right hand rests in my left, fingers bare of rings. There is only one I want to wear, and it's been seared into the soil in far-east Germany.

Instead I hold the program for the service, which lists the names of every Alliance agent who died for France or who disappeared. Four hundred and six names are printed here. We're still looking for around one hundred more.

The first name is *le commandant d'aviation Léon Faye, disparu*. Disappeared. Without a body, they say, nothing else can be declared with certainty. They don't care that my world has lost an entire dimension, and that is proof enough to me that he is dead. There is no sepia love, just light brown. The sky is a ceiling rather than a miracle.

I can't look at tall men.

In the pews near me are the faithful and the faithless. I don't know which camp I stand in. Perhaps both. Just like I'm both stronger now and weaker. Conquered but victorious.

I escape before the ceremony is finished, stand on the forecourt and look out over Paris, just one of the cities we rescued. Does she know? Does she care?

Pinned above her is the blinding sun, where Léon now resides, trying to make us all sleep, wake, and turn with honor. But I can't sleep, and my heart orbits just the three souls of my children when I'd thought it could encompass the world.

I grasp the balustrade and see the first telltale redness of chilblains. I thought they'd end when the war did. But war never ends, not for those who do not die. I'll have chilblains each year for the rest of my life. Somewhere to focus the pain.

Suddenly the horizon unzips. From that far-distant line comes a flutter, then feathers. A bird. No, not just a bird. A bird of prey, like an eagle. It hovers above me, wings outstretched. I hold my breath. For a long time it doesn't move, just hangs there, suspended.

I reach out my hand. *Stay!*

It blinks one mischievous eye. Then the eagle dips its wings in salute, wheels around, and soars upward—a soul free of pain, riding forever on the wind in his beloved sky.

One day I will ride with him again.

Because Léon Faye and I were made for the purpose of meeting. It was our destiny, but I am left with its carcass.

A burst of sound. The doors of the church open and people spill out. Alliance agents and their families. There are so many. Everyone, every man and woman, is smiling. Unshackled. Alive. Free.

There's Jeannie Rousseau or Amniarix, the woman I'd wanted to meet and thank. I did that three months ago, when she returned against all odds from Ravensbrück Concentration Camp. There's my mother and sister. Maurice and Marguerite and their children and mine, all hand in hand.

There's Magpie, beckoning me over. The look on his face is half thrilled, half afraid. What does my practical Magpie, who survived sixteen months in prison, have to be afraid of?

It's only when I reach him that I remember his name is Ferdinand Rodriguez. He's a man, not a bird.

We aren't animals anymore.

He stands to attention, in deference to the military uniform I'm wearing, and I'm about to tell him we're well past formalities when he takes not just my breath, but all of my words away by saying, "May I ask you for Monique's hand in marriage?"

Oh!

"Monique!" I call, and at last I'm on the verge of smiling.

She bounds over.

"Magpie has a question for you," I tell her.

She shrieks, "Yes!" and Magpie picks her up and twirls her around, and their happiness is so obvious that the world turns, just a little, showing me another perspective to lay beside all the others I carry in my head. A vista—no, a realization—that is sad and beautiful, wretched and wonderful, like the tiny scars left behind by a dead lover's kiss: That seconds might die, minutes and hours and years, too, but the consequences of our actions remain, not written down, not carved onto a stone tablet, but in the air around us. In the simple ability to step outside, tip back our heads, look up at the sky and breathe in.

The world is once again vast and illimitable. Because of Alliance.

Because of us.

That's the story I'll tell Achille when he asks about his father.

As my children take my hands, I remember words foretold to me not that long ago, but in another time entirely: *You will make it to the end of everything.* It had sounded like something almost impossible.

It was.

But at the same time it wasn't.

All I did was all I know how to do. I threw myself at life and I loved recklessly, and, my God, I was loved the same in return. Now I am once again limbless and bloodied and split wide open, and yet I will continue to love the way I always have, because it was worth it.

It was so worth it, Léon.

So nobody can say that any of it was wrong.

But please forgive me if sometimes late at night, when the children are asleep, I weep all the same.

If this novel—which is a work of fiction—inspires you (and I hope it does!) to find out more about Marie-Madeleine Méric (later Fourcade), then her memoir, *L'arche de Noé* (translated into English as *Noah's Ark*), is the best place to start. But even her memoir isn't solid fact; it contains conflicting names, dates, and accounts of certain events. And hundreds of paragraphs from the original French edition don't appear at all in the English translation, to the extent that the one conclusion I came to is that there is no "true" account of Marie-Madeleine's extraordinary life. Even the people who knew her can offer only a partial and outsider's perspective: What child can ever know what their mother told her lover; what sister can ever know what their sibling was like as a mother; what friend can ever guess what goes on in a Resistance leader's head at two o'clock in the morning when they've just learned their agents have died? I can't know any of that with certainty, not even after having read Marie-Madeleine's memoir from cover to cover more than five times in both French and English.

So I've written a novel using many so-called facts and definitely a dash of fiction.

The truest facts are: Marie-Madeleine was a remarkable woman who lived a life of such scope it takes my breath away.

She really was the only female leader of a Resistance network in France during WWII; she really did lead around three thousand agents, many of whom were conservative military men decades her senior; she did travel to Madrid while trapped in a mailbag for ten hours; she did have two children she was forced to send on to Switzerland after the Gestapo put them on a most-wanted list; she did escape from prison by squeezing out through the bars; she did fall in love with her second in command, Léon Faye, and she did have a child with him while on the run from the Gestapo. And the agents of Alliance did suffer as terribly as I've described—no one should doubt whether any of the murders, imprisonments, torture, and cruelty enacted by the Nazis happened. They did. Four hundred and thirty-nine of the three thousand Alliance agents were killed by the Nazis; some of their bodies have never been found.

If you find yourself shaking your head at any point and thinking, *That couldn't possibly have happened,* I hope you'll set your doubts aside. Marie-Madeleine, Léon Faye, and the agents of Alliance did extraordinary things. And in response, the Nazis did monstrous, abhorrent things.

I'm going to sound a warning at this point: If you haven't read the book yet, you might want to stop here (I know some people like to read the author's note first). There are spoilers ahead, so go on only if you're happy to know the end before the beginning.

Onward!

The question I've had to ask myself is: How much detail should I go into here? From all the feedback I've had about my previous books, I know my readers love my author's notes, and many of you seek out the sources I've used for further reading. If there's anyone you should read more about, it's Marie-Madeleine. I've never come across a more astonishing hero. It took me an entire draft to get over my hero worship of her, to pull her down off a pedestal and treat her like a character, which you have to do if you want to have any success in writing about someone. Still, it's tricky. I truly revere her for what she did, and Léon Faye, too. But I had to flesh them both out as three-dimensional characters, which meant coloring inside the lines of the historical record, creating dialogue without the benefit of any records of the private conversations that took place between them. Marie-Madeleine notes many operational conversations in her memoir; she expresses much distress and angst about Léon's fate—you can feel how much he meant to her. But she never says that she was his lover, and she never refers to their child.

Of course she doesn't. It was the early 1940s. She was already operating at the very edge of what was acceptable for a woman at those times; to then admit to an affair and an illegitimate child would have been to ostracize herself entirely. The child exists absolutely off the record. I can't even tell you his name; being born in wartime often means there's no paperwork to find in archives. I've named him Achille because that's one of Marie-Madeleine's son Christian's middle names, and I felt it suited this story about heroes.

In the end, I broke through my hero worship because of something very personal. Marie-Madeleine had hip dysplasia, as I describe in the book, and it often pained her. One of my daughters was born with hip dysplasia and had to have many operations as a baby and a child, just like Béatrice did. Hip dysplasia is genetic, and doctors constantly asked who in our family had it, given that my daughter suffered so badly from it. *Nobody*, I told them. But while writing the book, I discovered that the hip pain I've experienced for years was due to—yes, you guessed it—hip dysplasia that went undiagnosed and untreated when I was a child. I've always hidden my own occasional limp. And that connection to Marie-Madeleine as both a woman and a mother made me able to leap inside her, rather than view her from a distance.

The main thing I've changed from history is to reduce the

number of people in Alliance's core leadership team. For example, Henri Schaerrer was one of Marie-Madeleine's earliest lieutenants, and he did many of the things I describe, but he didn't accompany her to Madrid. Another Alliance operative, Jean Boutron, did that. So Schaerrer is largely himself, with elements of Boutron added to him. General Baston was in Vichy with Marie-Madeleine and Navarre right from the start, but Camille Raynal headed up the Vichy sector and was left to stand in the snow by the Nazis until he died. Alliance had several MI6 contacts—Richard, Ham, and Crane—and I've combined them all into Crane, as he was known by Marie-Madeleine, although his real name was Kenneth Cohen. The reason I've chosen to combine two or three people into one is that there were simply too many people for one cohesive narrative. Add to that the fact that everyone has a code name and a real name, and I knew my readers' heads would be spinning, like mine was, if I tried to include everyone in this story. Not to mention, just about every second person's real name was either Jean, Henri, or Pierre!

I've also reduced the number of times Alliance moved its headquarters. Yes, that's right: They moved more times than I've described in the book, probably around twice as many times, in fact. Detailing every move would have weighed down the narrative too much. And I've often changed dates and combined events into one larger event, again for the sake of narrative simplicity. For example, Marie-Madeleine went to Paris twice in early 1941 rather than once as I've described it. Navarre managed to escape and make it back to Pau after his initial arrest in Algiers but was then recaptured; I've combined it into one arrest. Maurice de McMahon, the duke of Magenta, and his wife, Marguerite, weren't married until 1937, but Marie-Madeleine did become friends with Maurice in Morocco. It wasn't Navarre but rather Marie-Madeleine's brother, Jacques (whom I've unfortunately had to excise from the narrative), who made the initial contact with the Allies in late 1940. Edouard Méric did meet Béatrice, but very briefly. It would be a dull exercise to list every single headquarters I didn't use, and every event I've combined or changed the date of, so I'll just say that, generally speaking, most of the events in the book did happen, but perhaps not in the exact order and with the same characters. My publisher has a record of every change in a footnoted manuscript, would you believe!

Lucien is my only invented character. He's based on several Alliance operatives, including Lucien Poulard, Georges Lamarque, and Helen des Isnards, whose code name was Grand Duke, but we already had a duke in the duke of Magenta—you can see what I mean about all the names being confusing! Much of what Lucien does in the book was done by these other men, but I wanted my readers to have at least one character who endured across a large part of the narrative. Like Lucien, Georges Lamarque died soon after he crossed into Germany, the village where he was hiding burned by the Nazis.

I used the French version of Marie-Madeleine's memoir as my primary source. As mentioned, the English translation is abridged and leaves out too many details. For example, while Alliance's operation to exfiltrate General Giraud from France to North Africa (which I've excluded from this book due to length) was called Operation Minerva, according to Marie-Madeleine in the French edition of her memoir, Léon Faye also called her Minerva, which I loved and decided to use in my book. Where she's referred to things by incorrect names, such as *le train bleu,* which apparently didn't run during the war, I've let it stand in her words.

I've taken occasional lines of dialogue, radio transmissions, phrasing, and description directly from Marie-Madeleine's memoir. I believe this gives a real sense of Marie-Madeleine's perspective on events and it's also nice to let people use the actual words they spoke in life. Taken from Commander Kenneth Cohen's Preface to the memoir are the words in the epigraph on page ix.

Similarly, I've taken snatches of dialogue and forms of expression from various other sources that detail reminiscences or conversations with Marie-Madeleine or her agents, including Michèle Cointet's biography, *Marie-Madeleine Fourcade: Un chef de la Résistance,* available only in French and based on Cointet's interviews with Marie-Madeleine; Navarre's (or Georges Loustaunau-Lacau's) autobiography, *Mémoires d'un Français rebelle*; David Schoenbrun's *Soldiers of the Night: The Story of the French Resistance*; R.V. Jones's *The Wizard War: British Scientific Intelligence 1939–1945; The Washington Post's* December 1998 article, "After Five Decades, A Spy Tells her Tale"; and Colin MacCabe's *Studio: Remembering Chris Marker.* The epigraph on page 229 comes from Pierre de Vomécourt's unpublished memoir held at the Imperial War Museum in the United Kingdom.

One other very important source of research, occasional phrasing, and the epigraph on page 395 is *Journal d'un Condamne à Mort,* the diary kept secretly by Léon Faye when he was in prison, which makes for distressing reading. His niece Madeleine's handwritten diaries, which are essentially a testimonial to a hero, are kept at the Archives Nationale de France and provided much useful information about her uncle, whom she clearly adored. Her handwriting is terrible, though, and she uses a lot of very archaic French, so I worked with my French tutor one hour a week for months deciphering the handwriting and the French. Also at the archives are many more useful documents about Alliance, including statements from some of the survivors, timelines, Gestapo records, and the program from the mass held at the Sacré-Coeur in November 1945. Another wonderful book that draws upon some of the same primary sources for dialogue from and information about the life of Marie-Madeleine, Léon Faye and the agents of Alliance is *Madame Fourcade's Secret War,* by Lynne Olsen, a truly gripping biography of Marie-Madeleine.

Descendants of the Alliance network keep an excellent website with many important documents; it's impossible to list them all, but I will say that *Memorial de L'Alliance,* which is dedicated to the 439 agents who died for France, will make you cry if you read it. But what happened to those men and women should never be forgotten.

More sources include *Hommage à Léon Faye* by Lucien Robineau; Barbara Bertram's oral histories kept at the National Archives in Kew, in which she says that Marie-Madeleine told her she was engaged to Léon Faye; Captain Rodriguez's (or Magpie's) memoir, *L'Escalier Sans Retour; When Paris Went Dark: The City of Light Under German Occupation,* by Ronald Rosbottom; newspaper reports from *Le Monde* about Lanky's trial; *La carrière militaire et de grand résistant du lieutenant-colonel Edouard Kauffmann,* by Louis Morgat; and Edith Wharton's *In Morocco.*

I also traveled to France in October 2022 to visit Vergt, Léon Faye's birthplace and the location of a monument dedicated to him; the Père-Lachaise Cemetery, where Marie-Madeleine is buried in a heartbreakingly badly kept grave; Aix-en-Provence, to see the apartment where she was arrested, the military barracks where she was detained, and the Mont Sainte-Victoire where she fled; Marseille, to visit the Corniche and the port du Vallon des Auffes, where Alliance had one of its early headquarters; Le Lavandou; Lyon; and various locations in Paris.

A lot of grubby politicking took place during the war while agents were dying, most of which Marie-Madeleine, with great dignity, did her best to stay out of. I've left most of that out of the book, apart from a couple of incidents involving General de Gaulle, whose intelligence agency at the very least treated Alliance in a shabby manner. I'll let you consider the fact that Charles de Gaulle created the Compagnons de la Libération to honor the Resistance fighters who struggled the hardest and were deemed most essential to achieving France's freedom. He bestowed this honor on 1,038 people. Of them, 1,032 were men, including three of Marie-Madeleine's lieutenants. Marie-Madeleine was not among them.

To finish, I want to say that I can't tell you the number of times I cried while researching and writing this book. The agents of Alliance, especially Léon Faye, who spent almost sixteen months in prison before he was murdered, and Marie-Madeleine, the only female Resistance network leader, were true heroes. How many people have heard of them, and the 439 agents who died? There were just too many souls lost to the war, but without those souls, who knows how many more people would have died, how much longer Hitler would have stayed in power, how much more horror the world would have faced?

Marie-Madeleine was finally honored by the French state after her death, becoming the first woman to be granted a funeral at Les Invalides. Hurray!

ACKNOWLEDGMENTS

First, as always, Kevan Lyon, my remarkable agent who, when everyone was saying that the industry didn't want any more WWII books, never told me to go away and write something else. Instead she believed in Marie-Madeleine's story as much as I did, and for that I will be forever grateful.

Hilary Teeman, editor extraordinaire, who also knew this was a story that had to be told and who believed I was the right person to tell it. Thank you for taking me on and for helping me transform the book into the best version I could make it.

The team at Ballantine Books, whose support of the book and belief in me have been unwavering and beyond anything I could have imagined. Thank you for the most glorious cover any author could ask for. Special mentions to Caroline Weishuhn and Corina Diez.

Rebecca Saunders and everyone at Hachette Australia. We've been together for many years now, and I thank you for staying with me and always supporting me and my books.

The team at Sphere, and all my translation publishers.

My readers and booksellers everywhere. You are the best.

THE
MADEMOISELLE
ALLIANCE

NATASHA LESTER

A BOOK CLUB GUIDE

WALKING IN MARIE-MADELEINE'S FOOTSTEPS

If you're anything like me, after you've read a book about real people and real events, you want to know more. So here are some of the places in France that you can visit if you'd like to walk in Marie-Madeleine's footsteps and find out more about her extraordinary life, the lives of her three thousand courageous agents, and the Alliance network. Whether you travel via the internet from the comfort of your armchair or you're lucky enough to have a vacation planned, I wish you bon voyage.

Port du Vallon des Auffes, Marseille

One of Marie-Madeleine's first headquarters was located in this part of Marseille. It's a small but beautiful harbor, filled with colorful boats and surrounded by high cliffs. Look up at all the blue and green shutters adorning the houses, bright squares of color offsetting the gold and terra-cotta tones of the buildings. There are a couple of Michelin-starred seafood restaurants to try here if you arrive at mealtime.

The Corniche, Marseille (now known as Corniche President John Fitzgerald Kennedy)

From the south side of the port du Vallon des Auffes, you can climb up to the Corniche, a 4.5-kilometer-long seaside promenade with some of the most spectacular views in France. The sea around Marseille is an incomparable shade of blue and when you get too hot, you can go for a swim at the beaches along the way. Marie-Madeleine lived in a house along the Corniche for a few months and one of Alliance's headquarters was also located here.

Hôtel Terminus, Marseille

The Hôtel Terminus, where Marie-Madeleine and Léon shared a bottle of Monbazillac and where she asked him to be Alliance's chief of staff, still stands. It's just opposite Saint-Charles station.

Aix-en-Provence

One of the most beautiful towns in France, Aix-en-Provence is also where Marie-Madeleine was imprisoned in a military barracks. The building at 13 Boulevard des Poilus is now the Lycée Militaire (military high school). You can easily trace Marie-Madeleine's flight path from the barracks to the Saint-Pierre cemetery by turning right at the end of Boulevard des Poilus onto the Avenue des Déportés de la Résistance Aixoise. From there, you'll be able to see the Mont Sainte-Victoire in the distance, where Marie-Madeleine camped out with the maquis after her escape.

Vergt

This small town is where Léon Faye grew up. In the center, at Place Charles Mangold, is a war memorial with a plaque dedicated to Léon Faye and an urn containing soil from Sonnenburg where he died. Make sure you pay your respects.

The Dordogne Region

After you've finished in Vergt, be sure to drive through the Dordogne region where Marie-Madeleine spent Christmas 1942 with her network. It's a secretive, shadowy place perfect for hiding out. The town of Sarlat-la-Canéda is close to where the Chateau Malfonds was located and is a lovely French town to spend a few hours in.

Resistance and Deportation History Centre, Lyon

This is a museum housed in the former headquarters of the Gestapo. You'll find incredibly moving and very informative exhibits about the Resistance networks that operated in France throughout WWII. You'll also see radios like the ones Magpie and Vallet operated for Alliance, as well as code books and all the other tools essential for fighting clandestinely against the Nazis. There is also a Rue Marie-Madeleine Fourcade in Lyon, commemorating her work for the Resistance.

Père-Lachaise Cemetery, Paris

This is probably the most famous cemetery in the world, with people making pilgrimages to the graves of Jim Morrison, Oscar Wilde, Edith Piaf, and many others. Marie-Madeleine is also buried here and it was one of the most affecting experiences of my life to stand before her grave. Sadly, the location of her grave isn't included in the tourist bureau's official map of the burial places of well-known figures, so it does take a bit of detective work to find it in Division 90 of the cemetery. There are also several WWII memorials; the monument to those, like Amniarix (or Jeannie Rousseau), who were deported to Ravensbrück Concentration Camp, is particularly moving.

Sacré-Coeur, Paris

This beautiful church is the location of the requiem mass held in November 1945 for the dead and missing agents of Alliance. Spend a few moments here thanking everyone in Alliance for their selfless heroism as they fought for freedom.

TIMELINE

1936

March 7: Hitler invades the Rhineland. Shortly after, Marie-Madeline meets Navarre at a party.

1939

September 1: Germany invades Poland.

September 3: Great Britain and France declare war on Germany. The Phoney War, a period of little military action by either side, follows.

1940

May 10: Germany attacks the Netherlands, Belgium, and Luxembourg, which all quickly fall to the Nazis.

May 13–14: The Germans enter France.

June 12: Marie-Madeleine leaves Paris, joining the exodus of people traveling to safety.

June 14: The French army abandons Paris and the Nazis occupy the city.

June 22: The armistice is signed. France is divided into a free zone in the south, governed from Vichy, and an Occupied Zone in the north, ruled by the Nazis.

1941

February: Marie-Madeline meets Léon Faye in Vichy for the first time. He agrees to head the North African arm of the network.

June 22: The Germans invade Russia, their former ally.

October 15: Navarre and Léon Faye sentenced for their roles in the failed coup in Algiers; Navarre for two years, Léon for five months.

December 7: Japanese attack Pearl Harbor; the United States officially enters the war.

1942

February: Marie-Madeleine makes Léon Faye her chief of staff after his release from prison.

August: Alliance lands the first moonlight Lysander flight from MI6.

November 7: The police burst into La Pinède headquarters and arrest Marie-Madeleine, Léon, Monique, and several more agents.

November 8: The Allies land in North Africa.

November 11: Marie-Madeleine and her agents escape prison with the help of the French police. Léon remains in prison in Castres.

November 23: Léon escapes from Castres prison.

December 25: Alliance celebrates having grown to almost one thousand agents.

1943

January 13: MI6 want Marie-Madeleine to go to London for her safety. She sends Léon instead.

January 14: Marie-Madeleine leaves Chateau Malfonds moments before the Nazis arrive.

March: Léon returns from London in his hunchback disguise. Marie-Madeleine arranges for her children to cross the border to Switzerland, but their guides refuse to take them all the way, so they make the crossing alone.

June: Marie-Madeleine gives birth to her son.

July 10: The Allies invade Sicily.

July 18: Marie-Madeleine flies to London. She meets MI6's Dansey and becomes worried about whether he really has Alliance's best interests at heart.

August 15: Magpie and Léon arrive, bringing with them Amniarix's reports on the V1 rocket.

September 15: After one failed flight, Léon and Magpie return to France.

September 18: Marie-Madeleine receives a transmission advising that the passengers on Léon's flight were all arrested, and that seven other sectors have fallen to the Nazis.

November 24: Léon escapes to the roof of 84 Avenue Foch. After only a few hours of freedom, Léon is rearrested and sent to Bruschal Fortress, Germany.

1944

March 16: Alliance agent Dragon arrives in London with a fifty-five-foot-long map of the Normandy beaches.

April: Marie-Madeleine strikes a deal with De Gaulle's Free French to make Alliance a part of their intelligence service.

June 6: D-Day; Allied forces land in Normandy and begin pushing back German forces.

July 5: Marie-Madeleine finally returns to France.

July 17: The Germans burst into Marie-Madeleine's apartment in Aix-en-Provence. She's imprisoned in a military barracks but manages to escape by squeezing out the window.

August 25: Paris is liberated by the Allies.

September: Marie-Madeleine is awarded the Order of the British Empire and reunited with her children.

September–December: The Allied advance slows because of supply issues. The Germans regroup.

1945

January 15: Magpie is freed following an exchange of prisoners.

January 27: Berlin radio announces that the Germans are prepared to exchange Léon Faye for a Nazi prisoner held in Paris. De Gaulle declines.

January 30: Léon Faye is shot by the Nazis. His body is burned by flamethrowers.

May 8: Victory in Europe Day. WWII in Europe comes to an end. Marie-Madeleine and Magpie set off into Germany to learn the fates of their missing agents.

August: Two atomic bombs are dropped on Japan and Japan surrenders. WWII is over.

November 30: A requiem mass is held at Sacré-Coeur Basilica in Paris to honor the dead and vanished members of Alliance.

QUESTIONS AND TOPICS FOR DISCUSSION

1. Before reading the book, had you heard of Marie-Madeleine Fourcade or of the Alliance network or any of its members? If you hadn't, why do you think that is?

2. In the early part of the book, Natasha Lester takes us back to Marie-Madeleine's life before the war in 1920s–1930s Morocco. How was this a foundational time for Marie-Madeleine politically, culturally, and emotionally, and how does it shape her decisions over the course of the story? How would the book have been different if the author had focused solely on Marie-Madeleine's life during WWII?

3. Marie-Madeleine had to make some difficult decisions in relation to her children throughout the book. Do you think she made the best decisions? How do you think her decisions might have affected her children? Is there anything you feel so strongly about that you would willingly step away from your loved ones for an unknowable period of time in order to pursue it?

4. Besides the two main characters of Marie-Madeleine Fourcade and Léon Faye, which of the characters made the deepest impression on you? Why?

5. Should Marie-Madeleine have ordered Léon Faye not to return to France? And should she have spoken up when she saw the field of pink heather in England right before Léon departed? Would it have made any difference, do you think, if she had?

6. What role does love play in this book? What kinds of love are explored and how do these different kinds of love drive different characters at pivotal moments?

7. Toward the end of the book, Marie-Madeleine reflects: *"Leadership means becoming a less moral person, not a better one"* (page 402). Were there any choices and decisions that she made, or any actions that she took as leader, that you thought were immoral? How did her leadership style change as the story progressed? And how do her thoughts

in this quote resonate (or not) with the state of the world today?

8. In one of the epigraphs in the book, Natasha Lester translates Marie-Madeleine's words: "*Soon, nobody will know what they did, nor why they did it, nor whether it was necessary to do it; you may even pity them for dying for nothing. I want to know that they will not be forgotten and, above all, that you understand the divine flame that burned in their hearts*" (page 315). Having read the book, do you pity the agents or do you feel some other emotion for them? Do you think they died for nothing? If not, what exactly is their legacy?

9. Do people in today's society have the same kind of "divine flame" in their hearts for the issues facing us as the agents of Alliance did? Who is a good example of someone in today's world who does have that same kind of burning passion for their beliefs? And is the "divine flame" always used for the purpose of good?

10. Do you enjoy reading fictionalized stories of real people? What other books like this have you read and enjoyed?

ABOUT THE AUTHOR

NATASHA LESTER is the *New York Times* bestselling author of *The Paris Seamstress, The Paris Orphan,* and *The Paris Secret,* and a former marketing executive for L'Oréal. Her novels have won several awards, been international bestsellers, and are translated into twenty-one languages and published all around the world. When she's not writing, she loves collecting vintage fashion, practicing the art of fashion illustration, and traveling the world. Natasha lives with her husband and three children in Perth, Western Australia.

natashalester.com.au
Facebook: Natasha Lester - Author
Instagram: @natashalesterauthor